MY BROTHER CHUCK

MY BROTHER CHUCK

A NOVEL BY
ANDREW EVANS

Stonehouse Publishing
www.stonehousepublishing.ca
Alberta, Canada

Stonehouse Publishing Inc. is an independent
publishing house, incorporated in 2014.

Cover design and layout by Anne Brown.
Printed in Canada

Stonehouse Publishing would like to thank and acknowledge
the support of the Alberta Government funding for the arts,
through the Alberta Media Fund.

National Library of Canada Cataloguing in Publication Data
Andrew Evans
My Brother Chuck
Novel
IBSN 978-1-988754-08-6

For my own brothers, Chris, Wyatt & Terence,
and all the games of touch football that we played in the yard.

CHAPTER ONE

It was several months before I got a good nights' rest. I don't think I slept at all the first week. It was lucky that I could sit and stare at a drafting table and not actually lift my pencil, without the need to interact at the office, for surely someone would have noticed my bleary eyes. They might have intruded into my self imposed isolation if I hadn't been known as the quiet one.

Even after exhaustion forced my eyes closed, I still woke five or six times a night thinking about what I'd seen. And now, years later, I lose another night if I let my mind go back to the quarry.

But Chuck; I don't know that he lost any sleep at all. I certainly couldn't tell from looking at him.

"How did you know I wouldn't say something?" I asked after Francis left.

He was puzzled by this strange question. I might as well have asked him how many fairies can dance on the head of a pin. "We're brothers," he answered, going back to his latest Meccano design.

"What would Dad say?" I had been looking at a maple tree out the front window for a couple of minutes. I hadn't intended to speak out loud; of course we could never know what Dad would say.

Chuck looked up from tightening the bolts on a scale model Titanic that he was building from old photos and a bit of assumption. It was complete with four smoke stacks, multiple passenger decks with silver railings, all the cabling and the famous radio antenna of the original ship and, most authentically, a rip along the hull that he'd cut with tin snips, even revealing the internal bulkheads. When finished it would undoubtedly be museum quality. "Dad says a man has to look after a woman. That's our job, right."

"But I don't think this is what he meant."

"Yeah, I think it is."

—

When I look back at it now, it's easy for me to understand how someone with so much ambition could lead such a life.

Chuck was born in January 1946, five years after me. He was adopted by our family as a newborn. I don't remember there being any lead up to the day he came home, other than Dad saying, "We're bringing home a new little brother to look after. It's a big responsibility. You can help us, right?"

From the time Chuck could talk, he was never shy. He would talk to anybody on the street or in a store. It's not that he'd talk a lot, although there were times he did that, but that he talked with such confidence. Mom said that he had the gift of the gab. Dad said that he was born to become a lawyer; a lawyer or a politician. But there was another job Dad had not considered.

"You know your brother's going around selling rocks?"

"What?" I said to Tom, answering his knock on our screen door.

"Chuck. He came to our place a few minutes ago selling rocks to my Mom."

"What are you talking about?"

Tom reached into his pocket. "He came to our door with some rocks he picked up down at the river." He pulled out his hand and showed me two small stones, each about an inch across. "He's selling them all over for a penny."

I took the two stones; one white and one reddish. I have to say that this didn't necessarily surprise me.

"You bought these from him?"

"It was my Mom."

"She bought these?"

"Yeah."

I paused again. Longer this time to think about a response. "So what are you telling me; that Chuck's a goof for selling rocks or that your mother's a goof for buying them?"

I'd seen salesmen coming to our door selling vacuum cleaners, brushes and other gadgets, insurance – lots of insurance, encyclopedias and lately even aluminum siding. These guys had the gift of the gab too. At least the good ones did.

In our younger years, Chuck and I raced to the door, he always got there first.

"Good afternoon, young man," said whoever was standing on the other side of the screen. They all looked the same; a tweed jacket with gray pants and a tie. They wore a gray fedora when we answered but took it off when Mom came to the door. And of course they always had shiny black shoes. They were somewhere between 25 and 40 years old and carried a big leather case full of whatever it was they were peddling. It started just after the war. I was pretty young then but remember we'd see one or two a week.

Chuck's natural talent for this door to door thing first amazed me on Halloween when he was just five years old. We went out with Tom and his little brothers and little sister. Chuck was the youngest of the group.

We had a real problem with his costume that evening. Chuck with determined to be a ghost. The *Peanuts* comic strip for the last couple of days had showed Charlie Brown's gang with sheets over their heads and the eye holes cut out. This is what he had in mind. But Mom was not about to ruin a perfectly good bed-sheet, even an old one. She dressed Chuck in a patched pair of white baker's pants that she'd picked up for fifteen cents at the *Sally Ann*, with at least ten inches of waist stitched together at the back, an old white shirt of Dad's turned around backwards, tucked into the pants and billowing out down to his knees, a small white pillowcase flopping from his head and white greasepaint over his face.

"There" she said. "You're a perfect ghost."

"No I'm not." Chuck was standing in front of the mirror. "I don't look anything like a ghost." He ran and got the newspaper, "I want to look like that!"

"I can't do that." Mom said, "You won't be able to see out the holes."

"But nobody will know that I'm a ghost!"

"Sure they will. You're all white, just like a ghost. Everyone will know and they'll be really scared."

"No they won't!" Chuck was getting more upset. He never cried. Dad wouldn't like that at all. Boys don't cry. But Chuck had a picture in his mind and nothing else was going to keep him satisfied.

The debate went on for several minutes until Dad intervened. "I'll fix it," he said. "Here, give me your shirt and I'll fix it so that everyone knows you're a ghost. Is that what you want?"

Dad lifted the huge shirt over Chuck's head and walked down the basement steps. "I'll be back in a bit."

Five minutes later he re-emerged holding the shirt at arm's length in front of him. "Don't touch it. It's still wet." Handwritten in black paint on the white shirt in letters six inches high: GHOST.

"It says ghost!" Mom said. "Everyone will know you're a ghost now!"

Chuck had the biggest smile. "I'm a ghost!" he shouted.

We were out for an hour and a half that night, going door to door. We climbed the steps of every porch with Chuck in the lead. "Trick or Treat," we shouted in unison.

When the door opened, Chuck was always first with his pillow-case opened. "Hi, I'm Chuck!" he shouted.

"Hi Chuck." was the invariable reply. "I see you're a ghost."

He was as happy as a clam and with every house he got bolder. Pretty soon it was, "Hi, I'm Chuck. What's your name?"

"Hi Chuck. I see you're a ghost. I'm Mrs. Wakefield," or "Hi Chuck. I see you're a ghost. I'm Mrs. Wellborn." Or "Hi Chuck, I see you're a ghost. I'm Mr. Schumer."

When the little kids got tired by seven-thirty we went home to sort the loot. Not only did Chuck remember every person's name;

he remembered what they gave him.

"This popcorn ball is from Mrs. Wellborn," he pulled it out of his bag and set it on the coffee table. We were both sitting on the floor of the living room. "This candy apple is from Mr. Schumer, and this chocolate bar is from Mrs. Wakefield."

I was astonished. I had gone to every house with him and received the same candy, but he remembered every name.

Now, four years later, the salesmen continued to flow past our door. "Good afternoon young man. Is your mother at home?" was always the line. "Would you be a pal and go get her for me?" If a hundred men came to the door, a hundred men would ask if our mother was home and ask us to be a pal. They had a pitch and they stuck to it.

So Chuck would run back to the kitchen to get Mom, leaving the salesman on the other side of the screen door. Mom had told us that we were never to let men into the front hall; it was okay to leave them looking into the screen. Then Mom would walk to the door, never in a hurry, wiping her hands on the front of her apron and picking up our toys along the way.

Mom was always casual when we came home. She usually had on an old plain skirt and top and flat wide shoes that she could stand in all day long. Just after school her hair would be falling from the bun on top of her head. It was normal to see specs of flour, gravy, spaghetti sauce or some other remnants of the upcoming supper on her face.

Mom was pretty. I'd met the other guys' moms and no doubt she was the prettiest in my small circle. She had high cheekbones with a nice glow, dark brown hair and a slim waist. Tom's mom was chubby and I was already taller than her, but I still had to look up a little when I was talking to my Mom. This time of day she never wore makeup or jewelry.

So Mom would open the screen door with one arm and stand on the threshold, placing her a couple of inches above eye level for all but the very tall salesman.

They would take off their hat and start on a well practiced spiel.

"Good afternoon, ma'am." A big smile. For some a natural look but by this time of day I could tell that most were struggling. "I'd like to present you…"

Chuck and I would stand back, two steps inside the front door, and watch.

If the salesman looked fresh and had a sincere smile, Mom would let him go through his full talk. But if he looked tired with a fake smile, she would listen for less than a minute before taking a step back into the hallway, saying to them "no thank you," closing the front door and leaving them with the screen door propped against their knee or their product display case.

Sometimes, not very often but sometimes, she bought something. It was usually small like Ajax cleanser or cleaning brushes. But I remember once when this guy sold her an entire set of encyclopedias. He must have been very good. We had lots of guys selling encyclopedias at the door but Mom had never let them inside. It was Chuck who saw what made him different.

Mom invited the man into the living room and they sat down on the chesterfield. He had the same tweed jacket, grey pants, fedora and shiny black shoes as all the other men, but Chuck noticed what made him stand out from the others.

"Do you remember the man last week?" Chuck asked me. Actually it was two or three weeks previously. "Do you remember how he gives you one of those books and tells you to look up jet airplane?"

Of course I remembered. He'd said "Do you like jet airplanes young fellow? Here take this and look them up."

"This guy isn't anything like that." Chuck said. "He's talking to Mom the whole time. He's giving her his whole attention. He's smiling at her."

It took me a while, but after Chuck brought it up even I could see that the difference between this salesman and all the others who came to the door was his smile. It was just pleasant. It wasn't too big. He didn't laugh too much or too little, just enough. I really think that it was his eyes that made the difference. The little lines beside his eyes showed that he was smiling with his whole face, not just his lips.

But Mom wasn't going to fall just for a nice face. He showed her volume A on atomic bombs and brought up the cold war. "This is in the news every day, isn't it?" he commented. "It's good to know that when something comes in the news, you can flip right here and find it."

He and Mom sat at the coffee table looking at his books for nearly 15 minutes while he thumbed through the pages. Chuck and I sat in the big arm chair beside the empty fireplace and watched them talk. In the end I remember the man said that Mom could buy the whole set of books and have them come one at a time, every two weeks for a year.

But Mom said, "No. I think I'd like to get them all right away. Can you do that?" she went upstairs and came down with a chequebook. Early the next week, I remember because it was just after Labour Day, a delivery truck dropped off a big heavy wooden carton. It took two men to carry it inside and they used a hammer to pry off the top.

It's hard to believe that two careers started on that day with Mom and the encyclopedia salesman sitting on the Chesterfield.

—

We already had the 26 volumes out of their crate and paper wrappings and lined up in alphabetical order on the coffee table by the time Dad came home for supper.

Dad was a tall man. So tall that Mr. Harris next door liked to say that Dad had outgrown his hair. This just meant that Dad was bald all across the top, with a ring of hair around his head at ear level. Mom told me that I didn't have to worry because baldness is hereditary from the mother's side of the family and her father still had a full head of hair.

Since the beginning of September, Dad always wore dark grey suits to work. He was the plant manager at the Goodyear Tire Factory in town. In the summer he wore light grey suits; he had three different shades of light grey suit. From September to April he wore dark grey suits. He had three different shades of dark grey suit. He had lots of neckties; red and blue neckties. He'd choose a different one of these every day. And he always wore tie clips so he had lots of these too. He said he had to wear a tie clip so that his tie didn't get caught in the machinery.

Dad had just been promoted to his position a few months earlier, when the previous manager was sent to the head office in Akron. I guess Dad was pretty young to be the boss, but this was a small plant and with his bald head, Dad looked a lot older than 37.

He had worked at Goodyear since before I was born. His bum leg kept him at home during the war but the work he did was crucial for the war effort. He told me that they made the extra tough tires used on big army trucks. There weren't many men, even older, who had as much experience at the factory as my Dad.

Dad came home that night and saw us sitting on the chesterfield looking through the brand new encyclopedia? "Hello," he gave his usual cheerful greeting. "They came already. That was quick, wasn't it?"

"Aren't they neat?" said Chuck. He had volume B on his lap.

Dad pulled the heavy armchair across the room next to the coffee table and sat down with his knees on either side of the corner. Reaching into the middle of the row, he picked up volume R. "Let's take a look at this and see what we've got." Leafing through towards the end of the volume, he settled on rubber. "Here's the section on natural rubber. We use some of that in the tires." He held up the book. "Look, Chuck, this is what a rubber tree looks like."

Chuck was puzzled "A rubber tree?"

"Yes," Dad replied. "Rubber comes from trees. It's sap. Just like maple syrup." He scanned the page further. "Over here is a section on synthetic rubber. It's made from oil." Dad held the book up to me. "See. Here's the formula for polybutadiene." He pointed at the page where I could see $CH_2 = CH\text{-}CH = CH_2$.

"Do you know what that is?"

I looked at the book.

"You take chemistry, right?" he asked.

"Yes." I paused "there's a C. That's carbon. And an H. That's hydrogen. And a little 2. That means there's two atoms of hydrogen for each atom of carbon. Then there's a whole bunch more C's and H's. But I don't know what all the equal signs and minus signs are for."

"That's good. You've got the basics. Polybutadiene is the main synthetic rubber that we use in our tires." He looked down at the book again and ran his fingers across the letters. "This is just a formula for how the carbon and hydrogen molecules are joined together to create a chain molecule."

I stared at the page to understand what he was saying.

"We've got a whole floor of chemists in Akron who work on this kind of thing all the time. I spent a day with them when I was down in June.

"These guys are real brains." He went on. "They've all got degrees from university. They've got chemistry degrees and physics degrees. All kinds of things." He looked at me again "You might think about something like this when you're ready."

"We're not into the chemical formulas yet. I'd need to understand it better before I think about that." We had just started learning the periodic table in chemistry class at school.

"Of course you would. Just something for you to think about. That's all." He turned the book around the continued to read across the page.

Back when I was Chuck's age, grade three or four, I had done a project on tires. Dad brought home four inch squares of the different types of rubber, coated fabric belts and wire beads that make up a tire. I used tacks to stick them all to a four foot plywood sheet to make a presentation to my class. My teacher was so impressed that she told the school principal and he asked me to give a presentation to the grade six class. I didn't give him an answer and after a few minutes he just let the matter drop. I don't have Chuck's "gift of the gab".

Dad spoke up again. "Your Mom and I talked about getting some encyclopedias over the summer, so I'm really happy she picked these up." He looked at me "You're in high school. Are you going to need these for your homework? This is a expensive set, so we expect you to use them." And he looked over to Chuck. "You're a little young yet but you can look at them too. If you need any help, I can help, or your brother."

Chuck still had volume B on his lap, but he hadn't opened it up. He was rubbing his hand along the cover and running his fingers on the golden edged pages. He was more interested in the look and the feel of the books than in what they had inside.

"Dad, can you teach me how to whistle?" he asked. This change in topic was sudden, even for Chuck.

"What brought that on?" Dad asked. He was surprised that Chuck had lost interest in the new encyclopedias so quickly.

"Francis whistles real good. Not as good as you but still real good. I want to whistle too."

Dad was a good whistler. He could hit all the notes and wiggle his tongue to make a really nice tremolo, just like the records. I remember once I walked into the house and heard Dad whistling a tune, but it wasn't him it all; Mom was listening to an old Horace Heidt record of the whistling cowboy. Dad was so good that I couldn't tell him from a professional.

"Sure, I can teach you." Dad said. "How about after supper?" Turning back to me "You think you'll get some use of these?"

"Thanks, Dad; thanks, Mom." I said. "These'll be good." And I meant it. The encyclopedias we had at school were old. They didn't even include the World War II and had nothing at all on jet aircraft.

—

When Chuck came home a few hours later I pulled him into my room, "Tom called me. He said you're bugging the neighbours; selling them rocks?"

"Not rocks. I'm selling them nice stones that I pick up at the river. Then I clean them up real good, see!" He took his hand out of his jeans pocket, clutching four smooth coloured stones. Two of them had a pale, blue colour. One was reddish and one was quartz.

I knew that for sure.

"Did you sell any?"

"Yeah, seven."

"At a penny each?"

"No, a nickel."

"A nickel? Tom said you sold them for a penny."

"No. I sell them for nickel. Mrs. Jenkins gives me ten cents for two."

"How much money do you have?"

"Thirty cents, see." He held the collection of nickels and pennies. "I've got some bubble gum." I could see that he was chewing a mouthful.

"What are you going to do with all the money?"

"I want a hockey stick. My old one is too short for me."

"Mom and Dad will get you a new one when the season starts."

"I want to buy it myself."

"It will take at least twice that much money." I paused. "Are you going to sell some more rocks tomorrow?"

"No. I'm finished on our street. I don't know anybody on the other streets."

"How many people bought your rocks?"

"Five." He thought for a moment. "Mrs. Jenkins buys two. And so does Mrs. Phillips. Mrs. McKenzie doesn't want to buy any. Either does Mrs. Horton, but Mrs. Tomlinson buys one."

"Hold on. Hold on," I cut in. Chuck would go forever if I let him. I knew there were least 20 houses on our street. "And everybody else said no?"

"Almost."

"But you didn't stop?"

"No." Chuck looked at me. I could tell that he was puzzled by the question. The idea of being self-conscious had never crossed his mind.

"Look. Don't sell any more of your rocks, okay?"

"Why not?"

"It's embarrassing to me when Tom comes over and says you're acting like a fool. And it's embarrassing to Mom and Dad. He's important now you know. You can't go around doing stuff like that anymore."

"Does Mom know?"

"I didn't tell her. Just don't do it anymore."

Chuck look at the four smooth stones remaining in his hand. "I'm done on the street anyway."

—

I was the type of person who embarrassed easily, so I took definite steps to avoid it. I was quiet in school. I kept my head down and was very good in math and science class. I didn't do as well in English because we had to stand up and read our stories and I didn't care for that. I had one close friend, Tom, who lived down the street, but most of the kids at school wouldn't recognize me if they bumped into me. And because nobody knew me, nobody made fun of me and I was never embarrassed by some joker.

"Are you still going to buy a hockey stick?" I asked Chuck.

"Yeah. I'll have enough with my allowance in a couple of weeks."

"Let me know and I'll go down to the store with you."

Chuck was a little below average sized for grade four. Mom and Dad were both tall, but I didn't start to shoot up until I was 12, so I mistakenly expected that Chuck would do the same. He had freckles across his cheeks and nose, but would probably lose those by the time he got to my age as well. His hair was dark brown, in the uniformly short cut worn by every boy in the 1950s.

Mom always bragged to her friends about how smart her boys were. In my case at least it was partially true, usually getting top marks in my math and science classes. But she was stretching matters more than a little for Chuck.

For the past couple of years we'd been sitting down together most evenings in our shared bedroom. Chuck and I talked about what was going on in school. It was when he had trouble getting past 5 in the multiplication tables that I started to understand he didn't have the same grasp of math that I found so easy. Even in grade four he was never able to memorize the tables. He always had to work his way up the numbers.

"What's 9 times 8?" I'd ask.

Under his breath I'd hear "8, 16, 24, 32, 40, 48, 56, 64," then finally "72," while he counted off each finger on the desk. Of course with this lack of speed he was very quickly eliminated from any desk to desk math quiz in his class.

Dad seemed to think that Chuck would reach the top of his class, like me, once he matured. But having spent many evenings with him in our room, I knew better. At best he was an average student. More likely he was below average. Of course I would never tell that to Mom and Dad. I took my duty to Chuck very seriously, helping him as much as I could. He spent time learning tricks to solve problems, not quickly but accurately. I was the one who taught him to do his multiplication tables by starting from the bottom and working up, using his fingers to keep track.

But as a confident speaker, Chuck had stood out in his class from the very start. When I was in grade six and he was just starting grade one, we were both assigned as class representatives in the Students Council. For me, in spite of the general shyness, I was selected because of my marks. For Chuck, the teacher's selection process was simple; from the very first days of class, probably from the first five minutes, he'd let his teacher know that he was more than happy to carry his weight in any discussion. He was not selected again in grade 2, when actual class grades became important.

Of course the one area where Chuck excelled was with school assemblies. Whether it was at Halloween, Christmas, Easter or the end of the year school play, Chuck was always front and centre. He was full of confidence in front of small groups of classmates or larger groups of parents. Whatever the production, Chuck always knew his lines and delivered them with a gusto that made the audience laugh, even when he was just playing the innkeeper who turned Joseph and Mary away at the Christmas pageant.

By the time he reached fourth grade, he was able to take control of his performances and not simply shout his few lines, but deliver them with an appropriate level of volume, if not yet emotion. It seemed that he was given a more important role in each new production as his skill grew.

When the grade four Christmas pageant came around, Chuck was given the most important role as the Angel of the Lord.

"Fear not! For behold I bring you good tidings of great joy," he echoed at the shepherds. Chuck stood with his arms spread open at shoulder height. He finally got to wear the bed sheet he had complained about years before at Hallowe'en. He was wearing the angel costume that had been passed down through years of Christmas pageants. I remember the same bed sheet from my own grade four class and I think it doubled as a table cloth for the Last Supper meal at Easter. "For unto you is born this day in the city of David a Saviour, who is Christ the lord."

This particular role was perfect for Chuck. It allowed him to use his powerful voice. "And this will be a sign to you. You will find the baby wrapped in swaddling clothes and lying in a manger." Chuck dropped his right arm and used his left hand to point at the inn and stable. As he said these final words five other children stood up around Chuck. Each was wearing their own version of the angel bed-sheet. They all spoke together. "Glory to God in the highest, and on Earth peace, good will toward men." Lights over that part of the stage faded off while Chuck and the other angels stepped backwards behind the curtain.

I'd played one of the shepherds in my own grade four Christmas pageant. We dressed in burlap sacks and sat on bales of straw with homemade shepherd's crooks in our hands. When the angel of the Lord appeared we fell to our knees and held our arms over our eyes in fear. When his command was completed, we walked slowly, in a zigzag path, from one side of the stage to the other while Mrs. Robinson played little drummer boy on a stand up piano at the bottom of the stairs.

With Christmas only a week away the subject came up at dinner. "Have you written your letter to Santa Claus?" asked Mom.

"I'm not gonna do that anymore." Chuck answered, "The guys

think it's stupid to believe in Santa Claus."

Dad had a smile on his face when he asked me "What about you? Do you still believe in Santa?"

"Well," I looked at Dad. "Every Christmas I wake up and find a present under the tree from you and Mom. And I find a present from Grandpa and Grandma. And I find another present under the tree from Santa." I looked over at Chuck. "If you ask me, it seems silly to question whether Santa brings you presents when every year you find a present with his name on it."

"Did you write a letter?" Chuck asked.

"Of course. I sent it off a few weeks ago."

Chuck was surprised by my answer. Surprised and doubtful. "What did you ask for?"

"I asked him for a microscope. So I can look at bugs and leaves and things."

Dad spoke up. "It's getting too late to send off a letter now."

"Yeah," Chuck spoke quietly.

"Why don't you tell me what you want. I can use the telex machine at work to send him a message directly."

"Will that work?"

"I don't see why not. I'll get Mrs. Ross to look up the telex number for the North Pole." Mrs. Ross was Dad's secretary at the factory. She'd been there for nearly as long as he had. She started at Goodyear when her husband left for Europe at the start of the war and she just stayed on when he didn't come home. "So what do you want me to ask him for?"

Chuck thought for a minute and looked back and forth between Mom and me. "I want new hockey skates and some Meccano."

Dad stopped him. "Which wrong with the skates you have now? Don't they fit?"

"They're hand-me-downs. I want some brand new ones all to myself. All my equipment is hand-me-down; the pants, the knee-pads, the shoulder pads, the skates, everything!"

Dad nodded quietly. "And Meccano. You've already got lots of that."

"Yeah, but I want to build bigger things. I want to build a Ferris wheel. I've got a picture from a magazine of a Ferris wheel and I want to build one like that."

"I saw it too." I said. "It was in *Popular Mechanics* a few months ago. Chuck and I were talking about how neat it was."

"I even have the plans." Chuck jumped in. "I sent away for them."

"I looked them over," I said. "It's pretty complicated but I can help him out."

"Okay," said Dad. "I should take a look at that. What else do you want?"

"I want a BB gun like Tom's got."

"Who's Tom?" Dad asked.

I spoke up. "Tom, my friend. He's got a BB gun."

"I think you're a little young for a BB gun just yet." Dad replied. "You're liable to take an eye out. What else would you like? How about a toboggan?" Dad was smart. He knew that by offering an alternative, any alternative, Chuck would forget all about the BB gun.

"No. I still got my toboggan. It's the fastest on the hill! All the other guys have that big curly thing in front. Mine is just pointed up a bit. It's a lot faster than all the other guys. But I have to wax it on the bottom again." He looked at me. "Will you help?"

"Sure. Let's do it right after supper."

"I see some of the other boys are using new aluminum toboggans." Dad said.

"Those are really slow. They stick to the snow real bad."

"Yes, you want to go fast." With the nix put on the BB gun and the toboggan, Dad was still looking for ideas. "Can you think of anything else you'd like for Christmas?"

"I really want the hockey skates and the Meccano."

"I got that. What else?"

"What about a bow and arrow? Like Tonto uses. I'd be real careful with it."

"Sure. That's a good idea. I'll put that in the telex. Anything else?"

"No. That's all I want."

"Would you like something scientific?"

Chuck looked at Dad but didn't say anything. He'd never even thought of such an idea before. What could possibly be scientific and a Christmas gift?

"Well," Dad went on. "We'll send your list off and let Santa choose what he thinks is best."

"Let's go do the toboggan right now!" Chuck said to me. "We can go out tomorrow."

"Sure." It was Friday so I didn't have to worry about my homework. With the holidays coming I didn't have very much anyway.

—

It was late in the afternoon, but already pitch black roadside, when Chuck ran home from the hill. Mom had a general rule that Chuck should be home before the street lights came on. I remember the same rule from my day. That was hard to enforce in the shortest days of winter when the sun sets by four-thirty, so the rule was relaxed as long as she knew where we were. Mom intercepted Chuck on the porch before he could step in the door. His pants, coat, toque and mittens were white with snow.

"You won't believe it!" he said. "Francis' arm is broken!"

"Oh my gosh." Mom held him back with the big straw broom that she used to sweep the floor. "Don't you come in here like that." She started swatting at Chuck's legs with the broom. "Tell me what happened."

"Out on the hill. Everyone's there. Bob and Francis and little Charlie and Liza and June. We're all on the hill and it's packed with a bunch of other kids from Saint Joseph's school too. It's really deep with all with snow so when we first get there after lunch it's real slow. We have to plow down the hill getting the snow packed under the toboggans but with so many kids going up and down after an hour we start going faster and faster and the packed part of the hill gets wider and wider. It's really neat. We race each other down the hill all afternoon and each time we go we pack the snow a little harder and we go a little farther.

"Then Bob goes home and brings a snow shovel. Not a small one but his Dad's big snow shovel. And we build a big jump on the far side of the hill where the little kids won't go. It's the biggest jump ever. It's really easy to build it with all the show. I bet you it's as big as me.

"And we go over the jump and fly through the air. It's fantastic. First we start two fence posts up the hill. Then we go up to three fence posts up the hill; I bet we're flying through the air at least five seconds. Then we go up to four fence posts above the jump. Little Charlie is chicken. He won't do it. He says he has a stomach ache but we call him a chicken and we flap our arms and we say 'bok, bok, bok', and then he says that he has to go home because his mom wants him home for dinner. But it's way too early for dinner so we call him a chicken again and we flap our arms and go 'bok, bok, bok', again.

"But Francis and Bob and me go over it a whole bunch of times. We must be staying in the air at least ten seconds and we laugh all the way down the hill and we can't go on our stomachs because it hurts too much when we land and so we have to sit on our bums on the seat. And when some of the little kids start to go home with their moms and dads and the top of the hill was clear I say, 'Let's go to the very top of the hill and start there. I bet that we go farther than anyone's ever gone before!'

"And Francis says 'I'll race ya,' but Bob doesn't say anything at all. And we all walk up to the top of the hill, and Bob says 'I'll start you.' And Francis and me lay our toboggans down beside each other on the top of the hill and we stand beside each other and Bob says,

'On your mark. Get set. Go!'

"And Francis and me run and jump on the sleds and we both take off down the hill and we have to make it around the curve near the top of the hill and I get there first 'cause I'm going so fast but when I get to the curve I know I can't make it and I roll off the side and that's why I got so much snow all over me but Francis he keeps going and makes it down the hill and he's going really really fast when he hits the jump but he doesn't hit it straight and he goes off the side a little and he lands and runs into the fence on the side and that's when he breaks his arm.

"He screams real loud and I run down and then Bob comes down and Francis is crying real loud and he isn't moving away from the fence post and we can see his arm is bent funny even in his snow suit. And we yell for help and Mr. Thorton is at the top of the hill with Johnny so he comes down and he looks at Francis and he asks him if he's okay and Francis just keeps screaming and Mr. Thompson can tell that something's really wrong with him so he picks Francis up and carries him down to the bottom of the hill and he tells me to tell Francis' mom that he's going to take him to the hospital and then he drives away.

"And Bob and me run down the street to Francis' house and we knock on the door real loud and then Mrs. Hopkins comes to the door and we tell her everything and she runs for her car and drives away and leaves us on the porch."

Chuck had rotated slowly through his story as, arm by arm and leg by leg, Mom swatted the snow onto the porch floor. I'd been through this enough times myself to know how much it burned to have Mom swat at my cold legs with a broom. By the time he was finished Chuck had peeled away the layers of clothing until he was down to long underwear and bare feet.

"Oh my gosh!" said Mom again. "Is Francis okay?"

"I don't know. He's at the hospital."

"This is just terrible. I'll give Mrs. Hopkins a call."

I spoke up. "Where's your toboggan?"

"It's at the hill."

"Okay. We can walk up and get it after supper."

CHAPTER TWO

Christmas came in its typical nervous fashion for Chuck. We went to the early church service on Christmas Eve, and even then he was a twitchy bundle of excitement. The Hopkins family sat behind us; Francis in a full arm cast and sling tucked inside his suit jacket beside his younger brother and sister and their parents.

We had just sat down from *Oh Holy Night*, the opening hymn, and I could feel the bumping of little hands as Francis and his brother started driving Dinky cars along the back of our pew. Chuck reached into both of his front pockets and pulled out two cars that he'd found in the park sandbox the previous summer and that Dad had allowed him to hang onto under the finders-keepers rule. I was nearly convinced that the friends had prearranged this impromptu sports car rally. Chuck had a pale green HWM Formula racer and a red Alpha Romeo with number 8 on the rear. Both had spent too many days in the sand and rain but were perfectly serviceable for pew top racing. Chuck twisted in his seat and the three boys zoomed their cars back and forth behind me. Dad allowed it to continue so long as they didn't start crashing with full sound effects, then his arm would come out and rub Chuck's back as a reminder to quiet down while the readings and sermon continued. Their rally concluded with the end of the service, after which every child in church rushed outside to slide down the snow packed sidewalk in their good shoes, before heading home.

There would have been no point in putting Chuck to bed at the normal 8:30, so we both went together at 10:00 in the hopes of falling asleep quickly. The late hour ensured that he was out after a few minutes of chatter.

The rule in our house is that we get up Christmas morning at six, but we didn't have a clock in our bedroom so six was something of an abstract number. Like every year before, Chuck first woke up at about three and asked me, "Is a time yet?"

I looked at my wristwatch and said "no," but that wasn't good enough so he went to ask Mom and Dad. A minute later he lay back down in bed.

"I told you so." I said.

Of course by this time he was wide awake and there'd be no more sleep for either of us. "What do you think I'm gonna get?" There was a long pause. "I hope I get new hockey skates." Another long pause. "Will you help me build a Ferris wheel?" A really long pause; perhaps a moment of sleep. "Can I look through your microscope?"

He went into Mom and Dad's room two more times to ask, "Is it time yet?" and climbed back into bed two more times before six o'clock arrived.

Finally we heard a shuffling in hallway and a soft tap that the bedroom door. "It's time to get up," came Dad's voice. I think that he was as eager to meet the day as we were.

We had a long-standing tradition of marching down the narrow stairs in a line, from youngest to oldest. This meant that Chuck couldn't start until Mom had her housecoat and slippers on and the family was all together at the top of the stairs.

It was still completely dark when we stepped into the living room. Dad plugged in the Christmas tree and the room lit up with red, blue, green, orange and yellow.

I knelt by the tree with my annual assignment to hand out gifts. I looked over at Chuck. "See, he came just like I told you. *To Chuck from Santa.*" I handed over the wrapped box. "*To Mom from Santa. To Dad from Santa.* And here's one to me from Santa."

I had to be fast handing out the first boxes. Chuck was ready to jump off the chesterfield in excitement. Once we each had our gifts in hand, we were allowed to open them up. We were not forced to watch as each opened theirs in turn, and we were not forced to carefully pull off the tape and fold up the wrapping paper like some other kids were.

Of course Chuck was the first to have his unwrapped. "Wow. I got Meccano! Set five!" He read off the front of the box. "I don't have that one!" The box showed two young boys in sweaters and ties playing with their Meccano model of London Bridge, including a ship passing underneath. Chuck had it open in a flash and was already fingering through the individual metal parts. I wondered if kids in ties really play with Meccano?

"I told you that sending a telex to Santa would work." Dad said as the first flashbulb of the morning was fired, but I don't think Chuck heard him and I don't think he looked up when the photo was taken.

By this time I had unwrapped a maple coloured wooden box; a little smaller than a shoebox. I clicked the latch and opened the top to stare down at my beautiful new Sans & Strieffe, 500X microscope.

"Is that what you wanted?" Dad asked.

"Just perfect." I said, carefully lifting it out of the felt lined box. "It's got extra slides and everything." We had used microscopes in school so I started putting it together right away.

Mom was very happy with the tall, blue vase she unwrapped from Santa, and Dad opened up a nice new Telix wristwatch with a brown leather strap.

"You're the boss now," Mom said. "It's about time you had a nice watch to wear."

"It's about time. Get it?" Chuck chirped in. With his face firmly planted inside the Meccano box, I was surprised that he had even heard Mom's comment, let alone been able to come back with such a witty quip.

We all chuckled. Dad put the watch around his wrist and held it out for us all to see. He was very proud.

"Okay," I said reaching back under the tree to hand out the gifts from Mom and Dad. "Here's one to Chuck; and one to me." It was small and flat. I looked further. "And here's one Dad; and this big one to Mom." I pointed to the large wrapped box up against the wall beside the tree. We all started the second round of unwrapping, and again Chuck was the fastest.

"Handy Andy Chemistry Lab" was written in big letters across the box. The picture showed a boy about Chuck's age staring, with deep interest, at a test tube half full of liquid. The words "atomic energy" were highlighted on the box.

"I thought you'd like that." Dad said "You can work on rubber compounds. I looked at the box and it has everything you need. I'll help you." Dad paused.

Chuck was looking up at him, but he wasn't smiling or reacting in any way, either positive or negative.

"Or you can work on it with your brother if you like." Dad went on. He looked over and me and smiled "I expect great things from both of you boys. You've got your microscope and you've got your chemistry set." He looked back at Chuck. "I didn't get to go to university, but you'll both go and become great scientists just like the men I work with." He was smiling broadly. "Do you know that some of them even have chemicals named after them? These are real compounds that we use in the rubber, named after the men who invented them."

By this time Chuck had opened the cardboard box and was looking down at a row of two dozen test tubes. Each was filled with a powered chemical of various colours. A paper label with "Handy Andy Chemistry Lab" and identifying the chemical inside was glued to each and a cork stopper scotch taped in the top. Chuck held up a test tube with a reddish powder inside. He shook it gently before putting it back in its place. "Thanks, Dad. This is neat."

I unwrapped the red and green paper that covered my gift "From Mom and Dad". It was a slide rule, about 10 inches long; bigger than the one that Dad carried in his shirt pocket at work every day. The name Pichett was stamped on the end. Dad had taught me how to use his slide rule the summer before so I knew how quickly it would solve math problems. He was smiling.

"This is great," I said "I'll be the first kid in grade nine with one." A few guys in grade ten had slide rules, and most of the advanced math students in grade twelve, but I really would be the first in grade nine.

"I knew you'd like this," Dad replied. He took the slide rule and moved it back and forth. "You'll be getting into trigonometry soon." He handed it back to me. "I use mine for basics, but I know the chemists have theirs out all the time."

Dad's gift to Mom wasn't much of a surprise. They had talked about it for weeks. The big wrapped box was lifted off the floor leaving behind a 17 inch RCA television. It was in a beautiful wooden cabinet with red stained doors. A few of the families on our block had television sets. I'd seen them in the store downtown and Mom had her eyes on one for some time. "You're the boss now," she had told Dad. "Isn't it time we had some nice things?"

By this time Chuck had closed the lid on his chemistry set and was back with the Meccano. He already had a few of the pieces bolted together.

"Hey Chuck," I said. "Look behind the tree and you'll see what I got you."

He stood up from the floor and walked around the tree. A hockey stick is not easy to cover in Christmas Paper, but I managed. He certainly did not need to unwrap it to know what it was. "You spent your money on candy, didn't you? I knew you'd want this."

He lit up. "Oh thanks!" he unwrapped the spiral of paper that wound around the stick from top to bottom. I'd already put black hockey tape on the blade and built up a tape knob for the top of the handle. "This is great." He bent over the stick in slap shot position and took a couple of swings. Mom jumped in "Stop, stop, stop. Do that outside or you'll break something."

"This is for you, from me!" Chuck showed his delight and handed me a small box that had been hidden inside the Christmas tree branches. I unwrapped the tin box of a *Hellerman* compass set, including a protractor, dividers, compass and triangle.

"This is great. With my slide rule and this I'll be the smartest kid in grade nine. Thanks."

Chuck had a smile stretching eight inches wide on a four inch face. This was his first big boy gift, bought with his own money.

After the excitement of opening presents was over, Chuck got down to the serious job of play. His shiny new Meccano set was quickly combined with the large box of pieces he already owned. There were a number of sets mixed into the box including small gifts from previous holidays, and a large set that he inherited from our cousins when they became teenagers. It was this first set that got him hooked on Meccano. It seemed that he never stopped in his quest to build a better car (or at least an eight year old's perception of a better car.) He had made dozens of airplane designs over the years, from swept wing jets that later proved to bear a striking resemblance to the Avro Aero, to biplanes and triplanes and even helicopters with spinning tops and rear propellers.

"Are you happy with your presents?" Dad asked

"I love my Meccano," Chuck said. "We're gonna start on the Ferris wheel after breakfast, aren't we?"

"Sure, I'll help you get started," I said.

"What about your chemistry set?" Dad asked again.

"Oh, it's nice too. And I got a hockey stick too. My old one is too short you know. I'm really glad to get a new one."

"You think you can score lots of goals with that?" I asked

"Oh sure. Just like The Rocket."

"You know we'll be able to watch the games on television," Dad said, "once I get it setup. Every Saturday night we can all sit down to watch the Leafs." Dad winked.

"Or the Canadiens." Chuck stuck in.

"I don't know if they show the Habs." Dad winked again. "Nobody wants to watch them." He paused. "Maybe if they are playing the Leafs."

"You bet we'll get to see them!" Chuck fumed.

—

With breakfast finished, Mom started on her first cleanup of the day. She was already talking about getting the turkey into the oven by one.

Dad sat down on the leather footstool next to the television with the RCA Manual.

Chuck and I retired to the big table with his box of Meccano and the *Popular Mechanics* plans in front of us. The plans came in a six by nine inch envelope with a photograph on the front. Inside were three sheets of paper, folded in half, with detailed drawings of each section, including detailed numbers and measurements of each required piece.

"Let's start with the seats," I said, pulling out the first sheet of the drawings. It showed each required piece very clearly, with each nut and bolt and the completed measurements for the finished unit. This was a professionally made set of drawings, as good as anything I'd ever seen Dad bring home from work, even if they were only on normal sized sheets of paper.

Chuck stared at it for 30 seconds, before laying it back in front of me and picking up the envelope. "Let's just use the picture," he said. He used a finger to tap on each seat on the picture and count quietly, "…, 8, 9, 10, 11 12. That's 12 benches."

"Sure. Can you see how each one is built?"

Chuck squinted down at the magazine. "Yup." He fished around in his box and held up a square piece. "It's got two of these for the sides." He dug around again, "One of these for the bottom." I looked at the detailed plans in front of me to confirm that he was right. He dug around again, longer this time, "And one of these for the seat."

As simple as Meccano is, it always takes much longer than expected to actually put the pieces together. Chuck sat in total concentration, carefully holding the pieces while he put each bolt into its nut, tightening by hand and then securing them with the little wrench. His fingers were still small enough to hold the nuts and bolts nimbly. I was already finding it clumsy.

As he concentrated, Chuck whistled his way through several passes of the Christmas carols that we'd heard on the radio over the past few weeks. His repertoire of a dozen or so songs included *Frosty the Snowman*, and *Rudolph the Red Nose Reindeer*, with the whole "You know Dasher and Dancer and Prancer and Vixen" part. But he was only whistling quietly, not intending for me, even right next to him, as an audience.

When we looked up, Dad was standing in front of the television set, ready to turn it on for the first time. Dad was a very methodical man. He wouldn't dream of even plugging it in until he had read the manual from cover to cover. He didn't just read it, he studied it with the concentration of a university student before final exams. He would certainly be as expert as the TV salesman by the time he had finished.

That was very particular of the way Dad completed every task. He could put his entire concentration into one thing and one thing alone. Sometimes, in the evening when he had brought home papers from work, I needed to disturb him with a problem from school. He would pick up all of the papers on his desk and place them neatly into a file folder or a big envelope, and carefully put the package in the side drawer of his desk. Then he would pull out a clean sheet of paper, and with pencil in hand say, "What can I help you with?"

After he had finished my problem, whether for two minutes or twenty minutes, he would hand me his worksheet. "Here, you keep this," open the side drawer to pull out the file folder or envelope, and carefully put each piece of paper back on his desk in exactly the same position it had been when I walked in. It was like I had never been there.

Dad pulled the upper button on the television set. In a moment a little white dot appeared in the centre of the grey screen. The sound of airwave static soon filled the room and Dad quickly rotated the volume button down.

Mom, Chuck and I sat on the chesterfield watching the glow. We had all seen televisions working at the neighbours' or at the store, so we knew what to expect.

When the screen was completely filled with flicking snow, Dad turned the channel dial to six. Through the sound of static we could hear a man's voice. Dad pushed in the outer ring of the channel dial, the "fine tuning," and rotated it slowly. First to the right, but the snow on the screen grew worse and the man's voice dropped away completely. Then to the left.

Dad was moving the dial very slowly, in his methodical and measured way. A fraction of an inch at a time. Slowly the man's voice became clear. We could tell that it was a Priest, reading from the bible. A moment later a picture worked its way out of the snow. A Catholic priest was standing at his pulpit, reading the bible verse for Christmas Day.

Our family is Anglican, not Catholic, but the services were similar enough for us to recognize. The Priest held his arms wide, his black robes hanging to the floor, "And behold the angel of the Lord came upon them and the glory of the Lord shone around them." Reading the same verses that Chuck had quoted one week earlier.

Dad continued to adjust the fine tuning and the circular antenna on top of the television until the picture was clear.

We were not transfixed by the television as later portrayed in family TV from the 1950s. This might have been because with only two stations available, the programming choice was limited. We watched the Christmas morning church service for about a half an hour until the communion started, and then we each drifted away from the living room.

That afternoon the station showed "Your Hit Parade," with the most popular songs of the year sung by the studio singers. They ran through a few Christmas favourites and the year's top hits; *Love is a Many Splendored Thing*, *Moments to Remember* and a soulless rendition of my personal favourite *Sixteen Tons*.

The television was turned on and off several times that day but none of us stuck with it for more than a few minutes. Christmas music over the radio was better background for our activities.

—

Boxing Day had another tradition in our house; Mom did absolutely nothing. We were allowed, no, *told*, to look after ourselves. We
did not sit down together for breakfast, lunch or supper. We just
picked away at the turkey leftovers until it was nothing but bones.
Three hungry guys and our assorted visitors will go through a turkey pretty quickly. Mom would turn the final carcass into soup the
next day.

In the real tradition of Boxing Day, members of our extended
family came by for short visits. My Dad's sister, Aunt Janet, her husband Uncle Ricky and our cousins Rob, Ray and Christine made
their visit. Once the preliminary greetings were out of the way, the
five kids sat around the dining room table for our annual game of
Monopoly.

"I'm gonna beat you guys," said Chuck, with his usual mix of
enthusiasm and confidence.

"You'll have to get by me first." Ray replied as he pulled the game
board out of the box. Ray was the middle child of the three cousins. Thirteen at the time; he had shot up by a few inches since our
last visit. He was tall for his age and had the light brown hair of his
father.

"I'm the race car!" was Chuck's response.

"I'm the top hat," Ray said.

"I'm the Scottie," Christine jumped in.

"I'll be the boot," said Rob.

I reached over to pick up the ship. It went without saying that
I acted as banker. I always was the banker in our annual game of
Monopoly even though we hadn't played for a year.

Christine was the youngest of the three, at eleven. She still had
the blonde hair of youth, but it would surely follow her brothers
to a light brown in her teens. She wore a dark blue dress with red
bows at the waist and collar. The kind of dress that would be worn
when visiting on a fancy occasion, which this was. Rob was just a
few months younger than me and almost as tall. He had a bad set of
pimples around his chin.

As banker, I counted out the opening $1,500 for each player. I was always careful to follow the rules precisely.

Sitting around the table in order by age, (our house rule,) Chuck rolled first. "A three. One, two, three," he counted off to land on *Baltic Avenue*. Chuck left his race car on the board, pulled his hand away and stared at the property. He didn't look to the left or the right, just directly at the property without blinking. We all sat quietly, waiting for him to say something. When ten seconds of silence had passed, ten seconds of awkward silence, Ray spoke "I'll buy it if you don't."

Another five seconds of awkward silence, until I leaned over to Chuck. "Buy it." I whispered audibly.

"Okay, I'll buy it." Chuck said out loud.

"That will be $60." I said. "Give me a 50 and a 10."

Monopoly is a good strategy game. I can look at the board and see where each piece is to calculate the odds of their landing on my properties (with a 45% chance of rolling a 6, 7 or 8) or my landing on theirs, and buy houses or hotels accordingly. With five of us in the game there was enough rolling of the dice, rents paid, houses and hotels bought and exclamations of *Oh No!* or *Oh Yes!* that conversation was limited to what was happening on the board. Every few minutes Chuck started talking about his Ferris Wheel or his hockey game or his friend's broken arm. I had learned to listen patiently to his stories with interest, but the cousins simply turned the conversation back to what was happening on the table.

Many roundings of the board later, it was Rob's bad luck to land on my *Atlantic*, then *Marvin Gardens*, in succession and paying me a total of $2,350 that was his downfall. He had to mortgage his most valuable set of hotels on the Orange set to make the second rent payment. This was just before Chuck, Christine and Ray all made visits to his properties and stayed rent free. When Rob landed on *Park Place* just a few rolls later, his fate was sealed.

Chuck covered the first side of the board with hotels. I had traded with him to build sets and helped with his decision making process. The cousins were not so conciliatory and worked against him aggressively.

"I'll give you *States Avenue* for your *Pennsylvania*." Ray offered. "That'll give you the whole corner of the board and you can put hotels on pinks too."

Chuck considered it for a few seconds and was picking up his *Pennsylvania Avenue* card when I intervened. "Hold on. Look at it. If you give him *Pennsylvania* he'll have the whole green set and he can put up hotels. Look at his pile. He's got lots of cash and you don't have much. So you won't be able to put up any houses until some people land on your properties and that won't be until we all get around the board again. But we're all coming around to his greens and if he gets hotels up, we'll get nailed. You'll be on his properties in a couple of rolls too and you'll get killed."

"Hey, this is between me and Chuck." Ray said. "You shouldn't have any say. I'm not talking to you."

Chuck put *Pennsylvania* back down on the table in front of him "No thanks," he said to Ray.

Chuck lasted longer than Christine, but landed on *Chance* and drew "Go To Jail." He used a "Get out of jail free" card on the next move, but that just put him back at the opening of the most expensive two sides of the board. He got nailed twice going around, leaving him a pauper with mortgaged properties. Ray soon picked those up and Chuck was gone.

With only Ray and me remaining, the game moved very quickly. At this point it becomes a matter of luck; me praying that he land on my properties and praying even harder to stay off of his. The problem was that while I owned much of the middle section of the board, Ray had complete control over the high rent district.

We circled, handing large rents back and forth; what I handed him always a few hundred dollars more than what he handed me. My neatly sorted cash reserves dwindled while his single stack grew. After a final minute of play it all came down to a bad roll of the dice. I landed on *Park Place*, then rolled snake eyes onto *Boardwalk* and was forced to mortgage my red and light blue properties. I conceded the game. It did not take many calculations to know that I had no ability to collect high rents, and there was no point in going further.

. We all retired to the living room where Dad and Uncle Ricky smoked their annual Christmas cigars.

"Why's your hand like that?" Chuck asked Uncle Ricky. He was missing three fingers from his right hand, holding the cigar between his thumb and index finger.

"You can thank Herr Hitler for that." Uncle Ricky said, looking at his hand. "Makes holding a pen damn tough." He was a lawyer.

"I don't get it." Ray asked. "How did a guy like Hitler ever get elected? Killing all of their own people; the Jews and all. Germany's a democracy, isn't it? How did he get elected in the first place?" World War II wasn't studied in history class yet, and I guess Ray didn't have the newest encyclopedias like we did.

Dad spoke up. "I think things were really bad in Germany after the first war. He came along and offered hope."

Uncle Ricky wasn't going to let anything remotely reasonable be said about Hitler.

"Let me tell you something, boys. The trouble with democracy is that fifty percent of the voting population has an I.Q. of less than a hundred. Every once in a while some huckster comes along and convinces them that all of their problems are someone else's fault. So they just fall in line behind him and goose step over a cliff."

Dad spoke again, "So what are you suggesting, that everyone with an I.Q. of less than one hundred doesn't get to vote?"

"No, I think everyone with an I.Q. that's one point less than mine. That sounds good, right?"

"Well that won't cut out many, will it?" Aunt Janet smiled.

—

Dad was right when he guessed that the encyclopedias would lead to my career choice. He was just wrong at the career. In grade eleven, our class was looking at the history of France. I was using our own encyclopedia as my main source of research and I found a lot of information about the Eiffel Tower and its designer, Gustave Eiffel. He designed more than just the tower. He was very famous for building railway bridges all over the world.

I knew that Tom's father was an engineer, but I didn't have any understanding about what he did, so the next time I was over, I asked him.

"Come back here with me and I'll show you." Mr. Jenkins said and walked into his den. "Take a look at this." He unrolled a large set of blueprints across his angled drafting table. "This is the new cement plant we're building outside of town."

"You're designing the whole thing?" I asked.

"No, no, no. I'm just doing a small part. Our company has the contract for the plant. I'm just working on the electrical wiring."

When I had read that Gustave Eiffel had designed railway bridges I had assumed that he did the entire job. It had never occurred to me that more than one man was involved.

What Mr. Jenkins showed me did not look anything at all like the towers that were going up at the cement factory out on Smyth Street, next to the river. The blueprints were criss-crossed with straight and curved lines, each one precisely hand-labeled. "What I do is pretty specialized," he said while I listened with my head bent down close to the page. "You won't be able to understand this yet. Tom says you're pretty good at mathematics, right?"

Tom cut in "Pretty good, he's top in the class!"

I smiled. Mr. Jenkins continued, "You understand basic calculus then. Let me give you an example that you'll be able to understand." He pulled out a blank piece of paper and began to write. "The men at my office who are building the towers work with this type of problem." He wrote $S=c(1-e^{-kt})$. "Let's say they're building with concrete. We know that concrete deteriorates over time, and the speed of the deterioration increases as time goes on. Understand?"

"Sure."

"This is the type of formula they would use to calculate the rate of deterioration." He wrote further on the page. "S equals the strength; that's what we're trying to find. T is the time and C and K are values of the specific type of concrete we're using. You know how calculus leads to curved lines?" He drew a curve on his paper. "We use this formula to determine how the concrete will break down over the next fifty years. So when they ask us to build a factory with a fifty year life span, we know exactly what we're doing."

This was really neat. The advanced group in math class was already looking at calculus problems even though the rest of my class wouldn't start on it until grade twelve.

"At school we've only been looking at numbers on a page. This really shows what it's used for."

"That's the difference between school and the real world," he went on. "Here, let me show you some more things that you might understand." Mr. Jenkins pulled an old university text book from the shelf in his closet. It was well used, with many sections underlined and many pencil notations along the margins. "This is from my first or second year of university, I think; a long, long time ago." He smiled. "You might understand parts of this."

We spent the rest of the evening flipping through the pages, looking at basic engineering problems related to buildings and bridges and dams. Most of the math was beyond my grasp, but at least I understood the concepts. He had me hooked in the first five minutes.

"Can I take this home with me?" I asked when nine o'clock rolled around.

"Sure. I haven't looked at it for at least twenty years. I don't even know why I keep it. Take these three books and look through them."

—

"Looks like Chuck's taking over my paper route."

It was Tom on the phone.

"You're kidding!"

"Nope. Not kidding. Mr. White told me when he dropped off my papers today."

"Wow."

"I don't know how he managed it. You're supposed to be twelve.

He's only eleven, right?"

"Yes, he's just eleven."

"Last week, when you and I were talking, I told you that I was giving up the paper route to take a summer job at the store. Chuck was there, right?"

"I don't remember."

Chuck had been in and out of the room a bunch of times when Tom and I were finishing up our science project.

"He must have heard, because this morning he walked into the office at the paper and asked for a job as a paperboy."

"Just like that?" I shouldn't have been surprised Chuck would do something like this.

"Well no, not quite. I guess he spoke to Mr. White about it. He must have told him that he knew me, because when Mr. White dropped off my bundle of papers this afternoon he hung around until I got there and asked me if I knew Chuck."

"What did you say?"

"Of course I said "yes." And I said Chuck was a good kid and I'm sure he'd do a good job and all that. And then he asked me if Charles Murray, was his father and I said "yes." And I think that clinched it."

Of course that would clinch it. Goodyear was the largest company in town. It contributed a lot to the community and was a big advertiser in the paper. It made sense that being the son of the Plant Manager would have some advantages.

"So now Mr. White wants me to take Chuck with me when I do my route next week," Tom went on, "and teach him how to do it and how to collect. Friday's my last day."

"You don't mind? Chuck can be a handful when he gets wound up, you know."

"I don't mind. I took over the route from my cousin four years ago. It's better that Chuck gets it than someone I don't know."

Chuck made his big announcement at the supper table.

"That's a lot of work you've taken on." Dad said. "What is it, six days a week? How long will it take you?"

"About an hour. More on Fridays when I have to collect."

"Well, I have to admire your ambition and your willingness to work. I used to deliver the paper when I was young too," he went on, "but I think I was a little older than you are."

Mom spoke up. "I'm fine with you doing it over the summer. But once school starts again you'll have to keep your school work up."

"It'll be fine. Don't worry, I promise."

"*Don't worry*. How many times have I heard you say don't worry. I'm your mother. It's my job to worry."

Later that evening, when we were alone, I asked him, "Tom said you're supposed to be twelve to get a paper route?"

"Well, I'm nearly twelve."

"You just turned eleven. You're not even eleven and a half yet. Did the man ask how old you are?"

"Yes." He was sheepish.

"Did you tell him you were eleven... or twelve?"

"Twelve."

"Oh."

"What difference does it make anyway? I can do it as good as anybody."

"I'm sure you can, but do you think it was good to lie like that?"

"They just don't want any little kids who can't even lift the paper bag doing it, that's all. I can lift the paper bag just fine."

It was impossible for me to scold Chuck for lying. He didn't lie to get out of trouble or dodge responsibility. He lied to take on more responsibility. That he had just walked into the office all by himself without Dad's help, without even telling me about it. Like Dad said, it was hard not to admire his ambition.

Chuck quickly became well known, practically famous, on the three blocks of his paper route. Other than quick breaks to say, "Hey!" to this person or that along the road, he whistled the entire time. It only took a few weeks for his customers to learn that they didn't need to check their front porch to see if the paper had arrived; they could hear Chuck's never-ending melody coming up the walk. He didn't do the old whistling standards. He was up to date with the hottest tunes from the Hit Parade. He heard them on TV and that was all it took. *Que Sera Sera* or *Blueberry Hill* or *Hot Diggity*. With an hour of practice, six days a week, along with all the other whistling he did around the house, he was becoming quite the expert.

I never learned to whistle myself. I think my tongue was just too fat. I couldn't curl it up into the roof of my mouth the way that Dad showed me. Everybody else accidentally blows a whistle at some time in their childhood and then just figures out what happened, but not me. Never once in my life has a whistling sound, even the most rudimentary, escaped my lips. Just a lot of air and spit.

—

Tom left Chuck with a daily route of 53 deliveries on three blocks of houses. By Christmas he had increased that to more than 80, but without adding extra streets.

"That's a lot of money." Tom said to Chuck one evening. "How did you get to that? I tried to sell papers to every house on the block, but 53 was the most I ever got."

"I don't do anything." Chuck said. "I'm just walking by and people step out on their front porch and wave at me. They say 'Hey Kid' and I say 'Hey' back to them and they tell me they want to get the paper too."

"You're just walking by?"

"And I'm whistling too. It's pretty hard not to like someone when they're whistling, isn't it?" Chuck smiled.

"Lord. Who would have guessed that you can get rich by whistling?" Tom replied.

Chuck laughed and walked into the back-yard, with *Mack the Knife* peeling over his shoulder.

—

A couple of years later, at lunch, Mom got the mail from the front porch. She held up the copy of *Sports Illustrated* magazine that came every week.

"Do you boys still look at this?" she asked. "Your father barely glances at it. I've got a stack of old ones in the closet. Do you still look at it, Chuck?"

"Not too much."

"Well, there's no use paying for a magazine that no one's reading. I get my magazines, and you still look at your *Popular Mechanics*. I think we're all covered, right?"

Chuck walked into the living room and picked up the newspaper that he had delivered to our house the previous afternoon. He rarely read anything more than the comic strips so I was surprised to see him flipping through the classified ads. He landed on one, larger, business ad.

Make Money Fast Selling Magazine Subscriptions, it said.

"We get five magazines every month, right?" he asked.

"That'll cut down to four if we stop getting *Sports Illustrated*." I answered.

"Do you think every house gets that many?"

"I see *Time*, or *Life*, or *Macleans* at my friends houses all the time. Do your friends get any of those?"

"There's always some magazines in the living room or the kitchen at Bob's house." He thought for several minutes before speaking again. "I've got 83 houses on my paper route. If every one of them gets five magazines that's ...., that's...." He was trying to do the multiplication in his head, but couldn't nail it down.

"415," I replied.

"415 magazine subscriptions. I wonder how much money I'd make selling 415 subscriptions?"

"I think you're being too optimistic." I said. "They're already getting 415 magazines. They don't need to buy them from you, do they?"

"Oh."

"I doubt you could sell them any more magazines than they've already got."

"Maybe one or two. That would still be okay."

"Sure. You'd still make some money, just not as much."

"I'm going to answer the ad anyway. It can't hurt to write them a letter. Will you help me?"

That afternoon we wrote a letter to Canadian Publishing, asking for their information package. A few weeks later, Chuck was equipped with a stack of subscription forms and a clipboard as he made his weekly newspaper collection rounds. His own whistling arrangement of *The Battle of New Orleans* announcing his way up every front walk along his route.

Later that day he told me how it went.

"I ring the bell and when Mrs. Wilkins comes to the door I say 'Hi Mrs. Wilkins. I'm collecting seventy five cents for the paper.' And when she comes back with the money I say 'I'm selling magazine subscriptions too. Would you like to buy some?' And I hold up the list of magazines for her to see.

"And Mrs. Wilkins takes the sheet and looks at it and she says 'I see you've got *Life* on the list. I just got a letter that my subscription is going to expire. I guess it wouldn't do any harm if I bought it from you instead of from them, would it?'

"And that's all it takes. Now I don't ask if they want a new magazine. I just ask if they have any subscriptions that are gonna expire? And if they do could they please buy them from me 'cause I'll be coming by to collect for their paper once a week anyway? And because I'm not asking them to buy anything right away, I'm just asking them to think about it in the future, how can they say no? So they all say, 'I'll keep it in mind,' or 'I'll think about it,' or something like that."

Sure enough, within a year Chuck had sold subscriptions all along his route. Most bought at least one or two and a few bought five or even more. He sold 187 subscriptions the first year, then they all came back for renewals the next year and he sold even more. And from what Chuck told me, he didn't need to do any work at all; just be ready with his clipboard every time he did collections.

—

When Uncle Bruce announced that his family was moving west, we decided to make Mom and Dad's 19th anniversary into a bigger event. The Grandparents, uncles, aunts and cousins from both sides of the family came by to make it a complete family reunion. At two o'clock we all headed down to the beach for an afternoon of swimming, a barbecue and bonfire.

As the oldest cousin, I reluctantly became a life-guard in the water. I spent most of the afternoon standing chest deep with my hands cupped for a half dozen five to ten year olds to climb on board and get tossed over my right shoulder. I'd swear that after my first fifteen minutes of this, most of the projectile children were not even relations, just strangers on the beach. I took a fair number of feet to the nose before learning that I should throw to the side.

With seven uncles and aunts, plus their husbands and wives and a total of 25 cousins, the day was exhausting.

At five-thirty, my uncles Mark and Bruce (Dad's brothers) lit up a large collection of charcoal barbecues brought by each family. By six o'clock the T-bone steaks for the adults, (thankfully myself included,) and hamburgers for the kids, were ready. We must have finished off half a cow that evening.

The aunts had set up picnic tables with the standard red and white checkered tables cloths, paper plates, mounds of potato salad and punch bowls of three-bean salad, and enough *Coke* and *Orange Fanta*, beer and wine to fill a swimming pool.

At the call for dinner, the whole family lined up to be served by Aunts June and Mary. (Mom's older sisters). All the men and boys were reminded that a shirt is required before being served, even for a beach supper. We sat on our blankets and towels on the beach with plates on our laps and cups dug into the sand nearby. My ad hoc babysitting duties had been passed over to my younger teenage cousins Janice and Julie, so I was able to sit with the adults, for the first time at a family event.

Uncle Bruce started off the toasts to Mom and Dad's years of marriage. He was a few years younger than Dad, with the same tall, slim build. After coming back from the war he'd gone north to work in the lumber business. "Lift your glasses everyone." He paused while we all recovered our beer and wine from the sand. "Here's to my brother and his beautiful wife, who is much too good for him."

We each clinked our glasses, (or rather tapped our paper cups,) with the few sitting relatives within easy reach. Uncle Bruce himself stood up and walked across the sand to tap cups with Mom and Dad.

Fifteen minutes later, with another case of beer passed around and several more bottles of wine opened, Uncle Mark stood to give his toast. Uncle Mark was just as tall, but much more solidly built than my Dad. "Built like a football player" we used to say.

"I remember when these two were married like it was yesterday. They were nice enough to rush the ceremony forward so Bruce and I could stand with them at the altar in our shiny new uniforms before we shipped out." He lowered his voice. "Of course their rush to the altar had nothing to do with the birth of their number-one-son." He winked at me. "And although none of us were here to witness it, we're told that he was born ten months later." General sly chuckles around the blanket.

"It was ten months and two days," Mom protested. "I know that because Goodyear's insurance would only pay for a baby born ten months after the wedding. I just kept my legs crossed for the last few days."

"Okay, okay, we'll believe you." Uncle Mark went on. "You've had 19 great years. Here's to the next 19 when we meet at this beach again."

Once more there was clicking of cups and Uncle Mark stepped through the soft sand and bent over to give my Mom a kiss on the cheek and my Dad a hug around his shoulders.

Another forty five minutes or so passed with more beer and wine for all. I was allowed to take part, but with Dad's close eye on me, I knew enough to take it easy. The uncles imbibed far more than I did.

In among the general conversation I heard Aunt June bring up

the topic of how Mom and Dad met. I had heard the general out-
line before but never in such detail and certainly never by someone
with so many cups of wine in her.

Aunt June was three years older than Mom. Not quite as tall
but every bit as pretty. She was wearing a yellow bathing suit with
orange flowers. When we were in the water earlier she'd had on a
matching yellow bathing cap with orange flowers sticking out of it.
She was a nurse until she married Uncle Jack in the late '40s. Their
three children, Gord, Tony and Jenny were among the cousins I'd
been throwing over my shoulder earlier that afternoon.

"I remember when Charles and Becca met. I was with her."

"Oh, God. Not this again." Dad said.

"What's the matter? It's a good story."

"Oh, please don't." Mom spoke up. She had an embarrassed
smile that just drew more audience interest.

"Let me tell the story," Aunt June went on, "And you two can
interrupt when I get something wrong."

By this time the teenaged cousins had come around the adults'
circle; the younger cousins were building sandcastles down near the
water. Janice and Julie kept one eye on them while listening to Aunt
June.

"I'd just returned home from nursing school. I'd been away since
Christmas. Becca and I hadn't seen each other for months so we
borrowed Dad's car and drove off to the fairgrounds."

"That was your grandfather's old Austin, with the inflatable
seats," Mom said to me.

"Inflatable seats?" I asked.

"Dad leaned over. "I'll tell you about it later."

Aunt June continued, "We stopped at the Shell station out on
Highway 7 to get some gas."

"It's still there." Dad said.

"We asked the fellow to check our tires as well." She took another drink of wine. "And while he was doing that, a very handsome
young man drove into the station on his motorcycle."

Mom blushed at Aunt June's use of the word "handsome."

"Oh come on, Becca! We both saw how handsome the young man was. You said so yourself at the time."

Dad interjected to relieve Mom's predicament. "That was my old Norton 350. Man, did I love that bike!"

"That bike almost killed you," Uncle Bruce jumped in.

"Let me tell you something, when I got on that bike, I felt free. You're driving a car, all sealed up and staring out the window, it's like you're in a cave watching the shadows of life pass by, but when you're on a bike, you move outside the cave; you see the world like it really is. You can feel the tiny change in temperature when you ride into a shadow. You can smell the hay in the fields or the lilacs pruned by old ladies along the streets. You can feel the morning dew on your skin or watch the moon coming up over the horizon. That's what it means to ride a motorcycle."

"Listen to this guy." Uncle Mike said. "One book on philosophy and thinks he's Plato. You talk about the dew on your skin, but I noticed you didn't mention the bugs."

"Just all part of the experience," Dad replied. "Once you move outside the cave, you have to take the bad with the good."

"Wasn't it looking at a full moon that busted up your ankle?"

"Like I said, it's all part of the experience," Dad said, taking another long pull at his beer. "It was such a hot day. I'd pulled in to take off my heavy jacket and I saw these two young beauties on the other side of the station. I was looking at them, trying to figure out a reason to go over and talk to them and they were looking back at me."

"We were not looking back at you!" Mom scolded.

"Well, two girls were looking at me. Are you telling me they were two other girls?"

Aunt June continued. "We hopped back in the car and drove off."

"That's when your Mom waved at me."

"I was just saying *hi*."

Aunt June continued. "And before you know it, this handsome young man pulls up along beside me, on his motorcycle, and we're driving."

Dad smiled again. "When your Mom waved at me, I thought,

'What the heck.' Actually "heck" wasn't the word I used, but you get the picture. I jumped on the bike and took off after them."

I had never heard this part of the story before.

"What exactly was your plan?" Aunt Mary questioned.

Dad laughed. "I really didn't have a plan. I just knew that I had to meet them."

Aunt June continued. "This handsome young man pulls up beside us, on his motorcycle and says 'Hi!'"

My mouth dropped. The straight-laced man I knew as Dad; the man who came home every day with his neck tie done up tight; the man who had taught us values and morals was, was... a hound dog.

"It was very hard to hear him over the noise of his motorcycle," said Mom.

"We said 'Hi back at ya!' said June, "then he shouted over at us 'Where you heading?' and I told him we were going to the fairgrounds and I asked if he was going."

"We thought he must be going. He was driving in that direction," Mom said.

"So I said 'Sure, I'll meet you there,'" Dad jumped in. "Then I fell back behind them and followed them to the fairgrounds."

"And the rest is history," said Uncle Bruce.

"Not quite," said Dad. "There were two cute girls but only one of me. We had some hot dogs and we walked around a bit. Then the band started up and I asked your Aunt June up to dance, but she said she was too tired."

"I really was tired. I'd just gotten back from college that afternoon, remember. Becca and I were only planning on going for a short drive before Charlie here showed up."

"So I waited a bit then I asked Becca up to dance and we spent the evening having a great time."

"Abandoning me on the sidelines," added Aunt June.

"And the rest is history." Dad concluded.

"You mean Aunt June could be our Mom?" Chuck asked.

"That's right," Dad winked at me. "But she was too tired to dance. You don't want to marry a girl who can't dance."

"And when was the last time we went dancing?" Mom stuck in.

"What year was that?" I asked.

"That was two years before we were married, so that would've been 1937."

"And when did you ask Mom to marry you?"

"A year or so later."

"And she said yes?"

"Oh no," said Mom. "Your Dad just had a nothing job at the clothing factory then. He wouldn't be able to support a family." She looked over at Chuck and me. "If there's one thing your Grandma taught me it's don't get involved with a fellow who can't look after you right."

Aunt June and Aunt Mary both nodded. They had obviously all been taught the same lesson by Grandma.

Mom went on. "Your Grandma had a hard time when she first married your Grandpa and she wasn't going to let us go through the same thing. So I told Charles here that he'd have to get a better job before I'd marry him, and he did."

"Gord Lock was working at the Goodyear plant," Dad explained. "He told me about their training program and he put in a good word for me. And I got in."

Gord Lock and Dad were very close friends until he died in a car accident when I was ten. I remember growing up, there was a big white bridge with concrete arches which crossed the river to his house. Even today we still call it, "Lock's Bridge." Until I was twelve, I thought that was its official name. Any time I told my friends that my Godfather lived on the other side of Lock's Bridge, they looked at me funny.

"My pay doubled overnight and that's when I became sufficiently worthy for your Mom to marry me."

When supper was cleared, the younger kids were sent to pick up one log each from the pile put by the roadside by park workers. Uncle Bruce dumped all of the still hot barbecue charcoal into the fire pit and stacked the kindling on top. It wasn't long until it caught and he was able to add the bigger logs.

The kids continued to feed the bonfire with fresh logs, and by the end of the evening it must have been six feet wide.

Many more bottles of beer and cups of wine were consumed. I even had three beers myself, which was a record for me at the time. We listened to all of the uncles and aunts tell stories of their younger days. Aunt June actually met Uncle Jack at the same fairgrounds a decade later.

By ten o'clock, with a bunch of sleepy children and tipsy adults, we all drove away to our various homes, (or motels for the out-of-town visitors.)

—

Just after school started in the fall, Chuck attended his first funeral that wasn't for one of our relatives.

"Can you let out my suit pants a bit?" He asked Mom at dinner. "I'm going to a funeral on Saturday and they're getting real tight."

"What funeral is that?" Dad asked, surprised.

"It's for Brian's Mom."

"Who's Brian?"

"A guy at school. His Mom's dead from cancer and he's not feeling too good."

"Well, that's very nice of you," Mom interjected as she put her hand on his arm. "Of course I'll take a look at your pants. Maybe it's time to buy you a new suit anyway. Let's drive down to Woolworth's after school tomorrow and see what they've got."

"Where is the funeral?" I asked.

"At Trinity Church." He replied. This was the oldest United Church in Bowmanville, with a history dating back to the early-1800s.

"Okay. I'll drive you there on Saturday," I said.

—

I let Chuck off at two pm and waited in the car. From the group that entered through the front door, I could tell it was a small service and would end quickly. I was a third of the way through *Fahrenheit 451* and appreciated the chance to read a couple more chapters while I waited.

Around two-thirty the front doors opened again and people slowly and silently walked out. At the tail end of the small group, Chuck came out with his arm around the shoulders of another boy; I could only assume this was Brian. They sat together on the church steps for five minutes, while pallbearers loaded his mother into the hearse and people got organized into cars driving to the cemetery. I looked up from my book from time to time and could see that the boys were only talking a little. Chuck was showing him some hockey cards that he'd pulled from his breast pocket. They handed the cards back and forth with little comment. When Brian's father tapped him on the shoulder, Chuck stood up slowly and walked over to our car.

—

We saw Brian at our house many times over the following weeks. At first he and Chuck sat in relative quiet building cars, rocket ships and jet airplanes with the still growing Meccano set. Their limited conversation was asking to pass a wrench or a certain length of Meccano metal strip for the model. After a week, he and Chuck played one-on-one ball hockey in the driveway, generating a bang on our garage door from every wrist shot that missed the makeshift net. The only conversation concerned the upcoming hockey season. After another week, the pair formed the nucleus of neighbourhood ball hockey games on our street with a dozen kids shouting and laughing at each goal scored.

Because of all of his friends and all of their families, Chuck went to a number of funerals over the years. There was at least one, and often two or three, every year from that point on. In almost every case we'd have the friend over, or Chuck would be at the friend's house, several times in the days and weeks following the funeral.

—

In spite of his academic struggles, Chuck continued to excel in any activity in front of a crowd. He was lead in the boys choir at church until his voice went flat at puberty. His real strength was with acting on stage. By twelve, he was cast in the lead role of every school production. In grade eight (both times), he played Scrooge in the school's version of *A Christmas Carol.*

In his first turn, the class did an abridged version of the play. In his second turn, a year later, only the other roles were condensed. The Scrooge role was extended to nearly its full length from the book. The final scene of the story was Chuck's acting masterpiece. By this point in the evening, he wasn't a boy playing Ebenezer Scrooge, he was Ebenezer Scrooge with the voice of a boy.

"I don't know what to do!" laughed Chuck, running around the stage in his nightshirt. "I'm as light as a feather, as happy as an eagle, as merry as a school boy, as giddy as a drunken man." He ran to the front of the stage and looked out an imaginary window, down to the gymnasium floor. "A Merry Christmas to everybody! You, boy," he shouted. "Yes, you. What day's today?"

"Today," replied the boy, played by one of the younger kids at school. "Why, it's Christmas day, sir."

"It's Christmas day!" Chuck said to the audience. "I haven't missed it. The spirits have done it all in one night! They can do anything they like. Of course they can. Of course they can."

In Chuck's first year in grade eight, he played the role well, but second time around, with an extra year of practice, he carried the entire production. It ran for three nights and most of the town showed up to watch. Our local newspaper, the *Canadian Statesman,* carried a photo of the entire cast with Chuck front and centre, page three.

He was naturally confident in front of an audience, and Dad was quick to stoke the fire even more.

"With confidence like that, you can achieve anything you want. I expect great things from you."

With me, Dad only changed the encouragement slightly, "With

intelligence like that, you can achieve anything you want. I expect great things from you."

I have to admit that I could never get a handle on Chuck's troubles at school. It certainly wasn't for lack of trying. Every night after supper we sat at our desks doing homework. I used to help Chuck with the first one or two problems on his page and leave him to do the rest. He'd stare at the book with pencil in hand for a few minutes before opening up in a monologue about whatever topic happened to cross his mind. His talking didn't bother me much.

After years of practice, I was able to just close my mind to Chuck's distractions and concentrate on my own books. I rarely had actual homework because I was able to finish most assignments in class. My home studies consisted mainly of working ahead in the advanced math and science classes that I enjoyed so much.

—

In January, Chuck had a group of friends and classmates over for a skating party on the rink Dad built in our back yard. With his gregarious nature, Chuck was always quick to make friends. "Hey Bob!" "Hey Jim!" "Hey Mike!" Chuck shouted out at what seemed like every second person on the streets downtown.

I'd always been terrible at remembering names and faces.

"Hey Betts! Will I see you this afternoon?" He could yell across Main Street. "Yeah, great. And don't forget to bring Jack!"

And a moment later, "Hey, Tom. How was Sudbury?" Did you have a good time at your Uncle's cottage?"

I'm sure Chuck would have liked more friends at his party, but even with fifteen our little rink was past its limit. They skated around in a tight circle with no room for tag or crack-the-whip.

Mom was the first to notice Chuck with Debbie, together on the ice, mitted hand in gloved hand. She called Dad and me to look out the window. "That's just lovely," she said, putting her arm around Dad's waist.

I had never been through the puppy love stage with a girlfriend, so I watched the young couple through the frosty window with some envy.

Debbie wore a dark blue, thigh-length wool coat with large round dark buttons. She had a brown, loose knitted hat and red scarf covering much of her face, and brown and black boys' hockey skates on her feet.

They stuck together for the afternoon, hands clasped on the ice and bumping shoulders when drinking hot chocolate beside the rink. It was not until Debbie came into the house and took off her coat, scarf and hat that I could get a look at her. She had a dark complexion, especially for January in Canada, and dark, curly shoulder-length hair. She wore brown corduroy pants and a checkered, heavy button-up shirt that looked like it was borrowed from her father.

When she pulled off her woollen hat her hair went in every direction from the static, but she didn't make the slightest effort to straighten it out. She just put on a big smile, stuck out her hand to Mom and said, "Hi there, I'm Debbie. I go to school with Chuck."

From that moment, the attraction between them was clear.

She continued, "He sits three seats behind me, over in the next row. Thank you very much for having us over for such a good party. I've had a very nice time. The hot chocolate was really good. It was cold out there and the hot chocolate really warmed me up, but it's good to come inside and get warm."

The rest of the friends followed through the kitchen, piling coats, hats and scarves on a single chair until they rolled onto the floor. They had all taken their skates off on the back porch so were walking in their heavy socks.

Mom said hello and handed each person a hotdog on a paper plate as they filed past the stove and into the living room, where a few took up the chesterfield and chair but most sank to the floor.

With fifteen young teenagers in the living room, the chatter instantly rose to the level of the exotic bird house at Bowmanville Zoo.

I stood, leaning against the kitchen doorway and watched the group. It seemed that every thirty seconds one section of the room or other broke into laughter. Several times the whole room started laughing at once but I could never quite make out the private joke.

Chuck sat on a big, brown leather footstool in front of Dad's chair on the far side of the room. Debbie was sitting cross-legged in front of the stool. She had her arm up on his knees and they both chatted non-stop with the two or three people nearest to them. They got into the laughter with all the rest.

Chuck had made it very clear to Mom that this was not to be an official birthday party with balloons and gifts, but he could not stop her from baking a cake. It was iced in white to recreate the skating rink outside. Around the rink were even higher piles of white icing to represent the snow banks that Dad shovelled every day. The most amazing feature was all the skating figures that Mom made from marzipan and food colouring. She had spent the entire previous afternoon on this project, keeping it secret from everyone, and to-day, when she saw the exact number of boys and girls outside, she put one figure on the cake for each with different coloured coats, hats and pants. Some were skating; a few were standing in the snow banks with tiny cups in their tiny hands; she had two that had fallen on their bums on the ice and one fellow who was stuck head first into the snow bank with only his legs and skates visible, and anoth-er boy trying to pull him free.

As soon as Mom walked into the living room with the big platter in her hands, Debbie jumped to her feet and led everyone in singing *Happy Birthday*.

When the party broke up, Chuck walked Debbie home in the early winter dark. She only lived a few blocks away, but it was after six by the time Chuck got back.

"Debbie seems like a nice girl," were Mom's first words when he walked in the door.

"Quite the Tom boy, isn't she?" Dad chuckled.

"Oh, she's real nice." Chuck said. "I don't think she's a Tom boy at all."

I smiled, but kept my opinion to myself.

CHAPTER THREE

With Debbie around, I didn't need to spend so much time helping Chuck in the evenings. She was more than a year younger than he was, but had a better grasp of their school work. On Sunday afternoons during the winter, and a couple of evenings each week once spring arrived, she and Chuck sat on the floor in the living room doing homework.

"Okay, we've got the fraction 2/3." Debbie wrote down. "What's that as a percentage?"

Chuck hesitated "23?" He asked with a quiet, high pitch. He knew it was wrong but Debbie wouldn't allow him to go with no answer.

"Can you tell me what percentage is ½?" She said. "Or ¼?"

"Let's go outside." Chuck said.

"Not until we're done here. I'll get you through this."

"Do you wanna watch TV? *Leave It To Beaver* is on. It's real good."

"Stop it, Chuck. We've got to get through this."

Mom was listening in the kitchen. "There's an old saying that behind every good man is an even better woman." The way she looked at me, I could tell this was as much a hint to me as a comment on Chuck's situation.

"It would be nice to see you with a girl," She went on. "Maybe you'll meet someone at university." She went back to cutting up potatoes at the sink. "Have you given any more thought to where you'd like to go?"

I was glad Mom had dropped the conversation about a girlfriend. She hinted at it once in a while. I was frustrated at not having a date for the school dances, but girls weren't interested in a wallflower like me. They wanted someone who was fun, not a guy buried in his books.

Chuck was busy most evenings and every weekend now. Dad insisted that we all eat dinner together, but as soon as his last mouthful was swallowed, either Debbie came over or Chuck was out the door and down the street. I knew that her parents did not want him there after seven o'clock, so most evenings he was with Francis and little Charlie, who was not so little any more.

If the weather was nice, street hockey was their game. As soon as they started slapping the ball, other kids, younger or older, would appear from their front doors to join in.

"Hey Jimmy!" Chuck shouted across the street. "Come on! You're on my team! You can play defence!"

"He's too young," Francis said. "He's only eight I think."

"He's fine. We'll put him back on defence and he can block shots."

"But he'll start crying. You know he will."

"He'll be okay. I'll make sure." He turned to Jimmy. "Hey, Jimmy, you know the rule about crying, right?"

"No crying allowed," Jimmy answered.

"That's right. This is a game for men. No crying allowed. You wouldn't see The Rocket cry, would you?"

Maurice "The Rocket" Richard, leader of the Montreal Canadiens and the best player in hockey in his prime (possibly the best of all time), was Chuck's idol. He'd retired that summer but his picture, with its glaring dark eyes, stayed on our bedroom wall for years afterwards.

Chuck turned back to Francis. "Jimmy'll be okay. You watch. And here comes Chris. Hey, Chris! You can go on Bob's team!"

Although his chums had moved one year ahead of him at school,

Chuck had remained the group's natural leader.

—

"Debbie's moving across *Lock's Bridge*." Chuck came into the house in late April. "I go over to her house and her Dad says she's moving into her Grandparent's house across the bridge. She's over there right now."

Mom and Dad looked at each other, but didn't say anything.

"She didn't tell you she was moving?" I asked.

"No. I'm gonna ride over and see her now."

"I'll tell you what." Dad said. "I want to change the oil in the car, and I need your help."

"But I need to go over and talk to Debbie."

"You know they don't like you visiting in the evening."

"That's Mr. Spinolli's rule. Her Mom never has a problem with it."

"All the same, I think that Debbie needs some time with her mother. I want you to give her some space; just until she comes back to school."

"What's going on?" I asked. I could tell that Mom and Dad had a secret between them.

"Mr. and Mrs. Spinolli have some problems," Dad paused, "I'm sure Debbie needs time with her mother."

"He's a hitter," Mom said quietly. I had heard that people can speak with venom in their voice but I'd never actually experienced it before. Her mouth was straight across and her eyebrows were furrowed. "Bastard," she whispered.

"Look, Chuck," Dad went on. "You can see Debbie when she comes back to school, but until she does, I want you to give her some space."

"Why, Dad?"

"Look, boys." Dad hesitated for some time. "You must never, ever, hit a woman. Ever." He paused again, looking us right in the eyes. "Do you understand?"

I nodded quietly. Chuck stared straight ahead. Mom didn't say anything, just kept flipping the pages of the newspaper without reading them.

"You know," Dad went on, "when you get married, and when a woman agrees to take on your name," he looked over at Mom, "it's important that a man understands the responsibility he's taking on." He looked back at Chuck and me. "In the old days people used to think that a man owned his wife, like he owns a dog or a cow or something."

Chuck and I both laughed a little, nervously. I think we were both surprised to hear Dad talking like this. He'd never had a serious, father to son, discussion with us before. I got the feeling that this was something he'd been holding in for a long time, just waiting for the right moment. He was speaking slowly, pausing to make sure that every sentence was saying what he wanted it to say.

He went on. "But that's not right, at least in this century. And lately, since all the women went to work during the war, we hear people talking about marriage like some sort of partnership. But that's not right either. Your mother and I don't think about each other like that; like we're business partners or something."

I noticed that Mom was not interjecting her thoughts on this. She was letting him explain something that was important to them both.

"It's better to think of a man and his wife as two halves of the same body. Like I'm one half and your mother is the other half, and the body just can't get anywhere unless both halves are working together.

"But you know maybe that's not right either. We're not halves of the same body. It's more like we're different parts of the same body; like I'm the arms and she's the legs. Yes, that's better. We each have different responsibilities but the body doesn't work unless we both hold up our responsibilities. The man is responsible for going to work and providing the family with a nice house and a nice life, and the woman is responsible for making sure the house is always kept up and there's nice meals to come home to, and of course she always has to look after the kids while he's away at work every day. And it's important that you both understand what your role is. Not just your role, but your duty. When you get married, you are promising your wife that you'll look after her, that you'll give her a nice house and security so she never has to worry about it. And your wife is making a promise back to you that she'll look after the house and give you a nice family life at home. And that's how you become different parts of one body. The body is the marriage, and one of you is the arms and the other is the legs.

"So if a man treats his wife badly, then he's not treating his partner badly but he's treating his own body badly. It's like the arm is stabbing the leg with a knife. Yes, it's hurting the leg but more importantly hurting the whole body. Do you understand what I'm trying to say?"

We both nodded. It would take some time for me to interpret what Dad said, but I was sure that both Chuck and I caught the basic message.

"You come out and help me change the oil." Dad said to Chuck. "It's time you learned to look after the car." Dad walked out of the room, putting an end to the conversation.

"I think you'd better go with him." I said to Chuck. He could tell that the situation had become serious and past questioning.

Mom continued flipping the pages of the newspaper. "The next time you see Debbie," she said, "you keep quiet about this unless she brings it up." She flipped a few more pages. "This is none of your business unless she brings it up. Do you understand?" She still had not looked up from her paper.

"Okay," Chuck said. He was confused by the whole situation. "I won't say anything. I promise."

Chuck didn't see Debbie at school for a few days. When she returned and they were back together in the evenings, I don't know that they ever discussed why she had moved across the bridge. Any time Debbie arrived at our house, Mom was very quick to invite her for supper, and quite often she stayed. They still joked and laughed together, but not quite as often.

—

In the summer after my first year of engineering at McGill University in Montreal, Dad got me and Chuck jobs at the factory. A new wing was being added to expand the passenger tire line. Dad had suggested to the building contractor that a place be found for his two boys. Miraculously, a position opened up for me the day after I returned home from Montreal in April and another position opened up for Chuck the day after he finished school in June.

I worked with Hans Schultz, the electrician. He was in his late 50s, dark black hair; very thin, like he saved money by scrimping on food, about five foot ten in height. Hans had fought for Germany and been a prisoner of war at Camp 30, just outside of town. He applied to immigrate immediately after the war. Because he was a skilled electrician and had learned rudimentary English from his time as a POW, he had no problem being approved. The building boom was on and there was a shortage of skilled tradesmen.

One time at lunch, Chuck had blurted out, "Ever shoot anyone?"

Hans answered very quietly, "The bullets didn't have my name on them."

I don't think that Chuck understood his meaning.

It was good experience for me to be involved in construction, even if I was just an assistant. I spent my day feeding electrical wires through pipes along the walls. I'd start at one end and push a long, flat fish wire into a conduit until it appeared fifty feet down the line. Hans would hook electrical wires to the fish and I'd pull them all the way back, then Hans would cut the wire, strip both ends and connect it to junction boxes. I was not allowed to do that part because I'm not a licensed electrician.

Hans kept very much to himself on the job site. Even then, fifteen years after the war had ended, there was still a lingering sense of resentment between Canadians and Germans. I remember one of the plumbing guys coming over one day and asking, "Hans, can I borrow your boy for an hour?"

"He stays with me." Hans replied and turned away.

Hans was very particular. We started working at exactly eight o'clock, even if he arrived a few minutes early. Once I arrived just at eight and went to put my lunch box down in the lunch room, so I got back on the floor about three minutes later.

"YOU START AT EIGHT O'CLOCK!" he yelled. "NOT AFTER EIGHT!"

"Okay, okay," I said meekly.

All of the other guys on the construction crew raised their heads to see the commotion. At coffee break, the plumber came over to me. "Don't worry about the fucking Nazi. Thinks he's still in the army."

I only heard Hans laugh one time all summer. Primo, Chuck's boss, was teasing me in his Portuguese accent. "So, you gotten laid yet? When I was your age I was getting laid by a different girl every night."

Everyone was shocked when Hans spoke up. "He's got hairy palms!" He roared with laughter like it had been bottled up in him since his arrival in Canada.

—

Every day the site engineer came by with his clip board. I tried to listen in when he talked to the workers. He often spoke to Primo about the cinder block walls they were putting up, making sure they had enough mortar or rebar supports. "He's a pain in the ass." Primo told me. "Are you going to be a pain in the ass when you are an engineer?"

"What's it like working with the bricklayers?" I asked Chuck.

"Jesus. These guys, I can't understand a word they're saying."

The bricklaying crew was entirely Portuguese. Only Primo spoke any English at all. "They only know three words." Chuck shouted, "'MOTAR! BLOCK! WATER!' To me it just sounds like 'BLAH!' So I can't figure out what the hell they want. They shout 'BLAH!' And I bring them more blocks and they look at me and shout 'NO – BLAH!' And I bring them mortar, and they shout 'NO – BLAH!' And I bring them water and they don't say a word. They just go back to work like nothing's happening. These guys are so fast. They're not paid by the hour you know. They're paid by the block. So they get real mad if I slow them down."

"You're the only one working for them?" I asked.

"Yeah. It's nuts. I'm supplying three different crews. Nine guys all shouting at me 'BLAH! BLAH! BLAH!' The ten inch blocks we're using on the outside walls are bloody heavy. I'm lifting hundreds of these every day. And not just the blocks, but the mortar and five gallon buckets of water."

"The BLAH, and the BLAH, and the BLAH." I laughed.

"Oh Jesus. I get enough of that at work."

"You're not wearing gloves?"

"No. I can go through a pair every two days. I can't afford to be buying gloves so I just go with my bare hands." Chuck held out his hands. The palms were callused and as tough as leather gloves themselves.

—

It was just a couple of weeks into the summer when Chuck came home about nine o'clock. He'd been out with his friends after supper. Usually he would be full of chat about whatever they'd been up to; something adventurous or stupid. Chuck was never shy about his adventures or goings-on, just as long as they were exciting, but this day he walked past the living room and just said, "Goodnight. I'm going to bed."

Mom and Dad looked up from their reading. "That was unusual." Mom said.

"What's that all about?" Dad asked me.

"I've no idea."

"Maybe you should check on him."

"I don't think it's anything. I'll go in as soon as I finish this," I said, holding up the newspaper.

I took my time to read every section, even sports, before I went up to our room at quarter to ten. The last of the daylight was setting through our bedroom curtains. Chuck had climbed into bed without even brushing his teeth, but it was still light enough for me to see that he was wide awake.

"What's going on?" I asked.

"I think I'm in trouble."

"Tell me about it." Chuck and I had always been as close as two brothers could be. He had never hesitated to fill me in on his tribulations, usually with a promise of not telling Dad.

"I beat up a guy."

"Who?"

"David"

"Who's he?"

"David Gillespie. He's in grade ten."

"Is he smaller than you?"

"No. He's bigger than me."

"That's good at least. What happened?"

"David and Bill and John are bugging Debbie. We're downtown roller skating and they come up to her and start bugging her about living across the bridge and they're saying, 'What's your Dad doing tonight Debbie,' and 'Has your Mom got a new boyfriend yet,' and stuff like that. And Debbie's real upset and we go to the other side of the arena to get a pop and they don't follow us over right away but later they come over to get some food and they start at it again saying stuff like 'Hey Debbie my uncle would like to meet your Mom,' and 'Hey Debbie why'd you move across the bridge' and Debbie is getting real upset again and then David says 'Hey Debbie, is your Daddy drunk again' and I jump up and punch him right in the gut and he bends over and I punch him right on the side of his head and he falls on the ground and then Bill and John start to grab at me but before they can pull me off I lean down and say to David in his ear, 'you shut up,' and a crowd of kids starts to get around us but then Mr. Pillis comes and breaks it up and he must think the three big kids are causing trouble because he tells them they have to get out right now and they leave, but we don't want to see them outside so Debbie and I stay for a while before I walk her home."

"So you said this David guy is bigger than you?"

"Oh yeah."

"And they were really teasing Debbie a lot?"

"Yeah. They're trying to make her cry."

"Okay."

"You're not going to tell Mom and Dad are you?"

"I don't think you've got anything to worry about. Go to sleep."

I left Chuck with the light off and went to have my bath. I've never been in a fight, before or since that night. My world is one of calmness and understanding, not spontaneity and passion. I could not understand how Chuck, or any boy, would suddenly launch out with his fists to solve a problem that could not be solved any other way. As far as I was concerned, his first action of walking away could be duplicated over and over until the problem was solved. I've never been in anything close to the situation that Chuck described but if I had, I'm certain that I would have given everything, even my own pride if necessary, to move away from the argument before it came to fighting.

After putting on my pyjamas, I went out to the living room to give Mom and Dad a brief description of the evening. I knew they would not be upset. "Some bigger kid was ragging pretty bad on Debbie, so Chuck set him straight." I said

"Did he deserve what he got?" Dad asked.

"Oh yes."

"Good."

A couple of days later, Dad squeezed Chuck's biceps. "Look at those muscles. You're putting your brother to shame."

Chuck's adult body was taking shape. He was not going to be tall and thin like Dad and me. People often referred to him as a fireplug; a little below average height but stout and thick, and by the end of the summer, after lifting thousands and thousands of ten-inch cinder blocks, he was solid muscle; immoveable solid muscle.

CHAPTER FOUR

In August, a couple of weeks before starting my second year at McGill, I had to make a quick trip to get set up in an off-campus apartment, near the Montreal Forum. Chuck was anxious to see what can only be described as a shrine to hockey greatness; the home of the Montreal Canadiens. I asked if he wanted to come with me on the bus and he said, "Why don't we hitchhike? It'll be a lot more fun."

"Are you sure?" I asked. "Who knows who we might meet?" Many of my friends hitchhiked regularly, but I had never done so.

"That's the whole point," he replied. "Who knows who we might meet?"

It's normally five hours of driving in each direction, so with hitchhiking delays, we planned on a day to get there, a full day in Montreal, and a day to get home. At eight o'clock on Wednesday morning we were standing beside Route 57 wearing small packs, our thumbs straight out and our backs to the South. Chuck was whistling *Saturday's Game*, the marching theme to the weekly TV hockey broadcast. The song didn't have definitive starting or ending points so Chuck could continue at it, over and over, without a break. I didn't mind.

The road was busy at this time of morning and it took a half hour for us to realize that standing just after a stop light was a bad idea. When the light turned green, the cars were too bunched together and too busy getting up to speed for one to safely pull off to the side. We saw many drivers give us a resigned look or a shrug as they drove past in the pack.

At eight-thirty we dropped our thumbs and walked a half mile further down the highway to a point where cars were spaced apart with a gravel pullout available. It only took five minutes for our first ride.

"Where you going?" the man asked over top of the boy who had rolled down the passenger window.

"Montreal!" Chuck blurted out. "Are you going that way?"

Even though I was five years older, Chuck had it all over me in confidence. He would talk to anyone, at any time and on any subject.

"Well I can get you down to the 401, but then I'm heading over to Toronto. Will that be good enough?"

"Sure!" Chuck said. He didn't ask me or even look at me before answering. He just opened the rear door and slid across the seat behind the driver. I followed without a word.

"So whatcha going downtown for?" Chuck asked.

"Well, we figure that if our tax dollars are paying for that new Don Valley Parkway, we should at least drive on it." He laughed. The brand new Don Valley Parkway joined highway 401 to downtown Toronto. "Then we're going to catch a ball game. I want to show my son here Sparky Anderson. He's something else."

"You bet he is," said Chuck.

"Oh, you follow baseball?"

"Not too much, but I hear his name on the radio enough. I'm a real Canadiens fan. We're going to see the Forum."

"You're hitchhiking all the way to Montreal just to see the forum? Boy, you must be a real fan."

"No, my brother's checking into university. I'm just tagging along."

"Didn't go to university myself. It is probably a good idea."

When our driver turned west, towards Toronto, we waited for a lull in traffic to run across the highway and aimed for Montreal in the east. The day was still cool with a nice breeze coming off of Lake Ontario. We walked a short distance down the highway, set our packs at our feet and stuck out our thumbs again.

Chuck was very excited about the trip.

"Do you think we'll see The Rocket? Or Boom Boom? Can I call them that? Do you think they'll mind? What about Jacques Plante? Do you think we'll see him?"

"Well, it's still August..."

"Oh yeah. They're probably not starting practices yet. What about the Forum; we'll be able to get in, won't we?"

"I don't think..."

"I'm sure we will, and even if we don't I'll still be able to walk around the outside. Maybe we can eat in a restaurant where the players eat. What are we going to do first? Do we have to go to the university first or can we go to the Forum first?"

"I have to get checked in at...."

"Okay, we'll go to the university in the morning and to the Forum right after, okay? It might not be open in the morning but I'm sure we'll be able to get in after lunch, don't you think? I wonder if we'll see anybody famous while we're there? We don't speak French. Are we going to be okay if we don't speak French?"

"Don't worry about that. I've been there for a year and never needed to speak French yet. If someone speaks to you in French, just say, 'Je ne parle pas Francais.'"

"Je-ne-parle-pas-Français." Chuck repeated slowly. "Je-ne-parle-pas-Français. That's it, right? I don't remember our last time in Montreal. Do you? Hey look, he's slowing down. Let's run."

The car that pulled over was something to see. A black Cadillac Eldorado sedan. It looked very new, with a smaller tail fin than the mid-1950's models. Chuck ran up to the front door and jumped in with a big "Hi!"

I climbed in the back with a smaller "hi."

"Hi fellas." The man answered. "Where ya going?" He was a big man; tall and heavy. He had the big, round face of someone who spends a lot of time eating restaurant food and the red cheeks of someone who spends a lot of time drinking restaurant whisky. He had red hair and complexion that Grandpa would call Irish. He was wearing a white button-up shirt with a dark blue tie loosened up around the undone top shirt button. His sleeves were rolled to the elbow.

We introduced ourselves. He reached over to shake Chuck's hand and back over the seat to shake mine, simultaneously driving up to speed and pulling back onto the highway, at the same time as moving his open briefcase over to the centre of the front seat.

"I'm Fred Willis. I'm going to Montreal myself. Sure I can get you there." A quick glance over his left shoulder as he pulled into the fast lane. "So what do you boys do for a living?" It was only a few seconds before we passed right through the 70 mph speed limit, before settling to a cruise at 80.

"I'm still in high school," Chuck said. "And he's in university. That's why we're going to Montreal."

"I remember those days myself." Mr. Willis glanced over his shoulder and swerved into the right lane. "Bet ya can't wait to get into the real world." We flew past a car and swerved back into the left lane, just missing the rear bumper of a transport truck that was only doing 60.

I gripped my seat-front tightly with both hands. This was several years before seat belts became standard equipment, even in a Cadillac. Chuck smiled across at Mr. Willis.

"You bet," said Chuck. "I don't get too much outta school anymore."

"Never finished myself. But a lotta boys didn't finish back in those days. I was up in Kirkland lake. Went to work in the gold mine to make some money."

"Gold mine! Are you rich?"

Mr. Willis laughed. "No, not me. I was just one of the grunts down in the mine. It was pretty disgusting. I was outta there as soon as I turned 17 and could join up; that was right near the end of the war."

"What do you do now?" I asked. From his car, I had the idea that Mr. Willis was pretty successful. Dad ran a factory with one hundred and fifty men, but we didn't have a Cadillac.

"I work for a company called Alside." He looked down into the briefcase and fished around in the pockets until he found his business card. We were still doing 80 and swerving back and forth between lanes to pass slower cars. He handed his card back over the seat to me. "Alside Corporation, Mr. Fred Willis, Regional Manager Ontario & Quebec."

"We do aluminum siding. Have you boys seen it?"

"What's that?" Chuck asked.

"You're from Bowmanville. Your house is made of brick, right?"

"Yeah."

"Well, these days nobody is using brick anymore. All the new houses being built around Toronto are using aluminum. Some of them are still using wood, but all the good ones are using aluminum."

I later came to understand that Mr. Willis was substantially exaggerating with his use of "all the good ones," but of course he was a salesman, so it can be excused.

"You mean like a can?"

"Something like that. We can paint the aluminum nice colours like white or light brown, and make the house look real nice."

I handed his business card over Chuck's shoulder.

"What does a Regional Manager do?" Chuck asked.

"I'm in charge of all the salesmen in Ontario and Quebec."

"So you have to drive all over?"

"Most of my business is around Toronto, with all the new houses going up. I'm going to Montreal to meet my boys there but things are pretty slow. There's nothing going on up North so I don't go up there at all. I spend most of my time in Toronto or Burlington or Hamilton or out this way; I was in Pickering first thing this morning. There's a new subdivision going up in Pickering."

"This is a nice car," Chuck said.

"This isn't a car, boys. This is my office." He patted his briefcase. His suit jacket hung from a little clip over the rear window on the opposite side of the back seat. "When you spend as much time driving as I do, you want something comfortable. Yup. After all my years on the road, I sure as hell want something comfortable to drive in."

"How long have you been on the road?" I asked, parroting his own words.

"Since the day I got back from Europe. I was one of the last to join up so I was stuck over there cleaning up for a while. I didn't get back until '47. Not that I had much to get back to, mind you. I sure as hell wasn't going back down those mines. So I volunteered to stay a while. It was nice to see the places without worrying about getting shot at. I was doing some of the cleanup in Paris and the smaller towns around there; got to see some of the countryside. Even learned to *parlez-vous* a bit; that's why the company put me in charge of Quebec too, because I can talk to the local construction bosses.

"What was it you asked again? Oh yeah. I came back in '47 and I needed to find work right away. All the easy jobs had been snatched up by the boys who came back in '45, so I was in a bind. I started walking between the companies, just going door to door, asking them if they needed any help. I was doing that for a couple weeks and I learned a few things along the way.

"First thing I learned was that people are too sidetracked to think about what they need, and most of them sure as hell don't know what they need anyway. So you gotta tell them what they need and you gotta show them that you can do it. So I figured it this way: With the war just over, there was a lot of guys coming back and starting their own companies. There were lots of little one-man companies and two-man companies popping up all over the place, but most of these guys were just off the farm. Well, not just off the farm. They'd come from the farm or from up North like me. And then they went to Europe, or some of them went to the Pacific. Then they came back and started up a business and they didn't know what the hell they were doing. They might know how to do some carpentry or some machine work, and a lot of them knew how to be mechanics; they learned that in the army. But all their businesses were doing bad. And you know why? Do you know why?"

Chuck shook his head.

"I'll tell you why. Because none of them, not one of them, knew how to sell. I'll tell you, you can be the best carpenter or the best machinist or the best mechanic in the world. But if you don't know how to sell, you've got nothing. Absolutely nothing but an empty shop with a lot of guys sitting around with their thumbs stuck you know where. And the reason they got no business going on is because they got no sales. Plain and simple.

"So after I'd been walking around for a couple of weeks I figured this out. So what I had to do was tell them that they needed sales and tell them that I was the guy to do it.

"So the next day, instead of going around in my work clothes and asking them if they need any help in the shop, well I put on my jacket and tie, and I carried my briefcase with me like I really knew something. I walked into the front door and I said, 'You guys need more business, right?' And they nodded their heads. And then I said, 'Do you like the way I came in here ready to sell myself to you?' And they nodded their heads again. And then I said, 'Well I can be doing this for you and bringing in business for you. Would you like that?' And they just couldn't stop nodding their heads.

"So I started doing this and I was getting lots of guys nodding their heads and I realized that this is my career I'm talking about so I didn't want to just take the first job that came around. So I took the third!" He smiled at Chuck beside him and at me in the mirror. I don't think the speedometer dropped below 75 the whole trip.

"So I walked into this shop out in Oakville. You know where that is? Well, I walked into this shop and these guys had the rights to sell linoleum around there. And they had all these machines to cut the linoleum and they had a truck and three guys to do the installations. All this and they were sitting there with their thumbs up their asses drinking coffee.

"So I walked in there, just like I told you, and before you know it I had a job. So I sat down with them that afternoon and I got them to teach me what linoleum was and the next day I hit the road and started making money!"

"Wow, that's really neat." Chuck said.

"I did that for five years and I was doing really well and making lots of money. Then I went down to a construction materials conference in Buffalo. I was walking around to all these booths that these companies had set up and I saw this company, Alside. So I stopped and talked to these men and apparently this aluminum siding was really taking off down in the States but there was no one selling it up here.

"I'd been reading about aluminum siding in the magazines and I read that it was taking off, so I talked to these guys for a long time. I told them all about what I'd been doing with linoleum and how I sold it to the contractors who were building the homes and I wasn't just selling it door-to-door to housewives like the other guys.

"A week later they invited me down to Ohio and I met the bosses and went through the whole story again. They offered me a job right there, on the spot.

"I'm the regional manager now and I've got eight men selling under me and nearly fifty men doing installation work. And I drive a great big car like this." He smiled an equally great big smile.

"Is that something I could do?" asked Chuck.

"You want to sell aluminum siding?"

Chuck nodded.

"You're pretty young for that." Mr. Willis chuckled. "But I admire your grit. You've got to be an experienced salesman to get into this business. Have you ever done any sales?" Mr. Willis presumed that this would put an end to the line of questioning.

"Selling pretty stones to the neighbours. And newspapers and magazines."

Mr. Willis looked over. "What?"

Chuck told the story of going door to door on our street selling his stones. Somehow the seven stones that he sold to five people grew into a whole bunch of stones to most of the people. As Chuck was speaking Mr. Willis looked into his rear view mirror at me. I nodded my corroboration at Chuck's story, but I was still holding the seat front with both hands.

"Well, you're quite the born salesman, aren't you."

"So, now do you think I can sell aluminum siding?"

"Don't get ahead of yourself, young fellow. You've got a long way to go before you get to that point. Do you like selling?"

Chuck nodded again, with vigour. "Sure do!"

"I'm going to want to see some real experience before I start talking to you about that." He thought for a moment. "You sold your stones door to door? Do you think you could sell something else door to door?"

"Oh yeah!"

"I'll tell you, you want to prove yourself to someone like me, you sell meat door to door. A man who can sell meat door to door can achieve anything."

Chuck was looking right at him.

"You do that for a few years. And if you still think you want to sell, then you come back to me then."

"What's it take to be a salesman?" Chuck asked. "Not just any old salesman, but the best salesman. What's it take to do that?"

"I'll tell you," Mr. Willis answered. "It's just like any other job. If you want to be really good at it that is. You can be an engineer," he looked at me in the mirror again. "Or a carpenter, or a musician or even a hockey player. The first one-third is just something you're born with. If you're not born with the gift of the gab then you can be a salesman but you'll never be a great salesman. I can tell right away that you've got it, so you don't have to worry about that."

"My Mom says I've got it; she says that all the time."

"The second third, that's experience. For a salesman, its straight experience selling, where you'll make lots of mistakes and learn what works and what doesn't work. It also means learning from other salesmen who've gone before you. It can take years to get the experience to be a great salesman."

He looked back at me again. "Of course for an engineer, that experience includes getting your education. For a musician, it means thousands of hours of practice. You get it, right?

"The final third; that's the hardest part and it's the part where most people fail. You've got to have the drive, this burning desire to succeed. If you want to be truly great at whatever you do, you've got to want it more than anything else. If you've got that burning desire, all the other things just fall into place."

"I've got a burning desire," said Chuck.

"Oh, you say that now, when you're just a kid and the world looks bright ahead with nothing but possibilities. But I'll tell you, it's a lot tougher to keep that desire burning after you've been at it for ten or twenty years and the world has thrown you some knocks. When nothing has gone right for you no matter how hard you work, regardless of if you were born with it or not or if you've got years and years of experience." He twisted slightly in his seat, reached into his pocket and pulled out a few coins. From these he picked out a quarter and handed it to Chuck.

"If you can keep that burning desire in spite of all the crap the world throws at you, well, even then, being truly great is just a flip of a coin. I hate to say it, but it's true. No matter what anyone says. Two guys start their own companies. One gets rich and the other goes broke. Was one of them smarter than the other? No. Did he work harder? No. Did he make fewer mistakes? No. In the end, he was just lucky. That's all there is to it. Pure dumb luck. Heads you win. Tails you lose. Just dumb luck. Nothing more than that. Flip that coin, go ahead."

Chuck flipped the coin. Not difficult to do in the front seat of a Cadillac.

"Don't look at it." Mr. Willis said. "Just put it in your pocket because you'll never know if you've flipped a heads or a tails. You'll never know until it's too late. But one thing's for sure, if you don't have the three thirds in the first place, then the flip of the coin can't happen at all."

Chuck handed him back the quarter.

"No, you keep that." Mr. Willis said. "It'll remind you of what we talked about."

Chuck fell silent for a while. "We're going to see the Montreal Forum," he said.

"Oh, you're a Habs fan are you. A lot of people down Toronto way wouldn't like that, you know. I saw them last year when I came down. Pretty exciting, I'll tell you. Saw them play Boston once. And New York too. I get to take customers out to the games and the company even pays for the tickets. That's what you get when you're a top salesman."

Chuck was entranced listening to Mr. Willis tell his stories about watching the Canadiens. At 80 miles an hour, the trip was much shorter than we had planned. We were into Montreal by one. Mr. Willis even bought us a smoked meat sandwich before he left for his meetings.

—

"Hey, Mom!" Chuck ran home from the first day at school. "You won't believe it! Mr. North wants me to come out for the wrestling team."

"You sure are built like a wrestler." Dad said at dinner.

And he was. He had a low centre of gravity that made it impossible to knock him off his feet. With his newly grown muscle bulk he would be fighting against tall, skinny, beanpoles - guys like me. He had matured very quickly over the past two years. At 15, he was already shaving every day; something that I only did twice a week at 20. His hair had darkened further and grown into tight curls; something of a swarthy look.

"With a build like yours, I expect great things. You could make it to the Olympics," Dad said.

"We practice every day after school, for an hour and a half, so I won't get home 'till dinner time."

"That's fine," Mom said. "I'll make sure to cook you lots of steaks. Just make sure you don't neglect your school work."

"Don't worry. Debbie is helping me."

—

There's an old saying about university. The first year they scare you to death; the second year they work you to death; the third year they bore you to death; and the fourth year you just want to get the hell out. My third year didn't disappoint. The good thing was meeting my first real girlfriend, and future wife, Kathleen Lawson.

I was living off campus in a boarding house on Rue Berger. I had a small room of my own on the second floor. There were three other rooms and a shared bathroom. The third floor was similar. It was an old, brick house dating from the turn of the century, very standard for the area. The central hallway on our floor had well worn hard-wood floors covered with a red area rug. The walls were plaster so we were not allowed to put in nails or hang pictures. All of the tenants met every morning for breakfast at seven, and again for supper at six. All but one of the tenants were McGill students, so we had a similar daily timetable.

With a greatly increased workload, the first time I was able to catch the bus home was for the long weekend at Thanksgiving.

Less than five seconds after walking into the house, Chuck had me down on the floor, his left arm under my armpit and twisting my forehead to the floor in a half-nelson position. He started laughing. The deep, uproarious laugh of someone twice his age. Three seconds later, and still laughing, he'd flipped me onto my back and had my shoulders pinned to the rug in a classic wrestling move.

"UNCLE!" I shouted.

Chuck jumped into the air with his hands waving above his head. "A new record for the fastest pin in Olympic history!" He danced around my prone body on the floor. "Ladies and Gentlemen, *Crusher Chuck* has done it again. Nothing can stop this man!"

I was hesitant to get up off the floor with his adrenalin pumped so high.

"Hey Buddy," I said. "It's good to see you. Tell me about your wrestling."

Chuck dropped down onto his bum on the rug next to me, with a mock elbow slam to my gut that made me cringe.

"It's fantastic. First day I show up with my normal gym shorts and a T-shirt and my sneakers on, but Coach North says 'No, that's no good. Here, come with me.' We go to his office and he throws a pair of wrestling trunks at me and tells me to put them on. No shirt at all. He says my high sneakers are okay because they go above my ankle.

"So I come back to the gym and there's a couple dozen guys sitting on the floor around a big wrestling mat that Coach has spread out. We're all wearing the same black wrestling trunks that Coach says I have to wear. And I look around and I don't recognize anyone except Bob is there. You remember Bob don't you. But he's in grade ten now.

"Coach says 'I want you rookies to watch this so you can see what's going on. Gary, Dennis, get out there and give these kids a show.'

"So Gary and Dennis go out to the middle of the mat and get into the neutral position; that's what it's called when we start a match. They're both standing in the middle of the mat and Coach says, 'Hold on a second. Okay, you can see that they're facing each other and they're crouching down a bit and they've got their hands in front and you can see that they've both got their forward feet in the green area. Okay, go ahead boys,' and he blows his whistle and Gary and Dennis starting grabbing at each other and a few seconds pass when they're just pawing at each other. Then, just like a cat, Dennis ducks down low and grabs Gary's legs and he picks him up in the air and in half a second he's down on the mat and Coach says, 'Hold on, hold on,' and they stop and Coach says, 'that's two points for the takedown. Okay, go ahead,' and they start at it again and they're kind of stuck down on the mat. Gary's on his stomach with his arms and legs spread apart and Dennis is laying across Gary's back with his arm under Gary's arm and he's trying to pry him over on his back, but nobody's moving, so after a bit Coach blows his whistle again and he says, 'We're going to stop here and move into what's called the *referee's position*. Gary, you get into the defensive position,' and Gary gets down on his hands and knees in the middle of the mat and Dennis gets down on his knees and puts one arm around Gary's stomach and the other arm on top of Gary's arm and

Coach blows his whistle and it's so fast I can't believe it. Gary twists around and grabs hold of Dennis and before you know it, they've switched positions and Gary's on top and Dennis is on the bottom and Coach says, 'Hold on. That's called a reversal and it's two points. Okay, go ahead.'

"And they keep going on like this for a while and Coach blows his whistle again and says, 'Okay, that's it. Take a seat, boys.' and Gary and Dennis stand up and they shake hands in the middle of the mat and they both sit down again with the rest of us and Coach says, 'That's what a wrestling match looks like, so everybody up,' and we all stand up. 'What we're going to do today is see what kind of shape you're all in and then we'll get some of the older boys to teach you rookies a few moves.' Then Coach shouts 'Everybody, ten laps around the gym!' and he blows his whistle and we all take off.

"We run real fast around both basketball courts and we touch our hands down on the floor at each corner and any time someone slows down Coach yells, 'Faster you candy ass!' and when we finish ten laps and we're all bent over double breathing real hard and Coach blows his whistle and he shouts, 'Everybody into pairs. You seniors, each of you grab a rookie and we'll go over some basic moves.'

"And Dennis comes over and he says, 'I'll be with you,' and I say 'I'm Chuck,' and I stick out my hand and he bats it away and he says, 'I know who you are. I'm going to teach you how to wrestle. Are you ready for that?' and I nod because I can still barely catch my breath.

"'You stand in front of me here' and he points to the mat 'and stand like this' and he gets into the crouch that Coach shows us earlier and I stand low with my knees bent and my arms out in front just like Coach says and Dennis says, 'Are you ready?' and I say, 'Ready' and he steps at me and grabs both of my legs from behind and picks me right up in the air and slams me down hard on the mat and I can't breathe at all and he says, 'That's a double leg takedown' and then Coach blows his whistle and he shouts, 'Dennis, what the hell are you doing! Are you trying to kill him!' and then Coach walks into the middle of the mat and everybody spreads out around him and Coach says, 'Let's work on the basic opening stance' and he looks at me and I can still barely breathe from getting thrown down so hard and he says, 'Get off the mat, Chuck. What are you, a candy ass?' And I stand up and then we start to listen to what Coach says and we learn the two basic positions; the *neutral position* and the *referee's position* and we learn how to keep our feet wide and our arms wide for balance.

"And when we're sitting there, Bob says to me, 'Don't you know who that is?' and I say, 'No' and he says, 'that's Dennis Gillispie. That's David's older brother.' And I say, 'Oh.' And I sit and watch Coach and listen to what he's telling us.

"And then Coach tells us to pair up again so we can work on what he's talking about and Dennis and I pair up and we're facing each other in our neutral position just like Coach says and I step in real close to Dennis and I punch him in the side of the head as hard as I can and he goes down on the mat like a sack of potatoes and I lean over him and I say, 'That's a one arm takedown,' and Coach blows his whistle and says, 'Dennis, get up off the mat. What the hell are you doing!' and Dennis and I are okay after that."

"So you took down Dennis and his brother David with these mighty fists of yours, and both of these guys are bigger and older than you?"

"I guess I'm just fast." Chuck smiled; a big, proud smile that pulled his entire face upwards.

CHAPTER FIVE

The daily trip to McGill was not far. I often walked, but if I was running late or the weather was bad, I caught the number 75 bus that took me right to the campus gate.

Meeting Kathleen was not some big romantic adventure like when Mom and Dad met. It was a normal situation, something that happens a thousand times a day in the winter. A dozen people, mostly McGill students I assume, were standing at the bus stop on St. Catherine Street. It had snowed heavily overnight. Snow plows had cleared the road, leaving 18 inch snow banks on the sidewalks that had yet to be shovelled away.

By nine in the morning the roads were a slushy mess. The sand that the city spreads on the roads had mixed with melting snow to create rivers of brown sludge running down the curbs. At each bus stop along St. Catherine, a narrow groove had formed in the snow banks from the footsteps of passengers crossing from the sidewalk to the street before getting on their buses. The groove in the snow bank was tightly packed and exactly one footprint wide, as each succeeding passenger put his foot into the same spot, over and over.

In better weather, when a bus arrived, the waiting men would stand back and allow women to board first. But when bus 75 arrived that day, it was simply more efficient for everyone to climb on without preference. The group had been standing on the sidewalk in a tight bundle, hemmed in by the snow bank in front, parked cars on either side, and pedestrians using up most of the sidewalk behind. There was just no room for men to stand aside and allow women to pass.

I was in the middle of the pack that trickled, one at a time, across the narrow footstep in the snow bank and then attempted to step across the stream of slush flowing down the road. I had just put my foot down on the road when I heard a woman's voice behind me. "Oh, I don't think I'm going to make it," the voice said, apparently to whomever was standing behind her.

Without thinking at all, I turned and held up my arm to act as a brace.

The woman was standing above me on the top of the snow bank. I did not look at her face, but saw that she was wearing a blue woollen coat that came down to her black boots. She rested her black, gloved hand firmly on my upheld arm for support and stepped onto the road.

"Thank you very much," she said cheerfully.

"Actually, you were supporting me," I replied, turning back towards the bus door, still without looking at her in the face.

Never in my life had I spoken so casually and so freely to a girl I didn't know. The quip "Actually, you were supporting me," had come without forethought. Months later, Kathleen told me that my charming comment had put her at ease and attracted her to my "quiet confidence," as she put it. It's funny, but I had never considered myself to have *quiet confidence*. She told the story of how we met many times during our marriage.

With Kathleen safely on the road and more passengers traversing the snow bank behind her, I allowed her to board the bus ahead of me. It was crowded with thick-coated and heavy-booted passengers. We were able to move five rows back before pressing up against each other in the aisle and grabbing the hand rail above.

The bus had a very distinctive smell, familiar to all commuters. It was a combination of hot air blowing from under seat heaters, rubber mats, slush and the odour of too many people packed too tightly, wearing heavy winter coats.

"Thanks for helping me out there." Kathleen looked at me. "I don't think I could have made it over that mountain without you." She stood five foot six, putting her eyes at my chin level. Of course I could not see her body under the winter coat but her face was slim with a very distinctive, upturned nose; 36 degrees from the horizontal. It was very attractive. She had dusty blue eyes and straight hair that hung down over her coat collar.

"It's pretty slippery out there," I said.

"Are you going to McGill?" she asked. It was an easy assumption since the bus was full of students. Working people were already at the office by this time.

"Yes, are you?"

"Oh, yes." She paused for a moment, "but I don't think we'll get there soon."

The bus had moved no more than seventy five feet down St. Catherine since we climbed on board. The road was clogged tight.

She went on. "What are you studying?"

"I'm in Engineering, in my third year. What about you?"

She continued to smile up at me, which was surprising given how closely we were standing on the tight bus. I tried not to stare right down at her nose, and turned a little bit to the left side of the bus.

"I'm working on my Bachelor of Education. I'm in my third year too."

I surprised myself with how well the chat was going. I'd never had a spontaneous conversation with a woman before (that is, without an introduction by a friend). Of course, there were no women in Engineering so our opportunities for interaction were limited. All of my classmates had girlfriends of one status or another but I spent my time in the library or studying at home.

"Are you from Montreal?" I asked. I was trying to keep the conversation going, but other than small talk, I had nothing else to say to her. She certainly wouldn't be interested in anything about my life and I didn't know anything about her courses.

"No, I'm from Moncton, in New Brunswick. What about you?"

"I'm from Bowmanville, near Toronto."

The conversation, such as it was, lulled at that point. The bus was barely moving in the traffic. Some of the more determined people on the sidewalk were moving faster through the crowds of pedestrians and snow than we were. We both stared quietly out the left side of the bus.

"Oh, look at that poor lady pushing her carriage in the snow!" Kathleen said to break the silence. "And the baby must be so cold. She should put extra blankets on. Poor little thing."

I was trying desperately to think of something to say, anything at all, to make her think I was interesting. But nothing came to me. Where was Chuck when I needed him? By this far into the conversation he could have recited her entire family history and her dreams for the future.

Several minutes passed.

"I think I'm going to miss my class," she said.

"Me too," I replied and continued to stare out the window.

Several more minutes passed. A few pessimistic riders got off and walked towards McGill, and a few more optimistic riders got on.

It seems the pessimists were right. The bus driver stood up, "I'm sorry people." He spoke with a heavy French accent, and paused for the various quiet conversations to stop. "I'm sorry but we're not going to be moving for a while."

All the passengers in the crowded bus turned to face forward. The street outside was no less slushy than it had been twenty minutes earlier, which slowed the process as each stepped gingerly to avoid the puddles.

After getting off the bus myself, I moved to the side while Kathleen stepped down. Without asking she held my arm as we stepped onto the sidewalk.

"Um," I said. "We're not going to make it to class." I hesitated.

"No, I don't think so." She looked up at me, but was still holding onto my arm. Kathleen guided us out of the main stream of pedestrian flow, over to the store front where we could pause. We were in front of a small fruit and vegetable shop, one of many in downtown Montreal. Normally the area under the green awning would have tables filled with boxes of tomatoes, cucumbers, potatoes, apples, turnips and squash, but the bad weather had delayed the shopkeeper from setting out his tables and we could stand close to the window, fogged over from the warm air inside.

"Would you–uh–would you like to stop for coffee?" I asked.

"That would be–very nice," she replied.

—

Chuck's Christmas report card did not show an improvement on any previous year. D in mathematics; D in English; D in history and geography. I suspect that his teachers might have been generous with these marks. No matter what we did to help, he just seemed to have a basic problem with understanding what he was looking at. It was almost like he could see nothing but Chinese on the page.

What I found especially odd was that in spite of his incredible memory for faces and names and an amazing ability to memorize the lines from plays he was acting in (so long as I read them to him) he absolutely had no memory at all for mathematical problems he'd been able to solve just a few days before. On a Tuesday, Debbie would work with Chuck to solve the equation $2/3 \times 4/5 = 8/15$. But on Saturday, looking at the exact same problem, it was as if he had never been taught the concepts at all. He just stared at the page until Debbie walked him through it, step by step, once again.

"Let's look at the numerator. What's 2 times 4?" She asked.

"Eight."

"Now the denominator. What's 3 times 5?"

"Fifteen."

Okay. Now what do you do with those two numbers?"

"Put the numerator on top of the denominator."

"So what have you got?"

"8 over 15. That's 8/15ths."

"There you go."

Debbie certainly had patience. She worked through each problem in their homework like this. Breaking it down into its basic components and talking Chuck through them step by step. Chuck seemed to be able to answer when she did it this way, but the moment he looked down at a new problem on the page, his eyes glazed over.

The issue was very similar with other subjects, like History or English. Chuck had real trouble reading what was in front of him. He certainly could read, but he had to work through each page paragraph by paragraph; line by line; often word by word. He spent so much time working through each word that he was not able to understand the topic of the paragraph, page or chapter. He really could not see the forest for the trees. I don't believe that he ever finished an entire novel.

"What do you think you want to do?" I asked across the dark bedroom a few days after Christmas. "The school's got a pretty good auto shop class, doesn't it?"

"I don't want to do that."

"You're really good with your Meccano. Auto shop is a lot like that, you know."

"The guys down there are real stupid and they just fool around all class. Every time the teacher goes over to work on one car, all the other guys just mess around. They push each other around and throw grease at the walls. Half the time they sneak out the back for a smoke. Some of them don't even come back inside, they just leave."

I nodded in the dark. "A bunch of losers, eh."

"Oh yeah. These guys aren't going anywhere. Dad wouldn't want me hanging around with them."

"Mom and Dad are both worried about how you're doing in school."

"They don't saying anything to me about it."

"You know Dad. He made it on his own and he expects the same from us."

Chuck imitated Dad's voice, "I expect great things from you."

"He sure does." I paused for a couple of minutes, "What do you want to do?"

"I don't think I can get better marks at school. Debbie helps me but I'm not getting anywhere."

"Sure." I believe we were both resigned to this situation.

This time it was Chuck who paused, five minutes at least. "Do you remember Mr. Willis?"

"No."

"From our trip Montreal, you remember?"

"Oh yes. What about him?"

"I'd like to do what he's doing."

"You mean be a business man?"

"A salesman. You remember his big Cadillac?"

"Yes, but he's been in business for a long time. What, twenty years at least?"

"I don't expect it to be easy. Now he's the manager of all of Ontario and Quebec. I've got his card."

"That's what you want to do?"

"Yeah."

"Okay." I paused again. "Let's see if we can get you through high school first. You don't have to go through the grade 13 classes like I did you know. You can just go through grade twelve and you'll still graduate."

He didn't reply.

"That's only a few more years."

More silence.

"I'm sure Debbie can help you out."

Still no reply.

"Do you want to go see *Hatari* at the movies tomorrow?" he asked.

"Sure. That sounds good."

CHAPTER SIX

I was told about the big change in family life when I got back to town at the end of February, during the annual winter break at university. I caught the first bus home from Montreal and walked in the door before lunch.

Mom was working in the kitchen. "I'm glad you're home," she said. "Lots going on around here and I could use a little calm in the house."

I put down my bag of laundry and sat at the kitchen table. "What's going on?"

Mom took off her rubber gloves, hung them on the edge of the sink and sat down at the end of the table. "Chuck's quit school and got himself a job."

"Lord," I said, dropping my forehead into my hands, with my elbows on the table. "When did this happen?"

"Last month."

"Right after his sixteenth birthday. So it's legal?"

"Yes."

I paused before asking, "What's he doing now?"

"He's a door to door meat salesman."

"Lord," I said again, more exasperated this time. "I know where this comes from."

"He told us the whole story," Mom said. "He told us all about Mr. Willis and how a man who can sell meat door to door can do anything."

"He even told you about Mr. Willis?"

"Don't you start. If I hear the name Mr. Willis in this house one more time I think I'll scream."

"And he's already got a job?"

"Oh yes. He had it all arranged before he left school. He started working the next day."

"Wow. At least he's determined."

"He's been working fourteen hours a day since he started. He leaves here at seven in the morning and doesn't come home until nine at night. That's why your father can't say too much, because Chuck's working so hard."

"He must have flipped when Chuck quit school?"

"Chuck didn't tell us until he'd already been working for two weeks. He was leaving so early and coming home so late, even on Saturday. We thought he was wrestling. Your father finally asked him what was going on and Chuck started telling us this story about your Mr. Willis and how he could be so successful in sales. And we were just talking about it like it was in the future, and then Chuck comes right out and tells us that he's already been doing it for two weeks. I said, 'That's why you're coming home so late, because you're doing it after school!' That's when he told me he wasn't going to school at all, he was doing it all day long."

"The school didn't call you when he wasn't coming in?"

"Oh no. Chuck had made it all official. He went into the office and signed the papers and formally left school, so there was no reason for them to call us."

"And Dad didn't flip?"

"He's upset about it, but what can he say? Chuck was doing so poorly at school, we didn't think he was going to last. And he's not lazing around the house like a bum, he's working so hard we never see him at all."

"What did Dad say?"

"Oh, you know your father. He said he expects great things and one day Chuck will be the best meat salesman in all of Canada."

"Lord." I said a third time. "Chuck will be the best meat sales-man in all of Canada and I'll design the next Eiffel Tower."

"You know your Dad," she switched to a deeper, authoritative, voice. "He expects great things out of you both. But at least Chuck's got one thing going for him," Mom went on. "Mr. Franks retired from his butcher shop right after Christmas. His son Robbie has taken over and I don't like him at all. I don't think anyone likes him. He's trying to skimp on every penny. I'm sure he's changed his meat scales to give less than a pound, and he's not trimming the meat the way his father did. I'd say that Chuck picked a really lucky time to get into the meat business."

I chuckled under my breath.

A little while later, Dad walked in for lunch and Mom set down soup and sandwiches.

"No Chuck?" I asked.

"We won't see him until tonight." Dad replied. "At least that's what he's been like so far."

I didn't ask Dad what he thought about Chuck, because I didn't want to hear the answer, but it came up in the conversation sort of naturally.

"Lots of boys drop out of school and most of them end up pretty badly," he volunteered, "but I'll say this about Chuck, he's got ambi-tion, he's got drive, he's willing to work hard and he knows how to talk to people. If those things count for anything at all, he should be okay."

"Tell us about you and Kathleen." Mom relieved us all by chang-ing the subject.

—

Chuck came home at nine, just as Mom had predicted. She had kept his supper warm and laid it on the table the moment he walked in. I sat down and watched as he emptied his glass of milk in one swallow.

"Man, that's what I need," he said.

"I'll bet." I paused. "So, tell me all about you leaving school?"

"Leaving school? That's all done and over. I'm onto better things now."

"But what did your teachers say when you quit? Or the Principal?"

"What does that have to do with anything? That's long gone."

Chuck wasn't being belligerent or trying to avoid a difficult subject. He lived for the now and had plans for the future. There was no such concept as regret in his mind. Anything that was past might as well of happened to another person far away. It had no bearing on him today or tomorrow. He had been this way his whole life and it was useless for me to ask for answers that he didn't have.

"I need you to teach me how to drive on Sunday so I can get my license next week, okay?"

"Teach you in one day?"

"I've only got Sunday off work, so you've only got one day to teach me. I need my license to drive around."

"Okay, we'll see what we can do. So tell me all about your new job."

"You remember Mr. Willis, right?"

"I've heard all about Mr. Willis. I think Mom would like to put her hands around his neck."

"Well he says that a man who can sell meat door to door can do anything. So that's what I'm doing, proving that I can do anything."

"I'll bet you are. How did you get into this?"

Chuck dove into his story with the same enthusiasm that he had any time he talked about something that really interested him. "Well, it's my birthday last month and I hitchhike down to Pickering. There's a company down there called Anderson Meats. I walk into the office and I say 'I'd like to speak to Mr. Anderson, please.' I'm wearing my jacket and tie from church so I look like a real businessman, just like Mr. Willis. The lady looks at me with a real surprised look like no one ever comes into the shop, and she says, 'Take a seat and I'll see if Mr. Anderson is available.'

"And I go and sit down. I don't think they get many visitors there because they only have one chair and there's all kinds of papers and files on the coffee table that look like they've been there for years. So I sit there for maybe ten minutes and then a man comes out of the back and he's wearing green coveralls but the top button is open and I can see that he's got a shirt and tie on underneath. And he walks over to me and says, 'Hello.'

"I stand up real quick and I stick out my hand and I say, 'I'm Chuck and I want to be a door to door meat salesman.'

"And he says, 'Wow, that's quite an introduction. Come into the back here with me.'

"We go through the door into his office and it's even more cluttered with papers and files and even more dusty than the front. And he picks a stack of paper off the chair in front of his desk and puts it on the floor and tells me to sit down and we talk for a long time.

"I tell him all about wrestling and school and working for two summers for the Portuguese guys and he sits and listens and asks some questions. After half an hour or so he says, 'I really don't know if we need anyone else right now. We get a lot of men come through here and they can't do the job.'

"And I say, 'I don't know what you want in a salesman but I cut my teeth selling stones door to door to the neighbours. Isn't that the kind of guy you want selling Anderson Meats?'

"And you know what? I think he's testing me or something because he says 'I think I'll start you with Gordon. I'll have you in training for a week or two with him and then you can be out on your own.'

"So I ask him when do I start and Mr. Anderson says 'Gordon's down in Florida right now. He takes a vacation down there every winter. You can start when he gets back.'

"And then Mr. Anderson walks out front and he says to the woman, 'Nancy, this is Chuck. He's going to be starting with Gordon. Can you get him set up?' Then he shakes my hand and walks back through the door and I haven't seen him since.

"So I talk to Nancy and give her my name and address and everything. She's surprised that I'm just turning 16. She says that Mr.

Anderson must know what he's doing and that she'll call me when Gordon comes back, and I say that I'll call her too."

I interjected. "You were still at school when all this happened? You hadn't quit yet?"

"Yeah, for another week and a half. Then I go into the office and I tell Mrs. LaPlante that I'm quitting and she says she's sorry to see me go and wishes me good luck. Then she fills out a piece of paper and I sign at the bottom and I'm all done."

"Chuck," I said, "you've got a lot more guts than I have. You just walked into the office and quit, just like that. You didn't talk to Mom and Dad about it or anything? I can't believe it." I paused to look at him across the kitchen table. He was finished the beef stew Mom had put in front of him. His entire conversation had been interspaced with bites of meat or potato, barely taking a second to chew before swallowing and continuing with his story. He was lucky that the stew bits were small; I think he would have choked if he'd needed more than three seconds to get each mouthful down. "So you've been there for three weeks now. What have you been doing?"

"That first day I get up early and I hitchhike down to Pickering to meet Gordon. He's a good guy. He's just back from Florida so he's got a nice tan.

"And I say, 'Hi, I'm Chuck' and he says 'I'm Gordon.' And he points at a stack of boxes and says, 'Come on, kid. Get those loaded. I've got a lot of hungry customers to feed.' All the time he's talking to Nancy about her vacation and drinking a cup of coffee.

"So I carry the boxes up into his van. It's white and says *Anderson Meats* on both sides in big red letters. The whole inside of the van is sealed to keep the meat cold.

"So after ten minutes, I've got all the boxes loaded and he says, 'Okay, kid, let's go,' and he jumps into the driver's seat.

"Once we're out on the road he says to me, 'So you want to sell meat, eh?' and he pulls a cigarette out of his pocket and lights it with a big silver lighter.

"'Yeah,' I tell him. 'A man who can sell meat door to door can do anything.'

"And he takes two or three drags on his cigarette and says, 'Well, I can sell meat. But after two weeks in Florida I sure as hell can't swing a club like Sam Snead. But then again, if I spent six days a week golfing, I just might be as good as him, and I doubt he can sell meat anyway.'

"We talk back and forth for a while until we get to a road full of houses. He tells me to wait in the van and he gets out and goes up their steps to the front door.

"He throws his cigarette butt in the garden and he pats his pants down smooth and straightens his tie. Then he knocks on the door, *shave and a haircut*.

"A lady comes to the door. She's older, maybe sixty or seventy, I don't know, but she's got on a long housecoat that goes right to the floor and a hairnet on her hair. She tells him to come inside, because it's cold on the porch. He stands inside the door, I can see them talking, but I can't hear what they're saying. I can see when she laughs a couple of times so he must be telling her a funny story or something.

"After a few minutes he walks to the van and climbs in the back and picks out some packages. Then he walks back to the house and taps on the door again, but he doesn't wait for her to answer he just walks in the front door. I can see him hand her the packages and she gives him some money and he gives her some change back. Then they talk for another minute and laugh a couple more times. Then he walks back to the van and we pull up to the next house on the road.

"Now he says I should come with him, but I have to stay quiet and not say a word so I walk up to the house and he goes through the whole thing again with another lady. This time she's not quite as old and she still has her housecoat on, but she doesn't have a hairnet on.

Chuck continued his story for another hour, describing in detail each house that they visited or, more specifically, each housewife they visited. In a short time, I knew more about every woman on Palace Street in Ajax than I know about any woman in Bowmanville, even our closest neighbours – except, of course, for the mothers of Chuck's friends. I know more about them than I know about my own Mom.

Chuck continued, "Gordon says that I have to keep my mouth shut so he can give his customer complete attention, and he wants her complete attention on him. He says that even though it looks like small talk, he's keeping control over their chatting so he can close a sale at the end. If I say anything, then he has to start it all over again.

"Let me tell you. We go up to a house on Kent Street and Gordon is talking to Mrs. Wolchowski. Right at the beginning, Gordon asks Mrs. Wolchowski if her son is back from university yet. They talk for a long time about how well Thomas (that's his name) is doing and Mrs. Wolchowski is really proud that he's going to be a lawyer because Mr. Wolchowski is a truck driver and it will be really good to have a son who's a lawyer.

"And after that they talk some more, Gordon says 'So, when Thomas comes home, are you planning to give him a T-bone steak for dinner, or maybe a nice chicken?' Gordon doesn't suggest pork chops because he knows Mrs. Wolchowski is Jewish. And she says, 'Nothing but the best for my Thomas. I'll be serving him steak, of course.'

"So Gordon says, 'Absolutely. And then you'll want a roast for the weekend, right? Something that will last all week while he's at home.' And we both come out to the van and he picks up a package of T-bone steaks and another package with a six pound roast. He jots some numbers down on a slip of paper and adds them up and hands it to her.

"When she takes the meat packages to take to her kitchen, Gordon uses it as a chance to leave quickly, and he shouts, 'Thank you very much and I certainly hope that you enjoy Thomas' homecoming,' and we leave quickly before she can come back to the front hall and start talking again.

"'The trick,' Gordon says to me, 'Is to know when a lady is busy and wants to get you out of the house as quick as she can while still being polite, and when she's not busy and will talk your ear off, in which case you need to get out of the house as quick as you can, while still being polite. If you make a mistake when she's busy, then she'll tell all her friends how you waste her time. And if you make the second mistake, then you'll spend all morning at her house and the neighbours will start to gossip about how much time you're spending over there. That's just as bad as the first.'

"He always tries to get his customers to talk about their friends. When he goes to get a new house he says something like, 'Hello. My name is Gordon. I'm a butcher for this neighbourhood and June says I should talk to you.' And sometimes they don't even know who June is but they know someone named June so they let him in and he talks to them about the neighbourhood and how long he's been the butcher around here and he would like it if they would just give him a try with something for supper."

"So you've got the whole thing figured out?" I asked.

"I'm paying real close attention to everything he says so I can be real good."

"But now you need your license? What are you going to do with that?"

"Gordon's got an old car that he'll give me cheap, and I can pay him from the money I make."

"What kind of shape is it in?"

"It's okay. It's got some rust but it will get me around."

"Did Dad see it?"

"No. I'm doing this by myself."

—

On Sunday, right after church, we borrowed Dad's car and I taught Chuck how to drive. He had watched my own learning process from the back seat five years earlier, so he knew the basics. He just needed to get behind the wheel himself and practice.

We went out to Lamps Road north of town. It was cleared of snow so I figured it would be safe. I got out of the front door and he slid into the driver's seat.

Dad had a nice Ford Frontenac. "You're the Plant Manager, you should drive a new car," Mom had said, so Dad went out and bought a new car. It wasn't fancy like a Lincoln Continental or something, but it was new, with red with light brown side panels. Dad liked it because he said it was actually built in Oakville, just on the other side of Toronto. Mom told Dad to buy the automatic so she could drive into town.

I remember how proud Dad was when he insisted that the car come delivered with Goodyear tires, and not the Firestones that were standard. Dad told the salesman that he would walk away unless it came with Goodyears. It seemed pretty stupid for a Ford dealer in Bowmanville to try to sell cars with Firestone tires on them.

Chuck had no trouble at all learning to drive. I'm sure the automatic helped because he didn't need to worry about changing gears like I had, with all of the clutching and grinding and stalling.

We drove up and down, stopping at every stop sign and slowing down at the railway crossings. I had trouble with these with the old manual transmission we used to drive.

"You haven't mentioned Debbie since I got home," I said.

"We're done for a while."

"That's too bad. What happened?"

"Her Mom won't let her go out with a guy who's dropped out of school. She says her Dad's got no education and her Mom pays for it every day."

I nodded, but didn't say anything.

"But it's okay. In a little while I'll be doing real good and I'll call up her Mom and tell her Debbie should be allowed to go out with me again." He paused. "A guy shouldn't have a girlfriend unless he has enough money to look after her anyway. Especially a guy who's out working and not just in school."

I nodded again as we came up to the next stop sign. By the middle of the afternoon I figured that he knew enough to pass his license.

Monday evening was quite an event at the house when Chuck

parked in the driveway. The car was deep red, almost a rust colour, which was probably best because it made it more difficult to distinguish the actual rust from the paint. All four fenders were badly pocked. Dad pressed his fingers firmly in the metal on the driver's side front fender and broke right through.

"How much did you pay for this?" he asked.

"A hundred dollars."

"I guess we'll have to see if it's worth a hundred dollars."

Dad had always taught us to be independent. He wasn't about to start interfering now, even if he thought Chuck had made a mistake.

Dad climbed behind the wheel and banged his heel on the floor to hear a distinctive rattle. He reached down and lifted up the mat to reveal a small piece of quarter-inch plywood. Lifting that up, we could see several small holes right through to the driveway.

"Looks like something out of the Flintstones here."

"It'll be just fine," Chuck said. He grabbed the plywood from Dad's hand and replaced the floor mat. "I can't walk around with a hundred pounds of meat in my arms, can I?"

"That's true. That's true."

"Do you have your license?" Mom asked.

"Not yet."

"I don't want you driving this thing until you get your license. Do you hear me?"

Chuck thought for a second. "Don't worry. I'm going first thing tomorrow."

"All right then."

We didn't find out that it was nearly three years before Chuck actually went for his driver's test. He drove well, but was so worried about taking the written test that he simply skipped the process altogether.

—

For the rest of the week Chuck was out selling on his own for the first time. I was given daily reports on his often futile efforts. "Gordon says I shouldn't try to make my friends into customers, I'll just lose a lot of friends. I should try to make my customers into my friends." With this idea in mind, Chuck started on the outskirts of Bowmanville, rather than on our neighbourhood streets, where he was so well known from his paper route.

"How did it go?" I asked on Tuesday.

"Not too good."

"Did you sell anything?"

"No."

"What happened?"

"Well, this morning I start by going to every house on Concession Street. Every single house. The first house on the North side is number two. Gordon says I should do one side of the street, then the other, and not go back and forth, just like we're trick-or-treating."

I knew Concession Street. Like most of Bowmanville's residential streets, it was filled with 2-story brick homes, each with a large front porch, several mature oak or maple trees, and large fenced backyards.

"I walk up to the door and ring the bell. It takes a little while, maybe half a minute, and a lady comes to the door. She's in a blue housecoat and blue slippers. I can see her legs and she's wearing light blue pyjamas too. She opens the front door, but not the storm door so I talk to her through the glass.

"'Good morning, ma'am,' I say. 'I'll bet your husband likes a good thick steak.' That's all I get a chance to say and then she says, 'No, thank you,' and she closes the front door in my face, so I'm left standing there on the porch with a nice steak wrapped in paper that I didn't even get a chance to show her.

"I stand on her porch for a couple of minutes; I'm so surprised by how quick she gets rid of me. Then after a couple of minutes I see her peeking out the front window at me and that wakes me up so I walk back to the car and get inside.

"So then I drive up in front of the next house. It's another brick house, only this time the porch is green instead of white like the first house. I ring the door bell and a woman comes to the door and she's wearing a pink house coat that goes right to the floor so I can't see what she's wearing underneath but she's got pink slippers on too. She opens the front door but not the storm door and I say, 'Good morning, ma'am. I'll bet your husband likes a big steak for dinner.' And she doesn't say anything at all. She just closes the door on my face without a word. Can you believe it? She doesn't say a word.

"So this time I walk back to the car right away because I don't want to look like an idiot standing on the porch waiting for nothing so I go and sit in the car for a while.

"Then after about ten minutes, I drive another thirty yards and walk up to the front door of the next house. This time the lady doesn't open the door at all. I can see the top of her head through the window in the door, but that's all I can see. And I'm standing waiting for her to open the door and nothing happens. Then I see the curtains in the living room move a bit and I realize that she's looking at me. I don't want her to think that I'm a peeping Tom or something, so I just walk back to the car.

"And it goes like this for all the other houses on the street too. Sometimes the lady says, 'No thank you' or sometimes they say nothing at all.

"Then I start with number three on the other side of the street. They haven't been out to shovel the sidewalk yet so the snow is half-way up to my knees. When the lady comes to the door I start to give my pitch and she just says, 'Oh my, would you look at all that snow. It must have been terrible for you.'

"She's wearing a blue house coat just like all the other ladies, even though it's a lot later in the morning, and she's got her hair covered in a big kerchief. She says, 'Look at me. I won't be able to get out and clear that snow at all today. I haven't been feeling well at all this week. I think I've got a cold. Did you slip on the stairs when you came up? I'd just be so upset if someone slipped on the stairs. My sister May will be coming by with some soup and I would be so upset if she slipped and hurt herself.' And she looks over at the garage.

"I can see there's a snow shovel propped up against the garage right next to the door, right where she's looking and I say, 'I can clear the walk for you if you like.'

"And she says, 'That would be so nice of you,' and she closes the door and goes back inside. So now I have no choice. I shovel the snow from her stairs and down her front walk and I'm thinking this will be great. She'll think I'm just the nicest guy in the world for doing all this work for her and she'll buy something from me.

"When I finish her front walk she comes out on her porch and she says, 'That's such a good job.'

"And I say, 'Thank you.' And I'm just going to tell her about our meats when she says, 'Do you think you could do the sidewalk as well? Those men from the town will come by and give me a ticket if I don't have the sidewalk cleared. You know how nasty they are.'

"And I say 'sure.' I've already spent fifteen minutes clearing her front walk and then I spend another thirty minutes shovelling the sidewalk because her house is right on the corner so have to do the sidewalk in front of her house and beside her house too.

"I'm wearing my jacket and tie under my coat and it's getting hot and I'm getting sweaty under my collar so I take my gloves off and loosen my tie.

"After a half hour or maybe forty minutes I figure that she'll be really grateful and buy some meat because I'm doing so much work for her. I walk back up her porch smiling and she comes out wearing a dark blue dress and she's got her hair fixed and she says, 'Thank you very much for helping me out. Now I won't get a ticket from the town men. You know how nasty they can be.'

"And then she looks over at the driveway in front of the garage and I can see tire marks in the snow from when her husband left in the morning and she says, 'Look at that. George is going to be in such a rush when he comes home for lunch. He's always in such a rush because it takes him fifteen minutes to drive home, if he's able to get away right at noon. And then it takes him fifteen minutes to drive back to work again and he has to be back by one o'clock. He barely has any time at all to sit down and eat his lunch so he won't have time to clear that away.'

"And I say, 'I don't mind helping you out.'

"And she says, 'Are you sure? You're being such a nice young man.'

"So I shovel the driveway too. Most of it's not too bad except under the tire marks where I have to push on the shovel to scrape it up. I work for maybe a half hour and my watch says it's eleven thirty by the time I finish. I put the shovel against the garage and I walk back to the front porch and the lady comes out, only now she's got a brown coat on and she's wearing her boots and gloves. 'You've done such a good job,' she says and I think she's so grateful that she'll buy lots of meat for sure.

"So I say 'I'll bet that George,' (I remember her husband's name from before) 'likes a big, thick steak, doesn't he?'

"And she says, 'Oh, yes. We buy all of our meat from Mr. Franks' shop over on Main Street. Do you work with him?'

"I say, 'No, I'm with Anderson Meats. I'm just getting started in town.'

"She says 'I really like the meat I get from Mr. Franks.' And then she says 'Look, here's May now.' And I look behind me and another lady has pulled up in a station wagon. And she says, 'I'm really sorry that I can't chat with you some more but we've got an appointment so we've got to get going right away. Thank you so much again for all the work you did. You're such a sweet boy.' Then she goes down the front walk that I just shovelled and she gets into the car and they drive away."

"It's just your first day selling." I consoled Chuck. "You'll figure it out."

Mom pulled a warmed over supper from the oven and he sat down to eat. There was no whistling this evening.

CHAPTER SEVEN

Kathleen and I continued to see each other back at school. We timed our morning bus rides to the same schedules. Afternoons were more difficult because of different classes and library study requirements. When the snow was gone we usually walked to the university together.

"It's so nice that spring is coming," she slipped her arm into mine as we walked. Kathleen was wearing a light blue, three-quarter length coat over top of her darker blue dress. "Let's go to the movies tonight. It's Friday and you can take the evening off studying."

"Sure," I said. "What would you like to see?"

"What's that one? *It's a Mad, Mad, Mad, Mad, Mad, Mad World* - or something like that. That should be funny."

"Sure. That sounds fine."

"It will be nice when it's finally warm out. You've never seen me in anything but my winter clothes. I've got a whole spring wardrobe that is just dear to look at. You'll find me so pretty then. I'd say we should go for a picnic this weekend but the grass is still too wet. I can hardly wait until we can sit on the ground with a blanket!"

"The April showers are coming soon, and then we'll be through with school. So I don't think we'll be doing any picnics this year."

"I'm going to miss you so much over the summer. I just know that you'll find some other girl to go out with back home."

Kathleen was teasing. She knew darned well that would never

happen. I only had a few guy friends, none of them close, let alone speaking to another girl.

"Do you promise to write to me? Every day?" she asked.

"Well..." I hesitated. "Every day?"

"You have to write to me every single day."

"What if I don't have anything to say?"

"There's always something to say. Why, on a day like this you could just say that the sun is out and the snow is nearly gone and everyone we see on the street is happy and smiling."

"Not everyone."

"Everyone that matters is smiling. The people who aren't smiling just don't matter, do they? And you can tell me all about your work. I want to hear every detail about what you're doing every day. You're almost a full engineer now so you'll be doing important work I'm sure."

Mr. Jenkins had gotten me on with his company for the summer. They usually hired one or two students every year. "I'm sure I'll just be doing the drudgery."

"I'm sure they'll have you building things in no time. Didn't you say that your company is designing the new city hall in Toronto?"

"I think we're just a subcontractor. Mr. Jenkins is working on the electrical system, that's all."

"I've seen the pictures. The new city hall is so modern. One day you'll be able to tell our grandchildren that you built that."

Kathleen had started to slip these little comments about our long term future into our conversations.

"One day," I conceded. She was probably right about our future, after all.

We were getting near the University gates and would be splitting off to our separate buildings.

"You can come by and pick me up at six," she said, "and take me out to a nice dinner before the movie." This was a directive; not a question.

"Sure." I replied.

Sundays were always dedicated to time together, even though it meant I missed out on a lot of studying time. I usually came up with an excuse, "I've got a big test tomorrow," or "I need to finish up a paper," or "I'm meeting with so-and-so this afternoon to study," but none of these were good enough for Kathleen.

"You've been studying for that all last week!" she'd say, or, "You can finish the paper tonight," or "you'll just have to tell so-and-so that I'm more important than he is, won't you."

Kathleen would knock at the boarding house door just after 9:30 in the morning, giving us time to walk down St. Catherine Street to Christ Church Cathedral for the ten o'clock service. We had tried me going to her door, but I was always up and studying at six in the morning and became so caught up in my books that I could never make it to her boarding house in time.

"Well, if the mountain can't come to Mohammed, then Mohammed can come to the mountain," she said, and her weekly 9:30 arrival was set. We never missed a service in spite of how busy I was at school.

Christ Church is the largest Anglican Cathedral in Montreal. It had just held its 100th anniversary when Kathleen and I started going. It had the classical, Neo-Gothic design standard to most Anglican Cathedrals in Canada, but the bell tower was an infamous engineering failure. Just like the Leaning Tower of Pisa, the Cathedral bell tower started to sink into the soft ground immediately after it was built. It had a four foot lean to the south before it was sixty years old. It was demolished and a much lighter aluminum tower, that looked the same from the outside, was built in the 1940s. The engineering failure of the bell tower construction was even something that we discussed at school as a classic case of what can go wrong in our chosen profession.

After church, Kathleen and I would choose one of the many restaurants on St. Catherine for lunch. I once suggested that we could save a bit of money by packing a picnic and sitting on a park bench, but she replied sternly, "You can pinch your pennies the rest of the week. On Sunday, you're taking me to some place nice."

Of course "nice" is a relative term and we were just students.

Restaurant *Robert's*, pronounced with a French accent, was one of a number of places where we could sit down to a smoked meat sandwich and chips with a big pickle, served in a basket lined with newspaper, and a Pepsi. The restaurants were always full from churches in downtown Montreal. *Robert's* was typical in the lower price range, with a glass case displaying all of their deli meats. There were nine small tables where three could sit if they squeezed their sandwich baskets and were careful not to push their drinks off the edge.

There were no table-cloths, but the yellow Formica table tops were in good shape and the red vinyl covered chairs were not ripped. Kathleen wouldn't let me take her to a restaurant with ripped chairs. The ceramic tiled floor was showing its age.

Customers who were taking their meals out ordered at the counter. Kathleen insisted that we take a table and place our order when Robert himself came over, which could mean a long delay as he filled the orders and ran the cash register. We would sit and chat casually as 15 or 20 minutes passed and my hunger increased, until Robert was able to take our order, and then wait another ten minutes until our lunch was ready.

We often spent the time watching passers-by out the window, many of whom would look back into *Robert's* in search of a vacant table. This was the fate of those who lingered to chat after their church service.

After lunch I was still not free to go back to my books. If the weather was nice, winter or spring, we caught the Number 11 street car to Mount Royal Park for a long walk on the pathways and through the cemetery.

Mount Royal Park was envisioned as a dense piece of nature in the middle of a modern city. In early days it became renowned as a make-out spot for young couples; so renowned that in the 1950s Mayor Drapeau's "morality cuts" thinned the trees and hedges to eliminate any opportunity for privacy.

Our Sunday walks through the park lasted three or four hours, including several stops on park benches and the invariable cup of tea from the pavilion. We drank coffee the rest of the week, but

Kathleen insisted that coffee was a drink for working and tea was a drink for relaxing.

During the cold of winter she had me carry our ice skates and we went out on the man-made lake for an hour or so. Often we would see families bring three or four young children out for their first attempts at skating. Kathleen was quick to volunteer and would skate backwards, holding the hands of the youngster to provide a little balance; but not so much to completely support the child's weight. She would work with each child for five or ten minutes, until they were tired, before moving on to the next, all while I skated in circles around the perimeter of the rink. After the last child was done, Kathleen would press in close to my arm and say, "I'm sorry. I've been completely ignoring you, haven't I?"

Kathleen had an unusual mixture of personalities that made her so attractive. A prim debutante at one moment and an active go-getter who was quick to jump at any chance for excitement the next. It was exhausting for me to keep up with her.

I think the only saving grace to my Sunday study plan was that, as a strict Catholic province, the museums, art galleries and stores were all closed. By six o'clock we both had to be back at our boarding houses for supper. I invariably stayed up until two in the morning to make up for lost time in my homework.

Neither of us had classes on Wednesday afternoons. I took this as an opportunity for quiet study at the library.

"There you are." Kathleen said. "I've been looking all over for you."

She couldn't have been looking too far because I always sat at the same table, along a side wall in the engineering section on the third floor. I could usually get this table to myself and sit with my back to the distractions in the book shelves.

"So what are we going to do today?" she asked.

"I've got to work on my calculus, I've got a test coming up."

"You've got a test every week in something or other. I'm not going to let it interrupt our mid-week breaks," she closed the binder gently on my hand. "The Art Gallery is having an exhibit by William Kurelek–he actually is insane. Apparently he did his paintings inside an asylum."

"I guess we could go for a little while," I said.

"Don't you worry. I'll have you back in plenty of time to study." She closed up my textbooks without replacing the book-marks and put them inside my leather satchel.

"That one stays here," I said, pulling the advanced calculus book out." It stays in the library."

"Do you need it again?" she asked.

"Yes. It's good."

"Okay." She looked around to see if anyone was watching. "We'll just put it right here." She put it up on the fourth row, at the very end of the shelf near my table. "It will be here when you get back and no one else will be able to find it."

"That's not too fair. A lot of people will be looking for it, I'm sure."

"Fair, schmair. You got it first so you get to keep it as long as you need it. Come on, let's go."

We caught a bus over to the Golden Square Mile, the district at the base of Mount Royal filled with mansions built at the turn of the century by the Montreal business elite. Calling it Golden was somewhat ironic since there had been no new development in the area since the depression and the younger generation of million-aires were quickly moving elsewhere. Many of the mansions were decaying.

The Museum of Fine Arts remained vibrant in the community. It was one of the most prominent art galleries in North America at the time. Kathleen often brought me to see the rotating exhibits there.

From what I could see in his paintings, Kurelek certainly was in-sane. "Look at this," I said. "It's the inside of his brain." I put my nose up close to the large painting to see the details. A security guard at the hall entrance coughed politely to let me know that touching is forbidden. The painting's details were so intricate that it was diffi-cult to see them without coming close. I'd say that from more than three feet away, it was impossible to recognize the details at all.

It showed a cartoon representation of the inside of his head. His brain was sectioned off into a dozen little rooms, like a maze. Each room represented a part of his life. In the middle of his brain–of the maze–was a white lab rat curled up in a ball. I have to admit that I didn't really understand the maze at all. In one room is a soldier being bayoneted, next to a crowd of people with 'War is Peace' banners. In another room is a boy in pyjamas being booted out of his house into the snow. I saw a carousel of people dancing with strings like marionettes, a boy in a test tube with doctors probing him–I guess that must be Kurelek himself–in another room is a man slicing open his arm while reading a book on anatomy; and in another room is a big, fly covered turd! There were other images that made even less sense than these.

I read the little card next to the painting and whispered to Kathleen, "It says here that he did this while he was at the funny farm. I can see why they had him locked up."

"Not the funny farm," she scolded, just as quietly. "A psychiatric hospital, in England. He wanted to show the doctors what was going on in his brain."

"So they could clean it out?"

"Exactly."

The steady crowd of visitors moved along to his other paintings, and my opinion of his mental status did not improve. One titled *Portrait of the Artist as a Young Man* showed his face in front of a collection of disturbing Satanic images. This was him as a young man?

In a corner of the gallery, where I could stand without being bumped by the passing crowd, was the painting called *I Spit on Life*. It showed bleak images of a man's life, starting from his childhood being bullied by other kids; sitting alone in a corner of the library, in a state of despair; toiling at a never ending woodpile reflecting his work; a reference to a play *My Lost Youth*; a repetitive, unending series of self portraits by Kurelek himself; an image of self-immolation; and, in the lower right hand corner, hanging by a noose from a desolate branch with a bag over his head and the sign *I Spit on Life* on his chest.

We moved past some twenty of his paintings in the exhibit hall. "He has quite a view on life," I said. "I hope they keep him locked up."

"Oh no," Kathleen replied. "He's fine now. He lives in Toronto."

"Were they able to cure him?"

"They gave him electro-shock treatment."

"Ouch. Maybe he just told them he was cured so they'd stop. I would."

The next morning, before my first class, I went back to take another look at his paintings without the crowds. I stared at every detail of *I Spit on Life* for some time, wondering if Kurelek was the only man who felt this way about his life.

—

The longer that I was in school, the more I enjoyed it. My marks were good and they were not difficult to achieve. I spent many hours absorbed in my studies at the library or in my room at the boarding house, interrupted only for classes, meals and walking out with Kathleen. I am grateful that she was able to take me out of my normal comfort zone.

—

When classes finished at the end of my third year, I was anxious to get home and hear how Chuck was doing. A letter from Mom had said he was coming along.

"Oh yeah. It's going pretty good now," Chuck confirmed when he came home at nine o'clock for supper on my first day back. "I get a couple of new sales every day and I'm getting lots of repeat customers now. Those are the best."

"What changed?" I asked.

"I've got to act like myself. I can't follow the rules that someone else tells me. Those rules are made for people who don't know how to sell at all, but I've got lots of practice. I know how to sell. I've just got to do it the way I know how."

"What does that mean?"

"I whistle a lot. People like it when I whistle. It shows that I'm friendly. They seem to really like it when I whistle the *Andy Griffith Show*. That's the best whistling song in the world. So I always whistle when I walk up to a house. It makes me sound real friendly. And then I don't ring the door bell any more. Now I knock on the door *Shave and a Haircut* just like Gordon does. He says that salesmen ring the bell but friends knock. And real close friends knock *Shave and a Haircut*." He paused to eat some supper.

"And another thing. I don't drive my car in between every house now. Now I park my car in the middle and walk to every house. And when I'm whistling all the time people can see that I'm being real friendly all down the street."

"So you're selling lots of meat now?"

"Not lots. Just lots more than before."

"So you're going to stick with it?"

"I have to now. Dad says I've got to start paying board to live here now that I'm out making money."

"Really?"

"Yup."

"How much?"

"Five dollars a week for now, but by September it's going to be up to ten dollars, then fifteen by Christmas."

Dad had long held that a man should be able to look after himself, so Chuck didn't see this as an unfair burden, but rather as a passage to manhood. I paid twenty dollars a week for my room and board in Montreal. "So you've got to get really serious about earning some money," I replied.

"Yup."

"Will you be able to handle it?"

"It'll be tough. I've got to pay for gas in the car, and I'm doing a lot of driving down to the warehouse and back, and the car is going to need some bodywork soon."

"Can you do that yourself?"

"I don't think so. There's lots of rust. There's a big hole in the bottom of the trunk and water splashes up and gets the boxes all wet. I've got another piece of plywood there."

"It's getting like the old Model Ts with wooden floor boards," I joked.

"Gordon says it's from all the salt they put on the 401. He drives that every day and gets lots of rust on his cars. And I need new tires too."

"At least Dad can get you a good deal on those, right?"

"A little bit. He says I can get the employee discount, but they'll still cost a lot."

"I guess you didn't think about all this when you started."

"I'm not worried. I'm gonna be rich. Just look at Gordon. He goes golfing down in Florida every year."

"You always talk about Gordon; are there any other salesmen there?"

"There's lots. I haven't even met most of them. They're out on the road all the time."

"Do they make as much money as Gordon?"

"I don't think so. He's the top guy. That's why he does the training of the new guys, so he can teach them. A lot of them don't even stay for more than a few weeks before they quit."

"Really?"

"Oh yeah. They just can't hack it. There's this guy, Brad. He's about 25, I guess. He gets hurt in construction so he can't do that anymore. So Gordon takes him out, just like me, but he's got a real bad feeling about him. After a couple of days Gordon tells him to go back up to the house and ask the customer something, but Brad's scared to talk to customers without Gordon there. When they get to the next house Gordon doesn't even go up to the door at all. He's worried about Brad, right, so he tells him to go up to the house and introduce himself. But he can't do it again. So Gordon tells him to take a hike, and says he hasn't got time for this. Then he just leaves him there on the street and drives away."

"So what happened to him?"

"Don't know."

"And the boss didn't say anything?"

"Nope. He knows that Gordon's in charge on the road. If he says you're not gonna make it, then you're not gonna make it."

"That's brutal."

"And another guy, Pat's his name. He goes through training with Gordon and he makes it through all right and Gordon thinks he's gonna do okay, but when he's out on his own, he goes to a few houses on his first day and gets shot down just like me and then he just stops knocking on doors at all. He just goes and sits in his car at the end of the street for the whole day, reading the newspaper and listening to the radio and looking at the meat order papers that we fill out. And he does this for three whole weeks and then he just quits.

"So after that Gordon says that he's sick of wasting his time training guys who are just gonna quit anyway and he tells Mr. Anderson to find someone else to train the new guys from now on."

"I remember when you started, you told me that you spent a lot of time sitting in your car when you didn't make a sale."

"Yeah, it's real easy to do. You pretend that you're working or something but really you're just wasting time. And before you know it an hour has gone by or even two or three hours and then it's time for lunch and you take another break because you don't want to disturb the people in case the husband comes home for lunch.

"That's why I don't get in my car and drive between each house on the street any more. It just gives you an excuse to spend ten minutes sitting there before you get out and go to the next house. At the end of the day, you find that you've only gone up to ten houses or something. But if you park in the middle of the block like I do and then walk to all of the houses, you get to do a lot more selling. What are you going to do? Stand in the street at the end of someone's front walk? Stand there for ten minutes? That would be really creepy, wouldn't it? Ladies would see you standing at the end of their walk and they'd never answer their door.

"So I get to call on a lot more houses every day, and because of that, I get to make a few new sales."

"Did Gordon tell you that trick?"

"That's my own idea. Gordon says that I'm coming along nicely and if I keep it up, I'll be doing real good soon."

After he finished eating, Chuck went upstairs to our room. While I was away he had taken over my desk for his latest Meccano project, a bulldozer. It was amazing. About a foot and a half long, the wheels turned and there was a track around them with individual sections that all rolled around the wheels. The shovel was lifted by a little lever right next to the driver's seat.

On the corner of my desk was another set of plans that Chuck had bought through the mail. He was just working from the picture on the front again, while the detailed drawings gathered dust.

He cleared a space out of the clutter of brochures on meat that covered his own desk top and moved the bulldozer over.

"Thanks," I said, unpacking the suitcase full of textbooks onto my desk. "I want to keep up on these over the summer or I'll be behind when school starts again."

CHAPTER EIGHT

I started working at Mr. Jenkins' office the following week. HBA is a large engineering company with offices across Ontario, created as an amalgamation of smaller partnerships so they could show enough experience to bid on government infrastructure projects.

Our office took up half of the second floor of an old, four-story stone building in the middle of Main Street. Small accounting and law offices filled the second and third floors, apartments on the fourth and *Paris Fashions* at street level. A half dozen drafting tables and large cabinets were spread on the interior walls. The west wall had racks stuffed full of drawings and blueprints, covered in dust and giving off a musty smell.

"This will be your first job," Mr. Jenkins said to me. "We're going to be starting on a big project, but we need to get rid of this mountain of old drawings. You'll work with Mrs. McLintoc, our office manager. She'll tell you what to do." He introduced us quickly and went back into his office.

Mrs. McLintoc smiled at me tightly. "Let's get to it," she said, "There's twenty-five years of drawings in here. I filed most of them myself, but we've got to get them all cleared out and over to storage. And not just these, but all the engineers' drawings in their offices as well."

For my first day of work I was wearing my gray suit, white shirt and tie, so I was not looking forward to handling the dusty drawing rolls. I used my fingertips to pull one up six inches, out of the slot.

She reached over my hand and grabbed the drawing, pulling all the way out of its slot and flipping it down in a clear space on the long table behind us. "Let's take a look at it," she said as dust drifted onto the table.

Mrs. McLintoc was in her early-sixties, I'd guess. She had short grey hair in tight curls, about five foot ten and very, very slim. Her face was drawn and creased; her shoulders pointed, her arms slim beneath a pale yellow blouse and her legs slim in dark blue slacks.

Dust flew once again as she unrolled the drawing. It was several pages thick. "What we need to do is properly identify and catalogue every drawing." She placed small shot bag weights on each of the four corners. The table had dozens of these leather shot bags spread across it. "Each project has several drawings. Some of them have dozens and the larger projects have more than a hundred." She pointed at the lower right hand corner. "If you look down here you can see the project name and number and the drawing number. But if you look here," she slid the right side shot bags over by six inches and held the drawing down with her hands to stop it from rolling, then moved her hand enough to allow the first, second and third pages of drawings to roll out of the way, "you can see that the drawings are all mixed in together. That's the engineers fault. They pull out all the drawings for a project and just roll them up together again and put them back in the rack." She slid the right side shot bags off the drawings and let the top sheets roll up completely, before placing the shot bags back on the last drawing. "So what you want to do," she said, "is to use your best draftsman's lettering." She looked at me again. "You can do that, right?"

"Yes," I replied.

"And write down the name of the project, the project number and the drawing number on the outside of the roll so that we can see it without opening up the roll. Right along here." She lifted the upper right shot bag and allowed the corner to roll over on itself. "Right along here," she repeated, sliding her slim, very slim finger vertically along the outer edge of the drawing. "And while you're doing that," she walked back to her desk on the far side of the room, and returned with a stack of file cards, "we want you to put the same information on these." She slid her fingers across one card. "The project name here, the drawing number right below that, and the drawing description over here on the left. Okay?" She looked at me again.

I nodded.

"Now make sure to leave the lower right corner of the file card open." She pointed at it. "That's where we'll put the drawing location down in the basement."

"Sure."

It took three weeks to move all of the drawings down into storage. After that first dusty day, I didn't wear my good suit to work; just casual pants and my white shirt and tie. I was still covered in dust at the end of the day, but I could take a bath and my pants and shirt went into the washing machine. I had to blow the dust out of my nose several times a day during this process. I didn't expect to be designing the Eiffel Tower on my first job, but I also didn't expect to be a file clerk.

I was disappointed again when that job was done. Mr. Jenkins called a meeting of the office.

"The Federal Government is building a new maximum security prison in Bath," he said. "We're going to bid on the design and construction. Our office over in Kingston is closer, but they're swamped with the cement plant, so it's up to us to get the bid in."

Mrs. McLintoc was in charge of the entire bid process, and I would be her assistant.

The first step was pre-qualification, proving HBA had the capacity and experience to take on such a large project. Mrs. McLintoc explained that I would call other HBA offices and get them to fill out detailed questionnaires about their largest projects. The projects on their own were not enough, but should qualify collectively.

She handed me a 65 page government document.

"That looks like a lot of information?" I asked.

"Yes, it certainly is," she paused. "It's not like the old days. During the war the government was spending money so fast that we didn't need any of this. The engineers had a quiet lunch with some bureaucrat and an hour later they'd shake hands on a contract. But that's all gone now. Fair and open bidding means we have to go through this every time we work for the government."

In three years of engineering studies at McGill, they taught us how to design buildings and bridges to the smallest detail, but not one single class on how to get the contract in the first place. This was not what I signed up for and I dreaded the thought of spending the remainder of the summer collecting paperwork and on the telephone with secretaries from far-flung HBA offices.

I spent that day at the large table in the middle of the office finding and preparing five projects that we had completed in the past ten years. We had to supply an incredible amount of detail for each, not on the actual construction, but on the process we used to manage the project, right down to the complete resumes of each of the engineers involved. Each resume would end up being 20 pages long for every project in each engineers' background. We had to hand in five carbon copies of the complete tender, each of which would end up being at least two thousand pages long.

Mrs. McLintoc gave me a handwritten list of the five projects that we would be using in our proposal:

Lever Brothers – a large soap factory designed and built by our Toronto office.

The Goodyear factory extension that Chuck and I had worked on here in Bowmanville.

General Motors offices designed and built by our Oshawa office.

Devey Paints, a small factory in Kingston that barely met the minimum requirement.

Adam Beck hydroelectric dam upgrades in Niagara Falls.

———

I mailed copies of the RFP to the other four offices.

"The biggest part of your job will be getting what we need from them. Can you manage that?" Mrs. McLintoc said.

I flipped some of the pages.

"Here." She handed me the company directory. "Here's a list of all the offices. Just call the Office Manager and make sure she understands what we need. Okay?"

I nodded. "Okay."

I spent two more hours reading through the document again. I had already studied it but wanted to be sure that I understood every detail before someone asked me a question.

My first call was to the Kingston office. "I mailed you the Bath Penitentiary requirements document. Did you receive it?"

"No, I don't think so," Miss Farmer answered.

"Okay. I'll call back again in a couple of days. Goodbye."

"That's fine. Goodbye."

I hung up the phone, relieved that she hadn't asked me any questions.

I spent a few more minutes familiarizing myself with the document, and then called Mrs. Ferguson in the Niagara Falls office.

"I'm afraid that she's away this week," the woman who answered the telephone said. "Is there someone else who can help you?"

"No thanks. That's okay. I'll call back next week. Thank you." And I hung up the phone.

Mrs. Labrough in the Oshawa office was next in the directory.

"I've got the envelope here on my desk," she said, "but I haven't opened it yet. "

"Um. Do you have any questions?"

"I guess I'd have to open it and look inside before I had any questions. Wouldn't I?"

"Yes."

There was silence on the phone.

"I'll try to take a look at it later this week. Is that okay?" she said.

"Okay."

"Okay. Bye bye." She hung up.

My final call was to Mrs. Maycher in the Toronto office.

"She's in a meeting right now. Can I ask her to call you back?"

the woman said.

"No. I'll call back later. Thank you."

Just before lunch Mrs. McLintoc asked, "How are things going?" and I explained my lack of progress. "We can't let this drag," she said. "We'll get behind if we let it slip, even by a week."

She told me that if someone is in a meeting I should leave a message, but not leave it more than a day before I call back myself. If someone is away on vacation, I should ask who is looking after their responsibilities. And I need to let them all know just how urgent it is.

That afternoon I was able to get through to Mrs. Maycher in Toronto.

"Yes. It arrived yesterday," she said. "It looks like quite a project."

"Do you have any questions about it?"

"To be honest I haven't had time to look at it very carefully."

"Okay."

"But I'm sure I'll be able to get on it soon." She sounded enthusiastic. The kind of response I was looking for.

I asked "Can I call you back next week some time?"

"Sure. That's fine. I'm sure I'll have read it through by then."

I called back to Niagara Falls and asked for whomever had taken over Mrs. Ferguson's responsibilities.

"I guess that would be me," said the woman on the phone.

"I sent a package to Mrs. Ferguson a few days ago with the RFP for the Bath Penitentiary project. Did you receive it?"

"Oh heavens," she said, "I wouldn't be looking after something like that. That would be up to Mrs. Ferguson. You'll have to call back next week and talk to her."

"Thank you. I'll call back next week then."

The following week I spent much of my time gathering information on our Goodyear factory project. To prove that we could properly manage a large undertaking, we were required to provide detailed timelines of our work. This included the bidding process, the moment the contract was signed, our own planning and scheduling, the lengthy design phase, all of the work with building contractors through the construction phase until the moment that the customer signed off on completion. It was vital to include every detail of our interaction with Goodyear management throughout the contract, just to show that we had the skills to do the same on the penitentiary contract.

Mrs. McLintoc explained. "We're dealing with the government here. They have staff devoted to reading these responses. I think sometimes that the selection process is to take all the responses to the top of the stairs and throw them down. The envelopes that weigh enough to slide all the way to the bottom can proceed. The light envelopes near the top of the stairs are rejected out of hand.

"You have to remember that the big engineering companies have been winning these things for years. They have a whole department to do nothing but respond to RFPs. They've got long relationships with the government. They even have the Ministers over for summer pool parties. We're newcomers, just trying to break into this type of work. The procurement department will be looking for ways to eliminate bids from interlopers."

Chuck continued to work his normal long days. He didn't get home until after we had finished supper and Mom and Dad had washed the dishes, but she always kept a plate warm. I was surprised that even though he was selling meat all day, he still enjoyed a good steak or pork chop or leftover pot-roast when he came home. "I gotta keep my strength up," he'd say, flexing his muscles at me.

He was making a little more money every day he went to work. It wasn't much, but enough to pay his rent and gas. By now it was warm enough to sit on the porch and watch the sun go down after supper.

"I guess the ladies aren't asking you to shovel snow anymore?" I joked.

"It's just as bad," he answered. "Now the old biddies are out in their garden all day and they expect me to help. This morning, there's Mrs. Schell on Douglas Street. She's planting flowers so I whistle my way up her front walk, just so I don't scare her. I'm telling her the special this week. It's salmon; we got a load in from the coast and Mr. Anderson says to push it. She's got a wheelbarrow full of little seedlings. And she gets up to move and she says, 'Would you mind coming over with the wheelbarrow?' So I put my clipboard under my arm and follow her. When we stop on the other side of the garden she says, 'Hand me the white chrysanthemum, would you? It's right there at the front.'

"So I pick up the chrysanthemum and she says, 'No, no. Not by the stem. You'll break it. Pick it up by the soil at the root.'

"And of course she's soaked all the flowers in water so the dirt is all wet and I get my hands all dirty and I've got nothing to wipe them on because I'm wearing my good pants."

I laughed at Chuck. "Now you know why Dad always has a handkerchief in his pocket. It's not just to blow his nose."

"Yeah, I guess. So I wipe my hands on the grass and it's all wet from the hose, but at least I'm not muddy any more.

"So she digs a little hole and puts the chrysanthemum in and she stands up and says, 'Follow me' so I get the wheelbarrow and follow her to the side of the house. She's got the whole garden dug up all along the side of the house. I ask her again if she's interested in the fresh salmon and she says, 'Wait here a minute,' and I think she's gone to get her money or something but then she comes back with a shovel and she says, 'Would you mind turning over the soil a bit?'

"I'm lucky that it's all muddy because it gives me an excuse so I can say, 'I'd better not. I'm in my good shoes.'

"And she says 'I guess you're right.'

"I start to ask her about the salmon again and she says, 'I'm kind of busy today. Perhaps you can come back next week and we can talk about it. I should have all my flowers in the garden by then.'

"And I say 'Thank you. I'll come back next week.' And I go on to the next house."

With his working twelve hours a day, six days a week, Chuck didn't have any time for a social life. He usually slept till noon on Sundays. Mom said, "Letting him sleep is more important than church right now."

In the afternoon he would get together with his buddies from high school for a game of street hockey or touch football. I had thought that this might be a little awkward, since he was no longer at school, but when I asked about it he didn't understand why it would be an issue. "Why would it be awkward to play hockey?" he asked.

Sunday evenings we usually went to a movie. He laughed so loud during the basketball scene in *The Absentminded Professor* that I thought he would bust open his spleen. Some might have been embarrassed to sit with him during this outburst but I admired his confidence and openness. Kathleen said Chuck had a laugh that could wake the dead.

Every time we were downtown, regardless if it was at ten in the morning, two in the afternoon or after the movies at night, Chuck came across friends. It wasn't just me who noticed, it was a point of conversation at the supper table. I have to believe that he knew the name of every kid in town between 12 and 18, and if they had a brother or sister who was outside of that range, he knew their names too. If I asked how he knew someone it was just, "He's at school," or "She's Bob's sister," or, "From Jackie's birthday party last fall."

Whenever we went downtown, I had to allow extra time for hand shaking, slaps on the back and quick "How-are-ya?"s that could stretch out to five minutes. Getting to the movie in time was not on Chuck's priority list. A few times we didn't make it at all when a group of friends were collecting in the park. There were just too many people to say, "Hey" to. I would sit down on a bench next to the hive of activity and admire Chuck making the rounds until it was too late to think about our intended destination. A couple of hours later we'd walk home and not even mention the movie, as if meeting his friends had been our goal from the start.

At the end of June, Chuck came home at his normal hour.

"Gordon says I know the business good enough now. I can start selling in our own neighbourhood and I won't screw it up too bad." Only six months earlier virtually every house on our block, and the streets next to us, had been customers of his paper route. So when he struck into, *I Whistle a Happy Tune* as he walked from house to house, most of the housewives met him at the front porch.

"I get lots of hugs from my old customers," he said. "They say how nice it is to see a nice young man making his way in the world. I think we've got a hundred Aunts living on our street."

"But do they buy anything?" I asked.

"Oh yeah. Nearly everyone. Mrs. Phillips says she and her sister just went together and bought half a cow so she doesn't need any beef for a long time. But she says I should come back when we get more salmon in stock."

"She bought half a cow? Where does she keep it?"

"At the butcher. He's got a big freezer and if you buy a lot of meat from him he'll keep it for you."

"That's a lot of meat."

"She's got six kids, so it will go pretty quick."

"So you can sell her some later?"

"I don't know. She buys it right from the farmer so she gets it real cheap."

"But everyone else bought something from you?"

"Almost. Some of them just buy some hamburger, but that's fine. We sell it just so that we keep the customer happy. I don't make any money on hamburger. We have to sell it at the same price as the butcher or no one will buy it. We want to get them used to buying from us. Maybe later they'll buy something else from me. We'll see."

"You should have started selling on the street months ago."

"Gordon says that if you make your friends into your customers, eventually you'll screw something up and lose both."

"I think everybody in the whole town is your friend."

"Yeah. But that doesn't leave much room for customers, does it? So after I bug him about it for so long, Gordon says I can sell in my own neighbourhood and I probably won't lose too many friends."

—

Chuck's income tripled over the next two weeks. He had just been covering his gas and board. Suddenly, he was making even more than I did at my summer job; five years older and with three years of university. He made a special point of taking us out to Sunday supper at the Chinese restaurant a couple of weeks later. Mom insisted that he save his money and Dad pulled out his wallet when the bill came, but Chuck was determined to prove that he could be successful after leaving school.

At dinner one day, Chuck brought up an interesting discussion. "Little Charlie needs to help his grandpa on the farm, but he's got no way to get out there every day. He's asking to borrow $50 to buy himself a car."

"That won't be much of a car," Mom said.

"His neighbour's got an old Ford he's giving him real cheap. It works. What do you think?" He looked at Dad.

Dad thought for a second. "You're good friends with Little Charlie, right?"

"Best buddies." Chuck replied.

"Are you willing to lose your friendship over $50?"

"What do you mean? We won't lose our friendship."

"Let me tell you something. If you lend him $50, then in all probability you won't see that money again. Then you'll fight about it and you won't be friends any longer."

"I trust Little Charlie. He'll pay me back. I'm sure of it."

"I'm glad you brought up trust. Here's a lesson both of you can learn." He paused. "I don't quite know how to put it. Don't ever mix up trust and money."

"What do you mean? I trust him." Chuck repeated.

"I'm sure you do, and I think that's great. He's a nice kid and I'm sure that if you got into a fight he'd be the first one to jump in and help you out. And if you got into a car accident, I'm sure that you could absolutely trust him to save your life. You trust him like that, right?"

"Yeah."

"Well let me tell you something. People behave differently when it comes to money. Everybody does it. It's a strange kind of thing. If you give him this money, when's he going to pay you back?"

"From his first pay that he gets from his grandpa. He's getting 75 cents an hour, so it'll only take him two weeks to pay me back."

Dad thought some more. "Let me tell you what's going to happen. I've seen it over and over again; any time anybody lends money to a friend.

"You're going to lend him the money and after he's been working for two weeks he won't mention a word about it. It'll be like he's hoping that you'll forget about it. So after a few days, you'll ask him about it and he'll have a perfectly legitimate reason why he couldn't pay you back right away. It'll be a good reason; something like his grandfather couldn't pay him on time so he doesn't have the money, but he'll pay you as soon as he gets the money. And that's a perfectly legitimate reason so you'll accept it. After all, he's your best friend.

"So then another couple of weeks will go by, and maybe you'll see him buying something in a store so you'll know that he's got some money, but he won't bring it up. And you'll see that he doesn't call you to hang out. Now we're into the excuse stage. If you ask him about it he'll make up some excuse why he doesn't have the money. He'll say something like he had to put new tires on the car because the old tires were ready to blow, and he had to pay for gas and insurance and a licence plate. And he had to buy work-boots because he couldn't work on the farm in his sneakers. It'll be things like that. It won't ever be something that's his fault, but life is expensive and once he starts working and gets his own car, then all of those expenses will catch up with him. Just think of all the things you needed when you started working.

"And here's where he starts to swing it back on you. You'll ask him when he thinks he can pay you back and he'll say, 'I'll pay you back. Don't you trust me?'" Dad looked at us. "I'll tell you something boys; don't ever trust someone who asks you to trust him. All that he's doing is taking the obligation off his back and putting it on yours. No person can ask for trust. He can only earn it through their behaviour. If you lend someone $5 and he runs up and pays you back the instant that he said he would, then he's earned enough trust for you to lend him $10, but still not enough to lend him $50.

"So let's get back to little Charlie. He's going to make you feel guilty because you don't trust him. Then after that you're going to move into the righteous indignation stage. This is where he starts to talk about you to his friends. He'll make it sound like he's an angel and you're a jerk. He'll say stuff like, 'Jeez, that Chuck is an ass. He lent me a measly $50 and now it's like he owns me, like I'm his personal slave.'

"But you're a nice guy and you still want to get your money back so you won't say anything bad about him. This is the problem. Because you want something from him, you'll be really nice. And because he doesn't want to have anything to do with you, he'll start to get nasty.

"Now we're into the final stage. This is where he actually convinces himself that he doesn't even owe you the money at all. He actually comes to believe it. He'll say something to you like 'that car you bought me is a piece of garbage. I had to put on new tires and it needs new shocks and the head-gasket leaks. That's all going to cost me at least $200. I don't have that kind of money and even if I did I wouldn't put it into that piece of garbage. If you want the car back, you can have it, but I'm not going to pay $50 for that pile of crap.' And maybe he'll say something even worse. Something like, 'What do you need the money for? You've got a good job. You don't need the money.' By this point he is absolutely certain that he's the good guy and you're the bad guy. After that, there's nothing you can do. The money's gone and so is the friendship. All for $50.

"Believe me, boys. I've seen this happen more times than you can imagine. One of the men at work lends money to someone else and a few weeks later they're slugging it out in the parking lot. It's bad news for everyone."

"So what about Little Charlie?" Chuck asked.

"Make up some excuse. Tell him you've got to take your own car into the garage because the brake line is ready to burst. Just tell him you can't afford it right now." Dad paused. "I know this isn't like you, Chuck. You're friends with everybody and you want to help him

out, but once you start lending money you're moving from friendship to business. Why don't you offer to drive him out to the farm
every day? That'll help him out."

—

It took three more weeks of cajoling, and calls from Mrs. McLintoc
to Toronto and Kingston, before the four other offices were completely cooperative with the penitentiary proposal. "Everybody has
their own priorities," she told me. "This just isn't one of them."

Slowly, very slowly, sections of each project description started
to arrive by mail. Sometimes just a single page or even only a paragraph or two at a time. My assignment was to receive them, make
sure they were exactly what we needed, and hand them over to Judy
Jones, our typist, for insertion into the larger project file.

"This goes on page three of Johnson's resume in the GM project,"
I'd say, or "This goes on page 15 of the administrative description
of the Lever project," or, "Here's a new costing analysis for the Beck
Dam project. It replaces the old one completely."

We did not want Janet to be typing and retyping the entire proposal over and over, so all of the individual sections, or pages, or
paragraphs were paper clipped, stapled or taped in their proper
place inside each labeled file folder. There were so many sheets of
paper being moved around the big table that Mrs. McLintoc insisted that I keep a constant watch on every folder.

I made up a sheet with rows for each required item and col-
umns for each project. I could leave each square blank for "nothing
received," 1 for "first draft," 2 for "second draft," F for "final," and
several other stages of completion that I made up as necessary. No
one ever told me that being an engineer meant being a librarian.

—

Kathleen and I exchanged letters at least once a week all summer
long; not the daily schedule she had set. She was working as a life-

guard and giving swimming lessons at a pool near her house. She'd been doing this since she was 16 and had a guaranteed job every summer. She said this was good experience for being a teacher and working with kids all day.

Towards the end of July she had her first really bad experience. "There was a family visiting from England," she wrote, "They were staying with their cousins, but they didn't know how to swim at all and the father drowned."

It was very unlike Kathleen to be writing in an unorganized, disjointed manner. I could tell that she was upset just by the way the sentences were put together.

"I gave him mouth-to-mouth resuscitation but he didn't come back. The two teenagers had been splashing around in the shallow end. It was so hot and the pool was so crowded, so we couldn't watch anyone very closely. But their cousins kept calling them over to the deep end.

"At first we didn't see anything wrong, but her father saw she was in trouble and he jumped in, but he couldn't swim either. With everybody splashing each other and riding on each other's backs, we didn't see what was happening.

"Then some kids in the water noticed. That's the first time I saw something. I blew my whistle and jumped down from my chair.

"They teach us not to jump in to save someone bigger than us or else he'll just drag us underwater, so I took the big hook and reached out to them. They were both all tangled up together flailing around and they couldn't see what was going on.

"The other lifeguard, Phil, jumped into the pool and got his arm around the girl. But the father was grabbing at them both and Phil was pulled under a couple of times. But he still hung on and pulled her away, to the side of the pool. Some people reached down and pulled her up and she was just lying on the side. And poor Phil was so exhausted that they had to pull him out as well.

"But I was still swinging the big hook out to the man in the water. He had nothing to hang on to since his daughter was gone and he had stopped flailing around and started sinking, so I had no choice but to save him.

"I jumped in and got my arm under his chin and pulled him up. He wasn't struggling any more. I towed him over to the side and right away some people grabbed him under his arms and pulled him out of the pool. I was climbing out but they grabbed me under my arms and pulled me out as well.

"Phil was giving mouth-to-mouth to the girl. We had trained for this so many times that it all just kicked in. I knelt down over the man and rolled him over on his side and gave him a couple of whacks on the back to expel any water, but nothing came out. So I rolled him over and pinched his nose and started giving him mouth-to-mouth.

"I just kept going and going. I don't know how long. I don't know how many breaths. I was getting dizzy but the man wasn't doing anything. Then my eyes started to go funny, like looking down a long tunnel. All I could see was a little bit of light at the end, but I kept going until Phil put his hand on my arm and stopped me. I didn't hear him say anything at all. I was so dizzy I couldn't see anything. I sat back on my heels and I just fainted and fell over on my side.

"Phil said I was only out for a minute, but he kept me lying down and he put a towel under my head. I opened my eyes and I was looking right at the man. I knew that he was dead so I closed my eyes again until I wasn't so dizzy.

"It was the worst experience in my whole life. I've pulled lots of children out of the water before. I've even had to slap them on the back, but I've never had to give mouth-to-mouth resuscitation other than in practice and I've never seen anyone die. It was my responsibility to save him but he died.

"My mother says that I should take a few days off of work, but they don't have anyone else to fill in for me, so I have to go back again tomorrow.

"I miss you so badly. I wish you were here with your arm around me, holding me close."

I wrote Kathleen back, telling her how badly I felt for her but she should be brave. It would only be a month until we were back in Montreal and I could hold her in my arms.

It's interesting how I could be much more expressive in my letters. Chuck would say I was being mushy. I could never say something like that to Kathleen in person, but in my letters, I put things down that were straight out of the movies. *Hold you in my arms.* Who actually says that in real life? For the first time I even signed the letter, *With Love.* Our entire marriage I don't think I ever said the word *love* to Kathleen, but I wrote it many times on birthday and anniversary cards. Perhaps saying it would have made the difference.

—

My last day at work was August 21ˢᵗ. By this time all of the necessary pieces had arrived from the other offices. The final few things were delivered on that day.

Since the beginning of the month, Janet had been typing up the proposal, with multiple carbon copies. We brought in a temporary typist to help her with the load.

She had a large pile of file folders of loose paper for each of the demonstration projects. She worked her way through each folder carefully so that every part was included. She had taken control of the folders to make sure that no one else accidentally moved something. I used my check list to confirm that everything arrived.

Mr. Jenkins and Mrs. McLintoc started the final proof-reading the second week in August. Although they did not have the complete proposal in their hands, they knew that Janet and I were managing it well. As each part arrived I would hand it to Janet with the appropriate instructions.

On my last day, I gave her two final pieces, carefully clipping instructions to each: "Add to resume section – Devey," and "New paragraph two of costing section for General Motors."

I was more than glad to be finished with that proposal. At the end of the day Mr. Jenkins shook my hand and thanked me. "You're welcome to come back next year," he said. "By then we should be starting on the penitentiary project and you'll be doing some real engineering work. How would that be?" His confidence in winning the bid was infectious.

CHAPTER NINE

The next day we left for a week up in North Bay on my uncle's houseboat. We had been doing this every couple of years since I was a kid. Chuck complained that he was missing a week of commissions and his customers would be going without food, but Mom was having none of it.

"We committed to this a long time ago," she said. "How was I to know that you'd be working?" Mom and Dad were careful never to mention that Chuck had quit school. "With you two all grown up," she went on, "I'm sure this will be the last time we can all get together for a week up there."

Uncle Ricky had built the houseboat himself. He started with a collection of oil drums that were welded together, six on each side to form the floating base, then painted red. On top was a wooden cabin with narrow open decks on the front and back. I should say "bow and stern," but this was more shoebox than boat. The minimal steering wheel and controls were in the small front living room. The cabins, with narrow bunk beds were strictly for adults. There was a small toilet room; so narrow that anyone more than fifteen pounds overweight had to back in. I didn't ask what happened after that. A pair of 10 horsepower two-stroke outboards on the stern moved us along at a very leisurely pace.

The highlight of the houseboat was the full upper deck, accessed by a narrow ladder at the stern. The inside of the boat was cramped and hot with more than three or four people, so we spent all of our time on top or on the beach.

I still remember, just after supper one evening, Chuck yelling, "Come on everyone, let's go!" He started at the front, ran past us and jumped over the railing about three feet high, diving head first into the water behind the boat.

Mom screamed and ran to the back to see that Chuck was okay. Aunt Janet yelled at Uncle Ricky to stop the boat and my cousin Ray shouted, "MAN OVERBOARD," so loud that I'm certain the cabins on shore heard him.

Chuck popped up in the water, laughing as usual. "Come on! It's too hot up there."

Dad was first to follow. He didn't take a running dive off the upper deck, but stepped over the rail and jumped down. Ray and Rob followed. Christine and I climbed down the ladder to the back deck and dove from a sane level.

It had taken a while for the boat to come to a complete stop, so we were spread across a hundred yards of Trout Lake. This late in August, the water was beautifully warm and was a refreshing break to the heat and black flies of a Northern Ontario summer.

Uncle Ricky shut off both motors and followed us in. Mom and Aunt Janet stayed on the upper deck. They didn't want to get their hair wet so late in the day.

The first over had the longest swim back to the boat, but even with their exertion, we all floated and splashed around for a good fifteen or twenty minutes before exhaustion forced us back on board.

We spent several days on James Island with the houseboat run up on the beach. "Do you think my treasure is still here?" Chuck asked.

"You're the only one who knows where it is," Mom said. "Do you remember where you put it?"

"Everything looks different."

"The waves and ice in the winter can move the beach around quite a bit," Uncle Ricky said.

"I remember it's between two big trees, near a big rock," Chuck said.

"There's lots of trees and lots of rocks."

"It's over there, I think." He pointed down to the left.

"We had a lot of bad storms a couple of years ago," Uncle Ricky said. "Some of those trees got washed away."

"I'm just going to have to look for it," Chuck said, getting up from the picnic table. He had not lost any of the muscle built up the previous summer. If anything, he had grown more of a barrel chest that reminded me of the old Tarzan movies.

Christine walked off after him, "It's my treasure too," she said.

"Sure," said Chuck. "Let's get started."

They spent the next two hours uncovering the tops of the rocks that jutted out of the sand, trying to identify the one that marked their treasure. We had a campfire going with marshmallows on sticks to call them back.

"Any luck?" I asked.

"They all kind of look the same after eight years, but don't worry, we'll get back to it tomorrow."

The men were up early to go fishing. Uncle Ricky was the only man I knew who could promise to catch some fish for breakfast and actually do it – every time. Years later, when Ray and Rob had become competitive bass fishermen, I mentioned this and Ray replied, "Yeah, but I'd ask what kind of fish you want."

We rowed back and cooked up some nice lake trout and fried potatoes for breakfast.

Even after another hour of work, when Chuck had revealed the top half of a dozen large rocks, he still seemed no closer to the treasure.

"It's between two trees, right in the middle," he said.

"But the trees are gone."

"Yeah, but it's three steps from the big rock, towards the water."

"You can't remember which rock?"

"No."

"Why don't you just start digging three feet in front of each rock?

I'll help." I stood with my heels against the rock we were working on and took three steps.

"No, no," he said. "It's three steps to an eight year old." Chuck took three half steps. "This should be okay."

I took the shovel from his hand and pushed into the soft sand. "How deep?"

"It's pretty deep. Maybe two feet."

"That's not too deep."

"It is to an eight year old."

"I'll go three feet just to make sure." The sand was very easy to move. In a few minutes, I had a hole three feet deep and three feet wide. "I don't think we're going to find anything here," I said. "Your turn on the next one."

Chuck took the shovel. Neither of us were wearing shoes, so we were digging with just our arms and backs. Chuck's shovelfuls were twice as big as mine and, after an hour of taking turns, the beach was looking like the D-Day invasion from a war movie.

Clink, we heard. At last the sound was unmistakably not a rock, but glass.

"I've got something," he said, crouching down inside the deep hole so that only his spine was still visible above ground level. "Give me a stick or something. It's packed in here real good."

I walked up to the trees and picked up a dead branch. Chuck bent back into his fox hole and scraped the jar free.

"This is it!" He pulled up an old mason jar. The lid was completely rusted over and coated with sand, but the jar itself was unmistakable. "I found it!" he shouted back to the houseboat.

Mom, Dad, Uncle Ricky and Aunt Janet were sitting in lawn chairs on the front deck of the boat. They looked up from their coffees and smiled.

CHAPTER TEN

The fourth year of university brought a nice change to our study topics. We had gone through the theoretical aspects and detailed mathematical studies. With my disciplined studying techniques and strong math background, I had enjoyed the work very much. But the fourth year brought a change to more applied problems. Because of my high marks, I was often asked to join study and project groups with other students.

"This is a good one," Barry said. "We have to build a bridge out of paper straws and then see how much weight it will hold." We were sitting on the worn brown couch and armchairs in the engineering students lounge. A few other study groups were meeting in other corners of the room. Barry had quickly established himself as natural leader in the group, in any group he joined for that matter. He did it without effort and, as far as I could see, without even being aware. He was always the first one to speak up in any situation; the first one to volunteer for a particular task, pleasant or unpleasant, the first one to raise his hand with a question when the professor was confusing us all.

"I snitched a box from the caf last night." He pointed to a large cardboard box full of straws at his feet. We had enough straws for ten bridges. "This should last us through a trial and error process."

Levy laughed. "You think that's how they do it in the real world? Build a bridge, watch it fall down, call it trial and error then build it again?" Levy was a local Montreal boy. He lived not far from Mount Royal Park, where Kathleen and I walked on Sundays.

"Sure makes it easy to finally get it right," said John. He had come to McGill all the way from British Columbia. He was living with some cousins in town.

"This is where you come in." Barry looked at me. "Do you think you can find the structural properties of a paper straw?"

I thought for a moment before answering. "Let's see." I bent down in my chair and picked up the box. It was very light.

Barry quickly put his hand on top of the box to keep it at our feet, "Shhhh." He held his finger to his lips and shifted his eyes towards the other study groups in the room. "We don't want everybody to know what we've got." He reached into his briefcase and pulled out a sharp, metal ruler, used this to slice open the paper tape that held the box closed and handed me a few white straws.

I tapped one on the table in front of us, scarred with a thousand coffee cup rings and many years of burning cigarettes that had missed the large ash tray in the middle.

"They have good compression strength," I said. "I could measure that." I held the straw between both hands and used my thumbs to press up in the middle, flexing it slightly, then further until it kinked and folded over. "Strong initial sheer strength but a low failure point. I could measure that too."

"What about torsional strength?" Levy asked.

I picked up another straw and twisted it along its axis. The small size made it difficult to hold, until I pinched the ends between my thumbs and fingers. I twisted until the coil of paper separated from itself. "Actually, pretty strong," I said. "I should be able to measure that in the lab."

"I doubt it," John said. "Those instruments are designed to measure metal beams, even just small ones. I doubt they are precise enough to measure the strength of a straw."

They all looked at me, but I was stuck. I knew exactly how to take these measurements, but there is a big leap between knowing how to do it and having the ability to actually do it.

After another thirty seconds, Barry spoke up. "I'm sure you'll come up with something."

"You know," John said, "if this is so difficult, then the other groups will have trouble too. This could give us a real advantage. It could be the main part in our report."

Ours was truly a Trans-National study group. John was from Newfoundland, with a very strong accent. Kathleen claimed that when he spoke, she could close her eyes and dream of Ireland. And if he'd had a couple of beers, it was hard to understand him at all.

"I'm sure that's the whole point," said Levy. "He's not just asking us to build a bridge, he's asking us to provide all of the engineering knowledge behind it."

We nodded.

"We've got lots of time on this one," Barry said. "Three weeks at least. How 'bout you come back after the long weekend with some ideas?"

"Sure." I replied.

Levy looked over at Barry and John. "You're not leaving the city, are you? Why don't you come over to my place on the weekend and we can come up with some design ideas and eat some Thanksgiving Turkey."

"That sounds great, thanks," they replied.

I reached into the box and quickly transferred a large handful of straws into my briefcase while the other groups were in deep discussion. "I'll need these for some destructive testing."

"Go ahead," Barry laughed. "We've got lots."

—

I caught the bus home on Friday. Chuck was later than usual getting in for supper.

"I'm taking orders for turkey," he said. "Every one of my customers. Now tomorrow, I've got to get up early and deliver them all. It'll be a killer, but I'll make it."

He had already sat down and was shovelling Mom's warmed

over supper into his mouth. She told us he had been late every night this week. I could see the combination of work exhaustion and excitement that Chuck carried into everything that he enjoyed. He was like a dog chasing a ball; he had no idea when to quit and would keep running until he collapsed, although I had never seen that collapse happen.

"What're you doing?" he asked.

The straws were in a pile, resting between the salt and pepper shakers so they wouldn't roll off the table. I picked one up. "I've got to figure out a way to measure the strength required to twist one of these." I held it between my hands and showed him.

He laughed, pieces of potato flying out. "What're you doing? Building a house of straws? Like the three little pigs?"

I heard Dad laugh from the living room.

"Actually, it's a bridge," I replied. "They want us to show how good we are at engineering principles by building a bridge of straws. And then the prof will put weights on it until it fails. The group that builds the bridge which holds the greatest weight wins."

"Wins what?"

"A good mark, I hope."

"And you need to twist the straw until it breaks?"

"The twisting part is easy," I said. "What I really need to do is measure the force required to twist it at each point until it breaks." I twisted the straw in my hands in a jerking motion, a few degrees at a time, to show him what I meant.

"Oh," he stared at the straw in my hands with a puzzled look. "Sure."

—

It was 2:30 in the morning when I rolled over and saw Chuck at his desk, working with Meccano. "What are you doing?" I yawned.

"Just messing around."

"You've got to get to bed. You've got to get up early again."

"Sure. I won't be long."

When I woke up again, he was already gone. He had built a rectangular tower of Meccano, about 18" inches high with four inch sides. The base was about six inches square. On top was a platform sticking out three inches. Directly below the platform, close to the bottom of the tower and protruding a couple of inches, were some Meccano strips held together with rubber bands. Scattered around his desk were a number of gears and axels. The tower was very solid, with crossbeams to opposite corners at six and twelve inches high as well as the top platform. Even with just the small Meccano nuts and bolts, it was quite strong and surprisingly heavy when I picked it up. Whatever he was building was not finished, but darned if I could figure out what it was.

It was nearly ten o'clock when Chuck got home from his deliveries on Saturday. "Nobody wants a turkey that's frozen and sitting around for two weeks." He took a long drink of milk and held up the fifteen pound bird he'd brought home for Mom, "Be careful, this guy's so fresh that he'll try to pinch your bum."

"Oh, Lord," Mom replied. "How many times did you use that line today?"

"'Bout a hundred."

"I'll bet the little old ladies just love you, smarty pants?"

"Yeah, but you gotta have a smile and a wink or it doesn't work," Chuck smirked.

After downing another glass of milk, he said to me, "Let me show you what I'm building. Maybe it'll help you."

We walked into the bedroom and he sat down. "What I figure is this," he picked up one of my straws and slipped the end between the two Meccano strips that were closed with rubber bands, with a short length of axel rod inside the straw to prevent the end being crushed. "We clamp the straw down here." He slid his fingers up the straw. "At the top here we put another clamp, but not attached to the tower. It's clamped to a bar that runs up to the platform here." He leaned the apparatus over so we were looking at the top. "We put some gears and a handle up here, but we gear it right down. Then you turn the handle and that twists the straw down here with this rubber band resisting. And somehow you measure how much the straw has twisted and that gives you what you need." He looked up at me. "What do you think?"

"I don't know. It's not really a proper measuring instrument."

"You have to use some imagination. What's that half moon thing you use to measure angles?" He stretched over to my desk, opened the drawer and grabbed the protractor. "This thing. These are angles, right? We could tape this up here. And when you turn the handle you'll know how much the top is twisted. Then you can see how much the straw is twisted. And then you can figure out exactly how much you need to twist it to break it." He paused again, showing me with his hands how the straw will twist. "That'll work, won't it?"

On Monday, I caught the bus back to Montreal with Chuck's invention in a cardboard box on my lap.

—

It was a month later, in November that I received a telephone call at the boarding house. I went into the central hall on my floor to pick it up.

"There's a problem with our proposal." Mr. Jenkins said. "We might not meet the technical requirements."

I waited for more details.

"We only had three resumes in the Devey Paints project. The requirement is for four."

"That can't be right." I replied. "I kept a careful checklist and everything was checked off. The list should still be there. I left it in my desk; in the bottom right hand drawer."

I heard him speak away from the telephone. "Can you get his checklist. It's in the bottom right hand drawer. Okay. Hold on for a minute," he said to me.

I could hear him speaking with Mrs. McLintoc, looking at my papers. I spoke up so they could hear me, "ON THE SECOND PAGE. HALF WAY DOWN."

"What's that?" he said.

"On the second page, half way down. You can see the section for the resumes on each project. I'm sure that all the spaces are checked in." I really was sure. I was completely confident that everything was done. I had been so particular with my records.

"Yes," he said, "I can see that it's all checked in. This is a very complete record that you've kept, and so precise. It almost looks like it was typed."

He was right. I had used my perfect draftsman's lettering throughout the document. Every letter was identical in style and shape to the strictest requirements. Every checkmark was exactly the same size and aligned precisely in the centre of its appropriate column.

I thought back to the summer. "I remember on my last day. Mrs. McLintoc had already taken charge of the proposal from me, but I had a few things left and I gave Janet a resume for the Devey project, and some other things. Did that get put in properly?"

"Hold on." I overheard them talking some more and call Janet into the conversation. "She doesn't remember that in particular."

"There was a lot of paperwork moving around in those last days." I said. "I don't think anyone could keep track of it all without careful notes," I had to make sure my position was solid, "but I remember quite specifically that I had paper-clipped a note to the front of the resume that it was for the Devey project.

"Could it have been misplaced?"

In that instant I knew what happened.

"Check the Lever Brothers file," I said. "Lever, Devey. The names are too similar and we had a couple of times when things got misplaced."

I heard them talking. "Do you remember who's resume it was?"

"No." I thought for a few seconds. "But it would be easy to see. All the resumes for the Devey project were from Kingston. The Lever project was in Toronto."

I overheard him say, "Bring the submission for the Lever Brothers project, will you?" I heard a knock as he put the telephone down on his desk while he flipped through the hundreds of pages in the project file. My ear was getting sore from pressing the telephone receiver against it. At one point, he picked up the phone again. "Hang on. Don't go anywhere," he said without waiting for a reply and putting the handset down again with another knock.

This would be an expensive phone call. It was stretching out with most of it being just empty air while things happened in the office.

"It looks like you're right," he said when he came back on the line. "There are five resumes in the Lever Brothers project."

"Is one of them from Kingston?"

"Hang on." And another couple of minutes. "Yes, here's one, Greg Franklin, it looks like..."

"That's it!" I interrupted. "I remember that name now. He should be in the Devey Paints project."

Mr. Jenkins did not reply. I could hear the movement of paper.

"Is this going to be a problem?" I asked.

"From what I understand," he replied, "they separate all of the parts of the proposal into different sections and subsections, and they have different people evaluate each one. So the man who evaluates the Devey Paints project is probably not the same man who looks at the Lever Brothers project, and they probably don't even talk to each other." He paused again, this time at least thirty seconds. "Each section needs to be complete on its own. It doesn't help to have five resumes in one project but only three in another. Whoever is reading our Devey Paints project will just mark it as incomplete, and that's bad." He paused again. "I don't know what we're going to do. Maybe we'll write a letter."

—

Kathleen and I went on one of our usual Sunday walks in late March. Spring had come early and hard, with two weeks of warming days to clear out the last of the snowy pathways of Mount Royal Park and kick off the buds in the trees. After church I had wanted to go back to my boarding house to study for the upcoming finals but she insisted that we spend the afternoon together on such a beautiful day.

"So what are our plans?" she asked after an unusually long period of silence as we walked one of the side paths. She had her arm through my elbow. She was wearing a three-quarter length, yellow, light wool coat over a tan dress. It was the first time since the fall that she'd worn shoes rather than boots on our walks.

"What do you mean?"

She didn't say anything for about a minute. "What are our plans? You know, for after school?"

I didn't say anything. Just kept looking straight ahead as we walked. I had a good idea what she was thinking of but I wasn't ready to broach the subject.

Another minute passed and she said, "Well, are we going to get married?"

"Um–I guess so."

"Aren't you going to ask me?"

"Didn't you just ask me?"

Another thirty seconds passed.

"I guess that's it then. We're engaged," she said.

"I guess so."

"Not quite the way I had in mind. I guess we'll have to start making plans."

"Sure."

"Oh, look! I think the tulips are coming up."

Later that evening, after supper at the boarding house and when I'd settled down with my books, Kathleen called.

"I spoke with my mother and she called the Minister. We'll get married on July 15th. It's a Saturday."

"In Moncton?"

"Of course in Moncton."

"I'll have just started at work. I don't know if I can get the time..."

She cut me off. "You've been there a year already. I'm sure they'll let you take a week off to get married."

"A week?"

"Yes. A whole week, at least. We have to take a honeymoon, you know."

"Do we have money for that?"

"It won't cost us anything. My uncle has a cottage on the ocean in Prince Edward Island. He's offered it to us."

"You arranged all of this today?"

"You really are clueless, aren't you? I've had this planned since last summer."

"What if I hadn't agreed?"

"Have you ever said no to me?"

"No– um–I guess not."

CHAPTER ELEVEN

The four of us left Bowmanville on Thursday, just before noon and spent the night in a motel along the highway in Riviere-du-Loup in Eastern Quebec. We could have made the entire trip in one long day but Dad said there wasn't much point in arriving just when everyone was going to bed. We left the motel early and arrived at Kathleen's house in time for lunch.

We could see that something was up when we found her address. The house had three cars parked on the front lawn and two in the drive. The street was packed with cars and pickup trucks taking up every inch of available space, even half covering the neighbours driveways. Several families walked towards Kathleen's, in each case with the woman carrying a large dish of food and the man carrying a case of beer or several bottles of some other refreshment in paper bags. It was like a line of ants marching back to their hill, each with a crumb of bread on its back.

Moncton was an important shipping hub, with railways from across Canada converging for goods coming from, or going to, overseas ports. Kathleen's father, whom I'd met when he made a business trip to Montreal, worked for the CNR, as did her two older brothers.

"Holy Cow!" Dad said when we pulled up to Kathleen's dark brown bungalow. "Where are we going to park?"

Mr. Lawson must have been waiting for us on the front stoop

because I caught a glimpse of him running out on the lawn. "Over there, Dad," I said. "That's Mr. Lawson waving at us."

He waved both arms and directed Dad to the last remaining spot on the front lawn. "Right here!" he shouted. "The place of honour for the family of honour!"

He was every bit the man I remembered, and even more energetic than Kathleen herself. "Welcome! Welcome!" he shouted, reaching through the car window and taking Dad by the hand in a two handed grip. "I'm Bernie. It's so good to finally meet you. Katie has said so much about you."

By this time Dad had opened the car door enough to put one foot out, but Mr. Lawson, still standing on the other side, their hands clasped through the window, made it impossible to move further until the grip was released and he ran around the front of the car to where Mom was getting out.

"And you must be Rebecca. Welcome! I'm Bernie. Welcome to Moncton." He extended one hand but, the moment she extended hers, pulled her into a hug. At least Mom was outside the car before the hug was attempted, or else I'm certain Mr. Lawson would have leaned right into the front seat.

"And there's my boy," he said as I got out of the door behind Mom. I extended my hand but he went right past it into a full, two armed hug. "How are you doing, my boy? Did you have a good trip?" He didn't wait for an answer before releasing me and running around the back of the car to meet Chuck.

He stuck out his hand for a good, firm handshake but no one, no one, could top Chuck in gregariousness. He deliberately pushed the hand aside and closed for a bear hug. I think even Mr. Lawson was surprised.

"My God, boy! You must be an East-coaster by heart. No one from Toronto ever hugs like that!"

"That's 'cause I'm not from Toronto, Mr. Lawson," Chuck laughed. "We're just small town yokels up from Bowmanville."

"Let me tell you, boy, everyone west of Quebec City is from Toronto as far as I'm concerned. And for God's sake, Mr. Lawson is my father, call me Bernie."

"You bet, Bernie."

We followed Bernie around the side of the house. "It's too crowded inside." He said, "We'll never make it through."

I was awestruck at what we saw. There must have been 75 people in the small backyard, and another 25 poured out the door at our arrival. Two dozen of the older family members, situated on folding lawn chairs, were spread with their backs to the fence in a manner that simply reduced the available yard space for others. There was no appearance of smaller groups or individual conversations going on because there was no room for separation. Just one large group with half the people talking and half the people listening.

"They're here!" Bernie shouted. He started to introduce us but was washed over by the wave of grandparents, aunts, uncles, first cousins, second cousins and third cousins that surged forward and surrounded Bernie like water past a lonely dock pylon.

I really can't distinguish what happened or who I met over the next two hours. A hundred people shook my hand. It started to hurt after the first twenty, but that didn't stop the next eighty from showing a good, firm grip. In most cases it was two-handed, so even when I relaxed my grip, the handshake continued. Every one of the men used their left hand to give me a good, hard slap on the back as he pumped my hand. My shoulder started to hurt as well. And every one of the women pulled me in for a hug and a kiss on the cheek. Mom had insisted that I shave before we left the motel even though I barely needed it. I now understood why.

Mom, Dad and Chuck had been shuffled to different points in the backyard, but they were also receiving handshakes and hugs. "Hi, I'm Katie's cousin so-and-so from Halifax. You can join Bernie and the boys at the CNR," was the gist of a comment I heard several times. I tried to explain that I wasn't that type of engineer, but I don't think I was understood in the hubbub.

Most of the conversations were a quick one minute with Aunt so-and-so or Uncle so-and-so telling me how lucky I was and that Katie was such a great girl, but several lasted much longer while they went on about some adventure they'd had with Katie when they were kids.

I vaguely remembered something being said about a dory and a storm, but by this point, I was in such a confused daze that nothing more could sink in. Two weeks later, back home, I brought it up and Kathleen just said she was really young and didn't remember it much, but Chuck jumped in, "That's your Uncle Dave from Cape Breton. The way he says it, when you're just a little girl, only five, you and your cousins are out fishing in his dory. A storm comes up and they have to row like the devil to get back to shore, and you're in the bottom the whole time bailing for your life with every wave. When you all finally reach shore they find you curled up asleep in the bottom of the boat."

Some time, half-way through the introductory ordeal, someone put a paper plate of sandwiches and potato salad in my left hand and a bottle of beer into my right. This just made it more awkward to continue with the hand shaking and hugging, so I drank down the beer as quickly as I could. Continuous *Hi's* and *Hello's* and *Nice-To-Meet-Ya's* had left me parched.

From time to time I caught a glimpse of Kathleen on the top of the back steps or looking out the kitchen window. She smiled and wiggled her fingers hello but did not make any attempt at a rescue until the last of her extended family had introduced themselves.

When the crowd around me had sufficiently thinned, she stood up on her toes to kiss me on the cheek. Our first contact in three months.

"What do you think of my family? I told you it would be an experience never to forget."

"I had no idea that anything like this existed," I said. "My family is friendly, but nothing like this."

"Welcome to the East Coast. We're all like this."

The introductions, eating and drinking went on all afternoon. At four o'clock Kathleen, her best friend Dianna, Chuck and I went to St. Andrew's Church to meet the Minister. St. Andrew's was a beautiful church, built of wood and with a small bell in the steeple at the front. The moment we walked in I could tell that it would be tight to fit Kathleen's family inside. "Oh, they'll all manage somehow," she said.

Overlooking the alter was a beautiful stained glass window showing Christ, with a red robe, holding a shepherd's crook in one hand and cradling a lamb in the other. Father Harkin heard us talking and came out from his office. He was about 35, with a dark, military brush cut.

Kathleen's family had been attending St. Andrew's only since they had moved to the new neighbourhood, and most of that time she had been studying in Montreal, so she knew Reverend Harkin but did not have a long family history.

He took ten minutes to go over how the service would proceed, what would be said and what our responses should be. Then he asked Dianna and Chuck to wait while Kathleen and I went into his office for a serious talk about the responsibilities of marriage. I was very glad that I'd only had two beers all afternoon, interspaced with several bottles of Coke. I was certainly alert, if not a bit jittery while he spoke.

—

The party had not stopped when we returned to Kathleen's house, if anything, the downing of beers while we'd been away had increased the revelry. Someone attempted to start a game of horseshoes but, with a hundred people crowded into the yard, the throwing lane was so narrow that shoulders, hips and knees were hit more often than the stake.

Several trays of hotdogs, fried chicken and corn on the cob appeared shortly after our return. The men stayed well away from the kitchen, and didn't even venture into the house for the bathroom. Instead, we made ample use of the alleyway and it was easy to recognize the attempts to write names on the brown paint of the fence.

As my best man, Chuck made sure that I was never without a beer in my hand, so I made as many marks on the fence as the next man, even if I was working to maintain my sobriety with Mom and Dad nearby.

Around eight, when a few of the families with small children left for their hotels, the party started in earnest. Out of nowhere fiddles, guitars, flutes and an accordion appeared. Kathleen had told me about the ceilidhs that were the sole source of entertainment in Cape Breton, but I could not truly understand until I saw it for myself.

It wasn't more than three seconds after the first notes were played that the entire family was clapping their hands and stomping their feet. I hesitated a bit until Kathleen reached around and started clapping my hands for me. She let out a deafening YELP next to my right ear. It was just a minute into the first song that couples started swinging each other around and the family cleared a small area in the middle of the lawn.

Across the yard I could see one of the second or third cousins pulling Chuck into the space. She looked to be in her late teens, about his age. She had dark hair tied up in a pony tail and hanging down her back, blue jeans, cut off just above the knee, a red button up shirt with no sleeves and white sneakers with no socks. "That's Georgette," Kathleen said. "From Halifax."

It wasn't important to Chuck that he didn't know the apparently complicated steps of this ceilidh reel. He had his right hand around her waist, his left hand holding her right, pumping up and down, back and forth with the beat of the music, and his feet bouncing around in no apparent direction at all. I think they were in the air more than they touched the ground. In general, Chuck and Georgette seemed to be turning at the same rate as the other couples, so only a few bumps occurred and both were talking and laughing as they moved.

"She's had her eye on him all afternoon," Kathleen leaned into me. "But she's lucky to have grabbed him first because a few of the others have been eyeing him too."

I leaned back a bit and looked at Kathleen with surprise. "Really?"

"Oh, yes. He's just got a way about him that's hard to resist," she paused while I continued to look at her. "But don't worry; he's good for a lark, but we're in this for the long run."

That didn't sound like much of a compliment. When the next song started up, Kathleen grabbed my arm. "Come on. I know this one."

We joined a dozen other couples in a circle with men on the inside, Kathleen and I holding each other around the waist. "Just follow what I do," she said.

We took three steps forward and hopped up. I tried to take another step forward but she held me tighter and we took three steps back with another hop. I could see Mom three couples ahead of us with Bernie's arm around her waist.

Kathleen dropped her arm from around me and gave me a little nudge. I followed the other men as we took a skip towards the centre of the circle and another skip out again – with a clap. This time Kathleen moved in front of me into a normal dance hold. All the couples twirled around a few times while the whole circle rotated counter-clockwise. We made it about half way around before the process started again.

It was a hot, sticky evening. We had several dances and several rests, and a couple more beers. "Have you seen Chuck?" Dad asked, looking over the crowd.

"No. I'm sure he's here somewhere."

"If you see him, tell him I'm looking for him." Dad said, walking towards the house.

"Georgette's gone too." Kathleen said. She had a smile on her face and a twinkle in her eye. "See what I told you? Let's have another dance."

Just before ten o'clock, Chuck reappeared. "Come here," he said. "I want to show you something."

"What?" I asked.

"Just come here."

Kathleen turned to me. "Go on and have fun." She gave me a kiss.

Chuck led me on the narrow walkway between the house and the side fence. It was nearly dark by now, but from the faded light I could see a dozen of Kathleen's uncles and cousins.

The instant they saw Chuck and I round the corner, I was jumped. Chuck grabbed me from behind, wrapping around me like a bear and pinning my arms to my sides. With his strength, I knew there was no use in struggling. Less than two seconds later a burlap feed sack was pulled over my head and shoulders and, while Chuck continued to hold me tight, some type of rope was wrapped around me four or five times. I'm sure I would have fallen over, or perhaps collapsed at the knees, if Chuck and the other men had not held me up.

"Hey! What's going on?" I shouted.

"Relax. We're gonna have some fun." Chuck laughed as he spoke into my ear.

By this time my feet were in the air. I tried to kick out but there were at least six hands holding tight to each leg, another four hands on each arm, and many more on my body. Whatever they were doing, they obviously had it well planned.

I was carried a short distance until the group of us, myself and my pallbearers, climbed into the bed of a pickup truck and I was held down on all sides. The ride was bumpy, with my head banging against the metal truck bed until someone slipped his foot underneath; it felt like a tennis shoe. There were lots of shouting and whoops of laughter from the guys. I could easily make out Chuck's voice so I knew that I wasn't in too much trouble. A few minutes later, I was picked up again and carried on their shoulders. There seemed to be fewer hands holding onto me, since I'd stopped struggling.

I could tell by the music that we had walked through a bar. I heard some voices shouting about a door and we went into another room that was quieter. "Right here" I heard Chuck say and they sat me down on a wooden chair. "Get it on." He said and I felt a metal clamp placed around my ankle.

The burlap sack was lifted off of my head. Chuck was right beside me with the sack in his hand. The dozen others all looked to be in their 20s or 30s. I had met them all earlier, but the names were a blur, not aided by the beer I'd been drinking or the disorientation of being kidnapped.

The only guy I remembered clearly was Kathleen's older brother, Ian. He was about thirty, as tall as I was with Kathleen's same dark hair. "Let's get going!" he shouted. "How 'bout some beer in here!"

As if on cue, a waitress walked in with a large tray held high. It was full of glasses of draught. Ian tried to grab a glass off the tray but she swatted his hand away. "Don't touch that unless you want the whole tray dumped on you." She scowled.

She looked to be in her late 50's; thin, her face lined and point-ed from a lifetime of sucking too hard on cigarettes. She had on a black, short sleeved dress that wouldn't show if beer had been splashed on it; her right arm was stringy and muscular from years of lifting loaded trays.

The room was the size of a small classroom, with a wooden platform up front. Wood-panelled walls were decorated with team sweaters; there were no windows, just a door from the bar and an exit out the side.

I looked down to see the ball and chain that had been clamped around my ankle, right out of a western movie. It weighed a good 30 pounds.

"What the heck is this?"

"We figured you'd better find out what marriage is really like," Ian said, "before you take that last step."

The conversation–no, *conversation* implies a sense of order–the *blather* took on a decidedly raunchy tone at this point. It reminded me of the talk between construction workers back at the Goodyear plant, where each tried to outdo the other in his level of supposed experience.

"So, have you nailed Katie yet?"

"You're not going into this blind are you? God! She might be frigid!"

"I remember my wedding night," one of the older cousins said.

"She squealed like a banshee. So I did her again and that shut her up. Now she can't get enough of me."

"That's not what I heard. I heard she's doin' the milkman 'cause you can't get her hot."

It went around the table in a haphazard fashion, with each of the married men giving their opinion on what the first night will be like, and each of the single men teasing me based on their own imagined experience.

"Leave him alone," Chuck butted in. "He's a gentleman and he's got himself a great girl."

"Ha! We all knew Katie back when she was just a teenager," another cousin teased. "You wouldn't be talking about her like that if you knew what we knew."

"And anyway," a different cousin chimed in. "Come tomorrow night, she's not going to be looking for a gentleman, is she?"

I was halfway through my second glass of beer when it went dark except for a single spot light over the wooden platform. We all stopped talking while decidedly female footsteps were heard crossing the floor. We couldn't make her out clearly until she reached the record player at the side of the platform. "Hey Boys! You up for a little fun?" She lifted the needle from the Elvis record that had been playing and put on her own stack of 45's.

"My name's Elizabeth. You can call me *Lady Elizabeth*. I hear that someone's getting married!" She looked around the table. Every finger was pointed at me. It had not dawned on me that I was front and centre of the table until she took up her position. "Well let's see what we can do to make your last night of freedom a memorable one!"`

Elizabeth was very attractive; I guess that helps in her business. She was in her mid 20s, about five foot eight, the epitome of an hourglass figure with a large bust, thin waist and large hips. She was wearing a tight gold sequinned dress that went down to her ankles with a slit, covered with a matching cape that was split all the way up the back so that the two halves swung wide like a propeller when she turned. She had on gold shoes with three inch heels and black gloves over her elbows. A big bouffant of wavy dark hair piled up on her head extended her height. She was heavily made up with matching gold eye shadow and dark red lips.

The first of her 45s, *Venus* by Frankie Avalon, dropped onto the turntable. Elizabeth started into a sort of Cha-Cha dance, holding her right hand against her stomach with her left hand extended. She was swinging her hips back and forth, but staying in the centre of the stage. She pushed the wings of her cape back to reveal her bare shoulders and the spaghetti straps of her dress. Half way through the second chorus, she unclipped the cape from her throat, letting it fall at the back of the platform. She started moving slowly from one end of the platform to the other, keeping the same Cha-Cha pose and swinging her hips as she gave everyone a close-up look at her figure.

As the song ended she stepped down off the platform and lowered herself onto my lap. Her dress was so fitted that she had to hitch it up to sit.

"What's your Sweetie's name, honey?" she asked.

"Um, Kathleen." I stammered.

"Is Kathleen your Venus?" she teased.

The guys started shouting.

"Woo Hoo!"

"Yeah!"

"Yes!"

"Well you can just forget all about her 'till tomorrow honey, because tonight, you're mine."

When *Smoke Gets In Your Eyes* started to play, she rose from my lap and gave me a kiss on the cheek. "You just sit back and enjoy the view, honey."

She moved much more slowly during the song. Her arms were raised in the air as she pulled the fingers of her left glove and then slid it off, then her right glove. She tossed them on top of her cape.

With her bare arms up above her head, the swaying motion reminded me of a cobra being entranced by a snake charmer. She turned slowly, giving us a very nice view of her shapely behind. She stepped down from the platform again and made her way in front of us, stopping with her back to me. "Give me a hand with that zipper, would you, honey."

I reached up to just below her shoulder blades and took hold of the zipper, being careful not to touch her back.

"Just give it a pull, honey. You'll need to practice for tomorrow night."

Chuck, sitting beside me, finished off his glass of beer and said, "Go for it."

She wiggled a bit as I pulled the zipper down to the small of her back and she took a step away. "That's enough for now, honey. Don't want to go too fast. You've got to learn that too."

She stepped back up on the platform and turned to face me. As she continued to sway back and forth, the spaghetti straps dropped off her shoulders. She held the front of the dress against her with her left forearm. A few seconds later, she reached back to lower the zipper and the dress dropped down to the floor.

She swayed in place, inside the circle of her dress, raised her arm back above her head and continued her snake charmers dance. She was wearing a black, strapless bustier, a black garter belt, black panties and black silk stockings.

The volume of shouts in the room increased dramatically. Chuck leaned over, "You like that? It's my present to you, big brother."

When the song ended, Elizabeth bent at the knees, to collect her dress. Her eyes were level with mine. "You enjoying yourself, honey?"

"Yes"

"Well you just wait."

Mack the Knife dropped onto the turntable and Elizabeth moved across the platform in a tango motion; taking long strides. The song isn't a perfect fit for the dance steps, but to be honest none of us were listening closely to the music.

After the first few bars she stepped off the platform and reached for my hand "Do ya tango, honey?"

I pulled my hand back, "Oh, no, no, no." I shook my head. The guys gave some whoops of encouragement but I shrunk back into my chair, looking for a way out of the embarrassment. I reached down and shook the chain attached to my ankle. "Can't," was all I said.

Elizabeth looked a little confused and hurt, then she turned to Chuck, "Are you the best man, honey?"

"Oh yeah!" He nodded vigorously.

"Well then, you just come with me and we'll see if you really are."

Chuck didn't need any extra encouragement to follow her. He practically led her back up on the platform. They joined together in the tango pose. Elizabeth, in nothing but her underwear, pressed up tightly against Chuck, nearly straddling his outstretched leg. With her height and high heels, she towered above him.

She pulled him even tighter as they moved. It was certain that she was leading the dance, but Chuck enjoyed every moment. I could see them talking as they held on closely. It was a clumsy tango, but they were stuck together like glue, and moved as one across the floor.

The guys continued their applause and yelps of approval. They had only met Chuck that afternoon but were already getting a real sense of his personality.

When the song ended, still tightly in each other's arms, Elizabeth kissed him right on the lips.

"Hand me that chair, will you, honey?" she said as he left the platform. She set it down directly in front of me as Elvis', *Love me Tender* started.

"This is all you got to remember, honey. Love me tender."

As the song played it's slow, monotonous tone, she unhooked her stockings and rolled them down, tossing the first one to her dress behind her. The second stocking she tossed, not to me, but to Chuck. "Thanks for the dance," she said quietly to him.

With her stockings and garter belt gone, she stood and swayed, just a few feet in front of me. She reached over to her right side and pulled the zipper that secured her bustier. Holding it in place with her left arm, and with her right arm raised, she slowly turned in a circle. With only a few lines left in the song, she raised her left arm and the bustier fell to the floor.

Her breasts were perfectly shaped. I'd describe them as melon sized if that doesn't seem irreverent. This was the first time I'd ever seen a woman naked in person, so I could not compare them to any others, but I sat staring while the guys around me continued their applause. The song ended and someone behind us turned out the spotlight, leaving only a dim bulb for Elizabeth to quickly gather her clothing and leave the room.

"You have a good day tomorrow, honey," she said as she crossed in front of me.

—

The wedding went as expected, aside from a bit of awkwardness when the Minister didn't say: "You may kiss the bride," at the end of the ceremony. I'd seen it on so many movies and TV shows, that I was expecting it. But I could always rely on Kathleen to handle any situation. When the Minister introduced us as Mr. and Mrs., she twisted my hand slightly, causing me to turn towards her. She stood up on her toes and leaned into me. I was quick to catch on and I doubt anyone in the church noted my hesitation.

The wedding reception was a complete success. Kathleen didn't want just another East Coast reception of local folk music (we'd had enough of that at her house) so she'd hired a disk jockey to play all the top hits from the past decade, mixed in with a few Cape Breton favourites to keep the older relatives up on the dance floor. Although Kathleen had family roots on the Island, she considered herself to be a fashionable city girl from Moncton.

As expected, Chuck had a great time on the floor. He didn't stick with Georgette but danced with many of the cousins, young and old, fat and thin. At about 9:30, he must have ducked away for a bit because at 10:00, Kathleen saw him come back into the dance holding hands with a new girl. "Who's that?" she asked.

"I've got no idea. Isn't she one of your family?"

"I don't think so, unless she's some distant cousin that I've never met."

The girl was our age, perhaps older and certainly older than Chuck, but of course he looked older than he was. She had dark hair with a Mary Tyler Moore curl at the bottom. She had light lipstick and no other makeup that I could see until Kathleen pointed out very subtle eye shadow. She was quite shapely, though she wore a conservative pink dress that went to just her knee. With just one inch heels, she was still a bit taller than Chuck.

She appeared to be quite shy, keeping her head low as she walked through the gathering without much notice. She only spoke a very quiet, "Congratulations," to me and, "My best wishes" to Kathleen when Chuck introduced her.

"This is Betty," he said. "I hope you don't mind if I bring her for a while?"

"Not at all," Kathleen assured him. "You are more than welcome to enjoy the celebrations."

They immediately went out to the dance floor and fell in with the crowd. Kathleen looked at me again.

"I have no idea who she is," I protested. "Chuck's been with me all day. Honest."

Of course we were busy making small talk with every single member of the family. Luckily, this time Kathleen didn't leave my side as we chatted with every cousin, uncle and aunt whom I didn't know other the indistinguishable introductions from the previous afternoon.

"So what are your plans for the future?" Uncle so-and-so would ask.

"I guess I'll stay with HBA Engineering for now," I'd say in reply. "It looks like I've got a good future there."

"When are you going to have children?" Aunt so-and-so would ask.

"I'd like to get in a few years of teaching first." Kathleen answered. "But don't worry, it'll be soon. We both want children when we're ready."

I don't remember having that specific conversation with Kathleen, but it was a reasonable assumption on her part.

We tried to break away for our own dances, but inevitably would be drawn into a new conversation with every family member we passed. My only relatives in attendance were Uncle Ricky and Aunt Janet who had left home after work on Friday and driven through the night. The plan was for Mom and Dad to join them on an East Coast vacation while Kathleen and I took Dad's car to our honeymoon at the cottage on Prince Edward Island.

The reception was enjoyed by everyone, with thirty or forty people out dancing at any given time and swelling to sixty or seventy when a special hit was put on the record player. *Teenager in Love, Tequila, Tutti Frutti* and *Great Balls of Fire* brought out the big crowds.

Chuck and Betty stayed together the rest of the evening. During the few times they sat down for a cold drink, I saw Betty shy away from other men asking her to dance. Likewise any time one of the female cousins approached, Chuck took Betty's hand, as his own way of warding off predators.

It was well after midnight when I heard the first few beats of *Mack the Knife* coming from the stage. Chuck and Betty were on the far side of the dance floor, but with my view over the crowd, I could easily see him pull her in tight and take the first three or four steps of a tango. As soon as Betty realized what was happening, she pushed him away into a more traditional dance position.

My jaw dropped, which I immediately covered with my hands. I looked around and a few of the other men had caught the same thing. All of us, or at least those of us who knew what was going on, stopped dead in our tracks. Of course this caused our wives or dance partners to look up.

"What's wrong?" Kathleen asked.

By this time Chuck and Betty were moving with the same steps as everyone else.

"Nothing," I said. "Let's dance. I like this song."

CHAPTER TWELVE

The three of us had rented a small house on Church Street near the middle of town. I was able to walk to work and Kathleen could walk, or ride her bicycle in good weather to her new job as grade three teacher at Charles Bowman Public School. She got the job because the previous teacher quit to have a baby after just one year, having replaced another teacher who had left after only a few months for the same reason. Kathleen promised the Principal that we did not plan to have children for a while. She wanted to make good use of her teaching degree before starting a family. The fact that she had a university degree, rather than just two years of college, was sufficient to convince the Principal that she was serious about the profession.

I was very surprised when Chuck came home earlier than usual one Friday evening in mid-February. He jumped right into the tub and even shaved for the second time that day. Then put on a clean shirt and tie and his best suit.

"What are you up to, getting so dressed up?" Kathleen asked.

"I'm taking Debbie to the dance," he said. "I have to dress up."

"It's the mid-winter ball at the Elks Club," I clarified for Kathleen. "It's been going on for years." I looked at Chuck. "You mean Debbie from when you were a kid? I thought you were forbidden to see her?"

"No, it's okay. We go out once in a while. Her parents are back together again. Her Mom doesn't think I'm such a bum anymore."

"I'll explain later," I said to Kathleen quietly. "They had some problems at home."

"Have they gotten over their... their issues?" I asked.

"Debbie says it's pretty tense. They argue all the time. It gets real bad at times."

Kathleen spoke up. "He doesn't hit her, does he?"

I nodded my head towards her.

"You mean he hits Debbie?" she exclaimed.

"No, her Mom," Chuck answered. "Sometimes Debbie stands in front of her Mom so he can't hit her."

"But he doesn't hit Debbie?"

"No."

"What a bastard. Deserves to have his nuts cut off." Kathleen said. A perfect reflection of what Mom had said a few years earlier, but I'd never heard Mom put is so succinctly.

—

Chuck and Debbie dated exclusively over the next few months, although she was still in school so it was only on weekends.

"We should have her over for supper," Kathleen mentioned to Chuck more than once. "I'd love to get to know her better."

After a few tries, we did manage to get her over but only for a barbecue, not a sit down Sunday dinner like Kathleen had hoped.

"So, you've got what, a year left at school?" Kathleen asked.

"If I decide to stay right through the end," Debbie answered.

"Oh. You haven't made your mind up yet. Do you know what you want to do when you're finished?"

"No. I haven't thought about it much."

"You should think about university. I really loved it. Gives you a chance to move out on your own. Wouldn't that be good?"

"I really need to stay at home, with my Mom."

"Yes. I understand."

When Kathleen was clearing up, I said, "Boy, she sure has

changed. I remember her getting up on the table in front of a crowd and singing. She was the centre of attention and loved it."

"Perhaps it's just around strangers. I barely know her. And I don't know her much better after tonight really."

"She certainly didn't let Chuck get out of her sight, did she?"

"I noticed that too. She wasn't going to let herself be left alone with us."

"Might have something to do with her situation at home. What do you think?"

"Perhaps when she's finished school, she'll get out on her own. That would be better than staying in a bad home. It's not up to her to protect her mother for the rest of her life." Kathleen washed another plate. "We should say something."

"I don't think we should stick our noses in their family business. We wouldn't want them sticking their noses in ours."

It didn't matter too much what we thought because a few weeks later, Debbie and her mother had moved out of the house again and Chuck was forbidden to come around.

—

It was just about a year later, on Dominion Day, that Chuck's stellar career in the meat business came to an end. Towards the end of June Chuck faced his annual rush on barbecue meats for Canada's birthday.

"Everybody gets the whole family together," he said. "Sometimes even whole blocks of people, but you know Mr. White from the newspaper? He wants me to supply all the hamburger for the barbecue downtown! He figures two thousand people will show up, so that's five hundred pounds of ground beef!"

"Two thousand people!"

"Everyone in the whole area comes for the music and the fireworks."

"You must be making a fortune on that order."

"No, I'm giving it to him at cost. That's the only way he'll give me the contract. He says it's my civic duty, but he says I can put up a sign that says Anderson Meats by the barbecue. Mr. Anderson says it'll be good promotion, just so long as we don't lose money. He's giving a good price."

"God. I'll bet the whole town is eating your hamburgers already."

"Hamburgers and steaks. Not the whole town, not yet. If I can just get those people who still buy their meat at the A&P, then I'll have everyone."

"You don't want much, do you?"

"Muahahahaha!" Chuck let out the trademark laugh of the evil scientist embarking on a scheme of world domination. "First we take Bowmanville, then Canada - That's not asking for too much, is it? I'll even be flipping the burgers myself, so everyone can see me."

"I thought the Boy Scouts did that every year?"

"Yeah, but I'll be there too. I want everyone to know whose hamburgers they're eating."

—

Bowmanville held typical small town Dominion Day celebrations. The outdoor pool was crammed with kids, and parents stood at the side trying to keep an eye on their own little monsters through the splashing and screaming.

"I always hated days like this when I was lifeguarding," Kathleen said, thinking back to the incident in Moncton. "There's so many children in there, and there's always four or five trying to show how long they can hold their breath underwater, but we couldn't see them anyway, so it didn't matter. Sometimes we'd blow our whistle and clear the pool just to calm everyone down, and get a break."

This must be a universal strategy amongst lifeguards because the whistles blasted out two or three times an hour. Once the pool was clear, the lifeguards took their time to walk around the pool carefully. Just as soon as the all clear was given, the kids were back screaming in the water.

The town men were involved with a hotly contested horseshoe

tournament. Twenty temporary pitches had been installed for the day by the local Rotarians.

Now that I was out of school and married, Dad figured we could enter as a team. Unfortunately, due to a total lack of practice, and Dad not being very good himself, we didn't make it past the first round. "He didn't want to get too deep into it," Mom made up an excuse. "It wouldn't look good for the plant manager to be competing against the workers."

"Oh, sure," I said, with an exaggerated eye roll. "We lost on purpose."

It was men from the plant who were always in the tournament finals. Dad had put a couple of pitches on the lawn right next to the lunchroom at the factory and it was used every day of the summer. He told me, "It's good to get the men out of the plant for a bit of fresh air; then they don't fall asleep in the afternoon." In the end, the team of Mr. Edley and Mr. Wilbur were presented a nice set of lawn chairs as first prize.

For women, the Rotarians sponsored an egg toss. A hundred women lined up facing another hundred women five yards apart. At the whistle they all tossed an egg to their partner; those who survived took five paces backwards and, at the whistle, tossed the egg back again.

It was easy to separate the women whose main concern was not splashing egg on their dress. When catching, they bent far over at the waist and locked their arms outstretched, but it was this rigid posture that was their undoing. Once the ladies got 15 or 20 yards apart, the eggs started to explode against their outstretched palms. As often as not, the yolks splashed up into their faces or at least on their sleeves.

Mom and Kathleen were among the more daring women. They understood that the key to successful egg catching is soft hands and bent elbows that absorb the force of the toss. But to be honest, I think that a carefree attitude is the most important aspect of the sport. I'm sure I could have separated the two hundred women into quartiles of egg tossing prowess just by timing how long each had spent doing their hair that morning.

The contest had thinned considerably by the 30 yard mark, with Mom and Kathleen among the dozen teams remaining on the field of battle. "Let's go, Rebecca!" Kathleen called when they were just 15 yards apart. At 20 yards, when she was tossing back she said, "Nice soft hands now." At 25 yards it was, "Put a bit of an arc on it. Don't come at me too fast." At 30 yards and with the crowds' encouragement increasing, she had to speak up across the gap, "I'm going to toss it nice and easy. Bend your elbows, Rebecca." And at 35 yards it was, "A little harder than last time. Just a little. And a little higher too."

One team, Mrs. Black, about 55 but looking older with pin-curled grey hair, and her daughter Brenda, only in her 30s but looking just as stern, had been taking advantage of the good-will of the judges by throwing their egg low and allowing it to bounce on the grass. But after using this technique several times through the 15 to 30 yard distances, the other women raised an objection and the judge ruled that bounces were no longer allowed. They were eliminated with a splash on the next toss.

The judges asked the remaining six teams to move back by five paces. They were 40 yards apart, which is a heck of a long way to toss an egg. The women displayed an odd mixture of feelings; somewhere between the giggling little girl inside who understood the inevitable mess to come, and the serious competitor, attempting to capture the prestige of the win and a set of lawn chairs.

The individuals in each of the two lines spread further apart to avoid bumping elbows or side splash. A number of Kathleen's students, who had left the pool to watch the event, were cheering her on. I even heard a few shouts of encouragement from inside the fenced pool area as they pressed their fingers through the chain links.

At the whistle, three of the six teams made their toss. Several hundred audience members had gathered now that the competition was getting exciting. There was an audible, "Whoa!" from the crowd as the eggs flew through the air and, "Oh no!" as two of them splattered on impact. At this distance, back splash was both horrible and inevitable. An egg might be small, but it carried a surprisingly large amount of sticky yolk and albumin.

Kathleen had held up her hand to delay Mom while the first three women performed their toss, then she looked at the other two pairs and determined that no one wanted to risk the next failure among the group. "Now's the time, Rebecca." She spoke loudly so that Mom could hear. "Higher this time, but not too high. Keep it nice and straight. Okay, let's go for it."

The toss was excellent. Mom took one step forward to improve the underhand distance. Kathleen took two steps backwards and slightly over to her left to get in proper position. The egg arced a good 25 feet in the air before coming down in seeming slow motion to Kathleen's soft catch. She held her arms out with a slight bend in the elbow that allowed her to cradle the egg gently and absorb the shock of the fall.

Immediately afterwards, the other two pairs also completed their tosses successfully. The audience had been quiet as the eggs flew across the widening gap, but let out a sudden, "Oh!" when the catches were made.

Mom, and the three remaining women beside her on the bloodied field of battle, took five paces back at the instructions of Mr. Jenkins, who was secretary of the Rotary Club as well as my boss. "Go for it!" "You got it, Mom!" and "Yeah, Teach!" were among the shouts heard from the crowd when Mr. Jenkins blew his whistle again.

Kathleen and the three other women at her end of the field looked at each other, no one wanting to be first. But she was not one to slack away from any challenge and stepped forward with a hard underhand swing that launched the egg on its trajectory, "Here you go!" she shouted.

From my position just a few paces behind, I could see that her line was perfect. The egg made a gorgeous parabolic curve towards waiting hands.

Mom barely had to move, taking just a half a step forward. She planted her left leg slightly ahead of her right and turned her body a little to allow her hands to soften the catch. When the egg arrived, Mom enclosed it carefully in her two hands as she turned her whole body to the right and swung in an arc.

There was a moment of suspense before she opened the covered nest of her hands to reveal that the egg had not survived. She let the shell and glob of yolk fall to the ground.

Kathleen cried, "Oh no!" and Mom exclaimed, "Yuck!"

With no thought of the eggs remaining to be launched over the battlefield, Kathleen rushed across the 45 yard no-man's land and gave Mom a hug. They found Dad and me in the audience and Mom held up her hands, threatening to wipe them on Dad's golf shirt, until he grabbed both of her wrists and held her at bay with a large smile.

—

Chuck had been busy preparing all afternoon. At five-thirty, multiple sack loads of charcoal were poured into three large barbecues, a gallon of starter fluid was sprayed and ignited.

"COME AND GET IT!" Chuck shouted at the crowd just after six. "BURGERS FOR EVERYONE, COURTESY OF THE LIONS CLUB AND ANDERSON MEATS."

He turned around to his crew of Boy Scouts. "Can you grab the buns? Tom, you put the burgers on and I'll hand them to the customers– er– um–to the visitors. How's that? Bob, you, Dan and Terry keep cooking. We need a real assembly line going here with the burgers going on the grill as fast as we're taking them off."

"Jeez, he'd make a good Production Manager," Dad said as we watched Chuck's team performing in synchronization. "He's got everything under control there."

"Let's hope they taste as good as they look," Mom replied.

—

We hung back as the hungry crowd took their place in line. Dad had brought some lawn chairs and a cooler of beer that made our own perfect little picnic table.

"Keep 'em going, Bob." Chuck encouraged his crew. "The lineup's huge."

"Hey, Mr. Bridges," Chuck turned back to the lineup. "How many for you?"

"Three please."

"Three. So is Dave back for the summer? Tell him to say hi to me later. Here you go. Hey Mrs. Phillips. Messed up pretty good in the egg toss, eh?"

She just laughed.

"You want two, right? Here's one for you and one for Veronica. Tell her "hey" for me. Hey Tilly. How many for you?"

"Will you look at him go!" Kathleen was watching the action. "Does he know everyone?"

"You know," said Dad. "There's guys at the plant that I've spoken to maybe once or twice, but they're good friends with Chuck."

"I think he dated their sister," I said. "Either their sister or their daughter."

Mom looked surprised.

"Oh yes. You know since he's lived with us, I don't think he's been home for dinner more than a dozen times."

"He's just working late." Mom said.

"He gets home at six or seven every night. Changes his clothes and he's gone again."

"Where?"

"He doesn't say. If it wasn't for our Sunday dinners with you, we'd never see him at all."

"He goes out on a date every night?"

"No. Sometimes he's just out with his buddies, bowling or at the bar."

"To the bar? He's not old enough."

I laughed. "Look at him. Do you think anyone is asking if he's 21?"

If Chuck didn't shave again in the evening, he could easily pass as 25 or 30.

Dad nodded. "Some of the younger men at the plant know him from downtown."

"And if he's not out with his friends, then sure enough he's on a date. At least two or three times a week."

"But he's dating all those women?" Mom went on. "What is he, some kind of cad?"

"A *cad*?" I laughed. "What is he, some kind of pirate?"

"You know what I mean." Mom furrowed her brow at me.

"Oh, don't you worry, Rebecca." Kathleen said. "I know one of the secretaries at school went out with Chuck and she said he was a perfect gentleman. You don't have to worry. You taught your sons well." She smiled at me. "They're both perfect gentlemen."

"Come on, Bob. Pick up the pace. This lineup's not getting any shorter." We turned back to Chuck. If anything, the lineup of hot, sweaty and impatient men, women and children had grown longer. "Come on, Dan. Come on, Jerry. Flip those burgers!"

Each of the three Boy Scouts was manning his own grill in a constant cycle; putting four long rows of patties on, flipping them three minutes later, and pulling them off three minutes after that. Chuck could have used three more helpers, but at the speed they were working I really don't know where they would have fit.

"Pick it up, boys." Chuck ordered again. "This line's still growing. Hey Mr. Tomlinson. How many for you today? Two. No problem. Give me two Carl. Pronto!"

An hour had gone by and Chuck still met every person in line with a smile, often a handshake if there was time.

—

Chuck's problems first appeared during the annual Lions Club versus Elks Club donkey baseball game. The irony of Lions and Elks riding on donkeys was not lost on the crowd and made up most of the jokes from the announcer.

The crowd had circled the ball diamond infield with lawn chairs to watch the ridiculous action. Being closely packed, it was easy to hear when the first children started to complain about stomach aches. Mothers held them on their laps and tried to settle their stomachs with water.

We heard the commotion when first one, then another child threw up. When a third child was struck and the first adults started looking green, we thought it might be a long day of heat taking effect. But looking around the crowd, there were very few smiles left on the faces that had been so happy an hour earlier.

"What's going on?" Chuck asked.

"I think we've got some sick people," Mom said. "I'm not feeling too well myself." She paused to look at Chuck. "You boys were moving pretty fast. Are you sure the burgers were cooked?"

"Yeah. I think so."

"You didn't leave the meat in the sun, did you?"

"No."

"Well, let's hope for the best."

—

Our telephone rang just before five the next morning, "Let me speak to Chuck." were the only words the man said.

"Um. Sure." I walked back to Chuck's room and knocked at the door. "There's someone on the phone for you. I think it's Mr. Anderson."

Chuck was up and in the kitchen in a matter of seconds. "Hello. Sure. Okay. I'll do what I can."

I could only hear one side of the conversation, but from the tone, and with the early hour, the matter was obviously serious. The call only lasted a few minutes before I got the full report.

"I have to go and get back everything since Tuesday. There's something wrong with the meat."

"With ALL the meat?"

"We don't know. We're getting reports of people sick everywhere. I gotta go."

"You can't go now. It's only five."

"Mr. Anderson says I gotta go right now. What if people are having sausages for breakfast?"

"You're going to wake people up for this?"

"Yup."

"How many houses?"

"At least two hundred."

I thought for a minute. "Okay, listen. You obviously can't visit that many houses before breakfast. You can't even do that in a whole day, can you?"

"If I hurry, maybe."

"Look, if we take a couple of minutes to make a plan, maybe we can do it better."

He looked at me.

"Think about it. Do you know who bought sausages? Who just bought steaks and other stuff?"

"It's on the order sheets."

"Well, if the first worry is about what people might have for breakfast, then start with that."

"Give me a sec," he sprinted out to the car, still in his short pajamas, and came back with a cardboard box of order papers. "Let's see," he fingered his way through the box, which was three quarters full, and came up with the top two inches. "This is since Tuesday."

"Okay. Give me half. Let's find who you sold sausages too."

It took several minutes to work our way through the yellow order papers looking for Chuck's scribbled sausages. There were times when I couldn't differentiate the word from bologna or steaks, but I referred these to him for clarification. We ended up with about 20 sheets.

By this time, Kathleen had been awoken by the noise of our search and joined us at the kitchen table. After a quick explanation, she said, "It must be the hamburger. That's what made everyone sick last night."

"Mr. Anderson thinks it might be anything. He doesn't know." Chuck replied.

"Okay, you should go now and get these back." She looked at the clock, and it was not yet five thirty. "Go get changed. I'll make you a coffee to take. Instant okay, right?" she put on the kettle.

Kathleen had the thermos ready by the time Chuck had washed his face and put on some clothes.

"You go and get these right away, and then come right back here," she said. "We'll go through the stack again and try to figure out who might be having what for lunch. That would be ham, right?"

"Ham and bologna."

"Okay. You hurry now, and come back here as soon as you're finished. Now you can't be "Mr. Nice Guy" and chat with everyone. You have to get in and get out, understand?"

"I can do that."

"Do you know what you're going to tell them?"

"Mr. Anderson says I should just say there's a problem with the meat and I'm supposed to take it all back and they'll get a full refund on their order."

"Okay, off you go, hurry now." She handed him the short stack of sausage orders and the thermos, and gave him a kiss on the cheek.

"Poor thing," she said as the screen door banged behind him. "He looks like a deer in the headlights."

"More like a rabbit in the headlights. A scared little rabbit." She poured two more cups of coffee. "There's no use going back to bed now. Let's work through these other orders and see if we can sort them for when he comes back."

—

Kathleen held out the afternoon newspaper when I came home for supper. The headline was clear and damning: "Meat Scare; Dozens Take Ill at Dominion Day Festivities." And it wasn't just Bowmanville that had been hit. There were reports of hamburger disease all along the 401, the exact territory served by Anderson Meats.

"Oh, shit," I said, reading through the article. "How's Chuck doing?"

"He got back from the breakfast round at about 9:30. He got to most of the homes, except for a few who are out of town. He said that he actually stopped a few who were about to serve sausages for breakfast."

"That's good." I looked back at the article, "but according to this, it's just hamburger."

"Who knows what goes into a sausage."

"Sure."

"Anyway, we didn't know that then. His boss wanted him to get everything, remember?"

"Did he have any problems?"

"A few people wanted their money back right away, but he convinced them that it would be okay."

"Who wouldn't trust Chuck? They all know him."

"So then I gave him the lunch meat group. He finished that about three. When he came back, I'd already seen the paper so now he's concentrating on just the customers who bought hamburger. I gave him something to eat and sent him back out again."

I looked at her quizzically.

"Peanut butter and jam."

"How's he doing?"

"He was still pretty nervous about it this morning. It can't be easy telling people the food you sold them will make them sick, but he seems to have caught his stride now. I guess you can get used to anything."

I looked at the paper again.

"He said he made two thousand hamburgers, right? And it says here that only 27 were reported seriously ill. That's just one in a hundred. Not too bad."

"I think that more people had upset stomachs, but that's all. Even I was feeling a little queasy, remember. Some people in Ajax got really sick; they're in the hospital."

"But none of Chuck's customers?"

"Not from what I've heard. Some vomiting. The doctors have been busy with house calls."

—

Chuck got home just before ten that night. He slumped down at the kitchen table and downed the entire glass of orange juice that Kathleen put in front of him.

"Let me scramble up some eggs, with toast." She pulled the frying pan out from the drawer under the oven. "What did you do with all that meat?" she asked.

"Straight to the dump." Chuck answered. "The rats'll be having a feast tonight."

"How are your customers?" I asked. "They must be mad."

"People are pretty good. No one's blaming me. It's in the paper and they see that it's everywhere, so they know it's not my fault." He put his glass down on the table and Kathleen left the frying pan heating while she refilled his juice.

"Did anyone get sick?"

"A couple of stomach aches. That's all. They're just asking when they'll get their money back so they can go shopping again."

"Did you talk to Mr. Anderson about that?"

"I can't get a hold of him. Must be busy I guess."

Chuck went silent, a real indicator of his exhaustion. I left Kathleen to make his dinner and soothe his wounds.

"He's really nervous about it all," she said, climbing into bed beside me. "I guess stunned would be a better word. He doesn't know what's happening or who's to blame."

"I guess he's done everything that he can."

"Yes, but that doesn't help the way he feels, with customers getting sick from the meat he's sold them, or even worse, with the meat he served himself."

"Maybe once it settles down a bit, I can take him out for a beer."

"That would be good."

Chuck's situation did not improve the next day. While he was picking up meat from the remaining customers, the newspaper made a damning report that Anderson Meats had slipped uninspected meat into their supplies in order to fill the Dominion Day rush. According to the report, old stock, which should have been discarded, was used to fill the demand. The hamburger disease was wide spread because the older ground beef had been mixed in with the recently inspected, newer meat. Mr. Anderson himself was not available for comment despite numerous attempts to contact him by reporters.

Chuck came home before supper. He had been told about the newspaper reports by his own customers.

"Everyone's asking about refunds," he said, "but I can't get a hold of Mr. Anderson myself. Nancy says he's not available."

"What are you going to do?"

"I don't know what I can do. They're not blaming me but they're still upset."

Two more days passed and still no word from Mr. Anderson. Chuck had driven down to the office and met with the other salesmen but no one had any idea where Mr. Anderson was or what to do about their customers.

"Gordon says I should visit all my customers again just to reassure them, but I've got nothing but bad news and I don't want to do that."

"He's got a lot of experience, right? Maybe you should listen to what he says, even if it is bad news."

"My customers won't like me if all I do is give them bad news. I want to wait for good news before I go see them."

Later that evening Kathleen and I talked about the predicament.

"My whole life, this has got to be the only time I've ever seen Chuck shrink away from a challenge."

"He's never faced something like this before, has he?" she replied. "People seem to forget how young he really is."

"A rabbit in the headlights, remember?"

The situation went from bad to worse over the next few days. The newspaper reported that an older man had died after eating the hamburger and the Ontario Provincial Police were called in to investigate the use of uninspected beef.

"The police are taking over the office," Chuck said. "They're taking away all the files and locking the doors. We can't get back in."

"You still haven't heard from Mr. Anderson?"

"Some of the guys think he's probably driving to Florida."

"What are you going to do?"

"What can I do? Wait, I guess."

And that's what he did; wait. Wait by the phone for a call that didn't come. Wait by the mailbox for a letter that didn't come. Wait for the newspaper, for reports and rumours that did come. Mr. Anderson was wanted for questioning by the OPP and the National Health Department. He had emptied the company safe, along with his bank account. His former wife, three years divorced, had no tips on where he might have gone and the rumours of Florida had escalated into print form.

Chuck stayed in touch with Gordon and the other salesmen but they offered no more information than what was being reported in the paper.

"I've never seen Chuck just sitting around before. He's really lost," I said to Kathleen.

"I think he's afraid. He's watching soap operas on TV now," she said. "Building things with his Meccano on the coffee table like a little kid."

I laughed. "I don't think he'll ever give up his Meccano. Keeps his fingers busy. What's he building?"

"He says it's a submarine. I don't think it will float though, with all those little holes."

"Submarines aren't supposed to float, are they?"

We smiled at each other.

Chuck's customers starting phoning the house over the next few days. "They're looking for refunds," he said.

"What do you tell them?"

"I say that we just have to wait for Mr. Anderson to get organized."

"Haven't they seen the papers?"

"Yeah, some."

"So are they buying it?"

"No, they don't believe it." He paused. "Here, come take a look at my submarine."

He held up his creation. It was at least two feet long. A complete cylinder with pointed bow and stern and a perfectly sized coning tower on the top, including fins sticking out the sides and rods to represent the various periscopes and antennae. It had twin propellers that he made by bending small pieces of Meccano into the appropriate shape.

Chuck smiled for the first time in a week as he described the features. "See, here's the ladder for climbing inside. See the little hatchway? And here, the deck gun for fighting off aircraft."

It truly was a feat of engineering. If not for the thousands of holes inherent in Meccano, I could almost imagine it sailing away to fight the Nazis.

He handed it to me. It must have weighed five pounds of strips, plates, nuts and bolts. "This is amazing," I said, and his smile broadened.

Another week passed with no news from Mr. Anderson, when Chuck caught me at the front door. "Gordon is working with Toronto Meats now. He says I should call them too. They're expanding out this way."

"Are you going to call them?"

"You bet. First thing tomorrow."

Getting the territory was easy for Chuck once they saw his sales numbers. He spent a couple of days travelling to Toronto before he hit the streets with his new product line.

"How did it go?" I asked when he came home before six o'clock on his first day on the job. "We didn't expect you home till later."

"Not so good," he was uncharacteristically quiet. "I'm visiting all my best customers first, but they want to hold off buying any meat for now."

"What does that mean?"

"Don't know. They want to hold off until they see that things are a little more settled, I guess."

The next few days didn't go any better. Of course some people were still looking to get their money back from Anderson Meats but Chuck couldn't do anything about that. Others said they wanted to stick with a big company, so they were going to buy their meat at the grocery store. But the majority just said they were going to hold off for a while.

Although the story had moved off of the front page, the newspaper was reporting that the Food Inspection Department was looking into all independent meat distributors. This didn't help his situation.

After a week of visiting every customer on his list with only a few small deliveries, Chuck spoke to Gordon. "He says he's keeping most of his customers, but they're not buying anything right now. He says I have to wait it out."

The next week Chuck was home by two in the afternoon. A few days later, he was home by noon.

"His ambition is gone." Kathleen said.

"Maybe he should think of something else?" I pondered.

"Things might get better if he sticks with it. It won't get better if he quits."

CHAPTER THIRTEEN

The chance to help came my way a few days later.

"Listen," I said, "One of the bricklayers needs a helper right away. His guy quit this afternoon. I'll bet if you showed up tomorrow, he'd hire you on the spot."

Kathleen scowled at me.

"Really?" Chuck asked.

"I don't get along with him, so don't mention that we're brothers."

"Why don't you get along?" Kathleen asked.

"Just the typical conflict between engineers and bricklayers."

"I'll be there first thing." Chuck jumped in.

"Don't you have to talk to your boss?" Kathleen asked.

"He won't care. I'm not selling anything anyway."

She turned back towards the stove.

For the past two months I'd been working with the site engineer at a new shopping plaza. The construction was just getting started so Chuck could have a job for the next year at least. It was a large project with an IGA supermarket at one end, a Simpsons Sears department store at the other, and forty five individual shops in between.

Chuck drove down to be front and centre at seven o'clock when the bricklaying team arrived. "I go up and tell him that I'm an experienced bricklayer's helper and I want to work for them," he said when we met a lunch, "but Adolpho says that he's already got someone coming in and they don't need me. But when he's talking to me, there's two of his guys working on a scaffold and they're climbing down all the time to get more blocks, so while he's still talking I bend down and pick up a twelve inch cinder block in each hand and I put them up on the scaffold. And the guys take them and I bend down and pick up two more. They're heavy you know, the twelve-inchers. After I've put eight blocks up on the scaffold Adolpho says I'm hired."

Once the surveys had been completed, my boss, Jack from the Pickering office, and I spent our days making sure that the construction work met all of the specifications of the plans. I was responsible to confirm that all materials met code. I generally was able to intercept every truck as it was being unloaded and before the materials were carted off to where they were they were needed. This often required me running back and forth between the ends of the plaza when two trucks arrived simultaneously, and undoubtedly meant delays for the crews as they waited for me to approve each shipment.

Complaints were common, but I was determined that nothing would get past my checklist. Jack told me several times that it wasn't necessary to examine every box, but I was not going to allow for any deviation from specs on my first project.

When the cool mornings arrived in late September, Kathleen presented me with a beautiful, hand-knit jacket that she'd been working on all summer. It was natural wool, off white colour with a zipper. There was a large elk on my chest and two Canada Geese flying across the back. All were done in dark brown with black. The wool was thick and itchy against my bare skin but fine over the shirt and tie that I wore to the work site.

"My mother taught me how to do these," she said. "Everybody has one out East."

"It's really beautiful." I gave her a kiss goodbye. "I'll wear it with pride."

It was just after ten that morning when the beautiful hand-knit jacket proved to be an embarrassment that lasted for the next year and continued sporadically for much longer. I was inspecting a load of pre-mixed concrete being poured from the truck directly into the framework of the foundation. There was a team of five controlling the pour.

"Hey! Look at this! We've got Daniel Boone here!" shouted Antoine to his crew. The men momentarily stopped pushing the concrete along with their shovels to look up at me. "Hurry up, Booney." he said loudly. "This shit'll turn hard in the truck if we have to wait for you."

Antoine was a Quebecer, recently moved to the area. His English was excellent and he obviously watched TV from the US side of Lake Ontario. He was about five foot ten, had the black hair and dark complexion of the French Canadian, but not as dark as the Italians of Toronto.

I'd seen other guys, and even some girls, with nicknames in high school and a few in university, but I had always assumed it was a gradual attribution. I had no idea that they could be created so quickly and stick so stubbornly. Within a few weeks, I was known as Booney to all of the workers. And as the various crews came and went from the site over the months, I'm sure that some didn't even know that I had a real name.

By the time three more mixing trucks had poured their loads and he had told me to, "Pick up the pace, Booney" a half dozen more times, the name was stuck fast.

"Well, there's nothing wrong with Daniel Boone," Chuck commented with a smirk.

"I don't think they meant it in a good way." My tall skinny frame had nothing of the rugged outdoor look of Fess Parker on TV. If anything, I'd be the character who sits at the back of the saloon and says, "Oh My," any time someone starts up a fight.

On October 28th of the year, the final concrete foundation was being poured. This was for a large storage shed behind the plaza, used for the smaller shops' garbage bins. The concrete pour was going well. Antoine had five men in his crew; enough to handle the mixing trucks as they arrived on schedule. It was a cool day to start, running at about 45°. The weather forecast had called for a cold front to come through that evening so the crew was pressed to complete the foundation in one day. Antoine even demanded that they skip lunch and coffee breaks.

With the rush, he pushed me harder than usual on my inspection routine. It wasn't the encouragement of earlier days. He had a deadline that would cost him real money and he was serious about making it.

I worked as fast as I could to take several sample cylinders from each load and examine them carefully for proportion of cement and water and particularly for the size of the crushed aggregate, which had been a problem in earlier deliveries.

"Let's move it, Booney. Move it!" Antoine shouted from the other side of the mixing truck. "We can't wait for you."

I had an inspection sheet to be completed for each load. Antoine would start the pour the moment he saw me put pen to paper, indicating that the load met specs.

At about one-thirty, the wind off Lake Ontario picked up considerably and by two there was a noticeable chill. The thermometre on my clipboard was reading 38 degrees and falling.

This was going to be trouble and I knew it. I walked, slowly, around the front of the truck to where Antoine was leaning on a shovel handle while his crew moved the pour along inside the plywood foundation forms. This close to the truck, I had to speak up to be heard over the sound of the gravel aggregate churning inside the drum.

"We've got a problem."

"Problem? We got no problem at all." He turned away from me.

The water hose was coiled on the ground in between us. I stepped over the loops. "It's getting colder," I said.

He didn't say anything at all, or even look at me.

"It's getting too cold to pour."

"It's just fine," he said. "We've only get three loads left. The trucks are already lined up. See?" He swung his arm to the trucks on our right side.

Past the trucks I could see a few of the other work crews having a coffee and cigarette. Chuck was there, wandering slowly in my direction. I held up my clipboard.

"Look at this. It's 38 degrees. We're not set up for cold weather." Standard construction requirements called for different procedures below 40 degrees.

"38, 40, what's the difference?" He turned away from me again. "It's gonna warm up again tomorrow anyway."

"Is that what you want me to put on the inspection sheet? 'Antoine says it's gonna warm up tomorrow anyway?'"

"Look, Booney. Where's your boss?"

"He's not here today." Jack was working back at his office for a few days.

By this time Chuck had made his way over, stopping to say, "Hey," to every man he ran into along the way. "Hey, Booney." He smiled at me. He didn't say, "Hey," to Antoine who was still facing away.

I had a serious look on my face; more serious than my normal look. Chuck was smart enough to read that look and stay quiet.

"I won't write anything on this truck," I spoke up, "but I have to stop it here."

Antoine turned around towards us.

"Look, kid," he'd never called me kid before. "It's just a garbage shed. Nobody cares."

I held my clipboard and shrugged at him.

"Do you have any fucking idea what it'll cost to dump these loads?" He waved his hands at the other three trucks again. "Who's gonna pay for that? You?"

I held up my clipboard and shrugged again. "I've got to fill out the reports." My voice was getting higher in pitch but not volume.

Chuck was standing right next to me, looking over my arm at the paper on the clipboard.

"Look, you little prick," Antoine said, taking a step closer. "I'm going to pour this shit and you're not going to report anything." He took another step in my direction with his hand raised and his finger pointing right at my chest. Just as Antoine came forward, Chuck stepped in front of me.

Although Antoine and I could see each other over Chuck's head, he definitely offered a solid barrier between us. Antoine stopped just an inch short of poking Chuck in the chest.

Chuck didn't say a word. He calmly stood between us with the plastic cup from his thermos of coffee in his right hand.

The two men had a similar stocky build, even if Antoine was taller. It was easy to imagine Chuck as a bulldog, standing between a Rottweiler and its dinner.

The closeness of the three of us calmed the anxiety a bit. Antoine took a half a step back. "Look, can you help me out here? I'm sure if Jack was here, he'd let it slide." He paused while I remained silent. "Will you at least talk to Jack before you fill in your papers?"

I thought for a few seconds. Chuck took step back to my left side. "He's at his office. I'll give him a call and see what he says."

"Thanks, Booney. You're a pal."

Antoine didn't stop the pour or the next truck from driving into place as I walked to the site office to call Jack.

"Let it slide." Jack said. "It's just a garbage shed, for heaven's sake. It's not like crowds of people will be in there. Just put it down as 41 degrees."

I didn't walk back to the shed after that short conversation, or inspect the final three loads of concrete at all. I left Chuck with his bricklaying crew and drove down to a coffee shop a few blocks over for the rest of the afternoon.

—

With more normalized working hours and a sharply lower income, we saw Chuck at the supper table most evenings, although he still went out afterwards. On nights with his buddies he'd have a few beers at the pool hall and come home at midnight with scrapes on his knuckles or a black eye, but never without a smile.

"We're just having fun," he'd say or, "Just a little dust-up."

At breakfast the following morning, Kathleen would shake her head and smile, "He's quite the rascal." (She said to me more than a few times over the years.)

On date nights, Chuck never had more than one or two beers. "You treat a lady like a lady and a guy like a guy," was his motto, "and you don't ever mix 'em up."

Given the small size of Bowmanville, I was surprised at his ability to keep the two from clashing until he clued me in. "Last night, Little Charlie and me are out with Lizzy and Betts, and Bob and his gang are bowling in the next lane and they're drinking a bunch and getting obnoxious and swearing in front of the girls. So when it's Lizzy's turn to bowl I excuse myself for a minute and I step over to Bob and put my arm around him 'cause we're friends and I lead him around the corner to the washrooms and set him straight."

I interrupted. "You hit him?"

"Just once. And his gang is all real nice after that and there's no more swearing or nothing."

"He certainly knows how to treat a lady," Kathleen said when I repeated the story. "Half the girls in town have been out with him and I've heard no complaints."

I raised my eyebrows.

"Don't you worry. When it comes time to get married, a girl wants someone stable, just like you. It'll be a long, long time before anyone calls Chuck stable."

Our life was certainly stable. Just a few months after graduation and not having my studies to keep me occupied in the evening, I took up astronomy as a hobby that became my lifelong passion.

Contrary to common belief, serious astronomy is 90 percent mathematics and 10 percent staring through a telescope. Even the 10 percent is just to confirm the predicted movements of the other 90.

"What is the angular size of Triton's orbit around Neptune as seen from Earth? Triton's orbital period is 5.9 Earth days and Neptune's orbital period around the sun is about 164.8 Earth years." This type of puzzle, involving Kepler's Third Law, was posted on the back page of Astronomy Magazine. It could keep me occupied for many hours over the coming month until the solution was posted in the following issue.

Of course it was impossible to see Triton with my own little 4 inch telescope, but when a question like that was posted in *Astronomy Magazine*, the observatory at Queens University in Kingston was often opened to the local club. Their 15 inch reflecting Feckler telescope had been installed in 1960, so was certainly the best available anywhere nearby.

A fellow that I'd met in Kingston, Guy Fleming, bought a brand new Minolta SRT camera to connect to his own 8" telescope. He was nice enough to give me his older Astro Camera 220 so I could try and get some decent shots of the night sky.

"You can keep it," he said. "It'll give you the same start that I had years ago."

It had the connectors to hook up directly to my own telescope with only a few minor parts to buy through mail order.

I was able to get a terrific photo of the moon in partial eclipse. The camera had settings for extra long exposures that would allow for detailed pictures of the stars and even distant galaxies. But I didn't own, and could not afford the equatorial tracking mount that would move the camera in perfect alignment with the rotation of the earth, thus keeping the star in one position for a long exposure. Without it, I simply got a faint white line across the picture.

I was looking at one of the Tasco units in *Astronomy Magazine* when Chuck asked about it. "How does it work?"

I pointed to the picture. "This dial face controls the speed of the movement. This dial sets the direction."

"How close does it have to be?"

"If it's not close, it's worthless. You don't get any sharp images at all."

"How fast does it move?"

"Really slow. The earth only turns fifteen degrees in an hour. So the movement of the camera is barely perceptible."

"And that's just an electric motor, right?" He put his finger on the page.

"Yes."

"Does it need to have dials? Can it use, I don't know, levers, or maybe bars, to set the speed?"

I could see that his mind was turning over. "As long as I can set it, it really doesn't matter how I do it."

"Let's take a look at what you've got."

In the corner of the living room, I had my telescope resting on its tripod.

"Hook the camera up," he said.

Once I did, the telescope was no longer balanced nicely on the tripod, but was much heavier on the viewfinder end.

"We'd have to fix that first," he said. "There's no reason to be carrying that weight when the stand can do it." He disconnected the telescope from the tripod and held it in a more balanced position. "Somewhere around here would be good."

Holding the telescope at its natural fulcrum, he moved the camera back and forth, four or five inches on each side of centre.

"How far does it have to move?"

I pointed at his moving hands. "That would be more than I need. Just an inch or two of swing would be enough."

He shortened his swing. "If we're going to do it, might as well do it right, right? This'll give you everything you need."

"I'm sure."

"Can I take this?" He picked up the telescope, camera and tripod and started back towards his room.

"Sure," I said as he closed his door for the night.

—

Chuck worked in seclusion for three evenings before calling me in to see his contraption. "The world turns around the North Star, right?" he asked.

"Polaris. That's right."

"It turns exactly around it?"

"Pretty close."

"Take a look here." He held up his collection of parts, some from Meccano and other metal parts that he picked up around the work site. "Look through this tube here."

I looked through a quarter inch copper metal pipe, about a foot long. "What am I looking at?"

"You look through this tube at the North Star. Now you see these brackets here, they spread apart like this." He had two brackets at right angles to the pipe. He spread them apart slightly, like scissors opening. "If this opens up by fifteen degrees, it matches the spin of the world, right? Now watch."

Through the lower bracket and fixed to the upper bracket, he spun a threaded rod. "See this," he said. "By spinning this rod I can open the brackets exactly the right amount, really slowly."

"Sure, but you'd have to spin the rod really, really slowly. And even more important, you'd have to be at the right speed. How would you do that?"

"That's easy." He pulled a small electric motor from the box of parts. "I can put a small pulley on the motor and a big pulley on the other side. And then just use a rubber band as a belt between them. I can control the speed that the rod spins just by changing the size of the big pulley. The little motor will spin like crazy and the big pulley will turn real slow."

"I think you've got the right idea, but this contraption isn't strong enough to hold up my telescope."

"That's no problem. That's why I need to know where it balances." He picked up the telescope, balancing it on one hand and moving it around with the other. "If I can hold it in the bracket here, I can run a cord up through another pulley up here." He held his left hand above his head. "With a weight that will hold the whole thing up so the bracket isn't holding the weight at all; it's just moving it."

I held the contraption up, sighting through the tube while I spun the threaded rod to open the scissors bracket. "You know. I think you've got something here."

He went on. "So what we have to do is figure out how to make the pulleys to spin the rod. You can do that with math, right?"

"Certainly." I thought for a moment. "You know, Chuck, this is bloody incredible."

He put his arm up high over my shoulder.

"Of course it is."

—

Once we figured out the speed of his little electric motor, we settled on two reductions involving four pulleys and a threaded rod. It took a week of evenings, many trials and many errors to get it right before we even attempted to connect the telescope in place with the counterweights. Of course at the very moment we finished, the clouds blew in for a few days. But with the combination of Chuck's seeming mechanical brilliance and my skills in mathematics, there was little doubt in the final outcome.

It didn't take long to figure out why Guy had bought his nice new 35mm SLR camera and abandoned the Astro Camera, with its 3¼" by 4¼" glass plates and rubber squeeze ball to control the shutter. He was nice enough, if that's the right way to say it, to include the plate developing equipment with the camera. I was soon spending more time in the bathroom-turned-darkroom, with black cardboard taped over the window and a nose full of chemical smells, than I was looking through the telescope at the stars.

I wanted to capture at least one good image, something I could show to Kathleen so she would understand the many hours I was spending on my hobby. I settled on Andromeda, the closest major galaxy to our own, at only two million light years away.

Andromeda is easy to find with a pair of binoculars, a little lower and to the right of the Cassiopeia constellation in the Northern sky. The entire galaxy is more than two hundred thousand light years across. I hoped to capture the central body, made up of one trillion stars, on a glass plate so that it could be projected on a wall. There would be no other way to appreciate its size. At least no other way than looking up at the night sky itself.

Chuck and I drove out to a farm, just north of town, to eliminate ambient light. It took some time to get the copper pipe of his, *Star Tracker* set up to face Polaris, and to offset the telescope to aim directly at Andromeda. It was big and bright when seen through my four inch telescope.

Andromeda is undoubtedly the distant heavenly body most photographed by amateurs like myself. Articles in magazines were correct in suggesting a nine minute exposure time. Once the galaxy was centred in the telescope, we removed the eyepiece and connected the camera. On my command, Chuck started the electric motor spinning, leading to the imperceptibly slow movement of the telescope-camera combination. Once we were certain of no vibrations, I squeezed the ball to open the shutter.

We didn't need accuracy greater than the second hand on my watch to keep time. We both stood back, lighting matches to look at my watch with the least extraneous light.

I will admit that after a few years, the long drive to Kingston to actually view a tiny dark dot of a distant moon, against a slightly larger planetary surface, became less worthwhile. Most of my satisfaction came from solving the mathematical challenges and my hobby become more specialized in that one particular area of astronomy.

The recent efforts of the U.S. and Soviet space programs, including a plan to put a man on the moon, had given rise to a much greater worldwide interest in astronomy. It was easy to fall into one group with an academic newsletter coming from the Massachusetts Institute of Technology.

I was not able to have an office of my own in our small house, but Dad gave me an old secretary's desk with a fold up front that I could work at in the bedroom. The light from a small desk lamp did not disturb Kathleen if I stayed up until one or two, although sometimes she complained at the prolonged scratching of my pencil and how it made the lamp chain jiggle.

CHAPTER FOURTEEN

The last of the winter snow had just melted away when Chuck told us of the change in his career. It was a Saturday afternoon. He was wearing his tweed jacket, white shirt and tie. With his stocky build and broad chest, Chuck was never able to carry off a sophisticated businessman look, even in his business clothes.

"I got a job with Morgan's Used Cars." He said proudly. "All his salesmen are old guys and he wants me to sell to anyone under thirty. He says they're missing all those sales."

"But you're only 21 yourself." Kathleen said. "Does he think you're old enough for this?"

"He thinks I'm older, I guess." Chuck spoke a little quieter.

"What did you tell him?"

"He thinks I'm 26," He paused. "And I'm not telling him any different."

Kathleen smiled her, "that little rascal" smile and put on her mother's voice. "Well, just make sure you don't get into trouble over this."

"When do you start?" I asked.

"On Monday. Mr. Morgan wants me all trained up before spring sales start to build."

"What about the plaza? We've still got a few months to go."

"You don't think I'm sticking at that for the rest of my life, do you?"

"There's lots of construction starting up. You could be a brick layer if you wanted. They make pretty good money." I thought for a second. "You should talk to your boss. He'd probably train you."

Chuck looked at me and tilted his head to the side. "Don't you guys get it? I'm a salesman, just like you're an engineer. That's what I am."

"For the rest of your life?"

"Why not?"

"Don't bother him." Kathleen said. "I'm sure he'll settle on something a little more stable eventually."

"But a used car salesman?" I questioned. "Is that a career?"

—

After the argument about concrete with Antoine, I made it my policy to confirm any questionable inspection results with Jack, or whoever the senior engineer was on a project, before approaching a construction contractor. I was able to stop a lot of arguments before they even got started by saying, "I've already spoken to Jack, (or Steve, or Frank, or Joe) and he said that you need to correct the problem before we can approve it."

Of course there were an equally large number of times when the project engineer just waved the issue off as inconsequential. I might have gotten a bit of a reputation as a nit-picker.

I went to Jack with problems about Chuck's boss and the spacing of rebar in the twelve inch concrete blocks on exterior walls, problems with electrical contractors about the placement of conduit in walls, and problems with plumbing contractors with the size of pipe in ceiling fire sprinklers. A few times Jack showed exasperation that I bothered them on these issues, but I thought it was better to bother an engineer than be yelled at by a contractor.

—

Not even a year had gone by at Morgan's and Chuck was once again earning more than me. Of course it helped that he knew everyone in town by name and was good friends with everyone under thirty.

"It's easy," he said. "You know how we have that cardboard sign on the front of every car?"

"With the price. Yes."

"When one of my friends comes in the first thing I do is take the cardboard sign and I turn it over and I say, 'That price is for people from out of town. That's not for you.' And that way they know that I'm going to help them out and be real fair."

"What does Mr. Morgan say about that?"

"That's just the way he does it. He sells a lot of cars and he knows everything about it."

"You mean he knows every trick."

"It's not a trick." Chuck looked disappointed that I questioned the integrity of his profession. "We have three prices. The first is the price on the sign. But that's only for people who act like an ass. Then there's the absolute lowest price and we only use that if we've got a car that we can't get off the lot. And then there's the price in the middle where I can make a bit of money and the customer gets a good deal so he's happy too.

"You know David Gillespie? He comes in the other day and I go through all of this just like Mr. Morgan says and I sell him a Fairlane."

"You mean David, the guy you punched at the roller rink?" I was flabbergasted.

"That's nothing. We're good friends. Some guys just need a lesson in manners once in a while. David doesn't have a good Mom so I can't blame him if he doesn't have manners like us. He just needs someone to set him straight once in a while. He won't act like that again. At least not around me."

There was no question that Chuck was right. Mom had taught us manners. More directly, manners towards women. It had become such a natural part of our upbringing that I had never thought about it before.

"Kathleen always tells me that you're a real gentleman when you take a girl out. Is that what she's talking about?" I asked.

"Well, yeah. What else. I see other guys and they treat girls real bad. They don't open doors for them or walk on the outside of the sidewalk. I even see some guys shout at girls or swear at them." He paused again. "I don't like that very much."

"I guess Mom wouldn't like it either."

"I guess not. I set 'em straight if I can."

"Is that why you've got so many dates?"

Chuck shrugged, "Like I always say, you treat a girl like a girl and a guy like a guy and you don't mix 'em up."

On the many evenings that Chuck was out on a date, Kathleen kept me informed about the latest talk around town.

"He'll take a girl out once every two or three weeks, with lots of other girls in between. I think it's his way of letting them know that he's too young to get serious about anyone, but none of them feel neglected because they know that he'll be calling them again. Actually, I shouldn't say that. From what I hear, he never actually calls a girl on the phone. It's when he meets then on the street downtown. You know Chuck. He stops and talks to everyone. Well, if he meets up with a girl coming out of a store or whatever, he starts chatting and before you know it, he's talking about bowling or a movie. I guess it's more like his dates are a casual coincidence rather than a formal undertaking. It would be pretty hard for a girl to think Chuck is serious if he's never actually called her on the phone."

"He comes home pretty late some nights," I said. "Does he ever try anything with them?"

Kathleen chuckled. "Honey, I know you still think it's the 1950s, but the 60s did arrive in Bowmanville, even if they did come a few years late."

That spring, Dad received a big promotion to Production Manager at the much larger Goodyear factory in Toronto, so they moved to a nice home near the water in Long Branch. We still made sure to travel down for a family dinner at least once a month.

When summer arrived, Kathleen insisted that we drive to Montreal for Expo. I tried to talk her out of it, saying that the crowds would be terrible, but she didn't give up. I was right about the crowds, but she had a great time anyway and insisted that we go back for a second trip and even spend the night and meet up with some of our university friends for the evening.

Levy from my engineering study group was doing very well. Although he worked for a small firm, he'd had a very successful project on the Montreal subway system. He pulled up to a restaurant in a brand new MGB that he'd bought with bonus money.

Levy had been nearly as bookish as I was in school, but seemed to have undergone a transformation after graduation.

"You can't sit back and rely on just regurgitating the text books now," he said. "You've got to start pushing the envelope and coming up with new ideas if you want to get ahead."

"You're just as likely to get in trouble with that approach," I responded.

"But that's why I've got this new car."

—

"Do you do anything like that?" Kathleen asked at our hotel.

"Like what?"

"Like what Levy said. About trying new ideas; innovating; you know?"

"I don't really get a chance. Right now, I'm just helping the construction engineer. I just make sure the thing gets built according to specifications."

"But didn't Levy get started like that too?"

"He must have gotten a promotion really early to be making those types of suggestions."

"Maybe he got the promotion because he made those suggestions."

"As an engineer, the most important thing is that the building stands. Any risk with that is just foolhardy."

"Yes," Kathleen said. "I understand."

—

The excitement of the Apollo space program had caught the attention of every astronomy hobbyist, to the exclusion of all other discussions. Those on the practical side spent their nights staring through powerful telescopes at the craters on the moon and debating the best possible landing sites.

Those of us on the theoretical side of astronomy spent our hours formulating and revising and reformulating orbital paths and velocities. It was a dream come true where we could come up with our own theories and compare them to the NASA experts who were regular contributors to the *Planetary Science Institute* newsletter.

I was able to calculate and plot the entire translunar phase predicted for Apollo 11 in fifteen minute increments for the entire voyage from leaving Earth's orbit to entering the Moon's orbit. I had the flight path, velocity, distance from Earth and latitude and longitude. Plotting a 3-dimensional voyage on 2-dimensional paper did not allow for a real understanding, so I plotted different views from the Earth's perspective, as well as from the Moon and two views from deep space.

With me concentrating intensely on my calculations every evening for several months, Kathleen kept busy with curling in the winter, golf in the summer and a book club all year round. She had curled as a girl in New Brunswick and slid, to use a pun, back into it quickly; Tuesdays with a ladies group and Thursdays with a mixed group. Several weekends over the winter, she was completely tied up with bonspiels, either locally or away.

Of course her evenings of curling ended with a few glasses of wine, so she didn't get home until after ten, giving me perfect silence for concentrating on the detailed, if somewhat repetitive, calculations necessary for the moon flight.

Chuck joked that my slide rule was wearing out from overuse. He was right; the etched lines and numbers were fading from time. I was still using the same slide rule Dad had given me for Christmas so many years before.

—

With a couple more projects assisting the construction engineer under my belt, I was moved back to steady work in the office in Bowmanville. I was assigned to complete sections of large projects coming from the Toronto or Hamilton offices. My aptitude for mathematics was recognized over the next few years so I was often tasked to work directly with a senior engineer on particularly challenging aspects of the design process, usually when large amounts of number crunching was involved. I did not have my own separate office space, but my desk in the corner was sufficiently distant from the rest of the room to allow me to concentrate for extended periods.

At 26, but already with ten very successful years of sales experience behind him, Chuck took a job selling new cars at the local Chrysler dealership.

"Mr. Kense says he knows all about my sales at Morgan's, so he walks right over to our lot and offers me the job." Chuck said.

"If you're selling new cars, then you won't be selling to people under thirty anymore. They can't afford it," I observed. Truth be told even just past thirty, I couldn't afford a new car. Kathleen and I had just made the down payment our own two storey house on Liberty Street with a 25 year mortgage, and we'd started to talk about having a family, although she was not expecting yet. That would cut our income in half.

"I don't think that matters to him," Chuck said. "He just wants a good salesman."

"But won't older men think that you don't know anything? What does Dad say, that you're 'still wet behind the ears.'"

"Let me tell you about sales." Chuck went on. "It's not what you know that counts, but how you connect with the man. I don't need to know everything. I can talk my way through most things that I don't know, and if I can't do that, then I just say so. People like it when you admit that you don't know everything once in a while. The worst thing is pretending that you know and then they find out that you don't know. You look like a crook. And once they think you're lying to them, they just walk away."

"You mean they don't even call you out on it?" I asked.

"No. They just walk away. I call it the walk of shame. But it's not their shame, it's my shame."

"So you never lie to a customer?"

Chuck laughed his deep laugh. "I lie to them all the time," he said, "but I do it in a way that makes them feel good." He paused again. "If a guy comes in and he's looking at a convertible, I'll tell him that it will make him a hit with the chicks, even though he's got a face that looks like it was smashed in with a baseball bat.

"Or if a couple comes in and the wife's expecting a baby, then I'll show them a car and tell them how safe it is. That's the kind of thing I tell them."

"Are those really lies?" I asked.

"Lies, stories, something," he said. "But the real trick isn't what you say but how you say it. I've got a pretty deep voice, right. So even if I talk really quietly, it still comes across like I know what I'm doing."

"With authority." I replied.

"Yeah, with authority. That's right. You know, I think that half of life is talking with authority. Maybe three quarters. If you can do that, the rest comes easy."

—

"I had an interesting day at school," Kathleen said as we were eating our meatloaf. "What happened?"

"It was Susan. I think her father works at the quarry. We'd just finished The Lord's Prayer and when I turned around to the blackboard I heard her crying, just softly."

"Oh," I replied. "Don't little girls cry all the time?"

"No, not Susan, anyway. She's usually pretty stoic. I thought I'd leave it for a bit but when I'd finished writing their lesson she was still crying. I crouched right down to her level and asked what was wrong. I didn't want to embarrass her in front of the class.

"She said her dog died overnight. I guess it always slept right in her room, sometimes right on the bed. She said she had to scrunch up when it was at the bottom. When she woke up this morning, it was dead. Pretty traumatic for a little girl."

"I'll bet."

"So I asked if she would like to come and sit up with me for a while. I pulled up a little chair beside my desk, but she stood right beside my chair and leaned against my arm for nearly the whole day. When I moved around she followed me like a little puppy, pressing against me; she didn't even want to go outside for recess, just stayed with me."

"Little girls," I replied.

"But you know what set her off: the dog's name was Wilby."

"Wilby?"

"Yes, Wilby. Just like in The Lord's Prayer. Thy Wilby done. Get it?"

She looked at me and I nodded but couldn't help smiling.

"Maybe she'll get over it by Monday. I felt bad, but It was so sweet to have a little girl stuck to me like a shadow."

Kathleen was bringing home these stories from school more often now. I don't know if this is some evolutionary urge in every woman, but she was certainly feeling a pull that I could not understand.

CHAPTER FIFTEEN

Any serious dialogue of astronomy and mathematics will soon turn to the advanced concepts of astrophysics, which of course quickly becomes a discussion on Einstein's general relativity. Everything on Earth, in our solar system, our galaxy and the universe as a whole is controlled by gravity. And unless we want to turn back the pages to Isaac Newton and an apple falling on our head then everything about gravity is dictated by Einstein. In fact, the origin of the universe itself, with the newly devised label "big bang theory," is a direct upshot of general relativity.

In 1919, Arthur Eddington used a solar eclipse to perform the first experimental confirmation of Einstein's general relativity. He used the brief dark sky, as the moon passed in front of the sun, to photograph distant stars peeking out from behind the sun. These photographs were compared to others taken earlier in the year to confirm the hypothesis that gravity from the sun could actually bend light itself. It's hard to imagine using old, silver nitrate covered glass photographic plates to measure a shift of just ½ of 1/1,000 of 1 degree. In fact the veracity of his own results was questioned because of the imprecision of the equipment.

A total eclipse was going to cross directly over Halifax on March 7. I already had the telescope and camera necessary to take photographs so I thought it would be interesting to replicate, perhaps even improve upon, the experiment. Although my camera was old, it was still several decades advanced on Eddington's, so perhaps could provide a record that more exactly matched with Einstein's calculations.

I wrote to George Slater, a member of the Royal Astronomical Society of Canada, who lived in the woods near Lawrencetown, just north of Halifax. George had a one man observatory dome in his backyard, directly in the path of the upcoming eclipse. Through letters back and forth, he agreed to dedicate his observatory to a six month long experiment. Our plan was to photograph four stars surrounding the sun during the eclipse: HD219215, HD217877, HD219877 and HD219402.

The first advancement was with Chuck's amazing star tracking invention that would allow for a steady exposure. I wanted to use Agfa Trockenplatten IIIa-F dry plates, which had a much finer resolution than anything available fifty years earlier. When considering the measurement of such a small shift in the star's positions, even the grain of the film will impact on results, but a high resolution film would require an exposure of two minutes, the length of the eclipse. Chuck's invention allowed my telescope to move with the rotation of the earth and remain aimed precisely at the stars during the entire period.

The second advancement over Eddington was that my telescope would be locked–virtually cemented into position–for the following 6 months and 12 hours, as measured in sidereal days of 23 hours, 56 minutes, 4.096 seconds, at which time the stars would be in the same position in the night time sky and could be photographed once again. A comparison of the two photographs would provide the most accurate results possible.

I pulled out Chuck's star tracker. It had been sitting in the back of a closet for some years. "We need to rebuild this; make it better. Do you mind?" I asked Chuck.

"What do you need?"

"I'm only taking a two minute exposure, but I need the most precision possible. And then I need to be able to reverse the rotation so that it moves back into exactly the starting position. Is that possible?"

"Sure," his response was immediate. "I could change the way the hinge is built to make it stronger, but it wouldn't move very far." He was holding his tracker and pointing to the various parts. "And then put in a smaller worm gear and larger main gear. That would give it a smoother movement with the spinning of the electric motor. But Meccano doesn't have that kind of worm gear. I'll have to get one built at a machine shop. Do you want me to do that?"

"I'll pay for it. Whatever it takes."

"Don't worry about it. My buddy Nick works down at Custom Machine. He'll do it for you. We just need to tell him what we want."

"That's great. Thanks."

Over the next two months, Chuck redesigned his tracker to a level of precision that would make any professional astronomer jealous. In addition to his gearing changes, he added a clutch that would start and stop camera movement with no shock or vibration. This also allowed me to open and close the shutter while the camera was in motion.

—

Kathleen was not able to take any time off from her teaching duties to join me in the Maritimes. I had hoped she would like to visit her family but she said, "I can't leave the children in the middle of the year. The Easter break is coming soon. We can do something then."

—

I left after work on Thursday, knowing I'd have to make a long overnight drive to reach Halifax in time to do a proper setup. I was bleary-eyed and pumped on coffee when I arrived at George's house.

It would be an understatement to say that I was disappointed with the state of his observatory. "Haven't used it for a few years," he said. "Makes a good garden shed though."

A garden shed was exactly what it looked like. The outside had a coating of moss topped with leaves and snow. The inside was packed with a wheelbarrow, garden rakes, shovels, hoes and picks and a dozen plastic bags of various types of potting soil and fertilizer. There was dust and cobwebs inside of the dome itself, but worst were the birds' nests in the structural framework with the associated white droppings all over the cement floor.

"It'll only take us a bit to clean it up. No worries." George said.

There was nothing I could say in reply. He had promised to dedicate his observatory to the experiment for the next six months and at this point, I had no alternative. I was prepared for disappointment due to weather, but I had not counted on disappointment from a fellow astronomer. I think Dad would have a lesson for this situation.

I was already past exhaustion when we started cleaning. His garden hose was still frozen so we could not spray the dome down with water. We just moved everything out and used a broom to sweep the snow off the dome and as much of the birds' nests, dust and grime from the internal framework and floor as possible. I did not partake in the numerous beers that George offered.

It was after dark by the time we'd positioned the telescope inside the dome. I wanted to let it acclimatize slowly to the outside temperature so there was no danger of condensation on the lenses.

Saturday was glorious for eclipse viewing, with clear skies. Totality would occur at five minutes to three in the afternoon, so we relaxed with a long breakfast.

By noon I had the telescope oriented correctly for the eclipse: Dec -05°13'05", Al +29°53'34". George's 50 pound bags of fertilizer were ideal to solidly hold the tripod in place. He promised that he would stay out of his observatory over the next six months. Based on its current level of use, I realized that I was not causing undue inconvenience.

I connected Chuck's tracker to a car battery, ideal for providing a constant, stable source of electricity to the motor. I was worried that if we connected directly to AC power, then street lights turning on automatically across the province during the eclipse might cause momentary flutters in the power grid.

I did three practice runs on the daytime sky without film in the camera. A two minute exposure would have turned film completely black, in any case. Simply by reversing the polarity of the wires, I reversed the direction of tracker movement and brought the telescope back to its original position. Everything was running perfectly.

We closed the observatory dome, closed the door and went for lunch into what passed for the Lawrencetown village centre, combination grocery store, gas station and pizza restaurant. I felt on the verge of a scientific breakthrough, at least within my own experience, and celebrated with a beer.

At twenty minutes to three we were ready. I covered my eyes with a black blindfold to acclimatize to the darkness. No flashlights would be allowed during the eclipse but I needed to be able to work all of the mechanisms on the tracker, camera and stopwatch.

I listened as George described the approaching darkness, the partial eclipse or "penumbra". At 18:55:30 Greenwich time the "umbra," or total eclipse started. I removed my blindfold and without even glancing up at the sky, connected the positive red wire from the battery to the tracker, released the tracker clutch to start lateral movement, compressed the air bulb shutter release on the camera and clicked my stopwatch.

A total eclipse is an amazing thing to see, completely different from a partial eclipse that most of the country experienced. It is not like the darkness just after sunset or just before sunrise. It is more like the darkness and the silence of the deepest part of the night. I don't remember hearing any birds chirping or animals moving, but perhaps this was my own emotional state rather than something that could be noted from a tape recorder. I imagine that the feeling is better compared to being inside the eye of a hurricane, absolute calm with the tempest blowing all around. I could hear the second to second click, click, click of my stopwatch, so I dropped it into my pocket to better enjoy the silence of the moment.

My eyes had completely adjusted to the darkness so I was able to clearly delineate every star in the heavens, including the four that we were concentrating on. The clear sky over all of Nova Scotia provided for a magical experience.

With two minutes complete, I closed the camera shutter. Just a few seconds later I could see, in the distance, a rush sweeping over the landscape. It came at us like a herd of white horses barreling at a thousand miles an hour. Once again we were in the daylight, with the sun still partially obscured by the moon but the eclipse experience complete.

I had brought a plate development tank and chemicals necessary to process the pictures immediately. We set up in his bathroom with black cardboard taped tightly over the window to block any possible light while loading the large format plate into the tank. A half hour later we had the single negative, the results of the last two days of work and months of planning.

"Let's take a look," I said, using masking tape to hold the plate firmly against a bright hole cut through our black window blocking cardboard. I had brought a high power jewellers' magnifying loupe with me for the purpose. I studied the film carefully for a minute or more.

"What do you think?" George asked.

"You take a look."

He put the loupe to his eye and examined the film in detail. "Is it just me, or does it seem slightly blurred?"

"That's what I was wondering." I replied.

"I think it is." He went on. "It looks a little fuzzy. What could cause that? You had the camera in focus. The tracker moved correctly."

"I tested it extensively at home. The photos were perfect."

"Let's take another look."

We went back out to his small observatory. We had to be very careful not to move the equipment, still looking forward to the matching photos in 6 months.

"Let's run it through another cycle and just watch it carefully." I said. "We can reverse it back again after."

I connected the power wire, released the clutch and leaned in closely to the tracking gears. George followed me.

"Look at that," he said. "It is vibrating? Look at the worm gear."

From such a close distance, with my nose nearly rubbing against them, we could see a slight vibration in the gears.

"Let me get the magnifying glass." He left the observatory and came back with a four inch magnifying glass while I re-engaged the clutch. "Take a look."

The problem was clear. A tiny spec of dirt; perhaps bird droppings, no more than the size of a grain of salt was stuck to the side of one tooth of the worm gear. Each time the gear rotated, that tiny spec caused the main gear to shudder, leading to the slightest vibration of the telescope lens. Neither of us had noticed the vibration in the darkness of the eclipse, but now that we knew what to look for, it became obvious. The end of the lens was moving, only by $1/16^{th}$ of an inch, but it was moving.

"Is this going to hurt us?" George asked.

"We're done." I replied with resignation. I looked up. "It must have fallen from the dome when we closed it, or opened it again."

"Oh, sorry about that."

When I drove away on Sunday morning, his only words were, "There's another eclipse in two years. We can try again then."

—

Late one evening in the summer, Kathleen and I were already in bed. Chuck's long time friend Francis, now a Constable with the OPP, brought him home. I could hear them talking from downstairs.

"Look, Chuck," Francis said, "no more of this, okay. I can't back you up anymore. If we get a call about you fighting again, I'm just not going to come and you can figure it out with whoever shows up. And you better pray it's not Mulroney because he won't put up with any of your excuses."

I couldn't make out Chuck's mumbled response.

"I don't care whose fault it is or who threw the first punch and Mulroney won't care either. He'll just throw you in the can and let the judge work it out. Is that what you want? A conviction for fighting on your record?"

Chuck was silent.

"Then no more, right? You can't act like a kid anymore because we're going to start treating you like an adult. And you don't want that, believe me."

Chuck remained quiet, very unusual for him, while Francis left.

At breakfast the next morning, I could see the results of Chuck's antics; a large bruise from his right cheekbone down to his jaw.

"What happened?" I asked.

"I'm playing pool and this guy challenges me to a game. His name's Randy. Must be new in town. So we're playing and I'm beating him by a couple of balls and when I turn away to pick up my beer I catch him moving the cue ball with the tip of his cue. So I don't say anything at all. I just walk over and move it back where it was before and he says, 'What the fuck do you think you're doing?' and I say that I think he accidentally moved the ball, but it doesn't matter because I fixed it. Then he grabs me by the shirt and tells me to move it back and I'm not going to give him the chance to hit me so I hit him real hard in the stomach just to cool him down, but he doesn't cool down instead he slugs me in the face here." Chuck rubbed his cheek while he continued talking. "And that starts both of us off real good and nothing will come of it but Francis is already there talking to some other guys so he sees the whole thing and before it gets too serious, he steps between us and busts it up and he tells Randy to go home and then he drives me home too."

"I could hear you two talking when you came in last night."

"Yeah. He says I can't get into fights anymore and I've got to grow up and stuff like that."

"He's probably right."

"Maybe."

When I came home for lunch Chuck was sitting in front of the TV. "How come you're home?" I asked. "Didn't you go in?"

"Mr. Kense says I can't sell cars at his place with a big bruise like this. He says I'm not selling used cars anymore and I have to look like a professional. He says I can come back when the bruise is gone and I can look respectable."

"I guess you'd better watch yourself, can't be getting into trouble."

"Yeah." He sounded resigned to his fate.

"How are things going over there anyway?"

"That Kense is something. That's all I can say."

"What do you mean?"

"Let me tell you. Our secretary Julie, she quits and he's gotta hire a new girl. So I'm sitting in his office and he calls up some agency he knows and tells them to send over a new girl right away. But get this. He tells them that she's gotta be willing to screw. He says it right over the phone!"

"Are you kidding? He's married isn't he?"

"And then he winks and says if I get the numbers then I can take her out on his boat for the weekend."

I was dumb struck. "What did you say?"

"Nothing. What can I say?"

"I can't imagine what Dad would think. Can you picture him and Mrs. Ross?"

"I think if Mom caught him doing something like that she'd cut his nuts off."

"That's for sure." I thought for a second. "So are you making any sales?" I wasn't asking to see if Chuck was eligible for the bonus, I just wanted to move away from a distasteful subject.

"It's a lot different. Everybody's older than me."

"I thought you were friends with everyone in town?"

"Yeah, I know everybody that comes in, but I'm not the only one. Grant, he's the senior guy, he's on the Chamber of Commerce and the Elks Club and he plays baseball too. So all the men who come in want to talk to him and not me."

"The Elks Club?" I questioned. "That's a bunch of old fogeys, isn't it?"

"Those are the guys who buy new cars."

—

For the first time in his sales career, Chuck struggled to make a living. "I go around to all the businesses in town and I talk to every owner and I give them a sheet on the New Yorker 'cause it's got better mileage and I think that should be real important with gas going up. And a couple of the men even come into the shop. Like Mr. Zwicky from the hardware store. He comes in and is looking at the New Yorker two-door we've got on the floor. But then Grant, he steps over and he starts talking to Mr. Zwicky and I guess they're friends and before you know it, he's made the sale and he gets the commission.

So I ask Mr. Zwicky why he bought from Grant and not from me and he says, 'Well, you're Grant's assistant aren't you?'

Then I go up to Mr. Kense and I tell him that Grant's stealing my sales and he says, 'You all row your own boat here.' That's what he says; you all row your own boat."

I guess the natural enthusiasm that made him a success in the day to day meat sales, and the incredibly long list of friends that was the impetus for his success in used car sales, were not enough to carry Chuck through the high dollar new car purchases by men twenty years his senior.

"Nobody wants to talk to me when they come in," he said. "It's like they think I'm the shop boy or something. I'm surprised they don't send me for coffee and donuts."

Although the commission on a new car was substantial, selling only one a month, or none at all in some months, did not meet his day to day expenses. He was soon eating through his savings. "Well at least you don't need to worry about being offered your turn with the new girl."

Chuck laughed. "I hope I never get so mean that I have to be like that."

—

After Francis had put a damper on his evening activities, and with many of his friends entering the age of home ownership, Chuck often spent evenings or weekends working on their various repair projects.

"I'm helping Bob replace his kitchen floor," Chuck would say as he hurried out the door. "I'm real cheap. All it costs him is beer and roast chicken." Or on a Saturday it might be, "I'm helping Ray put in a whole new bathroom so his Mom can move in. See you tonight."

"You know how to do this?" I'd ask.

"No, but you talk to a few guys down at the hardware store and you can learn anything."

He was always quick to volunteer for any job that would keep him busy for an evening or a weekend. Word of his generosity with a hammer got around among his friends and it wasn't long before, "Why don't you call Chuck? He'll give you a hand," was commonly heard around town. He didn't mind in the least. He really liked keeping busy and anything that allowed him to socialize while working was vastly preferable to staying at home with an old married couple.

—

The OPEC energy crisis was the final nail in Chuck's new car sales coffin. The unexpected rise in the price of gas decimated sales in big cars, which were the ones with the biggest commissions. The Goodyear plant, the largest local employer, laying off a fifth of its employees sent a nervous shiver to every worker in Bowmanville, and sales of everything from TVs to kitchen appliances to new cars suffered.

"Mr. Kense says he doesn't need me anymore." Chuck said, coming home early.

"But you're on commission. What does it matter to him if you sell a car or don't?" Kathleen asked.

"He says he has to look after the guys who've been there the longest. They've got families and houses and he doesn't want us competing with each other for sales."

"That's too bad," she said. "Well, you deserve a break. Why don't you take some time off?"

"You can just go back to used cars, can't you? You did really well there," I suggested.

"I don't think I want to do that." Chuck answered, "I can't move ahead if I'm just moving backwards. I want to move ahead."

CHAPTER SIXTEEN

The truly crushing news came in a telephone call from Mom, just after ten on a Sunday night.

"You boys have to come down here right now," she said. "There's something wrong with your father. We think he's had an aneurysm. He had to be taken to the hospital in an ambulance."

"Is he okay?" I asked.

"It's really bad. He's unconscious. The doctors don't know if he'll make it. They're working on him right now."

"What do you mean?" I was flabbergasted. "Is he going to be okay?"

"I just don't know, dear. Come down right now please. I need you here with me."

The second that I said, "Dad's in the hospital..." Chuck cut in with, "Let's go. Tell me on the way."

With no traffic and no police that late on a Sunday night, Chuck flew into the heart of Toronto. He did most of the 401 at ninety miles an hour and turned onto the Don Valley Parkway without slowing at all. Being the children of Goodyear, at least we had snow tires. The highways were mainly clear, except for a few areas where the wind off Lake Ontario had blown patches of snow across; Chuck didn't seem to notice these at all.

I had my seat belt done up tightly and was clenching the dashboard. I was lucky it was so dark in the car that Kathleen couldn't see my face. She was in the back seat, but huddled up against ours, urging Chuck to swerve this way or that to pass any car in our way.

Normal visiting hours were long over, so we had no trouble in parking on Elizabeth Street right in front of the Emergency entrance. There were only a few people waiting in chairs inside, so the receptionist was able to quickly tell us that Dad was in surgery on the second floor. We found Mom in a seating area in the middle of the floor.

Kathleen was the first to run up and wrap her arms around Mom, and Chuck was close behind. I held back a few seconds. "Is there any news?" I asked. "Have you heard anything?"

"Nothing yet," she said. Her face was a grey colour that contrasted sharply with her red dress and neat hairdo. "They're still operating on him. They had to call a doctor to come in."

The room would hold about a dozen, on five clinical green plastic couches, but we were the only ones there. Nobody would schedule surgery for late on a Sunday night. It was after eleven and the entire hospital was asleep, other than a few nurses quietly making their rounds.

"Oh, Rebecca, tell us what happened!" Kathleen said.

"We were at the movies. You know how much I wanted to see *The Sting*. We were just walking out when your father slumped down on the floor. He was leaning against the wall, all these people were going past. It was crowded and people were bumping into me. He was holding his head but he didn't say anything. I asked him what was wrong but he didn't say anything at all. He just held his head.

"Then some people noticed that we were blocking the way and they stood around us and asked if they could help. I said I didn't know what was wrong, and then someone shouted 'Is there a doctor here?' and a lady squeezed through and said she was a nurse.

"She took one look at your father. She didn't take his pulse or anything. She just looked at the way he was holding his head, and shouted 'Someone call an ambulance, right away. Please hurry.'

"A man who was standing over us ran into the crowd to call an ambulance.

"Then the nurse crouched down next to your father and she asked me his name. Then she said, 'Charles, can you hear me?' But he didn't say anything. His eyes were closed tight, but he wasn't moving at all. He was still holding his head in both hands.

"The nurse put her fingers on his neck to check his pulse, and she looked really worried and she shouted out again, 'Did someone call an ambulance?'

"I didn't know what to do. I was on my knees next to your father but I couldn't hold his hand and I didn't want to get in the way of the nurse.

"It seemed like forever until the ambulance came and they just pushed me right out of the way. They ripped open your father's shirt and put these little things with wires on his chest and looked at a machine. And the nurse said something to them but I couldn't hear what it was. Before you know it, they had him on a stretcher and they took him away.

"It was the nurse who told me they were taking him to Toronto General. She was so nice. I never got to thank her. She walked outside with me and jumped in front of another couple that was getting into a taxi and she said to them, 'this lady needs to get to the hospital,' and they backed away. Then she told the taxi driver to take me to the hospital.

"I haven't seen your father since I arrived. The lady in the emergency room said they brought him right up here. When I got here, a nurse came out and said Charles had an aneurysm and they were calling in a specialist to operate on him. That's all I know."

Mom was shaking visibly when she and Kathleen sat down together on the couch nearest the hallway. Her colour had not improved and I noticed wrinkles on her face that I'd never seen before. Kathleen had her arm around Mom, and Chuck sat down on the other side and held her hand. We were all still in our coats and boots. I think Mom actually needed hers to reduce the shivering, even inside the warm hospital.

More than two hours later, after one in the morning by that time, a doctor walked into the hallway in his operating scrubs.

"Mrs. Murray?" he asked, looking at us. "I'm Doctor Black." His voice didn't indicate anything other than the normal tiredness of the hour.

"Yes," Mom answered. She looked up but did not rise from the couch. Chuck and I stood up.

"He's had a ruptured aneurysm." Dr. Black paused. "And some bleeding on the brain. We've operated and stopped the bleeding. It was not a very large rupture and we think we've stopped any further damage." He paused again to let it sink in. "He's still under sedation right now, so I can't give you any better information until we see that he comes out of it okay."

"When will that be?" Kathleen was the first to speak up.

He looked over his shoulder at the wall clock. "At this point I don't think we'll see anything until the morning."

Chuck was next to speak. "You have to tell us more than that. Is Dad going to be okay?"

Dr. Black looked directly at Chuck, as if he was trying to avoid seeing Mom's face. "I'll be honest. If he hadn't gotten to the hospital so quickly, his prognosis would have been much worse. But since we were able to operate so quickly, I think we've reduced the risk considerably. The next step is to see that he regains consciousness. Once he does, then we have to check for any permanent damage."

"Is that likely?" Kathleen asked.

"I really don't like to say with a situation like this, until we've given him a chance to regain consciousness. We should know something in a day or two."

Nobody said anything for a moment while we let it sink in. Chuck finally asked, "Can we go in and see him?"

"He's still being cleaned up from surgery right now. And then he will spend some time in the recovery room. So right now I'd say it's best to wait until morning. I'll be back to check on him first thing. I can report to you at about seven, right here, if that's okay with you."

"We'll be here."

"There's nothing more that you can do right now," he went on. "You're welcome to wait here if you like, or you can go home and come back at seven. It's up to you."

"Thank you very much for your help," Kathleen said.

Dr. Black turned slowly and walked down the hall.

We remained silent for a moment before Kathleen asked Mom quietly, "Would you like to go home and get some sleep for a few hours?"

Mom shook her head. "No. I think I'll wait right here."

We sat through a long night together without much discussion, and what conversation we had was little more than whispering. With a little wandering, I found a coffee machine on the first floor, near the cafeteria. But just coffee. There were no donuts or anything else to snack on overnight.

Although Mom spoke little during the night, I don't believe she slept at all. Certainly the rest of us didn't. Of course this made her look even worse, with dark bags under her eyes when nurses, orderlies and doctors started to walk past just before seven o'clock.

It was nearly seven-thirty when Dr. Black walked out of the main hallway in his white coat, stethoscope around his neck and hanging into the breast pocket and a clipboard in his hand.

Mom stayed seated, if a little more upright. Kathleen was still next to her while Chuck and I stood again.

"He hasn't regained consciousness yet," Dr. Black said. "Normally the sedation would have worn off by now so I'm a little concerned. But with a ruptured aneurysm, it's often difficult to estimate." He looked at all of us and could quickly see that we didn't know what to ask. "What we're going to do is keep a very close eye on him throughout the day, and just see how he progresses."

"Can we see him now?" Kathleen asked.

He thought for a few seconds. "He's still in the recovery room and I'd like to keep him there. It's not really set up for visitors; there's lots going on in there." He looked over at a pair of nurses walking past. "Nurse," he spoke up to catch their attention. "Would you please take Mrs. Murray to see her husband in Recovery C?"

The nurse looked questioningly at him; obviously this was against normal procedure.

"Just for a five minutes," Dr. Black said. "They've been waiting all night."

"Can we all see him?" Kathleen asked.

"I'm sorry. It's pretty busy down there. Everybody's preparing for their first surgeries. Just two of you, if that's all right."

Chuck spoke up. "I'll go with her."

"Fine," Dr. Black said. "Please take them both down and stay with them for five minutes."

I was relieved that Chuck had spoken up so quickly. I did not look forward to seeing Dad in his condition, whatever condition that was.

—

Dad stayed in the hospital for a year and a half. All of his relatives visited in the first two weeks, but there was really nothing for them to see. He was in a coma with breathing and feeding tubes.

For the first month or so, Mom spent all afternoon and evening at his bedside, reading to herself or to him. But over time, that reduced to a couple of hours per day. There didn't seem to be any point for her to stay longer.

With no job holding him in Bowmanville, Chuck immediately moved in with Mom. She had lost much of her ability to function during the ordeal, so he took over most of the household chores.

The recession had laid off men in all walks of life, particularly construction, across the country, so Chuck was not able to pick up any kind of work that he wanted to do. His friends in Bowmanville had many brothers, cousins or fathers-in-law in Toronto and they were happy to pass on a reference, but even these could offer nothing better than a store clerk position. There were simply too many qualified men looking for the same position. In the end he decided that staying with Mom was more important.

In our whole lives, Mom and Dad had never spoken to us about their financial situation, not once. We had lived the same middle class childhood as all of the other kids at school. They had helped

me through university, not complaining when I needed money for
rent or food in the second semester, after my summer earnings had
run out. I think they knew I hadn't wasted any money on beer, like
some of the other guys had.

It wasn't until three or four months into Dad's coma that Mom
brought up the problem and she was very reluctant to impose her
situation on us. It had become dire by this time.

"The long term disability only pays us half of what your father
used to earn," she said. "And you know that Goodyear never paid
well in the first place. When we sold the house in Bowmanville,
we didn't get nearly enough to buy a house here, so it took all of
our savings and we still have a big mortgage payment to make every month. Your father's future looked so bright that we just hadn't
planned for anything like this. Now he's still in the hospital and the
money is gone. I don't know what I can do."

Kathleen didn't even look at me before she spoke, "Well, Rebecca. You don't have to worry about that at all. Of course we'll help
you out."

"No, dear. That's just not right. You two have your own problems
paying for your house yourselves. It's just not right that you should
worry about this. It's our own duty to look after ourselves."

"Don't be silly. You're family; that's what family is all about."

This was Kathleen's east coast heritage coming out. The idea of
extended family looking after each other is ingrained in their cul-
ture. But here in Ontario, the WASP ethos of stoic independence
was more prevalent. A person is better off to suffer in silence than
to ask a friend, or even family, for assistance.

"Charles wouldn't like it at all," Mom went on. "You will have
your own family soon to look after yourself. We raised you boys
to be independent and to look after yourselves. I can't come to you
now with my hand out."

"Don't be ridiculous." Kathleen came back. "We're both working, at least for now. There is absolutely no reason why we can't help
out for a little while, until Charles is back on his feet."

"But I don't know if that will ever happen."

Kathleen had to concede a little if she wanted Mom to accept our support. "Well, then just until I have to leave work to have a baby. How about that?"

"Well, it will just be a loan then. I'll think of it as a way for you to save for the future."

"That's fine."

I took a look at Mom's monthly expenses. It was quite a chunk out of our pay to make up for just the necessities that were missing from Dad's monthly disability payments. I guess that like most people, they had been living paycheque to paycheque with only a small reserve built in.

Chuck did get himself a minimum wage job with a local hardware store. With so many men out of work, even that was tough to get with his lack of formal qualifications.

—

Kathleen and I drove to Toronto every Saturday to visit Dad in the hospital and have supper with Mom and Chuck. After the first few weeks of the routine, Kathleen started to suggest that we take advantage of the trips to see a concert or play or even a new movie release that hadn't made its way out to Bowmanville yet.

She laughed like crazy at *Blazing Saddles*, even if it was something of a guy's movie and I really didn't enjoy the fart scene at all. For the next two weeks, I heard Kathleen's rendition, complete with a fake German accent, of Madeline Kahn's, "I've been with thousands of men; again and again, they promise the moon. They're always coming and going and going and coming and always too soon."

She dragged me to see Crosby, Stills, Nash & Young at Varsity Stadium. I'd never enjoyed that type of hard rock music, so I sat in the huge crowd while she jumped up and down on her seat. I think she would have had more fun with one of her girlfriends. I found David Bowie was a little better. I still didn't enjoy the music, but at least it wasn't in the football stadium and the formal seating of the

O'Keefe Centre kept the audience in their seats. I didn't smell any marijuana until we were out on Front Street after the concert.

The George Harrison – Ravi Shankar concert at Maple Leaf Gardens, with its East Indian music, could only be described as weird, but she certainly enjoyed it. It might have been better played in the meeting hall of a public library rather than in one of the largest hockey rinks in Canada. The stinging, off-key twang of the sitars and singers gave me a headache for the next month. I still revert back to that concert every time I have a tooth drilled at the dentist.

—

One Saturday, seven months into Dad's coma, Chuck and I were sitting next to his bed. It was getting on to supper time when the nurses would kick us out to look after the patients, even if Dad didn't take much attention. They liked to roll him from side to side several times a day to ease bedsores.

"What time is it?" Chuck asked.

I looked at my watch. "We've still got ten minutes left," I said and we continued to talk about Chuck's work.

It was creepy. That's the only word for it. To sit next to Dad with his eyes wide open but not moving from side to side at all. We were sitting in chairs on either side of his bed and talking across, but he didn't react to us speaking. Until seven minutes later. I know it was exactly seven minutes because I looked at my watch.

"Two o'clock."

It was a little quieter than a normal conversational voice, but it was distinctly clear. Chuck and I looked at each other.

"Was that my imagination?" I asked.

"Not unless I'm imagining it too."

I bent over and looked right into Dad's eyes.

"Dad, can you hear me? Can you hear me?"

Chuck leaned over too. "Dad, are you there?"

We got no answer, other than his continuing blank stare. We repeated our question over and over again with no response.

In a few minutes, we heard the gentle chime that gave notice it was time to leave. We walked out to the nurses' station.

"You didn't tell us that our father's talking?" I asked the nurse behind the counter. She was quite young, probably right out of school.

"I'm sorry. I'm only here on weekends and I don't know the patients' conditions very well."

"Can we talk to the Doctor?" Chuck asked.

"I'm sorry. He won't be in until Monday," she replied. "Our long term patients don't require daily visits unless something comes up."

"Is there nobody here we can talk to?"

"I'm sorry," she said for the third time. "We're very short staffed on Saturday evenings. You might be able to find out more on Monday."

—

I took the day off work and drove back into the city very early on Monday to try and sort out the situation. Chuck had to work but Mom and I were at the hospital before nine, when the doctor came for his quick check on Dad's condition.

Dr. Davidson looked after all of the long term patients on the floor. He was in his late 50s, completely bald on top and not much of a gray fringe around the sides. He was heavy and wore black-framed glasses.

"You didn't tell us that Dad was speaking?" I said when he walked into the room.

The hospital cleaning lady moved away from washing under the bed when the doctor walked in. She had arrived just a couple of minutes earlier with a cheerful, "Good Morning, Mr. Murray. Oh, I see we've got visitors today," before getting down to her work.

"I don't know about that," Dr. Davidson said. He picked up a chart from the end of Dad's bed. "There's nothing in the reports about it."

"I heard him talking on Saturday," I said.

"Just hang on for a minute." He looked out into the hallway and waved his hand to attract the attention of a nurse. A woman in her mid 40s with her hair all tucked up under the traditional nurses' cap.

"I understand that Mr. Murray has been speaking?" the doctor said. "There's nothing in the chart about it."

She answered cautiously, while taking the chart in her hands. "I'm sure we would have reported it if we'd ever heard it ourselves."

After a pause when they both stood side by side looking at the chart, he said, "Perhaps it was just spontaneous. A one time thing."

The cleaning lady had been making herself busy wiping the window blinds at the side of the room. "Oh, he talks to me every day," she spoke up, "Or nearly every day; when he's awake at least."

"What does he say?" I asked.

"Oh I say, 'good morning,' and he says, 'good morning,' back. It takes him a few minutes to get going. And then I might say, 'It's a beautiful day outside,' when I open the blinds and he usually says something back, like, 'it's raining out,' or, 'yes it's nice today,' but I don't think he really looks because he's wrong as much as he's right."

"How long has this been happening?" Dr. Davidson asked.

"A couple of months now. It started slow but he says a little more each week."

"But you didn't tell anyone on the nurses' staff?"

She shrugged. "I just assumed you knew."

Right on cue, Dad chose that moment to make himself heard. "Good morning," he said.

"See," the cleaning lady said. "There he goes. It takes him a little while to warm up, but eventually he comes around."

After a bit of discussion, we saw that in their normal routine, Dr. Davidson and the nurses pop in and out of Dad's room quickly and never initiate any sort of conversation with him, so he probably never spoke to them and even if he had, they would have left the room long before.

Dr. Davidson leaned over with his elbows resting on the safety railing and putting his face just twelve inches from Dad. He spoke very clearly.

"Charles, can you hear me?"

I'd say that we all held our breaths but the delay lasted much longer than this was possible, so I'll just say that we barely breathed and certainly didn't move over the next few minutes. Dr. Davidson continued to stare at Dad, looking for the slightest sign of recognition or even an unexplained movement of the eyes.

When Dad replied, it was quietly but much more than a whisper and could easily be heard by everyone in the silent room. "I'm here," he said.

"Charles, can you tell me what day it is?" Dr. Davidson asked, once again leaning in closely.

Once again we stood silently around the bed.

"Tuesday," was Dad's reply. The fact that it was Monday didn't bother us as we looked at each other with half-smile-half-question-half-relief expressions on our faces.

"What does this mean?" Mom was the first to speak. "Is he getting better?" She reached onto the bed with her right hand and took hold of Dad's, then reached over to me with her left. I moved over until we were pressed together.

Dr. Davidson went on. "I'm going to set up a treatment plan based on this improvement and we'll see if he continues to make progress. I don't want you to get too excited, but it does lead me to be optimistic."

—

I still believe that the majority of Dad's improvement, and the reason he was able to go home nearly a year later, was due to Mom's constant presence at his side, rather than from the doctors' or nurses' help. From that day on, she spent every minute of the allowed visiting hours at the hospital. It took days and weeks of her talking directly to Dad, and then waiting for an answer, before they were able to hold a slow, stilted conversation.

Kathleen and I still went down to Toronto every Saturday and took our turn to help out.

"Scores of North Vietnamese tanks, armoured vehicles and camouflaged Chinese built trucks rolled into the Presidential Palace. The President of the former government of South Vietnam was taken to a microphone by North Vietnamese soldiers for another announcement. He appealed to all Saigon troops to lay down their arms." I read from the newspaper. "Here's a picture of the last helicopter leaving from the embassy." I held it up.

Dad leaned forward enough to see the paper.

"Fucking Communists." He was furious. "They should all be shot." He went silent again.

Mom was worried that he became emotional at anything political in the news. She had asked me to stick to good news stories, but I thought that the end of the war was a good news story.

"Here. Let's take a look at *Peanuts*." I read again. "In the first square, Lucy is passing a ball to Charlie Brown on the pitchers' mound. She says, 'The first batter hit one over my head,' and then she says, 'The second batter hit one in front of me. The third batter hit one to my left and the fourth batter hit one to my right.' And then in the last square, she says, 'I'm looking forward to this next batter.' And she's walking away, see?"

I held up the paper and Dad looked over again.

"Old Lucy. She always gets Charlie Brown." He sat back with a satisfied look. "Did she pull the football away from him again?"

"I think that happens in the Fall; when football season starts."

Now that Dad was communicating and able to follow instructions from the doctors and physiotherapists, he made slow and rather unsteady progress towards recovery. It started with just having him open and close his hands; then moving his arms and legs. Unfortunately, he was never able to get back the use of his left hand. The physiotherapist positioned it in a natural, slightly closed position with his arm bent at the elbow. He could squeeze larger things between his arm and torso and use his right hand for finer work.

Mom spent all day, every day at the hospital.

"We need him to get better and get back to work," she said. "The physiotherapist only spends forty-five minutes with him and that's not enough. He gets so frustrated and so angry sometimes," Mom went on, "And then we have to take a break and come back later."

It took three months of constant effort to get him moving his legs and bending his knees in bed before he tried to stand for the first time.

"It hurts," he said. "I'm going to fall."

"Don't you worry. You just hang onto the bed and I'm right here to hold you up." The physiotherapist was a big woman, six feet tall and with a strong build, shaped more like a man from the back, and I guess from the front as well.

"I said it hurts," Dad said a little louder.

"Of course it hurts a little. You've been on your back a long time. We have to get those muscles working again."

Dad hadn't even taken a step yet. He remained standing in his pyjamas and open backed slippers, holding the bed with his right hand, "LISTEN, YOU BITCH! IT HURTS!"

"Okay, okay. Let's sit down and try it again in a little while."

She turned to Mom and me, "I'll try to come back in a while, once he's calmed down," and she walked off to her next patient.

"She won't be back today," Mom said. "This happens. Your father gets frustrated and there's nothing she can do with him, so she just walks away."

"Every day?"

"Well, not every day, but often enough. He gets so frustrated. I guess she can't deal with it, but I'll give him a few minutes to cool down and we'll do some other exercises."

—

Like every Saturday night in Toronto, Kathleen insisted we go out to dinner. "It sounds like there's something wrong in his brain," she said, "The way he loses his temper like that. I've never seen Charles swear like that before. It's just not like him at all."

"That's what the doctor thinks. The same reason he can't move his hand. Some part of his brain was damaged by the aneurysm."

"Will he get better?"

"Doctor Davidson said that the brain can't heal itself like a cut or something, but what does happen is another part of the brain can take over and compensate. That's what we've been doing all along; retraining the different parts of his brain to take over."

—

With the expense of driving down to Toronto every week, (especially since gas price had risen so sharply) and then going out to supper at a Toronto restaurant and inevitably to a movie or a club or a concert, all on top of what we were giving to help Mom, money had certainly become tight. We were eating into our savings.

Kathleen said, "I don't know what the big deal is. We don't have children yet. I'm starting to think we might never have them. It's not like we need to save for that."

"Dad always told me that we should start putting money away for retirement as soon as we start working. That's on top of saving for vacations or a car or kids. Right now we're not saving for anything."

"Well, maybe if your father had put more money away for himself, we wouldn't need to be giving so much to your mother, just to live," she was getting cross.

"They can't help that. It costs so much just to live in Toronto. Just look what their house cost; you know that."

"Well, I don't think we should be forced to sacrifice our lives just for them."

"You insisted, remember? You told Mom that we'd look after her."

"I didn't think this was going to be permanent. I didn't volunteer us for that."

"I'm not saying we need to sacrifice on the basics just for Mom and Dad to live. But maybe on the extras, like going out to dinner and the shows."

"So what if we go out once or twice a week; we deserve it."

"It's not just once or twice a week, is it? You're curling every Tuesday and Thursday. That costs a lot. And you always have drinks after, right? And your book club on Wednesdays. You always take a bottle of wine to that too."

"What do you want me to do?" She was getting very angry, "Sit at home and watch you scribbling at your desk every night? You've got your hobby, and I've got mine."

"But my hobby doesn't cost any money."

"Don't you start talking about money. I make my own money and I can spend some of it on me."

"I'm just saying we should try a little harder to put away some savings, that's all."

"Saving is your job, remember. You're the man. It's your job." She paused, "What are you going to do when we have children? I won't be working then." She thought for another second. "And when are you going to get a promotion anyway? Your pay isn't even keeping up with inflation. We're having to cut back left and right and we should be moving ahead, not behind."

"Sure, keep bringing this up. I like what I do. I'm sure they'll give me a raise when they think I deserve it, but that's not likely now with the recession. With all the cut-backs in construction, I'm lucky to have a job at all. They've already let some of the younger guys go in Toronto."

"Of course they're not going to let you go. They'll never be able to get anyone else for what they're paying you."

"Listen, I just don't think we should be going out every night. That's all I'm trying to say."

"What are you going to do, chain me to the house?" She was furious.

I tried to calm things down by relenting a bit.

"Maybe Dad will be able to go back to work again soon, then we won't need to be giving any more money to them."

"I hope so." Kathleen was exasperated.

CHAPTER SEVENTEEN

In January, I was looking for a snack in the pantry. In between the homemade strawberry jam and Mom's pickled beets, I discovered three dozen jars of baby food. They were stacked three high, pressed against the back wall with each jar aimed outward, the Gerber brand name and baby smiling straight at me.

I brought one into the light; applesauce. Three dozen jars of baby food applesauce. And it was empty. Half of the jars were empty, rinsed out and dried.

I found a box of Oreos on the second shelf and, slowly and thoughtfully, carried my cookies and the empty jar into the living room where Kathleen was watching TV.

"What's this?" I asked hesitantly.

She thought for a few seconds. "Oh, just some applesauce."

"It's baby food?"

"I picked it up on sale. I thought we might need it some time."

"But some of them are empty?"

"I have some once in a while if I'm blue."

"Oh," I sat down. "Is it supposed to help you get pregnant or something?" We had been trying to have a baby for many years, without success. We had both gone to the doctor and he said that I had low motility. The only advice he gave us was to take a multivitamin and keep trying, but after fourteen years, we had pretty well given up hope.

"I don't think that applesauce can help me get pregnant," she replied. "I just like the taste. And it's healthy."

I held up the jar and looked at the baby on the label. Kathleen had spoken often of babies after her first few years of teaching. We looked at magazines and talked about how we would decorate a small bedroom for a boy or a girl. On summer evenings, she took me for walks down to the park at the end of our street where we could see other young couples playing with their children; pushing them on the swings, tossing a ball back and forth or watching the kids play tag in large groups.

Of course most of the houses on our street had at least a few children by now, often more than a few. It seemed the block was filled with people from our generation, so the children ranged in age from babies all the way up to older teenagers. The street was filled with kids running up and down every evening.

"Cute baby," I said, holding the jar towards Kathleen. The Gerber baby was the definition of cute. He had a little round face that filled the round circle framing the label, short blonde hair sticking out in every direction. His eyes and mouth were open in a look of astonishment. 'What is this wonderful food that you are about to give me?' his expression seemed to be saying.

"That's little Reggie."

"Is that his name?"

"I like to imagine that's his name. I can imagine lots of things about little Reggie if I try."

I sat down to watch TV.

—

It was two months later that Dad did leave the hospital and move back home. Chuck had added wooden pegs inside their bed frame to raise the level of the mattress by six inches, making it easier for Dad to get in and out of bed. He could shuffle himself into the bathroom and slowly, very slowly, make his way up and down the stairs. At first he demanded that Chuck move the television set to their bedroom and had Mom bring his meals up. But it was only three days before she saw through his ploy and put an end to that.

"If he wants to eat, he can damn well come downstairs to the kitchen. He'll never get back to work if he doesn't keep improving. And I'm not going to let him wear his pyjamas all day either, he can get dressed like the rest of us."

—

Just a week after Dad returned home, and only when he was sure that Mom could cope, Chuck made his announcement that he was going travelling for a while.

"I want to see the country before I get old and married like you." He was 31 and had already had several careers, if that's what they could be called. He wasn't ready to settle down, but he also wasn't doing anything to build himself a future.

"Chuck's a rogue and always will be," Kathleen said with a smile. "I don't think any woman will ever tie him down. Certainly no job ever will."

"It's lots of fun now, but what about when he's 50 or 60? What will he do then?"

I dropped him off on Highway 7, aiming towards Ottawa. Looking in my rear view mirror, I could see him standing with his arm extended perfectly horizontal and his thumb vertically erect.

"You see these guys with their arm down at the side, trying to look cool," he used to say. "They can't get rides. People want someone who looks clean cut, like he's awake and alert. That's what people want."

All of his belongings, including a tiny nylon pup tent and a tightly rolled sleeping bag for nights when he was stuck on the side of the road, were packed into the same hockey duffle bag from when he was a teenager. It was red and blue with the crest of the Montreal Canadiens prominently sewn on the side.

"That crest gets me more rides than anything else," he told me. "Habs fans are everywhere."

Chuck's desire to communicate conflicted with his hatred of the written word in the many postcards that we started to receive immediately after his departure. The first was just three days later from Ottawa. "I'm walking up the front steps, like in the picture. I can see Pierre Trudeau getting into his car with five security men around him. I've got some new friends and I'm staying with them."

The second card was the famous Wawa Goose. "No one picks up hitchhikers in Wawa. Maybe today I'll get a ride."

A few days later we got a card from Thunder Bay and then a week later from Ignace.

"I'm up in a fire watch tower a thousand miles from nowhere. I'm staying in a log cabin at the bottom of the hill."

Two days after that we received a postcard with the bears from the Winnipeg Zoo, and five days later, a postcard of a train. "On my way to Hudson Bay. My friend Tom is letting me ride in the baggage car. He does this trip every week."

"Who's Tom?" Kathleen said.

I shrugged. "I guess he works in the baggage car. Chuck probably met him in a bar or something."

"Do you think he's riding the train for free?"

"Sounds like it."

She paused. "How much money did he take?"

"I have no idea. But from the sounds of it, all he needs is enough for beer."

"A pretty cheap way to live."

We had long ago ceased to be amazed by Chuck's ability to make new friends. Outside of work, I might talk to two or three strangers a year. I'm sure that Chuck met that many every day. Or even more, in the right circumstances.

"It's not just women he can charm," Kathleen went on. "He makes friends with men, kids, the elderly, everyone."

"I've watched him my whole life and I still don't know how he does it."

"A big smile goes a long way."

"I smile."

"Yes, but Chuck's smile is so big, so genuine. His eyes light up like Santa Claus or something. When he smiles, you just know that he's really interested in talking to you. It's hard to resist. It's impossible to resist."

—

Chuck's postcards continued. Never less than once a week and often two or three days in a row as he made his way out to Vancouver. Twice we received a small box with ten rolls of 35mm film with a note, "Hold onto these until I get back."

"Can you develop these?" Kathleen asked. "You've got all the equipment, don't you? We could find out what he's been up to."

"No, these are colour. I can only do black and white. Colour's a lot harder."

"Why don't we send them out then?"

"Twenty rolls would cost an arm and a leg."

She didn't say anything else.

—

On a hot Saturday afternoon that summer, I was mowing the front lawn and Kathleen was working in her flower beds along the porch.

Even above the unmuffled noise of the lawnmower, I heard a "clunk" from the street. I turned to see a light grey Volkswagen Beetle coast to a stop near our driveway. I shut off the lawnmower and walked over. A young couple, (he looked 18 or 19) and she even younger, was talking inside. The girl held a baby on her lap.

"It sounds like you've got a problem," I said, through the open window. The car's motor was not running. I don't know if it had quit on its own or been shut off.

"I think so," he said, getting himself organized inside and opening his door. "Do you know anything about cars?" We walked to the back and he opened it up to reveal the VW engine. He was small, about 5'6" with a light build, light brown hair over his ears, but neat-

ly cut. It was parted in the middle. He was wearing jeans and a black
Star Wars t-shirt.

I could tell by the styling that this was an older VW, possibly
from the early '60s. There were no headrests on the front seats and
the general body styling had an older feel, even for the unchanging
Beetle.

"No, sorry, I don't," I said.

We both looked at the small motor for a bit. He crouched down
and looked at one side, then the other.

"I think the noise came from back here," he tugged the fan belt
and it was still tight.

I looked back at the house. Kathleen had stopped digging in
her flowers. She was kneeling on the grass and sitting back on her
haunches. The girl opened her door and got out with the baby in
her arms. She was about 5'2" and just as lightly built. She was wearing tight cut off jeans and a loose "peasant" blouse.

"What's going on?" she asked.

Kathleen had stood up and was walking over.

"We don't know yet," he answered.

"Oh, what a beautiful baby!" Kathleen gushed. "Is it a boy or a
girl?"

The baby looked about six months old. It had just a diaper on.
Because of the heat, nothing else was needed. It still looked uncom-
fortably warm.

Kathleen reached out and the mother instinctively took a step
backwards.

"He's a boy," she answered.

Kathleen put her arms down, but still took another step closer.

"What a beautiful little boy."

The girl had looked concerned when she got out of the car, now
she was downright nervous.

"What about our car?" she asked.

"I don't know anything yet," the boy said. He lay down on his
back, sticking his head under the motor. It was too hot to touch, but
he looked around for at least a minute before crawling back out. "I

just don't have a clue," he said as he pushed himself up off the hot asphalt. "I never took auto shop."

"What are we going to do?" she asked.

He didn't answer.

"Where are you going?" Kathleen asked.

The girl hesitated. "Mount Forest."

"Is that your home?"

"My grandparents have a farm there. We're going for a visit."

"To show them the new baby; isn't that nice."

"That's quite a ways," I said. "Could you call and ask them pick you up?"

"They're pretty old," he replied. "I don't think they would drive this far."

"Where are you coming from?" Kathleen asked.

"Cornwall," she answered.

"That's not much closer. Is there anyone you could call?"

"No, not really."

They looked increasingly worried.

"I'm sorry I don't know anything about cars," I said. "I can call a tow truck if you like?"

She tugged at his t-shirt sleeve and they walked around the front of the car.

Kathleen leaned over close to me. "They don't have the money for a tow truck. Isn't there anything you can do?"

I shrugged my shoulders and shook my head. We both stood, looking at the car motor and deliberately trying not to eavesdrop on the couple talking quietly in front of their car.

After a couple of minutes he, walked back. She stayed in front with the baby. "Do you know how much a tow truck would cost?" he asked.

I was just about to say, "maybe ten dollars," when Kathleen jumped in, "Don't you worry about that. We'll look after that for you."

"That would be really nice. Thank you. Are you sure? You don't have to do that."

"Don't be silly. We've got a friend. I'll bet he won't charge us anything at all."

I looked at Kathleen, very surprised. She knew I would never contradict something she'd said.

"In that case, thank you very much. We really appreciate your help."

The girl had been listening. "Yes, thank you very much. That's very nice of you."

"It's too hot to stand out here," Kathleen added. "We can wait for the tow truck up on the porch." She looked over at me, "Go up and call the tow truck, honey. I'll get some lemonade."

"Volkswagens don't have air conditioning," the boy said. "It's been a long drive so far."

They sat on the wicker chairs on our porch while Kathleen and I went inside.

"Find out how much it will cost," she said to me while I looked through the phone book.

When I came back outside, Kathleen had completed the introductions.

"Honey, this is Carson and Jenny and their little boy Curtis."

"The tow truck won't be long," I said, sitting next to Kathleen on the wicker loveseat and picking up my lemonade.

"So how long have you two been married?" Kathleen asked.

They didn't answer, just looked at each other.

"Oh, that's fine." Kathleen went on. "Times certainly have changed, haven't they? Listen to me. I sound like my mother. We're not that much older than you are. I can tell you my mother would certainly be shocked, wouldn't she?" She looked at me and I nodded. "So how old is baby Curtis?"

"Five months," Jenny answered. She was still nervous about her situation, sitting stiffly and holding the baby a little less tightly.

"Oh, that's a wonderful age, isn't it?"

Kathleen went on about this and that for ten minutes until the tow truck pulled up on front. Carson, Jenny and I stood up, but Kathleen said, "Oh Jenny, let the men look after this. It's their job, isn't it?"

Carson and I walked down to the street. I went right up to the driver's window and slipped him twenty dollars before he even stepped out. He was just a teenager, with a face full of freckles.

"Can you tell us what's wrong with it?" Carson asked while they walked around to the open trunk.

"I doubt it," he answered. "I just clean up around the shop. I'm only driving the truck because it's Saturday. There's no one else around."

"Will anybody be able to look at it today?" I asked.

"No way, man. Not 'til Monday. The mechanics don't work on weekends."

Carson asked, "Is there anyone else who can look at it? Any other garage, I mean?"

"Not in Bowmanville, man. Nobody works on Saturday here."

Carson was certainly worried by this. He walked back up towards the porch and Jenny met him at the bottom of the steps. I couldn't hear what was discussed quietly between them, but after a couple of minutes, they both walked up the steps to Kathleen.

Thirty seconds later she yelled down at me. "Honey, Carson and Jenny are going to stay with us until they get their car sorted out. Isn't that wonderful?"

I turned to the tow truck driver who had been hooking up the VW. "I guess you can take it away."

"No problem, man."

"Will they be able to work on it first thing on Monday?"

"Can't say. I only work part time. But I'll put a note on it and maybe the boss can get it fixed first thing." He handed me a clipboard. "Here. Fill this out and he'll give you a call."

"It's not my car, it's his." I said, pointing up the walk. "Carson, you need to fill out some paperwork," I called.

"Oh, you look after that, honey." Kathleen replied.

Kathleen was in heaven with a baby in the house. Once they became our guests, Jenny let the baby be held and bounced and snuggled and fed. Carson and Jenny seemed to be relieved that, at least for a little while, they didn't have to mind him every minute of the day.

I finished mowing the lawn, Carson clipped the hedges on both sides and behind the house, and Jenny spent Sunday in the vegetable garden in the backyard. It had never been weeded so thoroughly. Kathleen spent the entire day with baby Curtis. In the middle of the afternoon, she brought out a tray of lemonade and donuts that she'd made, along with a jar of her applesauce.

"Can I feed Curtis?" she asked, even though she had already put on his bib and had her spoon in the jar.

"If it's not too much trouble," Jenny answered. There was already a spoonful of applesauce hovering in front of the baby's mouth by the time she had finished speaking.

Kathleen had Curtis on her lap in one of the wicker chairs, supporting his back with her left arm, holding the jar of applesauce in her left hand and the spoon in her right. It was one of the little silver coffee spoons that we only use when we have guests, when Kathleen brings out the silver coffee set that her grandmother had left to us.

"Open up, sweetie," she cooed. "If you want to grow up big and strong like Reggie here." She held the jar so Curtis was looking right at the Gerber baby on the label.

Jenny spoke up, "You know that baby, in the picture?"

"Oh, yes. That's little Reggie. But he's all grown up now." Kathleen used the spoon to catch applesauce that squeezed out the sides of Curtis' mouth. "I remember when he was just this age." She adjusted Curtis on her left leg. "All the other mothers were so jealous because he was just so cute. Look at his eyelashes; they're just so long, and his nose is just such a little button." She was looking closely at the jar herself, and not holding it up for anyone else to see.

"Oh, but when he was born his mother had such a hard time. Her labour lasted nearly a whole day. I remember it started just after supper and the baby didn't come until the next afternoon. She was just so exhausted when she was finished. And of course in those days the husbands weren't involved at all." She looked over at me with a scowl. "Her husband went to work just like any other day.

Men are so useless at times like this. He was just getting off work when little Reggie was born so he went down to see him for a few minutes. Then it was off to hand out cigars to the fellows like he had done something amazing and she wasn't involved at all.

"But Reggie was such a happy baby, right from the start. He hardly ever cried, except when he had the croup when he was just four months, but that didn't last long. He hardly cried at all.

"So, when he was six months old, she entered him in a beautiful baby contest. We used to have those, you know. I don't think they do them anymore, do they? But back in the '50s, we used to see that kind of thing all the time. Baby companies would put them on just to get publicity.

"All these mothers, hundreds of them, were crowded into the Horticulture Building at the Exhibition down in Toronto. It was more like a cattle show than a baby contest, with everybody just milling around and not knowing what to do.

"But their biggest mistake was holding it in the middle of the afternoon. All these babies should have been down for their naps but the mothers had to keep poking them to keep them awake for the judges who were walking around. And of course the judges were nothing special, just the local ladies from the Rebecca's Hall, that's all.

"But maybe they weren't so dumb after all because all of the babies who were crying were just eliminated right away and they got to go home. That was a simple way to cut the numbers by two thirds at least, and the mothers couldn't really argue, could they?

"And then some of the babies were just too young and couldn't sit up by themselves. They were eliminated right away too. And of course, some of the babies were just not very good looking at all. I know that as a mother, you think every baby is beautiful, but when you're looking at dozens of them in a line, you just realize that some are not as beautiful as others.

"The ladies from the Rebecca's Hall cut the number down to a couple of dozen or so of the really cute babies who were all sitting quietly on their mother's laps. And three people from the Gerber company came out, two women and a man with a camera. All the mothers were sitting in chairs in a big circle and the Gerber people walked around inside the circle. They stopped at every baby and they shook a little rattle in front and watched what the baby did. And of course some of the babies scowled and some of them cried. But some of them laughed and some of them smiled.

"The people from Gerber, they're professionals at this so they know that they have to move quickly. You can't keep babies waiting forever you know. They talked to each other for just a minute or two while they were looking at all the babies. Then they called out five names. I don't remember what the names were, but Reggie was one of them.

"These five mothers and their babies came forward and sat down on five chairs. Most of the other people had left by then. No one wants to wait around in a big room full of babies. There was always at least one or two crying.

"The two women from Gerber crouched down in front of each baby with a little jingle bells on a bright red ribbon. They shook it and watched what the baby did. As soon as the baby reacted, the man with the camera took a picture. He had a big camera with a big flash.

"And that's why little Reggie was chosen as the most beautiful baby. When they jingled the bells in front of him, his eyes opened big and wide and he gave out a squeal of delight and the man took his picture right at that moment. And that's what you see here." Kathleen was still looking closely at the jar, not holding it up for Jenny to see. She had only given Curtis a couple more spoonfuls of applesauce while she had been talking.

She went on. "Maybe they should have called it a *Happiest Baby* contest instead of a *Beautiful Baby* contest. But isn't that just the same thing anyways?

"Reggie's grown up to be such a nice young man. He's studying law at the University of Toronto now. I'm sure he's going to be very successful."

"Oh, look at the time." Kathleen said. "I'm going to put a nice roast in the oven. I know it's a hot day to be having a roast, but I think you two need a good home cooked meal and I'll make up some nice sandwiches to take with you when your car's fixed tomorrow."

Carson and Jenny nodded as Kathleen ended her tale. I sat, resigned, sipping my lemonade.

—

At nine in the morning, Carson, Jenny and I drove down to the garage to check on the car. It was a small shop with just two bays, owned by the Johnson Brothers, according to the sign. I remember when I was young it was just called *Jack Johnson's*. He must have been their father.

"You've got a real problem here, kid," the man said as he walked into the front office. It was a small reception area with just enough room for the three of us to stand on our side of the counter.

He was in his mid '30s, a few years younger than I was. He had a brown, bushy moustache that covered his top lip.

"Didn't you change the oil on that thing?" he went on. "It's nothing but sludge."

"We just bought it last week. I haven't had time to look after it yet." Carson replied.

"Well, what happened is your engine seized up. Not permanently, mind you. But it was so hot here last week and this thing's just air cooled, you know. And then when you add in the sludge, the pistons seized right up."

"Is it bad?" Carson asked.

"Well, we can turn the engine over now slowly, so it's not shot or anything like that. I'd have to open it up and take a look at the cylinders, but you can bet at the very least we'll have to replace the rings, just to get some compression back. And if the cylinders are scored, then you've got a bigger problem on your hands."

"How much is this going to cost?" Carson asked.

The man thought for a moment and started jotting down on a

scrap of paper. "Well, if we're just looking at replacing the rings, that means the head gasket too; and we'll have to do a real good job to flush out all the old sludge and the filter. I'd say we're looking at $325. But of course that's if it's just the rings. It'll be more if we need to work on the cylinders too."

"How much more?"

"Another couple hundred, at least."

"We only paid three-fifty for the car," Carson said.

"It might have been okay if you'd changed the oil on it right away. Hard to say."

"It's only got 78,000 miles on it."

"Is that what you were told?" Johnson said. "What's the old saying? 'In a pig's eye' it does. That car's fifteen years old. It's been past a hundred thousand at least once. It was worth $350, but no more, that's for sure. Now…" he paused. "I'll be honest with you, it's not worth putting that kinda money into."

Carson looked relieved that the decision had been made for him.

"We don't have the money anyway."

"That's that, then." Johnson said. "I'll tell you what I'll do. The fenders are all rusted out and the seats are completely worn through, but I might be able to sell the bumpers to someone; they're pretty good. And the wheels too. We can always use those." He thought for a few more seconds. "I'll give you 25 dollars for the car as scrap." He looked at Carson, then Jenny. "How's that?"

The two looked at each other. Jenny shrugged her shoulders.

"Okay," Carson resigned himself.

"Let's see now," Johnson reached down into a drawer on his side of the counter and fingered through a number of file folders until he found the paper he was looking for. He wrote, "1962 VW Beetle – Grey," in the vehicle description section and turned the paper around to Carson.

"Sign here," he pointed to a line on the bottom and Carson signed it. Then he pulled a stack of bills out of his cash box and handed 25 dollars over. "I'm sorry for your trouble, kids. Maybe this'll get you where you're going."

We drove home in silence; Carson in the front seat and Jenny in the back. Their plans had obviously been flipped upside down. When we got home, I took Kathleen aside and gave her the story.

"But I've got to get to work," I said. "I'm already late."

"If he gave them $25," Kathleen said, "Then that's all the money they've got in the world, I'm sure. We'll have to put them on a bus to their grandparent's house or they won't get anywhere at all."

She pulled out the telephone book and made a call to the Greyhound station. "Jenny! Carson!" she shouted and they came downstairs. "There's a bus leaving at eleven. You can be in Mount Forest by supper time. How's that?"

"Do you know how much it will cost?" Jenny asked.

"Oh, don't you worry about that. We'll get you on the bus." Kathleen was always sensitive to people's feelings. She would never say, "We'll give you money," or, "We'll pay for you," or anything that might make someone think they were receiving charity. She just said, "We'll get you on the bus," like it was no imposition at all.

I drove them down to the station and bought tickets for Mount Forest, stopping in Toronto on the way.

We did get a nice card from them a few months later. They were living in a room above their Grandparent's garage. It was a nice apartment that had originally been built for Carson's Great-Grandmother. Carson was working at his Grandfather's feed mill. They thanked us for all of the help.

"That was such a sweet little baby," Kathleen said. "It's nice that they landed on their feet after all that."

—

Since Dad had returned home, our trips to Toronto and the subsequent expenses had decreased. It made me happy to finally be putting a little money away again even if we still contributed to Mom and Dad's mortgage payment. It was quite a shock, both to my understanding of the business world and to my wallet, when they renewed the mortgage with a 12 percent interest rate. Mom was very apologetic, saying that it should not be up to the children to look after their parents, at least until they were older. But she promised that Dad was improving and would be back to work soon.

Kathleen did not take well to our reduced night life once we were stuck back in Bowmanville on the weekends. She compensated by going out Saturday nights with some single girlfriends from her school.

"What am I supposed to do? Sit here and watch TV while you're upstairs with your pencil scratching?"

When autumn came, Chuck made his way down into the States, but the big surprise was a collect call from San Diego, just before Christmas.

"I need you to send me my passport. I'm working on a freighter over to Japan. I need it right away, so send it by courier."

"How did you get that job?" I asked.

"My friend Juan," he said. "He says they need an extra man right away because one of their guys is sick. They're leaving in three days, so if you can send my passport, I can go too."

"Okay. I'll send it down right away. Let me know where you end up."

We cut the call short because of long distance charges.

—

Chuck sailed a circuit from San Diego to Tokyo to Seattle then back to San Diego before heading across the Pacific again. Every few weeks we'd receive a new postcard from one of the cities, with a couple of lines in his irregular printing. Every card depicted one of the cultural or tourist sites of the city he had docked at, with a note about his latest new friend, often a girlfriend. "I'm up the Space Needle with Janet," or, "Kyoko and I are at this shrine in the picture," or, "I'm at Disneyland with Carol." It appeared that neither nationality nor language were barriers to Chuck's smile. Never once did he forget to send us a card as he closed the circle around and around.

—

Dad started back at work, half days.

"The insurance company has been putting a lot of pressure on him to get back so they don't have to keep paying on his disability." Mom said. "Their doctor said he's ready and they're going to cut off payments altogether, so we have no choice."

But it was only a few weeks before the trouble started.

"He came home at ten-thirty this morning," Mom said over the phone.

"What happened? He only works 'till noon anyway."

"I don't know. He won't tell me anything and he's in a really bad mood so I don't want to push him. You know how he gets. I sent him upstairs to lie down."

Two weeks later, he was home early again.

"He said that he was arguing with one of the workers and they sent him home." Mom told me. "I don't know any more about it, and he won't say any more."

"Do you think he's losing his temper?" I asked. "Why else would they send him home?"

"I hope not. You've seen how he gets."

The third time it happened, the company ruled that he was not ready to come back and they wouldn't let him return unless he was completely over his temper problems.

Mom said, "Mr. Olivier, the new Plant Manager, called me to discuss it. From what he says, your father was upset with how the man on the calendar line was slowing the line down to cut between rolls. He started yelling at them about how they don't slow the roller down in Bowmanville. But when one of the men said they were told to do it this way for safety, your father picked up a crow bar and swung it at him. The other men on the crew grabbed hold of your father and held onto him. He didn't calm down for some time. Apparently, it took three men to hold him or he was going to hurt someone. They put him in the nurse's station for a while. Then Mr. Olivier had someone drive him home."

"Have you talked to the doctor yet? About Dad's temper?"

"Oh, yes. We've spoken about it several times. He says that some

part of his brain was damaged. It may take some time for it to get
better, if it ever does."

"You mean that it might never get better?"

"We just don't know. That's the hardest part. We just don't know
what's going to happen with him."

"So what do we do now?"

"We have to go back to the doctor again and get him to write a
letter to the insurance company that he can't go back to work because of a medical condition. Then we can only hope that they are
willing to accept it and start paying us again. I'm sorry, Dear, that we
have to keep coming to you for money, but I just don't know what
else to do. I can't go out and get a job because I have to stay home
and look after your father, or who knows what might happen."

"You don't have to worry about that, Mom. That's what family's
for. That's what you always taught us."

"Yes, but children shouldn't be burdened with their parents
while they're still able to work."

"But Dad's not able to work. That's the whole problem."

"Nevertheless."

After a collection of letters back and forth with the insurance
company in which they claimed that Dad's inability to work was
because of his own combative personality and not caused by the
aneurysm, they settled on a payment of just half the earlier amount.
This meant only one quarter of his previous salary, certainly not
enough to live in Toronto. The help Mom and Dad needed from us
only increased.

Kathleen was not at all happy.

"Why don't they move out of the city?" she complained. "They
could live much more cheaply back here?"

"Mom keeps hoping that Dad can get back to work. I think she
feels that if they move out of the city, she's resigning herself to Dad
as an invalid for the rest of his life. Goodyear has promised they'll
have something for him if he gets better."

"Do you really believe that? He's over 60 now. Do you really
think they're going to take him back now with just a few years until

he retires anyway? They gave him a chance and he failed miserably. I somehow doubt that they'll give him another chance, and in the meantime we're stuck here paying their bills and we can't look after ourselves.

"And what happens when he turns 65 and the insurance stops altogether? They'll have to live on his Goodyear pension then. And that won't be very much at all with all the time he's been out of work."

"We might be able to put some money away if we cut down on entertainment expenses a bit." I didn't look at her in the face.

"Oh, here we go again with that old argument! I'm not going to give up my life just so your parents can live in the city!"

I knew enough to stay away from this discussion again and tried another tack, "Do you want them living back here? Just down the street from us where Mom can drop by every day? Is that what you want?"

Kathleen was fuming, but did not answer.

"Or maybe they could move right in with us, into Chuck's room," I continued. "Is that what you want?"

"What I want is for us to live our own lives and not have to keep shelling out for them. Your mother is right. It's not up to us to support them. We've got our own problems."

"But isn't that what family is for? You've got your whole family back East. Don't they look after each other?"

"Well, it sure as hell looks like we're never going to have a family of our own," she brought up a sore subject again. "We might as well adopt your parents and we can treat them like our own children. Complete with your father's tantrums like a two year old."

"Well, if we don't keep helping out a bit, that's exactly what will happen," I said. After hundreds of arguments that I'd conceded, I finally was able to get in the last word.

Kathleen looked at me and stormed out the front door. Gone out to visit her girlfriends once again, I imagined. It was past 11:00 when she walked back in. I could smell the wine on her breath as she walked past my desk on her way to bed.

CHAPTER EIGHTEEN

In September, Mr. Jenkins called me into his office.

"Do you know anything about computer aided design and drafting?" he asked.

"Only what I've been reading in the *Civil Engineering Magazine*." I said. "There's something about CADD every month now. It's the hot topic." I started to rise from the wooden chair in front of his desk. "Do you want me to find you something?"

"No, no," he stopped me. "I've seen the articles. I was just wondering if you've been looking into it."

"Well, I've certainly read the articles. But it's the kind of thing that you can't really understand until you do it. My own computer at home is too small."

"You've got a computer at home?"

"Yes. I've got an Altair," I said. "I bought it from one of my astronomy friends. He struggled with it for a year and finally gave up in frustration so he gave it to me for a good price. I've been using it to calculate the movements of stars and planets." I stopped myself before going into a long explanation. I knew from past experience that Mr. Jenkins was not interested in my hobby.

"Have you used it for any engineering work?" he asked.

"Not yet. It would take me longer to set up the programming than I could do it with my own pocket calculator." A little Texas Instrument calculator had replaced my slide rule in 1975. Mr. Jenkins and the other, older engineers in the office were still using their slide rules. "That's the thing with computers," I went on. "They're great for doing the same thing over and over again, like the movement of stars, but they're no good for doing a wide variety of different tasks like we do here."

"Nothing can replace a smart engineer with a pencil," he smiled.

"Not so far," I replied. "But I have to admit that what the magazines are saying about the CADD systems is pretty interesting."

"Well, listen," he said, "the reason I'm asking is the head office is talking about it and they've sent out feelers to see if anyone is interested in getting something going. With your strength in mathematics, I thought you might be interested. And now that I know you've actually been working with a computer, I guess I was right. What do you think?" He looked back at me.

"Sure. That sounds interesting. Do you know what they're doing?"

"Not very much, but I'll get you on the phone to Toronto this afternoon. They've hired a fellow to put it all together. He's some sort of expert. Right out of university, I guess. He's going to be managing the project, and they want to train some of the younger engineers, like you. Old guys like me will never get the hang of this. They want to train guys for some of the new projects we're bidding on for the government. I've seen the James Bay Dam tender and they're actually requiring that the work be done on a CADD system." He paused again. "Just another way to make sure all the work goes to the big companies and the little guys can't catch a break. What do you think? Do you think you know enough to impress them over the phone this afternoon?"

I hesitated. "If this fellow is a real expert, I don't know if I'll be able to keep up with him."

Mr. Jenkins thought for thirty seconds. "I don't think there's anyone in the whole company who's as sharp as you with mathematics; at least not from what I've heard. Why do you think they keep sending all this work over from the other offices for you to do? What are you working on now?"

"The Jameston Centre Mall," I answered.

"That can wait. Why don't you go over everything you can find on it. I'm sure we've got years of magazines stacked in a closet somewhere. Then when you talk on the phone, you'll sound like an expert. How's that sound?"

"Okay."

"Can we set up the call for later this afternoon?"

I hesitated to answer.

He understood my personality. "What about tomorrow morning, then? I don't want to leave it any longer and lose the chance to put you forward."

"That would be better," I answered, relieved that I'd have 24 hours to study up.

"Listen, you make sure to give it your best. With your experience I think this could be a real chance for you. If we can pick up a nice contract, that is. This could be the opportunity for advancement that you've been waiting for."

I spent the day and long into the night reading through a stack of engineering magazines from the past three years. CADD was the hot new topic in the industry. Even if it was still in its infancy, there were articles in every issue.

The next morning I spent an hour on the telephone with Dan Keys. He had been hired directly out of the University of Toronto Computer Program to build and manage our new CADD system at the head office. With my strong penchant for mathematics, my limited abilities at programming in Basic and the seemingly knowledgeable questions I was able to ask, along with Mr. Jenkins' recommendation, I was an easy selection to start training on the new system.

"It's been a long haul, nearly fourteen months since I started," Dan said. "but I'd done a lot of this work while I was still at school, so we're just about ready. I'll have you and Brad from Kingston and Tony here in Toronto all in for training and we can work out any problems with the program. I imagine it will be three or four weeks. Are you okay with that?"

"Sure," I said. I was looking forward to it. With the tension at home, a break from each other might be just what we needed, although I was sure Kathleen wouldn't miss the opportunity to come down for weekends in the big city.

—

My introduction to the coffee fuelled fanaticism of computer programming was abrupt. Brad Wahl came in from Kingston to join the training. He was taller than me, which made me uncomfortable at first. As a tall boy and then a tall man, I was used to looking downwards in every conversation; it was unusual to be tilting my head upwards to speak with Brad. I'll always remember the first time we walked onto an elevator together. Looking up at him from only one foot apart was disconcerting. I tried to take a step backward but the crowded elevator didn't allow for it, so I kept up the conversation while looking straight ahead in the elevator and speaking out the side of my mouth.

Brad had joined HBA about the same time that I had. The Kingston office was larger than Bowmanville with greater opportunities and he had already been made Partner.

"I brought in a couple of nice sized projects," he told me. He was married with three young children.

Tony Perillo was local to Toronto. He was much younger than Brad and me, and had been with HBA for just five years. He was young enough that he had actually studied some computer programming as part of his engineering degree.

"It's the future," he said. "They're teaching it to everyone now."

The entire CADD program had been written by Dan and was far from perfect. I was used to the frustration of running my little Altair with programs shared amongst the astronomical community by mail. It could take hours for me to discover and correct a single missed switch. But Dan's program had tens of thousands of lines of code. It seemed that every day we discovered a new problem and with Dan's expertise and our amateur knowledge, we would work late into the night to solve each one as it arose. We never once left the office before eight o'clock. Many times we were there until midnight or even until three or four in the morning, only to start up again at eight or nine the next morning.

I think that management was surprised at the state of unreadiness of Dan's program. One of the secretaries who kept us supplied with coffee christened the program itself, "DannyCADD" and the name stuck for several years until an off-the-shelf program was purchased. But we were in an office by ourselves, so most of the senior partners had no idea what we were actually doing or how late we were working. Dan explained that pain is a normal part of software development, but we couldn't know if this was true or just his way of giving excuses.

Brad, Tony and I had started the training in our normal suits and ties, but after our second run past midnight, we imitated Dan and just stuck to our shirtsleeves unless a senior manager was making a formal appearance. Of course, we were back to business wear once the training was completed.

The James Bay Hydroelectric Dam bidding specifications required that our company have proven abilities with CADD. Management felt that three trained engineers, along with our own CADD development department (even if that department consisted solely of Dan) would be sufficient to meet the bid requirements. In the end, the proof of the company's abilities amounted to several hundred typed pages of documentation.

I invited Kathleen down for my second weekend in Toronto. I promised her that I wouldn't work past four on Saturday and we could have a nice night at my hotel and go out for drinks, but she was tied up with an early season curling bonspiel and couldn't make it down.

I invited her down again on my third weekend, but the weather was nice and she had promised to spend Saturday golfing with her friends.

I did get a chance to spend a Sunday dinner with Mom and Dad. In spite of the money I'd been sending to them regularly, the stress of their financial situation was evident. The roast that Mom pulled out of the oven was very small; just enough for the three of us, rather than the eight pounders of days past when we'd have a full dinner with vegetables and potatoes on Sunday, hot roast beef sandwiches with gravy on Monday, stew with large chunks of meat on Tuesday and soup with barley on Wednesday.

Dad and I sat in the living room while Mom did the dishes. We chatted and watched Suzanne Pleshette in *The Shaggy DA* on Walt Disney. I always had a crush on her, with that deep, sultry voice.

Dad sat in a rocking chair that had been part of their furniture for as long as I could remember. It was the type with springs that squeaked with a low metal tone. He kept up a constant, short rocking motion so the squeak never stopped. I believe that the low volume noise gave him more comfort than the actual rocking.

"Katie couldn't make it down?" he asked.

"No. She's tied up with golfing."

"That's too bad. It's been a while."

Our conversation, about nothing particular, went on while we watched the movie.

"Have you heard from Chuck at all?"

"Just another postcard. We get one every week or so."

"Yes, so do we. It's good that he keeps in touch like this. Your Mom appreciates it."

"Last I heard he was just leaving San Diego again for Japan."

"Sure."

"You know," Dad continued, "your Mom and I really appreciate all the help you and Katie and Chuck have given us over the past couple of years. I know it's been a lot of money."

He continued to look at the television, as did I. A commercial for toilet paper was showing.

"It's no problem. We've got two incomes so we can manage." The one thing we'd learned was to never discuss anything contentious with Dad that might set off his temper, just keep all conversation pleasant and light.

"All the same," he went on, "we certainly appreciate it. But I don't know what's going to happen if the interest rates keep going up."

"You don't have to worry; we'll manage."

"We really appreciate it," he said again. "And I really appreciate the way you've looked after your Mom while I've been sick. It's been really good of you and Katie." His voice went quiet.

—

A week later, we finished our CADD training with enough knowledge and experience to make a claim of proficiency on the bidding documents. It had been exciting being part of something new, but it would be good to get back to the normal 9 to 5 routine of the Bowmanville office. Of course the training was essentially wasted when we lost the bid to Legault et Associate, a Quebec firm.

"We didn't have a chance with The Parti Quebecois in power," I was later told. "They sure as hell weren't going to choose an English company, from Ontario no less, to do the work."

It was only years later, when we stared to hear about the widespread bribery scandals involving construction companies that we understood the real situation in Quebec.

—

We had tried to finish the CADD training on Friday afternoon, but a new set of problems had us staying one last night at the hotel and working until noon on Saturday. The drive home was easy and relaxing.

"Hi!" I shouted, walking through the front door, "I'm home!" I opened the closet door to hang up my jacket and saw that it was three quarters empty. All of Kathleen's coats and jackets were missing. Even the coat hangers were gone, leaving a stretch of bare wooden rod with my few coats taking up only the far left quarter of the closet space.

I heard Kathleen's footsteps crossing the tile floor of the kitchen and heading into the hallway at the back of the house.

"Hi," she said, walking up the hall, and past me without a kiss, then into the living room. "I need to talk to you about something."

I followed her into the living room.

"What's wrong?"

Kathleen sat down in the armchair and I sat on the chesterfield. We used to sit together on the chesterfield but that had slowly dwindled over the years.

"I might as well get right to the point," she said. "I'm moving out."

She paused to let me respond.

"What do you mean?" I sat with my hands pinched under my knees.

She didn't answer right away, but looked down at the floor in front, between us, "I've been seeing someone else for a while. I'm moving in with him."

"What do you mean you've been seeing someone else? Who else have you been seeing?"

"I might as well tell you. You're going to find out eventually anyway." She paused. "I've been seeing Rob Enright."

"Who's he?"

"You remember, you met him at the bonspiel dinner last spring."

"You curl with him?"

"Yes. He's on my team."

I thought for a few seconds. "How long has this been going on?"

"It doesn't matter, for a while now."

"What's a while? A month? A year?"

She paused again, calculating what to say. "A year. Or so."

"So now you're just moving out?"

"I've already taken my things over to his house."

I looked around the room. "What do you mean?"

"My clothes. Everything from the bathroom. Everything else that I want."

From her answers, it was clear that she had prepared well for this conversation. She wasn't speaking in anger, but in sadness. She continued to look down at the rug in front of us, with just occasional glances up at my face. Her eyes had turned red and she was fighting tears.

So was I. "After all the time we've been together, you're just walking out?"

"I'm not just walking out," she said slowly. "I've been thinking about this for a while now. I just can't think of spending the rest of my life like this."

"What do you mean? Haven't I been a good husband?"

"You've been a wonderful husband."

"Then what's the problem?"

"It's just not what I'm looking for. Not for the next 50 years of my life."

"You're one who asked me to marry you, remember, what's changed?"

"Things were different then. When I met you, I could tell right away that you would be the perfect man; the perfect husband to raise children. The way you used to talk about Chuck and about your parents. It was clear just how important family was to you. I could just tell that you would be a good father to our children. I've seen other men. Men who were out running around. I knew you would never be like that; I knew you would always be home. And you have been. When a woman is looking for a father to her children, that's just what she's looking for; a man who will be stable with a good job who will always be able to provide a good life. And that's just what you've always been, stable.

"But we've been trying for so long to have children, and it's just not going to happen." She stopped for just half a second. "With you." She paused again, longer this time. "And it's just not going to happen, so I needed to look somewhere else for what I wanted out of life. Having a stable husband but without a family just wasn't what I'd planned for.

"So, what?" I asked. "This Rob guy is Mr. Excitement? Is that what it is? You know, if it's more excitement that you want, then I can be more exciting. Haven't we been going out all the time in Toronto? We've been to all kinds of shows and plays and things.

We've been eating out at restaurants. I even invited you down last week but you didn't want to come. I thought that you wanted to be completely settled, so that's why I was always worked up about saving our money. But if that's not important to you, then I don't have to worry about that. We can have all the excitement that you want."

"No, you don't understand. It's not excitement that I want. I don't want that at all."

"I don't get it. You say that you don't want excitement but you're going out every night at your golf and now I know why you've been going out with your curling all the time, just to see this Rob guy. But you say that you don't want excitement. I don't get it."

"No, it's not that. Not at all. But look at us now. Every night we come home and eat supper and you go and sit at your desk and work at your astronomy all night and I watch TV all night or sit in silence. So it's no wonder that I like to go out sometimes. It's just that I can't stand to sit around every evening in silence, listening to you scratch your pencil. And now it's even worse; I get to sit and listen to you click the buttons on that machine of yours."

"I still don't get it," I said. "You say that you don't want excitement, but you go out practically every night. You say that you want stability and I give you stability. But now you're moving in with this Rob guy because he gives you stability too?"

"Don't you understand?" she was crying by this time. I could see the tears rolling down her nose; a few dropped to the floor before she caught them with the Kleenex that she'd pulled from her sleeve, an old teacher's trick. "I don't want stability. I want a family. You know I come from a big family. I want a big family of my own."

"I know you want that, Kathleen. We've been trying for years and it looks like it's just not going to happen. I'm sorry. I'm really sorry. If it's that important to you, then I don't see why we can't adopt a baby."

"We've talked about this. I don't want to adopt. I want my own babies."

There was a long silence. "I'm, sorry Kathleen. I'm sorry that we haven't been able to have children. I know that it's important to you." I stopped for a moment. "Listen. There's all kinds of new treatments for people like us. There's lots of couples who are just like us and there's new treatments the doctors can do to make it right. Maybe we should talk to the doctor again? It's been at least five years since we talked to anybody about this and they've come up with lots of new treatments since then. Why don't we talk to Dr. Pilson about it again? Maybe he can help us."

"We don't need to talk to Dr. Pilson. I saw him last week." She spoke quietly.

This got my hopes up a bit. Perhaps she was working on a solution. "What did he say?"

Kathleen looked right at me. Her eyes were completely red and the stream of tears had left a line down her face.

"I'm pregnant. Rob is the father."

Our marriage ended with those words. She hadn't said it defiantly like "I've got you now." Nor had she said it apologetically like, "I'm really sorry, but I made a mistake." The way she said it was a reflection of its importance to her very being; her sense of self worth. It came across as, "This is something I needed to do, so I did it."

I guess it really was the best thing for Kathleen. She had four children, three girls and a boy, one after the other, over the next five years. Every once in a while, I ran into her at the grocery store and there was always a child with their legs sticking out of the shopping cart, usually with a sucker in their mouth or a cookie in their hand and looking up at me wide-eyed while Kathleen and I exchanged a short, "Merry Christmas," or, "Hot weather lately." Kathleen herself always seemed happy on the occasions, as if having kids really had fulfilled her life's purpose.

CHAPTER NINETEEN

My second shock came just a month later with Dad's death.

"You have to come right away," Mom said when she called me at work early on a Tuesday afternoon in November. "The police are here. Your father's killed himself."

"What do you mean?" was the only response I could come up with.

"The police want me to come down to the morgue with them to identify your father. I said I wouldn't come without you."

"Did you tell them that I'm in Bowmanville?"

"They said they'll wait."

The mid-afternoon traffic was light and I made good time into Toronto. I arrived to see that Mom had been serving coffee and cookies and making small talk with the police man and police woman since her phone call.

"There he is now," Mom said when I opened the door and gave her a hug.

The police woman was the first to speak up, "My name is Officer Sarah Goode, and this is Officer Meyers." They stood up from the chesterfield.

I looked over at them, relaxing my hold on Mom but not stepping away from her.

"I'm sorry to tell you that your father has died," she continued. She knew that I'd already been told. "We would like you and your

Mother to come down to the hospital with us to identify your father."

"What happened?" I asked. "How did he die?"

Mom still held an arm around me. "He stepped off the pier at the park and drowned." Mom must have been referring to Marie Curtis Park, just a few blocks from their house.

"What, into Lake Ontario?"

"Yes."

"Just this afternoon?"

"Actually, it was this morning." Officer Goode spoke again. "It took a while for the fire department to recover the bo–' she paused briefly, '–to recover your father from the lake."

"You're sure it's him?"

"Yes. He was carrying identification. But we need you to confirm that, of course."

I had had the whole of the drive to consider what Mom had told me over the phone, so this was not a shock and I had no reason to doubt what they were saying.

"You're sure he killed himself? He didn't just fall off or something?"

"Several people saw him walk straight off the end of the pier. And when he was recovered, we found that his coat pockets were filled with stones." Officer Goode spoke calmly. I could tell that she'd done this kind of thing before.

"And he left this on his desk." Mom handed me life insurance papers. It was a dozen pages thick, stapled in the upper left with a blue triangular cardboard corner.

Paper clipped to the document was a handwritten note, a little more shaky than the perfect script that Dad had written with before his aneurysm.

"I love you, Becca. Thank you for our life together. C."

I unthinkingly flipped through the pages and could see that, in the middle of the document, Dad had used a pencil to draw brackets around "Section 28 – Suicide." Dad would never forsake his duty to Mom, even in death.

We drove to Toronto General in the back of the police car. When we pulled into the service vehicles area, I realized that there were no handles in the back seat, so we waited for officers Goode and Meyers to open our doors from the outside. For all the many, many times we had come to the hospital during Dad's recovery, we had never come in through this entrance.

The hospital morgue was similar to what we had seen dozens of times on TV shows. The room has a very strong smell of disinfectant cleanser. There were three examination tables with lamps. Only one table was occupied. A man in a white jacket introduced himself but I don't remember his name.

Mom took my left hand and pressed herself tightly up against me as we walked nervously up to the table. Dad was covered in a heavy powder blue sheet with, "Toronto General Hospital" stamped on the top seam. Officers Goode and Meyers stood nearby, but respectfully off to the side. Officer Goode nodded to the man in the white jacket and he folded down the sheet just to the shoulders so we could see Dad's face and neck.

Mom pressed herself even tighter up against me as we looked down.

I had expected his face to be swollen from the water, but he looked quite normal. I guess it takes longer than an hour in the water to make a permanent change. The mortician had even been nice enough to comb Dad's hair, although he put the part on the wrong side.

With Mom's head down, I could not see her eyes, but I could hear her soft sniffles.

"Is this Mr. Murray?" Officer Goode asked quietly.

I waited for a few seconds for Mom to answer. When she didn't, I said, "Yes," only to have her also say it at the same moment.

The police and mortician left us alone in the room for a few minutes. I didn't know what to say so I remained silent. Once again this was a situation where Chuck would have been perfect. He'd been to many funerals over the years.

Mom kept holding my left hand in both of hers. After a couple of minutes of quiet, she said, "He was a really good man, you know. He tried so hard. He worked so hard and it just didn't come out the way we expected. But he was a really good man."

The police and mortician seemed to take that as a cue to come back in.

"We'll write up a report. So there won't be any issues about this. Someone from the hospital will be in touch–" Officer Goode looked at her watch, "–probably tomorrow morning, about making arrangements. But you don't have to think about it; they will guide you through the entire process."

When we stepped out of the police car at home, one of the neighbours, Mrs. Hunt, quickly came out of her front door with a coat pulled over her shoulders. "I saw you leave in the police car earlier. Is something wrong?"

"Charles is dead." Mom said. "We're just returning from the hospital."

"Oh dear, oh dear. That's just horrible, Rebecca. I wondered if it was something awful like that when I didn't see Charles with you." Mrs. Hunt had put her arm around Mom and pulled her in close as we walked up to the porch.

It was already dark in the late autumn and we hadn't left the porch light on so it took me a few tries to put the key in the front door lock.

Mrs. Hunt walked right in, still with her arm around Mom. I had only heard Mom and Dad mention the Hunts as casual acquaintances. Something like this must bring out the sympathy in people.

"Here. Why don't the two of you just sit down and I'll make some tea. Would that be alright?"

"Thank you." I answered, "I'll help you find everything."

"No, no. You just sit with your mother. I'll be fine."

I heard her run water into the electric kettle and then a few cupboard doors opening and closing while she looked for teabags and cups. Like every other woman of her generation, Mom kept her brown teapot on the kitchen counter, covered with a macramé tea cozy.

"I should call Chuck," I said to Mom.

"Do you know how to reach him?" she asked. "He's probably out on the ship somewhere."

"The last card was from San Diego. He might be in Japan by now."

"How will you find him?"

"I'll call his company. It's *Matson*, isn't it? They'll know how to reach him."

I called directory assistance for San Diego and got the number for *Matson*. It was still afternoon on the West Coast so I was able to speak with a woman in the office and tell her that I needed to find Chuck urgently because of a death in the family.

A half hour later she called back.

"We've located him. Right now he's in transit from Tokyo to Seattle, but it will be sixteen days before he arrives. I can send him a radio message, if you think it's best?"

"Yes. Just tell him that our father has died and he should call me as soon as he can."

"Certainly, sir. I'll make sure that he receives the message. And my condolences to you and your family."

"I guess I should call the rest of the family," I said to Mom while we were eating spaghetti that Mrs. Hunt had brought over.

"Not tonight, dear. I really don't think I could spend all night on the phone with everybody. Maybe tomorrow, but not right now." She paused, "What are you going to say?"

"What do you mean?"

"I don't want to tell people how he died. Your father wouldn't like that at all."

"I'm sure they'll figure something out with the police being here."

"Why don't we just say that he was out for a walk and he had another stroke. That would be good enough, don't you think?"

The next morning I called Aunt June with the story we'd agreed on. Her husband, Uncle Jack, died of cancer a year earlier so I figured she was the best to handle the situation. Mom and her sister had remained very close during Dad's aneurysm and Uncle Jack's sickness. Aunt June arrived just after lunch and quickly took charge. Before we knew it, she had spread the word to all of the other relations on Mom's and Dad's sides. Mom spent four full hours responding to the many calls of condolence she received, repeating the same fib over and over again.

Mom felt strongly that we couldn't hold a funeral without Chuck. She and Aunt June had a long discussion with Father Stemming at our church in Bowmanville and decided that it would be acceptable if Dad was cremated immediately and the funeral was put off until Chuck could return. Cremation would save a large amount of money that Mom didn't have, in any case.

—

Chuck docked in Seattle on schedule and immediately flew home. I drove down to pick him up at the Airport. His full beard had grown in; two inches long but neatly trimmed. It was as dark as the rest of his head. He still carried the Montreal Canadiens duffle bag over his shoulder.

"Dad took his own life." I had waited until we were out of the public area and sitting together in the car. "He filled his pockets with stones and walked off the pier." I couldn't get myself to say the word suicide; I don't know why. Perhaps it's too clinical. Maybe it had too many negative connotations, but the word itself just bothers me. It's not the action that offends me, but the word itself. It physically hurts my ears to hear it.

"Oh, no, no, no." Chuck thought for a second. "That's bad. How does Mom feel about it?"

"It's hard to tell. You know how she can be. I get the feeling that she resents it. She gave him her whole life and he just abandoned it, like it didn't matter at all."

We both sat quietly in the car, driving up highway 400 to the 401, until Chuck spoke again.

"You know, a guy doesn't define himself by his past. Maybe when he's 85 and can look back at his life. But that's not until he's old. When a guy's young, like us or maybe even Dad's age, he defines himself by his future. By his plans and how he's going to make life better.

"Think about it. When you're talking to a bunch of guys, they talk about the past, sure. But what makes their eyes light up is when they talk about the boat they're gonna buy when they retire, or the car they're fixing up. Or they talk about the cottage they're gonna build up on the lake. Or even at work, they don't talk about what they've already done. They talk about what they're gonna do to make things better. It's all in the future.

"When you think about it, life can look pretty crummy if a guy spends his time thinking about the past. He struggles from one job to another hoping to do something important. When he looks back, he has nothing good to look at. All he sees is the long hours of work and the fights with his boss. Look at Dad. He works so hard for so many years. He comes home late. And he never grumbles about it 'cause he always has a plan for how life's gonna be better in the future.

"But then he gets sick and the future's all gone. And if a guy doesn't have a better future to look forward to, then he doesn't have anything at all, does he? His reason for living is gone. It just becomes—what's the point?"

"Do you think that's what happened to Dad?"

"Maybe."

We drove quietly for several more minutes before I spoke again.

"I've got more bad news. Kathleen left me."

"Oh shit." He twisted in his seat and put his hand on my shoulder. "I'm really sorry; just out of the blue?"

"She'd been seeing this guy—for a year. I didn't know anything about it. And now she's pregnant; so she just packed up and left."

"Oh man, that's a punch in the gut. Pregnant, eh?"

"It just didn't happen with us. You know how hard we tried, and she wanted a baby so bad." I was resigned.

"That's really tough." He paused again while I stared straight ahead at the road.

"I don't think I'll ever understand women," Chuck went on, "I don't understand how they think. I don't understand how they feel. I don't understand why they do anything they do. She wants a baby so bad, and then she just gives up everything for it. How can we understand that, and how can we judge her if we can't even understand her? That's what I figure.

"This will go down as a bad year for our family, won't it?" he continued.

"A death and a divorce. I guess so."

"So it's what I say. The past can be pretty crummy but the future is always bright."

"My future looks pretty bleak right now."

"Are you planning for another divorce?"

"No."

"Or another death?"

"No."

"So maybe things don't exactly seem bright right now, but you've got to admit that at least the future is brighter than the past, right?"

"It's pretty tough to look at any sort of bright future right now," I said.

"I don't think we can expect to be all sunny today, but once we're done with this we'll be able to see the sunrise again. And that's something to look forward to."

"That's quite poetic." I smiled, for the first time in weeks.

"You spend enough time on a ship and sunrises and sunsets take on a new meaning. In the summer, when you're halfway back from Tokyo, you're about as far north as you can get. You can see the sky start to glow just after three in the morning. Everybody else is still asleep but it's the start of a whole new day. Everything is brighter; the future is always brighter. At sea it happens every 24 hours. On land, I guess it doesn't happen so often, but the sunrise is still there. You just gotta get out of bed to look at it."

—

The evening before the funeral, we had a reception at the Morris Funeral Chapel on Division Street. It was very nice to see a number of people from the Goodyear plant come, both his former managers and his employees. They had nothing but nice things to say about him.

Dad's ashes were kept in a wooden box. It looked like a jewelry box. There were bouquets of flowers in vases on either side. I looked at the cards; there were some from his friends and a nice bouquet from Goodyear. Even Kathleen was thoughtful enough to send a small bouquet. She'd handwritten, "I'm thinking of you at this time of sorrow, Kathleen." Mom commented that it was nice of her not to include Rob's name on it.

Father Stemming led a very nice funeral service at church the next afternoon. All of Mom's and Dad's brothers and sisters and most of our cousins came into town. Christine even flew in from Calgary.

Standing around the funeral home afterwards, we quietly swapped the same old stories of Dad's younger days. The same old stories that his brothers shouted and laughed at many years earlier.

Chuck noticed the change in mood.

"When we're growing up, our friends laugh at all the crazy things we're gonna do. But when we get old, the planning stops, doesn't it? That might be just what getting old is. It's not when you can't run or jump any more. It's when we can't make plans anymore."

"Maybe we'd all be happier if we spent less time making dreams and spent more time living for today, like John Lennon says," Christine replied.

"That song's a load of crap," Chuck said. "It's only drug addicts and alcoholics who live for today. Spend some time hitchhiking and meet these guys and you'll know what I mean. It's the people who live for tomorrow, who have families and build bridges and fly to the moon. These are the good people."

Christine replied, "I think he was talking more about after we're dead; about going to heaven or hell."

"It's all the same thing," Chuck went on. "When we're young we make plans for our own future. Then when we get to middle age, we make plans for our kids. And then once we retire, we can plan for a better future in heaven."

"I didn't know you were so spiritual," she observed.

"We're Anglican, aren't we?" He shrugged. "We keep our religion quiet."

—

It was only two weeks after the funeral that Mom had the insurance settled and the house up for sale.

"June and I are going to get a nice place up in Peterborough," she said. "It's in the middle between you boys and her family, so we'll be able to visit any time we want. But it's far enough from the city that we can afford something on our savings, and use our pensions for travel if we like."

"Don't you think you should take some time before you made any big decisions?" I asked. "With the insurance, you don't have to worry about staying where you are for a while."

"Why wait?" she said. "There's nothing keeping me in Toronto. We want to take a trip to Ireland next summer."

"You're planning that already?"

"Sure. Why not? I've already written a letter to the tourism board asking for information. We'd like to do a rail tour if we can and see the whole country."

"You're not letting any grass grow under your feet, are you?"

"For the past forty years I've been looking after you boys and your father. Cooking and cleaning and worrying about whatever you were up to. Even if we went on a vacation somewhere, I still had to look after the three of you, didn't I. And then your father got sick and I had a whole new set of worries. Well, I'm done with that now. No more worrying for me. After forty years of looking after everyone else I'm going to spend some time looking after myself."

"I didn't realize we were such a burden," I chuckled.

"Not a burden, dear. Just constant worry. But I'm done with all that now."

"Won't you want to settle down again? Maybe get married again some day?"

"Absolutely not. For a woman, marriage is nothing but work and worry. Hopefully I'll meet a nice man, and if I want a roll in the hay, so be it."

I was stunned that Mom could say such a thing, but she went on.

"But I'm not going to be washing anybody's dirty underwear again. Not this girl. Life's too short for that."

CHAPTER TWENTY

"Hey," Chuck announced. "Do you remember Fred Willis?"

I thought for a second. "No, who's he?"

"You remember, from hitchhiking to Montreal, the salesman."

"You mean when we were kids? That was years ago."

"Yeah, that's right. You remember him, don't you?"

"I can barely remember someone I met last week. What about him?"

"I'm working for him now. I'm the new sales rep for Superior Flooring. That's his own company now. I handle everything from Bowmanville to Kingston."

"How did you find him again?"

"I still got his card."

"From all those years ago?"

"Sure."

"Did he remember you?"

"Oh yeah. Guys like him remember everyone."

"And he gave you a job right away?"

"Pretty well. First I go to the address on his card, but the guy there says he's moved down the street. So I go there and he's sitting in his office and I walk in and I say 'Hi, I'm Chuck. Remember me?' And it takes him a second but then he says 'Sure, I remember you. You're the Habs fan.' And then I tell him all about selling meat door to door like he says, and selling cars too. And then he says he needs a Territory Manager, but that's just a fancy name for salesman in Bowmanville, so he hires me on the spot.

"And then we talk for a while about flooring and it's time for lunch so he takes me out to a pub right next to his shop. We have a few drinks and he's all happy about having a new salesman 'cause they've got nothing going on out here and he wants to get something going."

—

I set my computer up in the living room and had all my books, both on astronomy and computer programming, in stacks on the floor. The Altair had quickly become a favourite among astronomers like myself. Programming instructions for orbital calculations on the planets, the stars and all of the known comets were being mailed back and forth across North America. Each of us would make changes, adjustments or improvements before sending them onto the next man in the chain. Programming was a very slow process at the birth of the personal computer. I spent hours in thought and experimentation before each incremental improvement.

Chuck set up his Meccano on the opposite side of the living room. He had a swivel chair set in a corner between two small tables, one for parts and the other for whatever model he was building. At first he created scale models of various freighters and tug boats that he'd seen during his voyages. He had collected enough pieces that he could display several before cannibalizing them for parts for his next creation. He built container ships, including the containers, oil tankers, grain haulers with cranes and vehicle transport ships. With each ship, he'd build a tugboat to pull it out of the harbour.

After these, he moved on to more detailed models of the ships' engines. These would end up being about a cubic foot in size with as many moving parts as possible. Axels turned, pistons went up and down and propellers sticking off the side of the table rotated as he turned a hand crank.

It took him several weeks to finish each model, working three or four hours a night. We sat at either side of the room. Chuck chatted away about his traveling adventures, pausing once in a while to say, "Come 'ere. Take a look at this," while he held up his newest invention. He bought stacks of old Meccano magazines from a used magazine store in Toronto and used these as a source of inspiration.

Chuck's chatter, and when he wasn't talking, his whistling, might have been distracting when I tried to concentrate on a new programming problem, but there is a level of comfort between two brothers that isn't possible in any other relationship. A brother will never accuse a brother of, "not listening to me," just because he doesn't get an immediate response to whatever he was saying at the moment.

—

One evening in July, Chuck had barbecued pork chops for supper. We were nearly finished eating when the phone rang. Chuck picked it up and listened for a minute.

"I've got to go over to Debbie's," he said, grabbing his keys. "Something's wrong."

I finished the dishes and was well into my evening of programming when they returned. Debbie sat in one of the wicker chairs on the porch while Chuck came in for iced tea.

"It's real bad," he said on his way back outside.

Although the front window was open I could only hear mumbles and sobs and long periods of silence from the porch. Chuck pulled his chair up to hers so that the arms were rubbing against each other with each slight movement of their bodies. They held hands. Debbie was twisted to her left to look Chuck directly in the face. She was crying slowly, and even in the dim light coming from the living room I could see a dark swelling on her cheek.

At 10 o'clock, Chuck came back in.

"I'm just driving Debbie home. Are you staying up?"

"Sure. I want to watch the news."

It was well after eleven when Chuck came back. Knowlton Nash was describing the latest in a never ending series of tragedies in Lebanon.

Chuck sat down next to me on the chesterfield as we watched another video of rocket launchers in the desert.

"What's going on?" I asked.

"Roy's hitting her now, and kicking her too."

"I could see in the window. How bad is she hurt?"

"She's got big bruises on her chest, and on her legs."

"That's terrible. Is this the first time?"

"Yeah."

"I thought he wasn't at home anymore?"

"Mrs. Spinolli kicks him out, and then a couple of months later he's back again."

"So she lets him come back?"

"Yeah. He promises he's stopped drinking and says how sorry he is and that he'll never do it again, so she lets him come home and they're fine for a while and then it starts up again."

"This has been going on since we were kids."

"Yeah, but this is the first time for Debbie. It's always her Mom. But now it's Debbie too."

"That's just horrible."

We sat watching the rest of the news and the opening jokes of Johnny Carson.

"Can you drive me downtown?" Chuck asked.

"Now?" I asked. "It's late."

"Yeah. I don't want to take my car."

"What are you going to do?"

"Teach him a lesson."

"Is that a good idea?"

"Somebody's gotta do something and it might as well be me 'cause nobody else will."

"But–"

"Don't worry." He stopped me. "You don't have to get into it. I just need you to drive me down."

We parked a half a block away from *The Imperial*, the local rummies' watering hole, waiting for closing time.

"How do you know he's here?" I asked.

"He's here every night. At least when he's drinking. He doesn't come when he's sober."

"Are you sure you should be doing this?" I asked. "You've been warned about fighting, remember?"

"Don't worry about that. I'm completely clean now. A perfect English gentleman."

"Will people still think that after tonight?"

"Oh yeah."

Shortly after closing time, at 1 AM, the last few men wandered out of the bar. When he caught a glimpse of Mr. Spinolli, Chuck jumped out his door.

"I need you to follow me, okay?" he said to me quickly.

"Where are you going?"

"Just follow me," he ran off.

"Hey! Roy! How ya doing?"

I could hear Chuck through my open window. Mr. Spinolli looked up just as Chuck caught up with him at his car. The situation actually looked friendly. Chuck put his arm over Mr. Spinolli's shoulder as they chatted. After a few seconds, Mr. Spinolli handed over his keys and walked around to the passenger side. It looked as if Chuck convinced him that he'd had too much to drink. Just before climbing into the drivers' seat, Chuck took a quick look back in my direction.

I started the car and followed them down the 57 to Waverly Road south of town, to the quarry. Although the east end of the limestone quarry was still operational, after many years of production, the west end was no longer being worked. A chain link gate had broken open years earlier, creating a hangout for teenagers. They'd sit on the pit's edge and toss empty beer bottles fifty feet onto the rocks below. The quarry's security guard was a man in his 70s, who had been injured years earlier as a shovel operator. He patrolled the East end, where all of the valuable machinery was located, but rarely came down to shout at the kids partying at the West end.

The area was empty at 1:30 AM on a weeknight when Chuck pulled up near the edge. I parked about twenty yards behind him. I was nervous that Chuck was going to use the remote location to beat the hell out of Mr. Spinolli. In the past, his lessons in manners consisted of a quick jab to the gut and a, "smarten up", but he had never driven to this distant location before. I envisioned Mr. Spinolli lying on the ground with his face swollen and lips split.

"Let's get out and have a drink," Chuck said as he rounded the trunk and opened Mr. Spinolli's door. "I've got a bottle of CC here."

"Okay, sure." Mr. Spinolli said as he stepped out of the car. "Why'd we drive all the way up here? I've gotta work tomorrow, you know."

Chuck pulled a full bottle of Canadian Club Whiskey out of his jacket and handed it to Mr. Spinolli. "Here, you crack it open."

Mr. Spinolli twisted open the cap and took one short pull on the bottle. "Can't have too much or I'll be sick as a dog in the morning."

"Sure thing." Chuck replied, taking the bottle back. "Here, let me have some."

Chuck took a few gulps of the rye whiskey, (it would have burned my throat terribly) and put the bottle on the ground. He slowly took five steps to the edge of the pit and Mr. Spinolli followed naturally.

I was expecting Chuck's lesson to start any second but what happened was over so quickly that I didn't believe it had actually happened.

Without saying a word, Chuck reached his left hand behind and grabbed Mr. Spinolli's belt. With his right hand, he reached up and grabbed his shirt collar. Although Chuck was several inches shorter, he was certainly more powerful and had caught Mr. Spinolli by surprise.

With two quick steps, Mr. Spinolli was over the edge. Chuck hadn't thrown him, but simply walked him right over the edge.

"Oops," was the only sound Mr. Spinolli made as he went over. There was no scream or "Aaaaahhhh!" we might see on TV. Just,

"Oops," as if he had missed one step on his porch.

I stared through my windshield for several seconds before I understood what I had just seen. It was so quick that if I'd glanced away, I would have noticed the pair happily drinking together one second and Chuck standing alone the next.

He leaned over the edge for a moment and turned back to Mr. Spinolli's car.

"What the hell did you do?" I stepped out of my car. "What just happened?"

"We're done with him now." Chuck stepped towards Mr. Spinolli's car and closed both doors. "Mrs. Spinolli doesn't have to worry about him anymore. Debbie doesn't have to worry anymore. He's just gone."

"But you killed him?"

"Just teaching him a lesson. Nothing else will work on a guy like him."

Chuck picked up the bottle of whisky. This was the first time I'd noticed that he was wearing work gloves. He must have put them on at the bar. He screwed the cap back on and tucked it into his jacket. He was very calm.

"You had this all planned?"

"Yeah."

"But that's murder!"

"He deserves it. No one is going to miss him."

"You can't do this!"

"It's already done, isn't it."

I was repelled by his complacency.

"Let's go, okay." He said.

"Chuck, we have to help him." I implored. "We have to see if he's okay."

I looked over the edge of the quarry. In the half moonlight, I could see Mr. Spinolli at the bottom, with his head towards the cliff wall. The surface was littered with rocks; some of them two feet across. His obviously dead body was bent over one of them.

Chuck walked over and put his arm around my shoulders.

"Look– he's gone. There's nothing we can do for him now; but he won't be hurting Mrs. Spinolli and Debbie anymore, will he? Let's go home."

He paused for a few seconds and pulled the bottle out of his jacket. He unscrewed the top and took another pull, then wiped off the bottle top and dropped it over the cliff edge. It smashed on the rocks, next to Mr. Spinolli's body. Then he wiped the cap on his pant leg and dropped it on the ground at our feet.

"Come on, let's go," he said. "We should leave."

He got into the driver's side and started my car. I was very shaky getting into the passenger side.

"Look," he said as we drove home. "A man's duty is looking after his family. You know that. A man who doesn't look after his wife and his daughter, he's not a man at all, is he? He's just an animal. And it's up to guys like us to do something about it, isn't it?"

Even though we got home very late and I didn't sleep at all, Chuck wouldn't allow me to call in sick. He wanted to behave completely normally. The best I could do is stare at my drafting table all day and hope that no one noticed that I rarely lifted a pencil.

—

Mr. Spinolli's body was found by a quarry worker the next day but it wasn't until Thursday that Chuck's friend Francis came over in uniform.

"I guess you know that Mr. Spinolli is dead?" Francis asked Chuck.

"Yeah. That's what Debbie says. Drunk again."

"That's what we figure too." Francis paused to look at us. "But we have to ask a few questions anyway. You were with Debbie on Tuesday night?"

"Yes."

"What time did you leave?"

"I don't know. About ten. Maybe 10:30."

"And did you come straight home?"

"Yes."

I noticed that Chuck's traditional "yeah" had changed to the formal "yes".

Francis looked at me. "Is that right?"

"Yes, that's right."

"And you spent the rest of the night together?"

"Yes," I answered. Chuck nodded.

"Okay then. Like I said, he probably just got drunk and fell over the edge. The guy was a bastard and no one at the station gives a damn."

"Was there nothing you could do about him?" I asked. "You must have known what was going on. Everybody in town knew, even if nobody talked about it."

"Look, we were over there all the time. I must have picked him up a dozen times myself. But Mrs. Spinolli would never lay a complaint against him, so there was nothing we could do. We'd keep him locked up until he was sober and let him go. We had no choice."

"That's crap," Chuck said. "He's beating up on her all the time and there's nothing you can do."

"Tell me about it. We would have loved to put him away for a long time. But she kept forgiving him and taking him back."

"How's she taking it now?" I asked.

Chuck spoke up. "She's really shaken, doesn't know what to do with herself now. She's kinda lost."

"I guess it will take some time for her to understand it all."

"Debbie will help her."

"I think that Debbie's got her own problems to work out, from what I've seen."

"Yeah. I'll help her as much as I can. She's got a lot of years of stuff to get over."

I had retained my composure while Francis was in the living room, but started to shake when he'd left.

"I didn't think I'd be able to hold it together." I said.

"I'm not worried about it." Chuck replied. "You can see that even the police don't care. The world is better off with him gone."

"Couldn't you have just beat him up or something? You said you were going to teach him a lesson, that's all…"

"No. Beating him up won't help. It's not like he has any control over it. He just loses his temper. Like a little baby or something."

"But even babies grow out of it."

"He's 65. He's not going to change. It's just a part of him and Mrs. Spinolli and Debbie don't have to live with it anymore."

We looked at each other in silence for a moment or two. To Chuck, it seemed that killing Mr. Spinolli was the only possible solution. There was no nervousness in his voice.

"Look," he said. "You don't blame a dog that's got rabies. You just take care of it. It's just the same thing here."

"But how did you know that I wouldn't say something?"

He was puzzled by this strange question. I might as well have asked him how many fairies can dance on the head of a pin.

"We're brothers," he answered, going back to his latest Meccano design.

CHAPTER TWENTY-ONE

Of course, Chuck excelled in the flooring game. He was a natural.

"All the people we knew growing up, they've all got their own houses now and they're fixing them up. All the guys I knew; all the girls. Everybody wants to have a nice house so it's easy to sell them a new floor.

"But the big sales come from contractors who are doing big housing developments. And they're my friends, too. You remember Tony Salco, from school?"

"Not really."

"He's a big contractor now. His Dad's company, but he runs it now. They're doing the new development out on Johnson Road. Twenty seven houses and I'm doing it all; carpeting, hardwood, linoleum, even ceramic tiles. His customer gets to choose what they want and he buys it all from me."

—

A new Managing Partner was brought in to our office at HBA. Ron Wilson was transferred from Niagara Falls to help us improve revenue. He was several years younger than me but was a real up-and-comer, as they say. He had been promoted several times and moved around through a few offices. Ron was about 5'11" with short blonde hair and a strong build. His specialty was in business development. I'd swear that he worked sixteen hours a day, seven days a week. No, I should say six and a half days a week because he always spent Sunday evenings with his wife, Leslie.

During the day, Ron was a whirlwind of activity. Talking on the phone to clients or prospective clients and then to the other offices as he put project plans together. He was always running out to meetings or lunches or golf games. He quickly fulfilled his role of doubling our office revenue with a number of new projects.

But at night, after the rest of us went home and the office was quiet, Ron put in another full day doing the same, normal engineering work that the rest of us did from nine to five. Any night of the week, other than Sunday, that I happened to drive through downtown, I could see the lights still on at eleven. More than a few occasions, I could tell that he'd slept on the couch in his office.

Ron was an avid trophy hunter and it wasn't long before stuffed animals appeared at the office. Every summer he took a trip up north and invariably came home with a few additions. He had three Canada Geese flying in formation on his wall, a wolf's head in the reception area and a black bear head next to his door. He spoke of mounting a moose head with a six foot antler spread but we had no place to put it. He settled for smaller animals eventually, like a weasel he'd shot in Timmins. He put the same passion into his annual hunting trips that he put into his work.

Surprisingly for someone so driven in his work, Ron was a really nice guy who often stopped to chat about his latest hunting conquest.

"You see this," Ron said one Friday afternoon as he pulled a bullet from the pocket of his denim jacket. He was leaving right after work for a long weekend of hunting up near Tobermory. "Sure, it's just a 22, right? Can't hurt a flea right?"

I nodded and shrugged in response.

"Well, that's just what the animals think. They look at me with my little pop gun and they laugh and say, 'you can't catch me.' But, oh, they are wrong."

He showed me the bullet more closely.

"This little boy's got 40 grams of lightening inside and a hollow point just to make sure the job gets done right. Fourteen hundred feet per second when it leaves the muzzle and it's still doing a thousand at a hundred yards. Say I stop on the side of the road and there's a coyote out in the field, maybe 100 or 150 yards away. He's looking at me like, why do you even bother. But I put this little fellow in the chamber and aim a little high and, 'pop'. Boy is he surprised!"

Ron had a faraway look in his eyes.

"I'll have to take you out one day just to show you what it's like."

I knew that he was just being polite, but he and Leslie did have the office over for dinner in January. The menu solely consisted of things that he'd shot, including venison, moose and beaver sausage. He even had the stereotypical polar bear rug laid out in front of the fireplace.

It was through Ron that I learned why I'd never become a partner.

"You're a great engineer," he said, "one of the best. But the senior partners are really looking for people who are good at business development. Bringing in new business. But don't worry," he said without a pause, "you'll always be looked after. We can't afford to lose someone as good as you."

—

It seemed that the remainder of Chuck's girlfriends had gotten married while he was at sea. And the guys he'd played pool with were stuck at home with children of their own by now. The new crop of bachelors at the bar was a generation younger than us so he was not interested in spending nights out on the town. He continued to see Debbie from time to time, but with her father gone, she felt responsible for looking after Mrs. Spinolli. The joyous teenage girl we'd met so long ago had been replaced by a demure spinster.

"She doesn't dream anymore," Chuck said one evening. "She's old now."

"Isn't that the definition of being an adult?" I replied. "Looking after your responsibilities?"

"Sure, she's got her responsibilities, but once we've done that, once we've paid the mortgage and put food on the table, can't we take a few hours and dream?"

"A few hours? After we spend our eight hours at work and make dinner and mow the lawn and fix the eavestrough, who has the time to spend a few hours dreaming?"

"The young," Chuck replied.

—

Chuck's success in the flooring game made him top producer at his company within a few years. In a business where knowing people at the right stage of their life, and being good friends with them was key, Chuck was simply a natural. At least once a month, I was approached by his latest satisfied customer, a long time Bowmanville resident who knew we were brothers.

"Say 'hi' to Chuck for me," or, "tell Chuck to drop by for a beer," or, "Mary sure likes the new tiles," or some such comment.

"Guess what?" Chuck said after returning from a meeting with Mr. Willis. "I'm the new Sales Manager. Fred wants me to teach all the guys my secret."

I laughed. "It's not really a secret, is it? You're friends with everyone in town. Who else would they buy from?"

"Shhhh." Chuck put his finger to his lips. "We don't want to let the secret get out. It looks like I'll be leaving you. I gotta move down to Toronto again. That's okay with you?"

"I think I can manage without your rent. Just think what I'll save on groceries and beer!"

He came back a few weeks later to pick up his Meccano collection, which by this time had grown to fill several boxes, even disassembled.

"So how's it going?" I asked.

"Real good. We've got nine salesmen, a couple of old guys and a bunch our age. Fred always goes on about what a great salesman I am so at least they know I deserve to be the boss."

"Well that helps."

"Yeah. None of them are making my numbers."

"So, you've got to train them?"

"Yeah, but it's not easy to get them moving. They're getting by. Making forty thousand a year. Once they reach that comfort level, it's hard to get them to move past it."

"It's a lot of work for them?"

"No, it's easy. All they've gotta do is get off their asses and knock on some doors. You can hardly call that work."

"It'd be work for me."

"No, sitting there with your pencil, staring at lines and numbers all day, that's work. What you do is hard. Sales is just talking, that's all."

"Then why can't they all do it?"

"They're always looking for reasons. They come in and read the paper and I ask what they're doing and they say, 'looking for new homes being built,' or something like that. And if they get an order it takes them all day to get it in, instead of just 15 minutes, which is what it should take them. Just excuses."

"Sounds like you've got your work cut out for you."

"Yeah. Fred wants me to fire the three worst guys. He says that'll light a rocket up the other guys' asses."

"That's not much fun."

"I gotta do it next week. It's not like a surprise. These guys know what their numbers are. They're just filling in time at work, not going anywhere."

"That'll still hurt."

"Yeah. Fred wants me to do it right away."

"So, what's he like?"

"He's okay. Drinks a lot."

"Oh?"

"Every day. No matter what we're doing. Twelve o'clock sharp we walk around the corner to the restaurant. As soon as we sit down he orders a gin and tonic. He finishes it before the food even comes and orders another one. He gets the same thing every day, a steak sandwich. And by the time he's finished that he has another drink. Every day."

"Three drinks, at lunch?"

"At least. Some days we stay till two and he has a couple more. He gets talking about what's going on and he just doesn't stop. He thinks the guys down the street have bugged our office."

"Really? You're bugged?"

"No, but it's a good excuse for us to have our meetings at the restaurant. He gets going about how bad things are and I let him ramble on."

"Is he always like that?"

"In the mornings he's sharp as a tack, has a real good eye for what's going on. But after lunch I don't even waste my time. Just try to figure out an excuse to get out of the restaurant and back to work. But he just keeps talking and I'm stuck there until he quits. Sometimes we're there all afternoon. He's usually griping about one of the suppliers or one of the staff. He's always got a complaint about someone or other."

"Is he an alcoholic?"

"I think so. Sometimes we stay after work and he keeps drinking. It's pretty bad."

"Does he at least buy you lunch?"

"Every day," Chuck smiled. "They have a great steak and kidney pie, so it's hard to complain."

—

The astronomy world was lit up that year with the first discovery of a planet orbiting a main sequence star, 51 light years from Earth. There had been discoveries of planets around pulsars a few years earlier, but a planet around a star was the first indication to the general media that life could possibly exist elsewhere in the universe. The planet 51 Pegasi-b was identified in the Pegasus constellation. It was labeled as a Hot Jupiter because it was located so close to its host star. But this was also the reason for its detection. Being so close to its star gave it significant gravitational pull.

Doppler spectroscopy was used to measure variations in light coming from the star. The gravitational pull of a planet orbiting the star causes a slight wobble in the star's own position, moving it slightly closer to or further away from the Earth and shifting the red-blue light.

The discovery led me to start researching the formation of planets, which of course leads back to the basic physical properties of solar nebula; the dust and gases that came together to form our own sun and planets. My thought, given the placement of planets around the sun, was that the physical properties of the solar nebula were very similar to those of an accretion disk. After the formation of the sun, or at least a proto-sun, the nebula flattened out from its uniform three-dimensional shape to the relatively flat two-dimensional shape that we know. This was caused by the sun's gravity pulling in the nebula particles into an inward spiral. The gathering of the material into bands allowed for the formation of planets. This might not have occurred if the materials had remained uniformly diffused around the sun.

Thus, my hypothesis was that a solar system essentially followed the same accretion disk pattern that we clearly see in our galaxy, on a much larger scale.

I spent several months looking at this, including numerous Saturdays at the University of Toronto library. It was a long trip down but I found that the quiet of the library, along with its studious atmosphere, helped to focus my thinking. The University has a highly respected Department of Astronomy and Astrophysics, including a large collection and connections to many other universities. I was surprised by the willingness of researchers as far away as London and Berlin to respond quickly to my questions.

Chuck and I ate together every time I went to Toronto; either pizza at his townhouse in Richmond Hill or a Mexican restaurant near the University. His ability to eat jalapeño peppers was astonishing. I broke into a sweat with my first bite of a burrito.

At the end of it all, I'd written a 7,000 word paper that I felt was worthy of publication in a scientific journal. I had read enough of these to know the peculiar writing style they were looking for. I sent off a copy to *Planetary and Space Science*, the journal that seemed most appropriate to this topic. I knew to be patient and three months went by before receiving a response.

"Thank you for your submission. Our editorial board has found that similar research was published in the journal *Protostars and Planets*; University of Arizona Press, 1985, pp 981-1072. Lin, D.N.C., Papaloizon, J. Therefore, we will not be examining your submission further at this time."

I mailed for a copy of *Protostars and Planets*. The findings presented in their paper were virtually identical to mine. It appeared that I'd missed out on publication by just a few months. I had enjoyed doing the research work but the slog of writing, editing, writing, editing again into a paper suitable for publication made the process disappointing. The discovery of planets had made this a popular topic with astronomers around the world. It was likely that every possible sub-sub category of study was already being examined by PhD students looking for something new.

—

Chuck was doing well in his new Manager's role.

"I'm pretty brutal with the guys," he said. "Brutal, but fair. I have this thought that if a guy does the work and isn't successful, then it's my fault for not teaching him the right way to do it, so I teach him. But if a guy's just dogging it, if he won't get on the phone or make house calls, then it's his fault and I just fire him."

"That's the brutal part."

"Yeah. Brutal but fair. I give him a chance, but I tell him straight out he has to visit 18 houses and one dealer every day."

"That's pretty specific."

"I know what it takes. I don't want these guys getting used to sitting around all day waiting for the phone to ring. If they do that,

I don't want them around. You know. It's not just the money. The money is just a score-card that shows who's winning and who's losing. When a guy pulls up in his new 'Vette, or when he buys a pool for his house, something he can be real proud of, that's like a trophy for a top salesman. He holds it over his head just like the Stanley Cup."

"But he still makes a lot of money."

"Hockey players make a lot of money. But they'd trade in every penny for the Stanley Cup."

"So that's what motivates your salesmen, the Stanley Cup?"

"Pretty much."

"Fred must be really happy with you if you're getting the sales up."

"Depends if it's before lunch or after lunch," Chuck answered. "Before lunch, he's great. We can have a meeting and go over each guy's numbers for last week and what I'm doing about it and he's got lots of suggestions. But after lunch everything changes; one minute he's all buddy buddy, telling me how great I'm doing and all that. Next minute he starts swearing and brings up something I said wrong and he's telling me how I'm tearing apart the company and everybody hates me. Then five minutes later he's all sweet again like nothing happened."

"Holy cow. That must be horrible."

Chuck shook his head. "You have no idea. The other day, we're sitting at the restaurant like normal but he won't get up to leave. So he's getting drunker and finally it's six o'clock and I wanna get out of there 'cause he's already switched back and forth twice."

"What do you mean?"

"Switched back and forth between being my best friend and my worst enemy, twice. I wanna get out of there but he's real drunk. Way too drunk to drive so I gotta drive him home. It's only ten minutes so it's no big deal. In the first five minutes he starts accusing me of selling our secrets to one of the other companies because we don't get this big bid. And he says I'm selling our pricing models. Five minutes later we pull up at his house and he wants me to come in and have a nice dinner with his wife and stay and have drinks and all that."

"What did you do?"

"I tell him that you're in town and I gotta go meet you."

"That's rough."

"Most days I try to spend the afternoons with the guys and out on sales calls. I try to get away just before lunch."

"So he eats alone."

"No, if I'm not around he grabs Russell, he's the Production Manager, or Linda, the accountant. And they're stuck with him for the afternoon."

"They must love you for that."

"Let me tell you, last Wednesday Fred's in a real mood and I can tell someone's gonna get fired. I can just tell it. And I say to myself that it's not gonna be me. He's just in this mood and he's got a look in his eye, you know. So I make up an excuse that I need to go see a guy about a new development over in Burlington. I get out of there and just go home and watch TV all afternoon. The next morning I go in and sure enough one of the installers is gone and Fred calls me in and tells me that he caught him stealing or something. He just makes it up on the spot and fires the guy."

"Jesus. I don't think I could handle it."

"I don't know how much longer I can handle it myself." Chuck answered.

"Shouldn't he be retired by now?"

"He's long past retirement age, but his kids won't have anything to do with him and I don't think he looks forward to spending all day with his wife. He'll keep working and drinking till he drops dead I guess."

"So what are you going to do?"

"What can I do? I'm stuck with it I guess."

"At least until he drops dead."

"With all the gin in him I think he's too well pickled to drop dead."

—

Chuck's situation didn't last. About four months after that conversation, he walked into my office at ten thirty in the morning.

I looked up. "What's going on?"

"Well, Fred's drinking has got the best of me." He pulled a quarter out of his pocket. "I guess its tails this time."

"What happened?"

"Well, last night about three in the morning, Fred starts pounding on my door. He's drunk as a skunk like usual. And I let him in so he doesn't wake up the neighbours and he starts ragging on me about how it's all my fault that we didn't win that contract six months ago and I'm not going to tell him that he's the one who set the prices on it and he keeps yelling at me about a lot of things I'm doing wrong and he just keeps going on for twenty or thirty minutes. So I can't take it anymore and I just say, 'Look, Fred, if you think I'm doing such a lousy job then I'll just quit. Do you think I'm doing a lousy job?'

"And he keeps going on and on. I don't know if he's even listening to anything I say so then I just say, 'Okay, I quit. Now get the hell out of my apartment' and I grab him by the shirt collar and by his belt and I bend him over and run him out on the front lawn and throw him on his face on the grass. And then I reach into his pocket and grab his keys and throw them way down the street so he won't be able to drive and kill someone. And then I go back and get dressed and I drive away. The last I see him, he's still passed out on the front lawn."

I looked at my watch.

"Where have you been all this time?"

"Driving around and drinking coffee, having breakfast, then coming out here."

CHAPTER TWENTY-TWO

It was only two weeks afterwards that Chuck had cleaned out his townhouse and moved back to Bowmanville. Our routine picked up as if he had never left, with evenings spent together in the living room. I had never taken down the card tables that formed his Meccano production factory. Once he'd moved my stacks of books to a shelf on the wall, he was back in business.

"I've got an idea," he said. "A new invention." He was drawing sketches on several sheets of white paper. "You know how the province has that wind mill down by the lake to make electricity?"

"Sure. The wind turbine."

"Well there's all kinds of problems with those things. They're noisy and they hit birds and kill them. I've got this idea for a better one. It's a lot smaller and it won't make as much noise and the birds won't fly into it. It doesn't have any blades. Let me show you what I've got."

He brought a sheet of paper over to my table. I slid my computer keyboard out of the way to the right and my mug of tea off to the left, to avoid spillage. At first glance, his pencil sketch looked like the contracting circles of a conch shell, held with a U shaped bracket.

"The reason for the problems, the noise and the birds, is because they need to make the blades so long. If the blades where shorter they'd spin real fast but wouldn't have any power to turn the generator. What I want to do is take all of the big size of the long blades and make it real compact into a smaller space. So this here," he pointed to the conch circles "is a screw thing."

"Oh, I know what you're talking about," I replied. "We'd call that an Archimedes screw. That's basic mechanical engineering."

"You know the blades on a wind mill, they're not just flat. They're shaped like the wings on a plane. They do the same thing on a sailboat. Doug Graydon, he owns Graydon Chemicals, they supply all the glue for our linoleum, right? Well, last summer he has me out on his sailboat, in a race. Well, the wind doesn't push on the sails like a bed sheet, that's in the olden times. The sails are shaped just like a wing and the wind actually pulls them forward. That's how a sailboat can sail into the wind." He drew a foil shape on his paper and added wind lines.

"But there's more to it than that," he continued. "And this is the neat part of my idea. There's a front sail and a back sail. The back one is the mainsail and the front one is the jib. Well, when the front sail overlaps the mainsail," he continued sketching while he spoke, "there is a gap between them. He calls that the slot.

"Wings work because there is pressure underneath them and less pressure on top, right? So when wind blows in-between the sails, into the slot, there's even more pressure than with a normal wing. This means that there is more lift than normal.

"Now look at this drawing here," he pulled out another piece of paper, "think if we had a wind turbine shaped like this–" he drew his spiral. "You can see that each part of it is shaped just like the sail on the boat. But let's take another step. Let's add another spiral inside the first one. What I've done now is make a slot between them, just like the sails." He shaded in the slot area. "I think this will give as much electricity as a big windmill but with really small blades. What do you think?"

"You're getting into aeronautical engineering here," I said. "That's out of my area."

We didn't even study that at school. After the Avro Aero debacle, no one was talking about aeronautical engineering in the 1960s.

"No problem, I can just build it myself with my Meccano."

"If we knew what we were doing we could probably perfect it on paper first. It would be much easier than building it over and over. That's the whole point of engineering, you know."

"Oh well. I've got nothing but time on my hands anyway, don't I?"

—

For the next few days, Chuck tried putting together his basic design using only the plates, strips, nuts and bolts from his Meccano box. Each day I'd come home to see another of his ships or motors in pieces as he cannibalized the required parts. He was, in essence, attempting to build one spiral sea shell inside another. After a week of attempts he realized that the Meccano plates, with all the nuts and bolts needed to hold them together, would not be flexible enough to create the required shape.

He pulled a plastic, 3-ring binder off my bookshelf. "Can I have this binder?"

"Sure. Just don't throw away my papers."

He opened the binder and put a rubber band around the hundred sheets of paper before putting them back on the shelf. In a moment he had pulled the rings and metal spine out, leaving just a sheet of red plastic with two creases where the spine had been.

"Maybe this will work." He said, curling it into a spiral.

Over the next week, Chuck went to the drug store several times and came home with more binders that he immediately pulled apart to create more versions of his seashell blades. What started as a simple idea in design became quite a challenge in practice. He was using shears to cut the thick plastic and his Meccano nuts and bolts to hold the pieces of plastic in place.

He ended up with a red plastic spiral, about 12 inches across, nestled inside another, slightly larger, blue spiral. The centre of the spirals was a coat hanger wire, about 18 inches long, supported on each end by a pyramidal shaped tower of Meccano. He brought a table fan from the basement and set it in front of the contraption.

"Plug it in," he said.

His wind turbine started to turn, reaching its maximum speed in about ten seconds. "See, it works," he used his pencil to point to the back half of the spiral. "This is the slot. It's what makes it go so fast."

"Is it really turning any faster than a normal wind turbine?" I asked. "Have you compared it?"

"You can just see it's going fast."

"Sorry, but in the engineering world we don't say 'you can just see it.' You have to test it and get real measurements and empirical proof."

"How do I do that?"

"Well, you could build a model of a wind turbine and take measurements to compare."

"But it has to be perfect to make the comparison any good?"

"I'll tell you what. On Saturday, let's go down to the engineering library at the University of Toronto. We can probably find something."

Of course academic research was beyond Chuck's ability, but the interest in wind power around the world meant there were numerous papers in engineering periodicals that U of T subscribed too. We spent the first hour looking through microfiche catalogues of the University's collection. Chuck sat in the stall beside me, completing pencil sketches of his ideas, while I stared at the glowing screen and moved the glass microfiche slides back and forth.

We settled on three articles published over the previous year and a half in *IEEE Spectrum* magazine. They were technical, but not to the level of an academic PhD thesis. I figured Chuck would be able to work through them.

"Go and copy these," I said. "Do you have any dimes?"

Chuck jingled his pants. "A pocketful."

"Okay. There's a photocopier over in that room," I pointed. "Go for it."

We stopped for burgers on the way home. It was mid-afternoon so the crowd was thin and we could spread the photocopies across a couple of tables, after wiping them carefully with napkins. With a pair of pencils, we both marked up the drawings as I interpreted the dimensions.

"You've got a diameter of about 12 inches?" I asked.

"12 ¾ for the outer spiral."

"Okay, if we look at these ratios here," I continued to work up the drawings, "I can give you the exact dimensions for a wind turbine with the same diameter."

"You want me to build that?"

"That's right. I don't know enough about it to model it on paper. And we don't have any of the computer programs at work, so that's the only way to do it."

"Okay. Whatever it takes."

When I got home on Monday, Chuck was carefully carving the turbine blades out of wax, using callipers to ensure the dimensions were exactly as I'd drawn out the day before.

On Tuesday, I found him creating a *plaster of Paris* mold of the blades. He'd mounted three wax blades in a shallow Tupperware tray that he carefully filled with plaster.

"What I'm gonna do after the plaster dries tomorrow," he said, "is heat it up in the oven really slow so it doesn't crack. Then the wax will drip out the holes on the end here. Then I'll fill the holes back up with epoxy, and after that dries I'll have perfect blades. I just have to break the plaster off."

He was out bowling when I came home on Wednesday, but by Thursday he'd made the next step. He had three perfectly shaped six inch blades in epoxy. He was using coat hanger wires to connect the blades to a central gear from his Meccano set. By eight o'clock, he had the mini-windvane set up in front of the fan.

"I've got a little piece of plastic sticking out from this blade here. It will click against this other gear here every time it goes past the bottom. That'll turn these counting gears so we know how many times it spins around in a minute."

He turned on the fan and we watched for a half a minute while his windvane got up to speed before he engaged the counter. He kept his eye on the second hand of the large clock that he'd brought out from the kitchen. At the one minute mark, he disengaged the counter gears.

"Okay. This 72 tooth gear has gone around 3 and a bit, that's 216 and we times that by 2." He was using his pencil and paper to do the multiplication. "That's 432. And this 36 tooth gear has gone around by 1 and–" he counted individual teeth with his pencil "–1,2,3,4,5,6,7 clicks, so that's 43. And the total is 475. Now I've got to do the same thing with my seashell turbine. That's what I'm calling it."

He moved the bladed vane off the table and put his new design in its place. He'd built them to exactly the same dimensions, so it fit perfectly into the counter system. He had always been meticulous about his Meccano contraptions. He ran the test again and came up with 513 revolutions.

"That's not much of a difference," I said.

"No. This count doesn't really matter at all. The vanes are just spinning free. But in real life they'll be turning a generator, right. So they'll have to turn against something. Resistance." He turned around behind his chair. "Watch this."

Chuck connected a string to the central shaft of the 72 tooth gear on his counter. The string hung down to the floor beneath the card table. Another Meccano gear was tied to the end of the string as a weight and he could add more pieces as needed.

"Each of these weights is about 4 grams, so what I really want to know is if the seashell vane can lift more than the blade vane, while they're still spinning at full speed."

He moved the blade vane back into place and started the fan. Once the vane was spinning at full speed, he started adding weights to the string. The clicking of his counter slowed slightly with each additional weight, but the 6th piece was the proverbial straw that broke the camel's back and the vane stopped completely. He removed the 6th piece and the vane slowly came back up to speed.

"So let's say it stops at 6. That's 24 grams. Now let's try the seashell."

The difference was immediately obvious. He kept adding weights until the vane stopped turning at 19 or a total of 76 grams.

"Well there you go," he said. "Not only does it turn faster but it can pull three times the weight. I think I've got the proof you're looking for, right?"

"I can't argue with the facts," I said.

"So what I gotta do now is make it better. This is pretty rough. I gotta make the shape just perfect. And I can't use these plastic binders anymore. It's gotta be out of tin or something. I've got an idea for a way to make it adjustable, so that I can turn a screw to move the seashells a tiny bit at a time to figure out the best shape."

Later that week, I came home to find a sheet metal roller and a sheet metal punch set up in the living room. They were well used manual models, at least 30 or 40 years old from the look of the cast iron. Chuck had moved the chesterfield back so that it was almost in the hallway. It didn't impact our television viewing anyway, since it was usually covered with my books or whatever jackets we happened to throw on it when we walked in the door.

"It's a good thing we're bachelors," I said. "I can't imagine a woman putting up with this."

—

It took Chuck months longer than he'd planned to create his perfect seashell turbine. He used the sheet metal roller to curl pieces of tin into shape, connecting them together with the hole punch and rivet gun. His work efforts were rewarded by a moving parade of Band-aids covering his hands from the sharp tin edges.

As weeks passed, failed attempts at his 24 inch diameter vane piled up outside the back door. His unwillingness to make detailed notes was a part of the problem. Each successive experiment was not an incremental improvement over the last, rather was a move in a completely new direction.

"I think it's better than number three but not as good as number five," was a typical comment.

"Do you know what made number five better?" I would ask, hoping for a more detailed answer.

"I think I'll just bend this a little more," was his answer, just before sliding a new piece of tin into the rollers.

Chuck was not the least frustrated by the slow progress towards a perfect design. For him, this was nothing more than an advanced Meccano. He was used to tearing down one of his models because two pieces could not be put together as he had envisioned. I gave up on convincing him that it could be done quickly with the proper computer program. With his reading difficulty, there was no way he was about to stare at a computer screen.

Often I'd come home to catch him whistling away at full force as he rolled a foil into shape. He could even be heard from the sidewalk if the windows were open. His version of *Walk Like an Egyptian* was dance-worthy, though he turned down the volume as soon as I walked in the door.

"This is the one!" he said after testing number 17. "It can't get any better. I count 627 revolutions per minute and it can pick up 844 grams of weight." He had changed the small table fan to a three foot diameter, square-framed floor fan for these later tests.

"That's amazing," I said. "I'd swear that you're getting out more than you're putting in. Of course that's impossible."

"That's the whole point of this. When you're sailing, you can go faster than the wind because the sails are working just like a wing. The wind doesn't push the sails, it pulls them. So with this, the fan isn't pushing the blades, it's pulling them. And the slot between the two makes it pull even harder."

A few days later Chuck recognized a problem.

"I'm testing with this one big fan. I have this little wind gauge from Radio Shack and it says the fan is blowing wind at 12 miles an hour, but the wind doesn't just blow at one speed, does it? So I figure I've got to test it at different wind speeds, right from one mile an hour up to say fifty miles an hour."

"You're going to need a heck of a fan to blow at fifty miles an hour," I said.

"That's nothing. I can get a big electric motor and hook it up with belts to this unit. As long as the blades don't blow off I'll be okay."

So Chuck spent another week building his high speed fan.

"I'm right," he said, when he had finished. "This vane works great at 12 miles an hour but it's pretty bad at lower wind speeds and doesn't get any better at higher speeds. So I call Doug and he says that he can't just set the sails the same all the time. When the wind is lower the slot is narrow. And when the wind is high he makes the slot wider."

"This happens automatically?" I asked.

"He has one of his crew whose job it is to pull the sail in and out when the wind changes. I gotta figure out a way for my seashells to move automatically any time the wind changes to open and close the slot."

"What are you going to do? Set up a computer with a wind gauge?"

"I've been thinking of something with springs. When the wind blows stronger the springs will just stretch more and that will open the slot. What do you think?"

"Your simple design is getting a lot more complex."

"Shouldn't be a problem."

"The devil's in the details, you know."

"I'll work on it and see what I come up with."

—

Chuck's variable speed turbine proved to be a greater challenge than he'd hoped, taking nearly six months to solve. He started by coiling his own springs from brass wire, mounted on metal shafts between the two seashells. After many trials and errors, he admitted defeat.

"You know," he said. "A clock keeps good time because it uses a flat kind of spring. They bend the same no matter how much they're stretched out. I'm thinking that might work."

He was right, but it still took him three months with his tin snips and sheet metal roller to prove it. By connecting the inner and outer seashells with several springs on sliding tracks, he was able to get the consistent narrowing or widening of the slot that he needed.

"Now that it works," he said, "I can fine tune it for every wind speed. That should be easy."

It was nearly a full year from the time Chuck started on this project until he was happy with his working model. The pile of scrap tin in our back yard had grown in height and width. Every time he threw his latest failure on the top, it rolled down the back side to make the pile wider.

"It's not going quite as quickly as you expected?" I had asked several months into the design.

"No, but it's a lot of fun. How many guys can say that they play with Meccano all day?" He held up another piece of tin in his Band-aid covered hands.

"Most men can't take a year off to work on a dream project. They've got mortgages and kids to pay for."

"I've got lots of money put away; that's the beauty of getting paid commission, if you're a good salesman."

It seemed true. The rent that Chuck paid me was more than half the mortgage and the utilities combined. And he never missed a month, even during one of his breaks in employment.

—

The big day came when we installed four units along the peak of his friend Dave's old hay barn.

"You're not going to burn the place down, are you?" Dave asked, as we stood watching Chuck shimmy his way across the roof. "Actually," he winked, "it might be better if you did. I could use a new barn."

Chuck spread his 12", 18", 24" and 36" turbines along the peak. Each was connected by a belt to a magnetic coil generator. The output wires were led to the upper hay-loft inside. I connected them to a four input data logger connected to an old Commodore 64 that Chuck picked up from a classified ad in the newspaper.

As always, the devil was in the details. Chuck had to construct boxes that allowed the belts to move freely but were weather proof against rain. And the entire unit had to rotate freely with shifting wind direction. A big part of the design time was used to reduce friction in the process. Chuck's natural mechanical aptitude significantly reduced the amount of trial and error.

Over the course of a month, we saw the full range of weather conditions including a thunder storm. I don't want to think what would have happened to the computer if one of the vanes had been struck by lightning. We had winds up to 37mph recorded on the roof top.

Chuck climbed the barn every day to ensure connections and mounting brackets were secure.

"Look at this," he said, holding a length of bent one inch steel pipe. "This is from the big one."

"That's a lot of surface area there," I said. "You'll have to make them stronger."

"I don't think we can. It's already pulling out the top beam of the roof. Maybe the 24 inch is as big as we can go, if we want to mount it on top of someone's house."

I did the calculations to prove that he was right. A typical framed roof with a 2x6 peak would not have the strength required to support his largest wind turbine.

—

The year had been a strange juxtaposition for Chuck. From his youngest days he truly had been the life of the party, able to fit into any crowd. He had then selected the perfect career for his gregarious nature, a salesman who was selling to the same people he associated with after work.

But he suddenly decided to withdraw from all of that and dedicate himself to working in our living room for hours, days, and eventually for more than 13 consecutive months, on his new project.

I came home every day at 12 minutes past five to find him whistling the latest tune from the radio, having not spoken to a single person all day unless he had made a trip to the hardware store for a new tool or scrap of metal. When I walked in, he would put down whatever he'd been working on and we'd turn the TV on and talk about what to make for supper.

At least once, and sometimes twice a week, he went to Debbie's house in the evening. They had stopped going out on dates some time earlier. "She doesn't like to leave her Mom alone," he said. "I guess she starts to cry. But if I'm there she just putters in the kitchen and we watch TV."

Often times he didn't come home until the next day.

All of Chuck's old friends were still around, although married with families. Once a month or so he was invited to dinner at one home or another.

"And bring your brother too," they would add at the last second.

After introductions came the inevitable, "Chuck, this is my cousin Nancy. She's visiting from Kitchener, or Ottawa, or Timiskaming," or wherever the latest version of cousin Nancy happened to be visiting from. "We thought you two would like to meet."

There was never a cousin Nancy for me.

"Hi there," Chuck would say with his amazingly genuine smile and tone of voice that had brought him so much attention from women in the past. "It's nice to meet you."

I'd sit quietly at a corner of the table while our hosts, Chuck and cousin Nancy held a lively conversation on the topic of the day. Chuck's ability to keep a party light and cheerful had never waned. Sometimes the cousin Nancy would giggle at Chuck's anecdotes, reminiscent of the last time she had been out on a date in her teenage years, before marriage, children and divorce had worn her down. Other times, the cousin Nancy was more cynical, reflecting how marriage, children and divorce had broken her trust in men. And finally, there was the cousin Nancy who had never been married and never would be married for a variety of reasons that I could not fathom other than that she just wasn't fun in the traditional sense. This is probably why I never re-married and was never introduced as a prospective husband.

At the end of the evening, Chuck and I would thank our hosts for dinner. Cousin Nancy would send Chuck off with a warm, long held handshake or a kiss on the cheek or a long, inviting hug. But not once did Chuck call her to ask for a date.

"I'm really tied up with work right now," he'd apologize if he ran into our hosts on the street. Or, "It's just not the right time since I'm not working right now."

It took me several such evenings to notice that whenever he was invited out for dinner, Chuck always spent the following night with Debbie.

—

"You should put a patent on that," I told Chuck as we watched his vane turn.

"I'm already working on it," he answered. "Do you know Martin Wakefield, from school? He's a big lawyer now. His office is just down the street from you. He's working on it for me. But it's not cheap, even if he is giving me a deal. I can't show it to anyone until he's got the application in. Then I can start selling."

"You mean you have to sit around and wait? How long will that take?"

"Sitting around doesn't sound like me, does it?" he asked.

"Have you ever sat still in your life?"

"You know, there's people who go out of their way to do something. And there's people who go out of their way to do nothing. I guess I'm just one of the ones who's always trying to do something, that's all. It actually kind of hurts if I've got nothing to do."

"It hurts?" I asked.

"Yeah. I get real antsy. My legs twitch. They need to be moving. I don't like it."

—

I ran into Kathleen doing back-to-school shopping for her children.

The youngest, a little girl, was hanging onto her leg and three older children were moving up the aisle. Kathleen had the harried look of any woman shopping with four kids, but was certainly the happiest I'd seen.

She introduced me to them as an old friend. They each stuck out their hand when she told me their name. "This is Bernice," she said, "she's going into grade four this year." She must have been named after Kathleen's father. "And this is Robin. She's in grade three. Henry is in grade two and little Dianna is just starting kindergarten. You remember Dianna, my maid of honour?" Kathleen asked.

"Sure."

"She died of cancer." She rested her hand on top of the little girl's head. "A nice way to remember my best friend from growing up."

"You've moved?" I asked. I'd seen a "for sale" sign up on their house some time earlier.

"Oh yes. The house was too small for all of us and the dogs. We've got a place out on Old Scugog Road. A few acres with lots of room for everyone to run around and no neighbours to bother. I've got a nice big garden too. I've just filled the freezer if you'd like some cauliflower." She looked at me.

By this time, the older two were moving further up the aisle towards the running shoes, so we said our goodbyes.

"It was good to see you again," she said, patting my arm. "Do keep in touch. I was sorry to hear about your father. Such a sweet man."

"Thanks," I said as she was pulled away.

—

Chuck ground away at his company, Live Air Industries, day after day, month after month, eventually passing a second year. He spent his mornings working through the Toronto or Hamilton or Windsor telephone books, searching for companies that might have some possible connection to his new design. He bought a $500 suit so that he could walk into an office at Ontario Hydro or General Electric or Magna or any of the larger companies that stretched along the Ontario to Quebec industrial belt. He spent the first year targeting the middle management level at these companies.

"What I want to do," he said, "is find some guy in the company who will champion my product up the ladder."

"So what's happening with that?" I asked.

"Let me tell you, I go and see this guy Bob Miller at Magnum Electrical Products. His card says that he's Manager of Technical Solutions, whatever the heck that means. It says he's a Manager, but I don't think he actually manages anybody. It's just a title to make him feel good. There's probably another hundred guys with the same title."

"Why did you see him?"

"When I call into the office, the receptionist says that he's the guy I should talk to. Or sometimes I talk to one guy and he tells me I should talk to this other guy. And when I talk to him, he says that he's not the guy I should talk to; I should talk to this other guy. It happens like that all the time.

"So I go see this Bob Miller. We're sitting in his office with his desk that's covered with paper. There's two small chairs in front of his desk but the door bumps into one when it's opened so he just leaves it open all the time. There isn't enough room for me to bring in my display trunk so I open it in the hall and just bring in the fan and my seashell vane. I ask him if he's got an extra plug in the wall for my fan and he moves his garbage can out of the way so I can reach the wall plug. There isn't enough space on the floor for me to set up the fan and my vane, so I put the fan on one chair and the vane on the other chair and I stand with my back pressed against the wall so I don't get in the way."

"How did you fit them on the chairs?" I asked.

"It's the same everywhere. I've got to put them on a chair or on top of a pile of papers on his desk or on the floor. They stand on tripods that I can fit on anything no matter how small it is. I can lower them right down if I'm putting them on a desk or I can raise them up if I'm putting them on the floor."

"You built these tripods yourself?"

"Yeah, but the tricky part is getting them to fold up real small so I can fit them inside the trunk that I can roll into the office. What I want to do next is put mounting supports right on the trunk and a little motorcycle battery inside so I don't need any power or anything. I'll use the turbine to recharge the battery."

"You're trying to invent a perpetual motion machine," I joked.

"So I'm in this Bob Miller's office pressed up against the wall for a half hour. He doesn't ask me to move the things off the chairs so I can sit down or anything. I give him the whole pitch and he asks lots of questions about efficiency and how much I've tested it in different wind strengths and things like that. The same stuff that everybody else asks me, so I've got the answers down pat. And he says he really likes it and it's got lots of potential and he's going to bring it up at the next committee meeting.

"And I ask him when that will be and he says they meet on the first and third Wednesday every month, so it's just a week away. I say, 'that's great' and I'll give him a call on Thursday or Friday to see if they like the idea and he says that's fine.

"So a week goes by and I give him a call and ask what the committee thinks and he says that they spent the whole meeting talking about some problem they're having with the power transformer at the St. Catherine's factory so they can't talk about it at all and I should call back in two weeks after their next meeting.

"So two weeks goes by and I call him back again and he says he made a mistake that there's five Wednesdays this month and they meet on the first and third Wednesday of the month so I should call him back in another week after their next meeting.

"So I wait another week and call him back again and this time he says that it's their annual budget review so they can't talk about anything else. I ask him if he'll be able to bring it up at their next meeting and he says he doubts it because this will be the second part of their annual budget review. So then he says I should just leave it with him and he'll get back to me when he can. And that just means that I'll never hear from him again."

"Holy cow!" I said. "It's nothing but a big run-around."

"I get this all the time. Lots of good intentions but it never goes anywhere."

"Did you see anyone over at Goodyear? They might still remember Dad. That'll get you in the door."

"Yeah. The production manager, Sean Gilmore. He's heard of Dad. But it's the same thing with him. Have a good meeting and everything, but it goes nowhere."

I did not mention to Chuck when I met Sean a few weeks later. I spent a day at their plant to discuss some new fire abatement systems we were designing.

"Chuck's your brother, right?" Sean asked when the two of us were separated from the group. "He was in a little while ago with his wind gizmo." It was after we'd had a few afternoon meetings over two weeks, and while we were both pouring a cup of coffee that he confided in me. "He's got a great little invention there but he comes across a little over his head getting into his own business. I don't know. I wish him good luck though. Hell of a nice guy."

"He's put a lot of work into it," was all that I could say.

—

Chuck racked up some twenty thousand miles on his car over the months. He sat down at the table in the living room with a simple goal every morning at 7:30. "I just keep making phone calls until I get a meeting set up. Sometimes I can do it on the first call and sometimes it takes 20, but I keep going until I get that meeting."

"You don't seem to be getting very far. What are you going to do?" I asked.

"I've had it with these middle management types. It seems that they're either just trying to put in time in meetings to waste their day, or else they're looking for that one brilliant idea that will make them stand out at work, or just trying to make sure that no one else gets a good idea ahead of them. But with all the meetings I'm going to I can't find a single guy who wants to step up to the plate and move it to the next level. I should say they'll step up to the plate but they won't swing the bat. Every one of them is hoping for a walk. That's middle management."

"You know a lot more about it than I do, but I'd think that it would be tough to get any sort of partnership going with a big company. The middle managers don't have that kind of authority and the bigwigs are not going to be looking for a new company with nothing more than an idea. Maybe you'd be better off looking at small companies. There are lots of them around. They might be looking for something new?"

I knew about these companies from many small design projects we'd done at HBA. It was the five and ten thousand dollar jobs, usually from manufacturers moving into smaller locations, that had kept us alive during the recession. For every Ford or GM or Chrysler plant, there were a hundred small operations, some with just a half dozen workers, putting together hydraulic systems or electric motors or conveyor belts. Fifty years earlier the big companies had done all of this work internally but with every downturn more and more of the sub-processes had been farmed out.

"Do you think they'd want to put up money for this?" Chuck asked.

"Well, when you look at it these are the real entrepreneurs. That's what you want, right? They make decisions on the spot, yes or no. I don't think you'll find any obfuscation."

"What?"

I chuckled. "They won't waste your time."

"Man, that would be nice. Right now I've got nothing to lose." Chuck replied. "I have to tell you that I'm pretty well ready to give up if this doesn't work. I have to get a job soon if nothing comes around."

—

My advice was right. Chuck switched his target to the smaller companies where he had no problem getting in to see the owner. His approach also changed. No longer was he wearing a three-piece suit. He had changed into a more comfortable light-weight bomber jacket, with "Live Air" embroidered on the front, but still with a tie. The men that he was visiting were more likely to be wiping away grease to shake his hand than any of the middle-managers he had been meeting previously.

"It's really something," Chuck told me three weeks later. "When I'm talking to them I can see the wheels turning in their head. It's like they're already two steps in front of me, thinking about where we could make money."

"Have you made any deals yet?"

"I got one Chinese guy, Gong Zheng, he's really interested."

"Is Gong his first name or his last name?" I had never been able to figure that out.

"I think it's his last name. Everyone calls him Mr. Gong and he answers, so it must be right. He calls me, 'Mr. Chuck.' I tell him to just call me Chuck, but he won't stop saying Mr. Chuck."

"What's his company?"

"He brings in motors from China and puts them together. Sells to the car companies. He's got 15 people working there.

"He says he's got lots of contacts in China and that he can sell lots of my turbines there. They're always having power shutoffs. It's really serious. The factories have big generators. Even the houses have generators. He says this is perfect for houses on the coast where the wind is always blowing. He says the apartment buildings will put them up on the roof."

"And he can help you sell them?"

"His family's still there and his brother runs a big electric motor company. He says it's the second biggest electric motor company in the province. That's where he gets his motors from. And he says his cousin is some important guy in the government. They're spending lots of money to build new factories and this is the kind of thing they want to do. Smog is a big problem and anything they can do to stop smog is good."

"China, eh. You've got to be careful there. Everyone says they'll steal your invention."

"Yeah, I know. I'll be real careful. We're meeting again tomorrow afternoon to talk some more. I'll see if it goes anywhere. I've got some other guys interested too."

—

Chuck's next meeting went very well.

"He says we can build them in China for one-quarter the price, and then we can sell them all over. He says the government will give us money to build a factory and everything. If we build them there the government will support it and make sure we sell millions in China."

"Has he spoken to anyone about it yet?"

"Yeah. He says his brother's real interested. He wants to look at it a lot closer. He's gonna talk to him again and I might have to fly over there."

"Wow. All of a sudden this is moving really fast."

"That's the way it always is. Things go real slow then real fast."

"Are you sure about this guy? Is he legitimate?"

"Seems so. How can I tell?"

"Is he paying to fly you over?"

"No. I don't expect him to do that."

"What's he like?"

"Talks real fast. Always business. Always working a deal." Chuck spoke in a quick choppy voice.

"Just like that?"

"Yeah. I have to listen hard to understand him, and he has an accent. We're meeting again on Monday. He's gonna get his brother on the phone and we can all talk. He wants me to have proper drawings, engineering drawings. Can you help me?"

"I don't have the software for mechanical drawing." I thought for a moment. "I know a guy who can probably help. He's a mechanical engineer, doing some work with us on contract, but he'll charge you something. Is that okay?"

"How much?"

"You'd have to ask him that. I'm sure he'll be fair."

I put Chuck in touch with Jerry Bosch and they spent Saturday going over the details of the seashell model. Jerry promised that he'd have the first drawings complete in a week. He was charging Chuck $1,500 for the work because there were so many individual moving components to the design that it would take him a full week of working evenings to finish.

On Monday Chuck came home from his meeting in high spirits. "I'm flying over to China in two weeks. He wants me to bring a business proposal and all the engineering drawings with me."

"A business proposal? How are you going to do that?"

"You'll help me, right?"

"I guess I'll have to, won't I?" I knew that Chuck could never write something so detailed, but it would be not much different from the many contract submissions I'd worked on at HBA over the years.

We worked on it over the next week. Based on his discussions with Mr. Gong, Chuck had dollar signs in his eyes. He started with too many different ideas about how production might be done in China or in Canada and who would be responsible for sales around the world. It becomes rather simple when one party to the agreement is an individual with a few thousand dollars to spare and the other party is a large corporation with limitless resources. In the end, we proposed a royalty agreement with all production done in China, Live Air Industries "LAI" would control of all sales in North America or Europe, Qingdao Electric Motors responsible for sales across Asia, but with LAI receiving USD $500 royalty for every unit sold.

Chuck was both exhausted and excited on his return from three days in China. "He agrees with everything I'm asking, but the royalty is too high, so we talk about it and agree that $200 is good enough. He says he can sell thousands of units so I'll make tons of money. They're having their lawyers look over the proposal and they're going to send me a formal contract."

"That's fantastic. The meetings went well?"

"Oh yeah. First I meet with Mr. Gong and his brother. His name's Han, but I just call him Mr. Gong too. Then in the afternoon he brings in a team of engineers and I show them my display unit and explain it very carefully."

"They speak English?"

"Mr. Gong and his brother do. And the engineers too. Everyone under thirty I guess, but not the older guys. They all talk in Chinese while I'm there–" I didn't interrupt to ask whether he meant Mandarin or Cantonese, "–they spend a lot of time adjusting the fan speed and looking at how the sea shells contract and expand with the springs I designed. And then spend an hour going over the drawings from Jerry. They say the drawings are real good."

"Wow. That sounds great. You did get them to sign the non-competition agreement, didn't you?"

"You bet. And then the next day we meet his cousin. He's a deputy minister for the whole province. But he doesn't speak English at all so we have to talk through a translator and that's real hard 'cause I have to speak one sentence at a time. He says that they will give us money for a factory."

"Really!"

"Yeah. He says the government wants all kinds of new businesses so they will give us a building."

"How do you handle all that?"

"I don't know yet. I'll have to talk to Mr. Gong about all that, but they're going to look after the production aren't they."

"Well, congratulations." I shook Chuck's hand. "You must be really relieved. It's been a long haul."

He smiled, "Thanks."

—

Chuck had several calls and meetings with Mr. Gong over the next four weeks and everything looked to be going well. He was getting more and more excited every day, talking about how he might have to move to China to manage the production, but the next minute talking about moving to Europe because they are a lot greener than we are.

Then very suddenly, "Mr. Gong doesn't want to talk to me anymore. He says someone else has my plans and they are already making the seashell vanes. He's blaming me. He says I'm wasting their time and he's mad."

"You didn't talk to anyone else did you?"

"Lots of people, but not in China. And no one has the plans."

"Is it an exact copy?"

"He says so. He says he's got a brochure and it looks just like mine. I'm going down tomorrow to pick it up."

Chuck showed me the single sheet of glossy red paper, folded in thirds. On the front was a photograph of a seashell turbine. The shape of the spirals and design of the spring mechanism were clearly identical to Chuck's patent pending invention. If it had not been painted a different colour, it could have been Chuck's own display model in the photograph. Opening the page, I saw a drawing depicting the turbine spinning in a breeze and connected by electrical wires to a house. Other than a few recognizable numerals, the entire sheet was printed with Mandarin writing.

"Mr. Gong is blaming me. He says I'm cheating them and wasting their time. He doesn't want to talk to me anymore, but it's not my fault." Chuck was clearly dejected.

"You should talk to a lawyer. What about Uncle Ricky?"

"He's retired."

"So? He might still be able to help you. Give him a call."

I got on the other line so we could both hear the bad news.

"I'd say you're screwed," Uncle Ricky told us after the situation had been explained. "I've seen this before and everybody is talking about it. Chinese companies are stealing our ideas left and right. And it's not just little guys like you; even big companies are being ripped off, but at least they can afford to hire lawyers down in China. But what's a guy like you going to do? You can't afford a team of lawyers and you just know it'll take years before anything is resolved. And even if they sell the product overseas, what are you going to do, sue a company in China for a sale they made in Portugal for a patent in Canada?"

"It's an international patent," Chuck said.

"Right now it's an international patent pending, that's all it is. You might have some protection in few years if the patent is granted, but until then you've got nothing. Like I said, you're screwed. Sorry, Chuck. But don't feel too bad. There is nothing else you could have done. To these Chinese guys, it wouldn't matter if you had patents up the wazoo. They'll just copy you anyway."

Chuck's dejection was palpable. The little rabbit in the headlights expression on his face had returned for the first time in many years. He had a dream for something really special; something he had made himself with his own hands. And it was gone.

He spent most of his time with Debbie after that. I didn't actually lay eyes on him for two weeks but I could tell that he had come home during the day when his tables full of Meccano were boxed up and put down in the basement. It was not until several years later, when Chinese companies appeared on the internet, that we discovered Chuck's seashell turbine being manufactured and sold by Qingdao Trading Company, Gong Han – President. He had been screwed over by his own partners. Chuck's only response was, "I'm over that. Holding a grudge never does any good."

CHAPTER TWENTY-THREE

"I'm back with Morgan's Cars," Chuck said a couple of weeks after closing the books on Live Air Industries. "The old man's long gone but his son Mike's in charge now."

"Oh," I paused, "Selling used cars again." I looked at him quizzically. I remembered what he'd said about always moving forwards.

"I guess a guy's gotta do what he's gotta do." He sounded resigned to the fate. "Gotta start making some money or you'll be looking after me."

"Well, you were always good at it," I replied. "Might as well stick with what you're good at."

Chuck stuck at Morgan's for the remainder of his career and excelled in the used car market. He just had that knack, I guess. Only a year later and he was earning more than me again. His income went up and down with the economy, but every year I did his taxes, so I knew exactly how much he was paid.

—

Chuck was all smiles walking in the door late in the summer. "Hey! Francis is retiring from the police and we're gonna buy some motorcycles and do a tour all over Europe starting in the spring. Do you want to come with us? It'll be great."

"I don't know how to ride a motorcycle, do you?"

"So what? We'll learn. No big deal. We've got the fall to learn, then we'll ship the bikes over and fly there in the spring."

"Where do we get these bikes?"

"That's the best part. Johnny, the dealer next door to us is shutting down for the winter soon. He's got a bunch of used bikes he wants to get rid of. With fall coming he can't sell them now. He's got three beautiful BMWs, just a few years old. He'll give them to us real cheap.

"These five rich guys come over from Germany in the spring and they start on this big trip across the country. It rains every day and by the time they hit Ontario they're sick and tired of it. So I guess they see his shop and ask if he'll keep the bikes until they can ship them back to Germany. He thinks it's just gonna be a few weeks or something, but after three months they tell him to just sell the bikes and send them the money. So he tells them a really low price and they say sure."

"So he's ripping them off?"

"He says with the way they look, with matching leather jackets and pants and the whole bit, that he figures they can afford it. They're just rich guys out for an adventure and over their heads. They've got no idea what riding in the rain is really like, and now they're home in their nice villas in the Alps or something. That's what Johnny says anyway.

"He's got three of the bikes left and they're in perfect condition. That's what starts me thinking about this. BMWs are what everyone drives in Germany. They're made there. So I ask Francis if he wants to come on a trip with me, and he says he wants to see Greece. So we get talking and we decide to do the whole thing. Take all summer. Maybe take a couple of years if we're having fun."

"Where are you going to stay?"

"We're gonna camp. There's all kinds of motorcycle camping all over Europe. Everybody does it. And there's hostels too. We'll stay there when we need a break."

"So you don't have any real plans, just wander around?"

"Why are you worrying so much? We'll figure it out when we

get there."

I thought for a bit.

"I'll be 65 next year. I don't think I want to spend the summer sleeping on the ground in a tent. My back couldn't take it."

"You'll be 65, not dead. We'll have air mattresses. We'll be rebels, just like Dad. The chicks love a guy on a motorcycle."

"That's right, and Dad broke his leg on a motorcycle, didn't he?" I thought for a bit longer. "You two go ahead and have fun. I'll hold down the fort for when you come back all crippled and out of shape from lying on the cold ground. Or with your broken leg."

The next day a truck came by and unloaded a shiny silver BMW R1100RT motorcycle. It had the trade mark cylinder heads sticking out the side and a beautiful fairing. It was a gorgeous bike and looked incredibly fast. Just sitting on the road it looked like it was moving at a hundred miles an hour.

"Holy cow!" I said, "Can you drive that thing?"

"Not yet, but Johnny's lending us a couple of old 350s he's got, and he's giving us lessons. He says we can use his bikes to get our license. It's a lot easier on a small bike."

On Saturday, Chuck walked down to the dealership. Four hours later, he pulled into the driveway on an old Suzuki 350. The gas tank was well scratched and dented from too many drops on the ground and the seat was faded to a dark gray with the seams splitting open to show the foam padding underneath.

He was wearing a black, full face helmet and a light blue jacket made of some high tech rip proof material, with hard padding on the elbows for when he hits the road. The brand name prominent on the jacket said, "Thor."

"That's for when you're riding all day and you get a 'thor' back." Chuck lisped.

He rode everywhere on that bike through September. He and Francis took the back roads all the way to Kingston and up to Peterborough.

"You don't want to take this on the 401," he said. "You'll get run over by a truck. But wait 'till we get the BMWs moving. Then noth-

322   MY BROTHER CHUCK

ing will catch us."

They passed their licenses at the end of September and immediately returned the small Suzukis to concentrate on riding the
BMWs. October was chilly, but the fairings allowed them to ride on
the highways in comfort.

"It's like flying," Chuck said. "The hardest part isn't keeping up to
highway speed. It's keeping down to highway speed. I can't wait to
get to Germany and get on the Autobahn."

"You're going to kill yourself if you're not careful," I replied.

"Stop worrying, Mom. You're like an old lady."

He was right. "You know," I said. "You guys are going to London,
right? Maybe I'll fly over and we can go to see the Royal Observatory in Greenwich. We can see the Prime Meridian. Would you like
that?"

"You're gonna come meet us? That'll be great!"

"Just for a few days. Just to see some of the history in London.
And I could do some research while I'm there."

"You'll have to get a helmet. You can ride on the back of my
bike."

I hesitated. "It probably won't be worthwhile. You'll have all of
your gear on the bike. And I imagine you'll be parking it most of the
time you're in London anyway. We can get everyone on the buses
or the subway. After that," I went on, "you two can go on your way.
I'd like to see Oxford University. You're probably not interested in
that."

"I don't know why you don't get a bike of your own and come
with us," Chuck said. "We're gonna have a blast."

"No, I don't think so. There's just a few things I'd like to see. Maybe I'll fly over when you get to Italy. There's a museum about Galileo
that would be something to see. It's in Florence. Will you be going
there?"

"We're going everywhere, or anywhere, we want. That's the
whole point of the bikes. We can go anywhere."

"That will be something."

Winter came and the bikes were taken off the road. Chuck and Francis re-installed the metal saddlebags and storage racks, turning them back into real touring machines that would look good at any camp-site.

—

He continued to see Debbie quite often, but she rarely came to our house. The bags under her eyes from a lifetime of worry added a decade and a half to her appearance. Meanwhile, Chuck's cheerfulness took at least five years off from his. I could never figure out if her influence made him older or his influence made her younger.

"Have you seen a change since her father, um…, died?" I asked.

"Her Mom is so damaged," Chuck answered. "Debbie worries about her all the time. She hates to leave her alone during the day but she's gotta go to work. She won't leave her alone at night."

"What's Mrs. Spinolli like? It's been years since I've seen here on the street."

"She sits in front of the TV all day; that's all she does. She watches game shows in the morning and soap operas in the afternoon. She's usually really quiet. Doesn't say anything for an hour at a time. She's always nice to me though. She says hello when I come to the door and she always makes my favourites any time I come for dinner."

"Oh, she cooks?"

"Only when I come over. Debbie cooks if it's just the two of them," he paused to explain. "She's trained to look after a man, isn't she? Trained just like a lion trainer. With a whip and a chair."

"Doesn't that make you feel bad? When you go over?"

"Not any more. When I come over at least she's got a purpose. She'll be busy all afternoon. Debbie says she's much happier."

"Have you thought of moving in?" I asked.

"That would be torturing her, wouldn't it. It's not too bad if I go over for dinner once a week. She's afraid of men, no question. But she knows how to make a man happy." He patted his stomach.

"So I guess you two are stuck. You can't move in and Debbie

won't move out."

"That's our life, isn't it. But it's getting kind of late in the game now. We're kind of used to it being this way. I don't know if it would work any other way."

—

In February, Tom won HBA another cement plant contract in Sarnia. I'd done enough of these in my life and didn't feel like spending six months rehashing over the same thing, so I decided to retire.

Under Tom's leadership, we'd grown to take over another floor of the building with a total of seventeen engineers, a dozen draftsmen, three IT guys and a complete support staff, although the traditional role of the personal secretary had passed.

The recession after 9/11 hurt the company badly, but Tom had kept our office busy by picking up every small engineering job in the region. We didn't make much profit but kept the young engineers on staff for when things turned around, which they did by 2003.

Tom was being promoted to a Vice President position in Toronto and his replacement as managing director of our office was a 45 year old fellow from Kingston. I didn't feel like going through the office politics or adapting to meet the demands of another aggressive youngster. This was the second reason for my retirement a few months early. And of course, I had nearly six months of unused vacation time awaiting me. To be honest, I'm sure the company was happy to see the old man off. They had no trouble approving my full pension a few months early, after more than 40 years of service.

The office manager, Jeanne, asked if I wanted the full dinner and dance that had been given to the long standing retirees before me, but with no wife to take dancing and no desire to spend an evening with a crowd, twenty, thirty, or even forty years my junior, I opted for a simple lunch down the street.

"So what are your plans for retirement?" Steve asked. He was the next oldest engineer at HBA, in his early 50s and still a long way from retirement himself. We'd developed a casual friendship at work, if not enough to be invited to dinner.

"I'm looking into astrophysics courses," I said. "I'm trying to get a deeper understanding of how gravity affects space-time. And how it relates to Einstein's theories on general relativity."

"Boy, you're right into this, aren't you. What are you going to do, study at University of Toronto? You'd be right back at school again."

"U of T has a course, but I don't think I want to be driving down every day. The University of London, in England, has an online degree. I'm looking into that. I can study at home."

"A degree? You're going to go for a whole four year degree?"

"I think so. Maybe even a Masters or a PhD. I've got to do something to keep busy."

"You could travel. That's what I'm going to do when I retire. See the world. That's what I've promised Brenda, anyway."

"That sounds good on paper. But you have to think about it. You take a couple of trips per year, two weeks each. That still leaves 48 weeks of sitting around to fill. What are you going to do with that?"

"I don't know. I'm sure Brenda will keep my busy. There's always something to fix around the house."

"Yes. There is that." I replied.

The highlight of the lunch, at least from the audience point of view, was rolling in a big cake with a picture of Daniel Boone in his buckskin jacket drawn comically in icing on the top, while a tape recorder played the TV theme song, "Daniel Boone was a man. Was a big man..." to much applause and laughter. Of course nobody in the room had the slightest idea of how I'd gained that nickname, which I hadn't heard for decades.

At two o'clock, people started to filter out of the restaurant back to the office. They all stopped to shake my hand and wish me well in retirement. I barely knew the names of a few of the younger staff who worked on the other floor.

"What are your plans?" Jeanne asked.

"Astrophysics." I replied. "Right now all the talk is about black holes, but no one's even seen one and we aren't even sure if they exist. It's all Einstein's theories and mathematics. That's what I'd like to work on."

"It sounds like it's right up your alley. I hope you enjoy it," she said.

By two thirty the few of us remaining walked back over the slushy sidewalk. The days of the company giving a gold watch at retirement were long gone. I doubted if any of the current crop of employees would stay at HBA for even twenty years, let alone their entire career. New employees were not even signed up for the company pension plan, but were just given matching contributions to their own retirement funds.

Back at the office, I collected a small box of my personal belongings and the drafting tools that I'd brought with me all those years ago, but had gathered dust since the computer age. The new Managing Director, who had just started the previous week, shook my hand when I walked out the door just before three. One of the few times in 40 years that I'd left work early.

In February, Chuck and Francis loaded their motorcycles and camping gear into a shipping container bound for Greece. By starting their trip in the Mediterranean, they could take advantage of the early spring, rather than waiting for the rain to stop in England. Apparently, Francis had distant relatives in Greece and they planned to use that as a base for day trips around the region.

—

I sent my application for admission to the University of London in early March; the same week that Chuck and Francis boarded the plane for Europe.

Even with the internet and the ability to send messages and photos instantly, Chuck reverted to his excellent habit of sending postcards from every place they visited. The messages were always short and his printing had not improved over time, but there remains a real warmth and pleasure in receiving a postcard in the mailbox. Since they were visiting so many places on their trip, I usually received one postcard a day, and with the vagaries of the mail service in Greece, sometimes two or three cards in one day even though they were posted days, or even weeks, apart.

"In Parthenon today. It's real old," was one postcard. "The Acropolis this afternoon. It's real old too," was another. "Mount Olympus. That's where the Gods come from. But not ours." It remains a contrast how a person as collegial and conversational as Chuck could be so limited with the written word. Of course, the spelling remained atrocious and he did flip his letters back to front from time to time. Perhaps if we had understood dyslexia in his youth, steps could have been taken to improve his abilities, but it was not being diagnosed in those days and he had no motivation to try as an adult. His was a verbal world.

Their hosts lived in Corinth, a thousand year old city in central Greece, 50 miles from Athens. From the cards, it seemed that Chuck and Francis hopped on their motorcycles immediately after breakfast every morning for the ride to whatever city they were visiting that day. I got the impression that they enjoyed spending three or four hours riding as much, or more, than they enjoyed the attraction. This confirmed my decision not to travel with them. The thought of several hours a day on a motorcycle, on ancient cobblestone roads, made my back hurt even from a chair in my living room.

After two weeks in Greece, they moved their adventure up to Albania, which was finally emerging out of the shadow of the Soviet Union. They stayed for a few days in Tirana, and spent a few more camping in the mountains. As Chuck's postcard said, "Nothing to see in these communist countries, but the mountains are nice." Then they continued the trip north to Serbia and I received a card from the town of Sibinjanin. "Really good view," was all Chuck wrote.

My application to the University College London as an external student was approved. Although it would be several months before the official course, I decided to get a head start and ordered the books I'd need for each class.

—

It was mid-August, just a week before my flight to England when I got the terrible long distance call from Francis.

"There's been a bad accident," he said. "The doctors don't know if Chuck's going to make it. He has a severe brain injury and fractures to his spinal cord. He's unconscious right now. Can you come over right away?"

I knew Francis was accustomed to giving this type of news to family members after traffic accidents. Very factual with as little emotion in his voice as possible. It was just a part of his job as a policeman. He must have done it dozens of times over his career, but I doubt he'd ever had to give such horrible news about such a close friend.

"When did it happen?" I asked.

"A few hours ago. We'd just arrived in England yesterday. Chuck must have gotten mixed up with driving on the left side of the road. He made a turn into the wrong lane and hit a truck head on. I was right behind him. The ambulance was there in just a few minutes and they got him into the operating room right away. I waited until I heard from the doctor before I called you. He just came out a few minutes ago. The situation doesn't look good. Can you come over right away?"

Francis had spoken slowly, with short pauses after each sentence to allow me to interrupt, but I didn't, only because I didn't know what to say.

"I'll have to phone Air Canada to see how soon I can get out," I paused. "Is it really bad?"

"Yes. I'm sorry; it is. The doctor said that you should come as soon as possible."

"Okay. I'll call Air Canada right now. What number can I reach you at?"

"I'm just at a payphone in the hospital. I'll call you back in an hour," he paused to think. "You'll have to fly to London and then down to Plymouth. I only have the motorcycle so I can't pick you up. You can take a taxi to the hospital."

"Yes, I understand. Call me back in an hour and I'll let you know when I'll arrive."

A strange feeling of numbness set in as I waited on hold for the next available Air Canada representative.

"Due to a high volume of calls, your wait time may be longer than normal," the recorded voice on the phone told me. I sat down in the kitchen chair and held the phone away from my ear, close enough that I could still hear the on-hold message repeated over and over and over again, every two minutes, with the perfectly formulated white bread on-hold music played in between messages.

After the fourth or fifth repetition, my numb, business-like demeanour started to fade and I realized that with Chuck gone I would be alone in the world. My only brother, and my best friend was being taken away. From what Francis had said, I thought it wouldn't be worthwhile to pray for Chuck's recovery, but I did speak aloud when I said, "Lord, if Chuck dies, can I ask you to please take him into heaven. Please ignore anything bad that he might have done in his life and accept him with you."

I added 'amen' at the last second. I really didn't know how God would feel about what Chuck did to Mr. Spinolli. Was that particular murder so bad that it could never be forgiven? Or was Chuck justified in God's eyes? It was really only God's eyes that mattered at this point. Any thoughts of human justice were long past.

I caught the overnight flight to arrive in London. Three times, when all the other passengers were sleeping, a stewardess reached across the seats to close the window shade next to me. Each time I waited for a couple of minutes and opened it to look out over the dark ocean. When we stood up to disembark, the business woman next to me said, "Have a nice day," and I mumbled "thank you," in return. Those were the only words spoken between us.

Eighteen hours had passed from my last talk with Francis by the time the taxi let me off at the hospital. When I asked for Chuck's room number at the reception counter, the woman asked me to wait a moment and she made a phone call.

"Someone will be down to see you in a moment," she said.

It was Francis who gently shook my hand two minutes later. "I'm sorry," he said, "but Chuck didn't make it through the night. He never recovered consciousness."

"Oh," I said. "I guess I expected it. Can I see him?"

"Sure. He's not in his room any more, but the doctor said I can take you down. We knew you were coming so they've kept him available."

Francis took my suitcase as we walked down the hall together.

"Here, let me carry that," he said.

"You seem to know your way around a hospital," I said to fill the silence as we walked.

"I've seen more than my share of accident victims," he replied, "And I've escorted more family members to see their loved ones than I'd care to remember."

I half expected to watch Francis open a freezer drawer to pull Chuck out. Instead, we walked into a small room, certainly hospital-like but not stainless steel. There were three plastic chairs against a wall and Chuck was lying on a gurney in the middle, covered in a blue hospital sheet and with his face exposed. He had on a hospital cap, as they had performed brain surgery.

His face was pale. He had obviously not shaved for several days before the accident and the grey stubble on his chin contrasted with the black hair sticking out from under the cap.

"Take as long as you like," Francis said. "I'll be just out here."

I put my hands on Chuck's shoulders. Even through the sheet, I could feel the coldness of his body. I remembered what the Minister had said at Dad's funeral. It went something like, "Do not stand and weep. I am not here anymore." I think it's from a poem, but I've probably got it wrong.

It seemed truly appropriate at that moment. I was holding onto Chuck's body, but he wasn't in the room with me. He had gone to his next adventure. Maybe he was at the pool hall, or maybe playing street hockey with the gang. But one thing was certain; he was with a very large group of very close friends and they were all smiling and raising toasts to their future plans. I guess it was at that moment that I knew Chuck had made his way into heaven.

About fifteen minutes later, Francis tapped on the door and walked in to stand next to me. I pulled a Kleenex out of my pocket to dry my eyes, but Francis didn't embarrass me by looking at my face.

"He was a hell of a guy," he said. "You know, he passed me at that corner and I could hear him laughing."

—

We arranged to have Chuck cremated a couple of days later. I knew it would be important to all of his friends to have a proper wake with him present, even if only in a small wooden box.

I didn't get a chance to see the observatory at Greenwich or to walk around the historic buildings at Oxford. I did make a special trip to Cambridge where so many famous astrophysics advancements had been made. Stephen Hawking continued to give periodic lectures on theoretical cosmology. I thought I could pick up an autographed copy of *A Brief History of Time*, until I found out just how exceedingly rare and valuable his signature had become. I even spent a couple of afternoons sitting at the ancient oak tables in the library trying to read through some of his papers, but I found it difficult to concentrate on his advanced mathematical theories, a new experience for me. There were more modern rooms in the library with more comfortable chairs, but I could get those in Toronto. I wanted to soak up as much of the historic university atmosphere as possible while visiting London.

It was very calming to be back in an academic setting. I wandered the halls and looked at photographs of people I never knew who had won Nobel prizes, been Knighted or made Members of the Order of the British Empire.

—

After a week, Francis and I flew back home with Chuck's ashes. There were a half dozen of Chuck's last postcards waiting in my mail box and several more arrived over the coming weeks, delayed in whatever country they'd been posted.

Francis had already been in touch with Little Charlie who arranged for a wake at the Liberty Bowling Alley. The owner, a Nigerian fellow, had been friends with Chuck since he'd moved to Canada ten years earlier, and offered the space free of charge. Our Minister, Reverend Thompson, gave the homily and included the poem I'd been thinking of. Over the course of a Saturday afternoon, nearly two hundred of Chuck's friends showed up, bowled a few lanes and drank a few beers in his honour.

What amazed me most, only because I had kept none of my high school contacts, was the number of friends from Chuck's teens and twenties who came by to shake my hand. They were all long settled by now, nearing or past retirement and with teenaged grandchildren of their own. It reminded me of the final scene from *It's a Wonderful Life*, when all of George Bailey's friends arrived at his house. If a bell had rung at that moment, I would have known that Chuck got his wings.

Kathleen spent the whole afternoon at the bowling alley. After giving me a long hug she realized that I was a little overwhelmed by the number of people arriving and took over the role of hostess, making sure there was a steady supply of snacks and beer coming out from behind the counter.

The most important role that Kathleen performed, which I didn't realize until well into the afternoon, was acting as interference. Any time a group of four or five of Chuck's friends circled around me with their stories, Kathleen would squeeze herself into the group and take over as the active audience for whomever was talking, enabling me to mumble "excuse me" and drift away without embarrassment. A couple of times, she even said, "Bob over there wants to give you his condolences," while pointing across the room, making my exit more expedient.

There were still a couple of dozen of Chuck's friends giving toasts and rolling balls into the gutter when Kathleen saw my exhaustion and led me out to the car by the arm. "You go home and have a nice nap," she said, kissing me on the cheek. "Call me if you need anything." I never called her.

CHAPTER TWENTY-FOUR

Of course Chuck died without a will. It was only a matter of some paperwork and a judge's signature to declare me, his closest relative, as his sole heir. The judge, Martin Wakefield, had been one of the guests at the wake.

Chuck had one hundred and fifty thousand dollars in his retirement account. I knew he'd had a greater amount in the past but had used some of it during his entrepreneurial gamble.

I used eight thousand to put a new roof on the house, something he had promised to pay for. The remainder I gave to Debbie. They never were married or even close to married, according to the few times Chuck and I had discussed it, but for more than 40 years, off and on, she was the closest thing he'd ever had to a wife, and I knew that if they'd both lived to old age, he would have made sure of her comfort even at the cost of his own.

Debbie's self imposed hermitage had grown even further since hearing of Chuck's death. She barely invited me in when I knocked on the door, just mumbled something softly and left it open as she walked towards her kitchen.

"Chuck left this for you," I said while holding out an envelope. After a few seconds when Debbie didn't move, her mother reached over to take it. She was into her late eighties by this time, but was still active enough to have cleaned the house and made coffee and cookies when I had asked if I could visit.

"Thank you so much," Mrs. Spinolli said. "It was so nice of Chuck to think of Debbie." I didn't mention that Chuck had died intestate. "He has always been so good to her," she went on. "It's such a shame that they were never able to get together."

I didn't know if, for all those years, Debbie had stayed with her mother out of her own sense of guilt, or if her mother had pressured her into staying, but I had the feeling it was the former. Chuck never mentioned Debbie having any resentment towards Mrs. Spinolli.

"Look, Honey," she handed the cheque to Debbie. "This will be your retirement fund. We can stop worrying now. Wasn't that nice of Chuck? He was such a sweet boy."

"Thank you," Debbie said softly. "It will be helpful." This was the first time she had looked at me in the eyes, if only for a moment.

"I'm sure that Chuck would be happy to know that you have some security," I said.

Just a few months later I attended Mrs. Spinolli's funeral. She caught the flu and didn't recover. Only eight people were there; Debbie and I and a few casual friends she had made since her father's death. I got the feeling that these other women were amateur mourners who would attend the funeral of any church member. The Minister didn't ask if anyone wanted to say a few words.

When spring came, Debbie sold the house. I'm sure the land had more value than the building as the suburbs of Toronto continued to stretch eastward along the 401. Eventually, the whole block was turned into townhomes. Debbie did retire and moved up to Lakefield, north of Peterborough. She had enough to buy a 500 square-foot cottage.

I didn't tell Mom about Chuck. She and Aunt June shared a small suite at an old folk's home up in Peterborough. Mom barely recognized me these days, and I saw no reason to upset her. On the few times that she mentioned Chuck's name, I just said, "He's really happy; traveling in England right now." And she'd smile. I pinned a rotating number of his postcards up on her wall.

—

Chuck had been in Europe for several months before his death and had been away most evenings even when we were together, but the house became surprisingly silent at his passing. It was a meta-physical silence rather than something that could be measured. He had always been a presence in the house, even if he wasn't there. I had just never realized that the anticipation, even if it was weeks or months away, of his whistling and laughter was every bit as import-ant as his physical presence.

When my courses started in September, I found it difficult to concentrate in the absolute quiet of the living room. I tried turning the radio on low but the conversational voices of CBC did not help. I discovered the public library to be a better solution. Bomanville's two-year old library on Church Street was perfectly modern and completely comfortable. I started spending my days in the science section on the 2nd floor, but in the middle of the day, when students were at school, this was nearly as silent as home, other than the few old men with their nose in a magazine. In the evenings, it was too busy and distracting when high school students filled the room with inane chatter.

A better solution was at a table next to the children's section on the first floor. The all-day chatter of children under five, of their own making or from their mothers reading, seemed just what I needed to concentrate on my studies, looking up from time to time when a giggle occurred.

Some of the mothers might have found it odd for a grey-haired man to be sitting, day after day, with a stack of books and a laptop computer, right next to the children's section. (I always arrived at opening at nine and stayed until five. Often in the evenings, if it was too quiet at home, I'd return for two more hours.) But Chuck had dated the head librarian, Janice Pennington, some years previously and I think she understood my situation.

One day, after I'd been coming for a year, Janice noticed me looking over and suggested that I might enjoy reading a book to the children. I moved into their section and sat down on one of the child sized chairs, with my bony knees sticking up high. There were a number of worn and torn books scattered on the floor. I picked up the nearest, Curious George, and opened to the first page.

"Just start," Janice said. "They'll know what to do."

So I started from page one. "This is George. He lived in Africa. He was a good little monkey and always very curious."

As soon as I started reading, several of the children sat down at my feet, as I had seen them do for many others before me. I held up the book to show them a drawing of the monkey, George, hanging from a vine and eating a banana.

A few mothers brought their little ones, some too young to walk, over as well. I went on. "One day George saw a man. He had on a large yellow straw hat...." one of little girls reached up and took hold of the bottom corner of the book. I held it down for her to look closely at the drawing of the Man in the Yellow Hat, looking up at George through a pair of binoculars. The little girl, with her sticky hands, grabbed hold of the page and seemed to fall down, creating a six inch rip.

I looked up and Janice smiled. "Don't worry about it," she said.

Reading to the children became my routine at 10:30 every morning and 2 every afternoon. Some children visited the library daily, others once or twice a week. Often they held up whatever book they wanted me to read, but if there were no other suggestions I returned to Curious George over and over again. I don't think I could calculate the number of times I went through that story. It was slightly annoying if the three library copies were out on loan or in the repair shop, so I bought my own copy and always kept it in my briefcase. Even it needed the assistance of scotch tape from time to time and a replacement after several years of use.

—

I've now finished my Bachelors and Masters degrees in astrophysics. On Tuesday, I'll be flying over to London to present a topic for my PhD thesis: "Measurements in the Equivalence Principle using Binary Pulsar Gravitational Lensing," to evaluate ideas of inertial and gravitational mass in four dimensions. In the end it all comes back to Einstein and Eddington.

This should be interesting.

THE END

About the Author

Andrew Evans, his wife Sharon, and their dogs Wally and Russell live in Victoria, BC, the only place in Canada where he can enjoy year-round sailing. He is known around the world for his 2014 best-selling book "Singlehanded Sailing; Thoughts, Tips, Techniques &

Tactics".